U0165908

英美文學

60大家

五南圖書出版公司 印行

姜葳・著

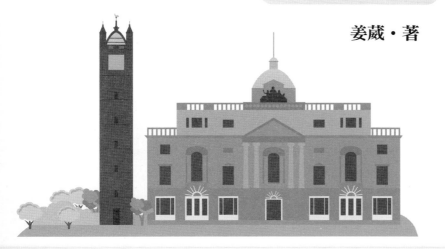

ENGLISH

preface 序

民國103年初，五南圖書朱曉蘋主編就書寫英美文學教科書之事相詢筆者，筆者自忖自民國93年起即在國立台中科技大學（當時的台中技術學院）應用英語系教授英美文學，遂應承之。

本書結構、內容根據下列原則設計：

一、循筆者課程設計，以作家爲單位，重點選擇作家，介紹其生平、作品、地位。《貝武夫》（*Beowulf*）、《高文爵士與綠騎士》（*Sir Gawain and the Green Knight*）兩篇作者不詳，則以篇名標題。

二、英國文學佔2/3，美國文學佔1/3。

三、資料來源與筆者課程相同，主要包括英語維基網站（wikipedia）、英語教科書（如Norton Anthology）、其他英美文學網站（如shmoop）、中文英美文學書籍等。

四、主要對象爲國內技職體系大專應用英語系學生。

五、文學、文化知識、語言並重，內容爲一般英美大學非文科學生應知者。

六、因全書篇幅有限，重要作家介紹較多，一般作家較少。作品也是擇重點介紹，非全部涵蓋。

本書特點在盡量爲每位作家選譯名作一兩段，中英並排，譯法稍偏直譯，以便讀者對照學習。譯文內容全由筆者自譯，作品標題則參考了網站譯法。

姜葳

民國一〇四年十一月二十五日於台中

目錄
Contents

目錄
Contents

～English Literature 40 scholars 英國文學40大家～

圖片來源：維基共享資源

1-1

貝武夫

Beowulf

羅馬帝國5世紀自英格蘭撤退，克爾特（Celt）原住民受北方蘇格蘭族群侵襲，邀請北歐盎格魯撒克遜人入住英格蘭東南幫助抵禦蘇格蘭人，反被盎格魯撒克遜人驅趕。《貝武夫》（Beowulf）即是盎格魯撒克遜人以其語言－古英語（Old English）－著作之史詩，於8-11世紀間為不知名文人記錄，敘述5-7世紀發生於丹麥之事，共3182行。

　　其內容為：丹麥國王霍斯高（Hroðgar）於雄鹿宮（Heorot）率眾居住，屢受妖魔獦婪殆（Grendel）夜間侵襲吃人，北歐亞塔斯族（古英語Gēatas，現代英語Geats）英雄貝武夫來援，赤手扯斷獦婪殆手臂，獦婪殆逃回巢穴而死。次晚，獦婪殆之母來報仇殺人，貝武夫等循跡追至其湖底巢穴，用宏廷劍（Hrunting）搏鬥，但宏廷劍無法傷害獦婪殆之母，貝武夫遂取湖底寶藏中神劍斬殺獦婪殆之母，再將獦婪殆頭砍下獻給霍斯高。霍斯高叮嚀貝武夫勿驕傲自滿、要賞賜部下。貝武夫返回亞塔斯部落，多年後成為國王；距離殺獦婪殆50年後，有部落奴隸從惡龍據守的寶藏偷了金杯，惡龍憤而噴火燒殺，貝武夫單挑惡龍失敗，屬下逃逸，只有維格拉夫（Wiglaf）協助貝武夫追至龍穴屠龍，貝武夫身受重傷，死後屍體火焚葬於海邊山上，過往船隻皆可望見憑弔。

　　古英語詩多壓頭韻（alliteration），即一行中多字起頭聲音相同，且每行節奏多分為兩半。茲選譯兩段，一為獦婪殆進犯雄鹿宮，一為詩末火葬貝武夫一段，左為古英語：

ða com of more　　under misthleoþum Grendel gongan,　　godes yrre bær; mynte se manscaða manna cynnes sumne besyrwan　in sele ðam hean. Wod under wolcnum to þæs þe he winreced, goldsele gumena,　gearwost wisse,	Then from the moorland, by misty crags, Grendel came, with God's wrath laden. The monster was minded of mankind now sundry to seize in the stately house. Under welkin he walked, till the wine-palace there, gold-hall of men, he gladly discerned,

fættum fahne.　　Ne wæs þæt forma sið,
þæt he Hroþgares　ham gesohte;
næfre he on aldordagum　ær ne siþðan
heardran hæle,　　healðegnas fand.

flashing with fretwork. Not first time, this,
that he the home of Hrothgar sought,—
yet ne'er in his life-day, late or early,
such hardy heroes, such hall-thanes, found!

來自沼澤，經過霧瘴山岩，
獷獒殆過來，帶天國之怒。
這時妖魔 注意到人眾
可供果腹 在高大宮殿。
蒼穹下前進，去到那嚐酒處，
眾人的金殿，牠開心看見，
閃熾澄光。這誠非初次，
霍斯高的宏殿 牠來禍害；
但是牠一生的時日，不論始末，
未得見此等英雄，此等鬥士。

最後一段：

Geworhton ða Wedra leode
hleo on hoe, se wæs heah ond brad,
wæligendum wide gesyne,
ond betimbredon on tyn dagum

The folk of the Weders fashioned there
on the headland a barrow broad and high,
by ocean-farers far descried:
in ten days' time their toil had raised it,

beadurofes becn, bronda lafe
wealle beworhton, swa hyt weorðlicost
foresnotre men findan mihton.
...
eahtodan eorlscipe ond his ellenweorc
duguðum demdon, swa hit gedefe bið
þæt mon his winedryhten wordum herge,
ferhðum freoge, þonne he forð scile
of lichaman læded weorðan.

the battle-brave's beacon. Round brands of the pyre
a wall they built, the worthiest ever
that wit could prompt in their wisest men.
...
They praised his earlship, his acts of prowess
worthily witnessed: and well it is
that men their master-friend mightily laud,
heartily love, when hence he goes
from life in the body forlorn away.

韋德族人 在彼堆起
於海岬上 宏闊皇陵，
走海者 遠距可見：
十日之期 即已築起，
勇士的營火，縈繞燔柴
築起木幕，至美至大
爲多才者 之大成。
……
稱其領導，崇其力德
眾皆昭見：極之得當
其友其主 齊歌頌祈祝，
哀悼以愛意，當其道別
離別肉身 孤獨上路。

《貝武夫》是英語文學最早史詩，古英語文學代表作，體現北歐早期封建文化。

圖片來源：IDJ圖庫

1-2

高文爵士與綠騎士

Sir Gawain and the Green Knight

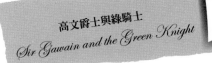
高文爵士與綠騎士

《高文爵士與綠騎士》（Sir Gawain and the Green Knight）屬於中古英語（Middle English）騎士浪漫文學，並屬歷險追尋文類（quest），共2530行，格律延用古英語頭韻，每段結尾還有古英詩的「紡錘紡輪」（bob and wheel）結構，即每段尾一、二字為紡錘，接續4行為紡輪，紡輪除頭韻外，還須與紡錘壓腳韻（rhyme）。此詩14世紀為不知名文人以英格蘭中西部方言記錄。

故事敘述亞瑟王（King Arthur）圓桌武士（Knights of the Round Table）聖誕節在卡美洛（Camelot）宮庭，有一綠色武士騎綠馬來挑戰，讓人以斧砍他一次，但一年後要讓他回砍一次。亞瑟王的外甥高文爵士出列應戰，一斧砍下綠騎士腦袋，綠騎士撿起腦袋，提醒高文一年後在綠教堂（Green Chapel）見。一年後高文赴約，途經城堡，堡主伯提拉克（Bertilak de Hautdesert）留高文暫住。伯提拉克提議與高文互換每日所獲，首日伯提拉克獵得鹿一頭，伯提拉克美貌夫人趁其夫打獵時挑逗高文，但僅得高文一吻，高文與伯提拉克互換所得，但未透露得吻於何人。次日情景類似，兩人互換野豬一頭與二吻。第三日，堡主夫人送給高文她自己的魔法綠色腰帶，可保護佩戴者，高文顧及綠騎士的挑戰，因而接受，當晚與伯提拉克互換狐狸一隻與三吻，但隱瞞腰帶之事。高文隨即至綠教堂赴約，綠騎士第一斧砍來，高文略微縮頭遭譏笑，第二斧則堅定不移，但綠騎士旨在測試、並未砍下，第三斧全力揮出，但只作皮毛之傷。綠騎士露出本來面目：堡主伯提拉克，他解釋挑戰只是亞瑟魔法師姊姊莫甘（Morgan le Fay）測試圓桌武士之舉。高文因隱瞞腰帶一事而羞愧，決定穿戴綠腰帶以自我警惕，圓桌眾武士決定共同仿效。

有議者解讀此詩暗含大自然（綠騎士）對文化（圓桌武士）之挑戰，也有人解讀綠騎士代表大自然生生不息，砍頭也會再長出。茲選譯近開頭兩段，左為中古英語：

高文爵士與綠騎士

Þis kyng lay at Camylot vpon Krystmasse	This king lay at Camelot nigh on Christmas
With mony luflych lorde, ledez of þe best,	with many lovely lords, of leaders the best,
Rekenly of þe Rounde Table alle þo rich breþer,	reckoning of the Round Table all the rich brethren,
With rych reuel ory t and rechles merþes.	with right ripe revel and reckless mirth.
þer tournayed tulkes by tymez ful mony	There tourneyed tykes by times full many,
justed ful jolile þise gentyle kni3tes	jousted full jollily these gentle knights,
syþen kayred to þe court caroles to make	then carried to court, their carols to make.
for þer þe fest watz ilyche ful fiften dayes	For there the feast was alike full fifteen days,
with alle þe mete and þe mirþe þat men couþe avyse	with all the meat and mirth men could devise:
such glaumande gle glorious to here	such clamour and glee glorious to hear,
dere dyn vpon day daunsyng on ny3tes	dear din in the daylight, dancing of nights;
al watz hap vpon he3e in hallez and chambrez	all was happiness high in halls and chambers
with lordez and ladies as leuest him þo3t	with lords and ladies, as liked them all best.
with all þe wele of þe worlde þay woned þer samen	With all that's well in the world were they together,
þe most kyd kny3tez vnder krystes seluen	the knights best known under the Christ Himself,
and þe louelokkest ladies þat euer lif haden	and the loveliest ladies that ever life honoured,
and he þe comlokest kyng þat þe court haldes	and he the comeliest king that the court rules.
for al watz þis fayre folk in her first age	For all were fair folk and in their first age
on sille	still,
þe hapnest vnder heuen	the happiest under heaven,
kyng hy3est mon of wylle	king noblest in his will;
hit werere now gret nye to neuen	that it were hard to reckon
so hardy a here on hille	so hardy a host on hill.

到聖誕時大王端駐卡美洛
和廣多甘美貴族，人中高士，
圓桌武士芸芸眾兄弟，
團團相聚同慶同享樂。
許多少男爭相比試，
優雅爵士歡聚騎馬競技，
過後更赴宮庭，高唱作樂。

盛宴水席碩然持續十五天，
瓊酒禽肉其樂無窮：
歡鬧呼嘯撼動人心，
白日喧嚚嬉戲，夜晚相擁舞；
高大宮殿中公侯共樂
男爵女士，盡能鬧騰。
世間所享，咸在一室。
天主關照下至佳爵士，
世間所見最靚女士，
還有治御全國最俊君主。
凡人皆風致豐美年華仍
　　　　少
　　世間最有幸者，
　　君主志最高；
　　他處難以尋得
　　如彼堡中虎賁同袍。

高文爵士與綠騎士

þer hales in at þe halle dor an aghlich mayster
on þe most on þe molde on mesure hyghe
fro þe swyre to þe swange so sware and so þik
and his lyndes and his lymes so longe and so grete
half etayn in erde I hope þat he were
bot mon most I algate mynn hym to bene
and þat þe myriest in his muckel þat my3t ride
for of bak and of brest al were his bodi sturne
bot his wombe and his wast were worthily smale
and alle his fetures fol3ande in forme þat he hade
　　　　ful clene
　　for wonder of his hwe men hade
　　set in his semblaunt sene
　　he ferde as freke were fade
　　and oueral enker grene

There hurtles in at the hall-door an unknown rider,
One the greatest on ground in growth of his frame:
From broad neck to buttocks so bulky and thick,
And his loins and his legs so long and so great,
Half a giant on earth I hold him to be,
But believe him no less than the largest of men,
And the seemliest in his stature to see, as he rides,
For in back and in breast though his body was grim,
His waist in its width was worthily small,
And formed with every feature in fair accord
　　　　was he.
　　Great wonder grew in hall
　　At his hue most strange to see,
　　For man and gear and all
　　Were green as green could be.

有陌生騎士一名闖入大廳大門，
其身材碩然高大 實舉世無雙：
從頸項到雙股 如此粗壯厚實，
那腰膀那腿臀 如此闊如此長，
我敢說他該算 世上半個巨人，
至少在世人中 絕對是最高大，
也是最崇美可觀的，騎乘馬上，
雖然後背胸脯 其身軀可怖，
但是其腰脊 卻細緻可讚，
其身軀上下相貌 其所具形體。
美俊
人們對其驚歎不停
見其具此身形，
其行動舉止有如仙人
全綠上下其身。

　　此詩為中古英語重要作品，是圓桌武士傳奇重要篇章，融合14世紀英格蘭、威爾斯（Wales）、法國文學特色。

圖片來源：IDJ圖庫

1-3
傑弗瑞‧喬叟
Geoffrey Chaucer

　　傑弗瑞·喬叟（Geoffrey Chaucer）1343年左右生於倫敦，出身中產階級，父親爲殷實酒商。喬叟幼受教育，能讀拉丁文，說法文、意大利文，14歲入愛德華三世次媳烏爾斯特伯爵夫人（Countess of Ulster）家服侍，得以接觸貴族，1360年於戰役中被法國俘獲贖回，之後周遊法、西、荷。1366年23歲出使西班牙，同年婚娶皇后近侍，日後王儲第三任妻子之姊，菲莉芭·羅艾（Philippa Roet）。約此時喬叟入內殿法學院（Inner Temple）學法，1367年入王府服侍，1369年撰寫《公爵夫人之書》（Book of the Duchess）哀悼當年去世的王儲妃，1370年赴法、意。其文學創作第一期摹仿法國文學，譯有法國寓言故事《玫瑰傳奇》（Roman de la Rose），爲時興的托夢文體，主角夢到爲心愛的玫瑰受苦。

　　1373年喬叟赴意大利，可能見到佩脫拉克（Francesco Petrarca）、薄伽丘（Giovanni Boccaccio）。此後14年間爲其文學創作第二期，摹仿意大利文人但丁（Dante）、佩脫拉克、薄伽丘。1374英王賜予典型的文人賞賜「每日一加侖葡萄酒」。同年就任倫敦海關長，掌管羊毛、羊皮進出口。1372-86年有大量創作，包括《義婦傳》（Legend of Good Women）、《飛禽議會》（The Parliament of Fowls）、譯作《哲學的慰藉》（De consolatione philosophiae）、《聲譽之宮》（The House of Fame）、《卓勒斯與柯麗希德》（Troilus and Criseyde）、《論星盤》（Treatise on the Astrolabe）。

　　《義婦傳》記述9位歷史、文學中因男人而死的女人，首創「英雄聯句」（heroic couplet）：五步抑揚格（iambic pentameter），每兩句同韻aabbcc…。此詩開啓後世英詩一句10音節典型格律。《飛禽議會》慶祝國王理查二世婚禮，描述眾禽鳥在情人節擇偶歡配，首創「王者韻」（rhyme royal，爲詹姆士一世所用得名）：一節七句，五步抑揚格，韻腳ababbcc。《哲學的慰藉》譯自6世紀羅馬文人博伊修（Boethius）作品，論現世名利虛幻，而靈魂精神永存。《聲譽之宮》作於1379-80，以托夢體審視「名」之虛幻。《卓勒斯與柯麗希德》作於1380-85，改寫佩脫拉克《歌集》（Canzoniere）部份詩句。《論星盤》爲最早英文科技論文。

喬叟後派任東南部肯特郡（Kent）郡官。80年代初著手巨著《坎特伯里故事集》（Canterbury Tales）。1386年獲選肯特郡國會議員。妻子可能次年去世。1387年後進入創作第三期，展現個人風格。1389年受任王家司工大臣（Clerk of the King's Works）。1391年出任北舶瑟屯（North Petherton）王家林場副場長。《坎特伯里故事集》敘述一位領隊帶著29位信徒，包括喬叟，由倫敦去坎特伯里，向1170年殉教的大主教聖湯瑪斯‧貝克特（Thomas Becket）朝聖，沿路為解悶，相約比賽說故事，每人來去途中各說兩篇，獲勝者由眾人返回後共饗一餐。預計共120篇，另加序和跋，喬叟只完成22篇，另有兩篇未寫完。朝聖者包含當時英國社會各階層人物，有騎士（knight）、磨坊主人（miller）、郡縣差官（reeve）、廚子（cook）、律師（man of law）、中年婦女（wife）、行腳僧（friar）、宗教法庭傳票人（summoner）、文員（clerk）、商人（merchant）、騎士助手（squire）、自由農（franklin）、醫師（physician）、贖罪券僧（pardoner）、水手（shipman）、女修院院長（prioress）、修士（monk）、修女告解僧（nun's priest）、修女（nun）、教區差人（canon's yeoman）、修院採辦（manciple）、教區神父（parson）。各別故事內容、語氣、文類搭配講者身份、個性，栩栩如生，故事之間互有對比、陪襯，文學成就出類拔萃。茲擇兩篇簡介：

浴場城婦人（Wife of Bath，Bath乃英格蘭西南羅馬人建的大浴場，一譯「巴斯」）40歲，自述從12歲起曾五度結婚，不同意基督教男尊女卑教條，認為男女應盡情享樂，否則上帝為何予人性器官？她認為五個老公有三個好（因為年老、溫順、又富有，她要求他們付錢才行房），第四任老公比她小，在外有情婦，但早死；現任老公20歲，是牛津大學（Oxford University）學生，床上功夫好，但會家暴。老公常引經據典要老婆順從，婦人一氣就撕爛老公的書，老公一巴掌打到她失聰，但懺悔表示以後服從老婆，從此婦人得償所願，兩人恩愛過日。婦人故事如下：亞瑟王手下一騎士強暴少女，罪應處死，王后為騎士請命，但騎士必須在一年內答出「女人最想要什麼？（What do women want?）」有老嫗知道答案，但要求騎士娶她為妻，答案是「女人要老公服從」，騎士得以保命，但嫌老婆又醜又老又窮，老嫗駁說上帝眼中不分貧富，並允他擇一：妻子或老醜但聽話，或年輕貌美但不馴。他選擇後者，接吻後老嫗化為美女，兩人快樂度日。訓曰：願耶穌賜福天下女性，讓老公聽話、滿足老婆性需求。

磨坊主人所敘故事為粗謔體（fabliau）：牛津城有一老木匠與其貌美少妻艾莉森

（Alison），租房給主修天文（星象）的學生尼可拉斯（Nicholas），尼可拉斯垂涎艾莉森，後者也答應伺機幽會。另一男子亞布索朗（Absolon）也追求艾莉森，夜晚在窗下唱小夜曲。尼可拉斯和艾莉森設計愚弄老木匠以便幽會：尼可拉斯整日閉房不出，木匠好奇詢問，尼可拉斯說觀天象將降洪水，須備木桶至屋頂避災，木匠依言而行，當晚木匠、尼可拉斯、艾莉森上屋一人藏身一木桶，木匠入睡後尼可拉斯即與艾莉森行歡。凌晨亞布索朗又來唱曲，尼可拉斯與艾莉森決定捉弄他，艾莉森假允一吻，但要求亞布索朗閉目，艾莉森脫褲讓亞布索朗吻臀，亞布索朗發覺受辱，去鐵匠處借了烙棒，回來要求再吻，這次尼可拉斯脫褲打算放屁，不料亞布索朗將烙棒插入，尼可拉斯燙極大呼：「水！」木匠驚醒以為洪水已至，急將綁住木桶之繩索割斷，三人跌下屋頂，鄰居聞聲群聚歡笑。

茲選譯《坎特伯里故事集》序文起頭，喬叟用的是中古英語（Middle English）：

Whan that aprill with his shoures soote
The droghte of march hath perced to the roote,
And bathed every veyne in swich licour
Of which vertu engendred is the flour;
Whan zephirus eek with his sweete breeth
Inspired hath in every holt and heeth
Tendre croppes, and the yonge sonne
Hath in the ram his halve cours yronne,
And smale foweles maken melodye,
That slepen al the nyght with open ye
(so priketh hem nature in hir corages);
Thanne longen folk to goon on pilgrimages,
And palmeres for to seken straunge strondes,
To ferne halwes, kowthe in sondry londes;
And specially from every shires ende
Of engelond to caunterbury they wende,
The hooly blisful martir for to seke,
That hem hath holpen whan that they were seeke.

當四月天攜帶著那甜美甘霖
將三月的乾旱深浸直到柢根
讓每株樹莖都以此津液滋養，
花朵因受此嘉惠而生發綻放：
當西風也以他那芬芳的氣息
在每個樹叢每處原野都激勵
稚嫩的細枝，再者，年輕的太陽
一年行程走了一半，位在牡羊，
各種小鳥禽雀紛紛展喉歌唱，
就連夜晚睡眠雙眼也不閉上
（大自然這般地激動牠們心情）：
當此時刻人們會想要去朝聖，
一眾信徒會想探尋異鄉異城，
去敬拜遙遠他方各國的聖人；
尤其，從英格蘭各郡角落他們
向著坎特伯里出發，迤邐前進，
去找那位神聖受福的殉道者，
他曾賜援手，在他們病痛時刻。

1399年英王理查二世被黜，喬叟失寵，遷居西敏寺（Westminster Abbey）。大約此時寫了《喬叟對其錢包抱怨》（The Complaint of Chaucer to his Purse）：

To yow, my purse, and to noon other wight	我對你，錢包，而非對他人，
Complaine I, for ye be my lady dere.	抱怨，因你是我至親夫人。
I am so sory now that ye be light,	我很遺憾你的體重變輕，
For certes but if ye make me hevy chere,	假使你不能鼓舞我心情，
Me were as leef be leyd upon my bere,	我還不如躺入棺木進墳，
For which unto your mercy thus I crye	爲此我懇求你慈悲恩賜
Beth hevy ageyn or elles mot I dye.	請再變重，否則我必定死。
Now voucheth-sauf this day er it be night	請在日落之前向我保證
That I of yow the blisful soun may here,	我可以聽到你美妙聲音，
Or see your colour lyke the sonne bright	或見到你太陽般的顏容
That of yelownesse hadde never pere.	金黄之色無人能誇等同。
Ye be my lyf, ye be myn hertes stere,	你主導我的生命，我的心，
Quene of comfort and of good companye,	你如皇后伴人度日，安適，
Beth hevy ageyn or elles mot I dye.	請再變重，否則我必定死。
Now purse that been to me my lyves lyght	錢包，你是我生命的光明
And saveour as doun in this worlde here	是我在人世凡間的救星
Out of this toune help me thurgh your might	請以大力助我脫離此境
Sin that ye wole nat been my tresorere	即使你不願幫我管錢銀
For I am shave as nye as any frere;	因我無錢如僧人無髮莖；
But yet I prey unto your curtesye,	我謹此虔誠祈求你護持，
Beth hevy ageyn or elles mot I dye.	請再變重，否則我必定死。
Lenvoy de Chaucer	喬叟附記
O conquerour of Brutes Albyoun	噢！布魯土斯傲白昂之王
Which that by line and free eleccioun	你因乃其後裔，因眾所望
Been verray king, this song to yow I sende,	而爲王，我將此詩送給你，
And ye that mowen alle oure harmes amende	你負責平反我等的冤屈
Have minde upon my supplicacioun.	請你關注垂聽我的祈盼。

1400年喬叟去世，葬於西敏寺，1556年遷葬該寺「詩人角」（Poet's Corner），為英國作家獲此殊榮第一人。

喬叟以當時地位低下的民間用語——英語——而非傳統的拉丁文、法文寫作，開創英詩多種格律，反映社會百態，人稱英國文學之父。

傑弗瑞·喬叟

圖片來源：IDJ圖庫

1-4

史本瑟

Edmund Spenser

史本瑟
Edmund Spenser

　　史本瑟（Edmund Spenser）1552年左右生於倫敦，父親是布商，入讀劍橋大學（Cambridge University）潘伯克學院（Pembroke College），1573年獲學士學位，3年後獲碩士學位，1578年任英國東南部羅徹斯特主教（Bishop of Rochester）秘書，次年任萊斯特伯爵（Earl of Leicester）秘書，同年結婚，並出版《牧人曆書》（The Shpheardes Calender），仿效羅馬詩人維吉爾（Publius Vergilius Maro，此處從英譯 Virgil）《鄉景偶拾》（Eclogues，又譯《牧歌》、《田園詩》），以牧人柯林（Colin Clout）獨白描述一年12個月的生活，頗受歡迎。

　　史本瑟1580年赴愛爾蘭協助英國駐愛爾蘭大臣，協助鎮壓有功，1587-89年獲賜愛爾蘭西南部莊園。

　　史本瑟寓言長詩《仙后》（The Faerie Queene）歌頌都鐸（Tudor）王朝，獨創史本瑟格律（Spenserian stanza）：每段共9句，前8句5步抑揚格，末句6步抑揚格（iambic hexameter），壓句尾韻ababbcbcc。全詩原訂24冊，只完成6冊，1590年出版1-3冊，1596年出版4-6冊。第一冊以紅十字騎士（Redcrosse Knight）象徵神聖（Holiness），敘述騎士與戀人嫵娜（Una，意為「唯一」）歷險，最終結合。第二冊以貴庸爵士（Sir Guyon）象徵中庸（Temperance），敘述貴庸抗拒各種誘惑。第三冊以薄麗妥瑪女爵士（Sir Britomart）象徵貞節（Chastity）。第四冊以坎博爵士（Sir Cambell）與崔蒙爵士（Sir Triamond）象徵友情（Friendship）。第五冊以爾特高爵士（Sir Artegal）象徵公正（Justice）。第六冊以卡禮多爵士（Sir Calidore）象徵禮節（Courtesy）。詩中仙后（Gloriana）象徵光輝（Glory），一般認為代表伊莉莎白女王。圓桌武士亞瑟王（King Arthur）象徵集大成的宏偉（Magnificence）。因歌頌伊莉莎白女王，獲賜年金50鎊。茲選譯第四冊、第五冊各一段。

　　第四冊一段：

> Yet all was forg'd and spred with golden foyle,
> That vnder it hidde hate and hollow guyle.
> Ne certes can that friendship long edure,
> How euer gay and goodly be teh style,
> That doth ill cause or euill end endure:
> For vertue is the band, that bindeth harts most sure.

> 但全都以金箔打造遮掩，
> 其下藏蓋仇恨、空虛計算。
> 如此絕對無法長保友情，
> 無論外貌如何令人喜歡，
> 因其作惡，出自不良居心：
> 唯有德行可以，穩固緊繫心靈。

第五冊一段：

> What though the sea with waves continuall
> Doe eate the earth, it is no more at all ;
> Ne is the earth the lesse, or loseth ought :
> For whatsoever from one place doth fall
> Is with the tyde unto another brought :
> For there is nothing lost, that may be found if sought.

> 雖然海洋不斷地以海浪
> 吞噬陸地，但海洋並不長：
> 陸地也不減，不少去分釐：
> 因為任何一地有所失亡
> 都會隨海潮去到另一地：
> 事物永不消失，求找即可尋回。

1594年史本瑟妻子去世再婚，1596年寫就政治評論《愛爾蘭現狀一觀》（A View of the Present State of Ireland），認為須徹底消滅愛爾蘭語言、文化，才能平息造反。同年出版《仙后》4-6冊。

1598年愛爾蘭人起義，史本瑟家園毀於戰火，次年返英去世，葬於西敏寺。

據說伊莉莎白女王曾應承賜予史本瑟100鎊，財務大臣嫌多，女王回應：「那就給他合理的數額。（Then give him what is reason）」史本瑟日久未收到錢，以詩上告：

I was promis'd on a time,	我曾一度獲應承，
To have a reason for my rhyme:	為詩受賜合理賞金：
From that time unto this season,	從那時一直到如今，
I receiv'd nor rhyme nor reason.	也無詩文、也無賞金。

女王即刻賜下100鎊；此為成語rhyme or reason（意為「理由」）之由來。

史本瑟仿習歐陸詩人與喬叟，為早期英詩創立格律，人稱「詩人中之詩人」（Poets' Poet）。

圖片來源：IDJ圖庫

1-5

莎士比亞

William Shakespeare

莎士比亞（William Shakespeare）1564年4月23日前後生於英格蘭中部史特拉福鎮（Stratford-upon-Avon），父親曾任鎮長，家人皆虔信天主教。英王亨利八世1532年發動英國宗教改革，其父事業與地位遽跌，莎士比亞約14歲退學幫助家計。其作品善揣摩多重觀點，可能因新教為主流，他必須兼俱強勢弱勢族群視角。18歲婚娶大他8歲的安·亨德維（Anne Hathaway），22歲左右加入倫敦戲班，後轉入王家管家大臣戲班（Chamberlain's Men），該戲班1598年興建了環球劇院（The Globe）。伊莉莎白女王1603年去世，詹姆士一世登基，提升該戲班為國王戲班（King's Men）。依當時習俗，莎士比亞兼任編劇、演員、股東，約1610年退休，1616年病逝。據說其個性「坦誠開朗，趣思妙想源源不絕，有時簡直氾濫成災……他沉浸其中，自己笑到不行。」

莎士比亞傳世之作有154首商籟（sonnet）、2首長詩、37齣劇本，包括10齣歷史劇，17齣喜劇，10齣悲劇。

根據商籟內容，莎士比亞32歲與「黑夫人」（Dark Lady）、「美少年」（Fair Youth）大談三角戀愛。次年有人委託他寫17首商籟（可能為慶賀「美少年」17歲生日），接下來7年間他為「美少年」、「黑夫人」寫出英美文學最有名的情詩，共83首。茲譯出給「美少年」的商籟兩首。

第18首：

Shall I compare thee to a summer's day? Thou art more lovely and more temperate. Rough winds do shake the darling buds of May, And summer's lease hath all too short a date. Sometime too hot the eye of heaven shines, And often is his gold complexion dimmed.	請容我將你以夏日比擬， 你比那夏日更美更溫煦。 烈風搖撼五月甜美花蒂， 夏季又苦短轉瞬即逝去。 有時太陽照耀過於強烈， 有時金芒又被烏雲遮掩。

And every fair from fair sometime declines,	美麗事物終有一朝消謝，
By chance or nature's changing course untrimmed.	漫由機運或隨大化流衍。
But thy eternal summer shall not fade,	但你的夏日將永不變易，
Nor lose possession of that fair thou owest,	你美麗的容貌勢將長存。
Nor shall death brag thou wander'st in his shade	死神將不得誇稱佔有你，
When in eternal lines to time thou grow'st.	因你存活於永恆的詩文。
So long as men can breathe, or eyes can see,	但使人間一息一念尚留，
So long lives this, and this gives life to thee.	此詩將讓你在世間不朽。

第20首：

A woman's face with Nature's own hand painted	大自然親手賦予你女性
Hast thou, the master-mistress of my passion,	容貌，我的情夫，我的情婦，
A woman's gentle heart, but not acquainted	你有女子溫柔的心靈，但
With shifting change, as is false women's fashion,	性情堅貞，不會虛情衍數，
An eye more bright than theirs, less false in rolling,	你明眸流盼從不顯輕佻，
Gilding the object whereupon it gazeth,	你目注之物皆蒙上金輝，
A man in hue, all hues in his controlling,	你身披光彩，握霞光萬道，
Which steals men's eyes and women's souls amazeth.	讓男性炫眼，讓女性神迷。
And for a woman wert thou first created,	你原應是身為女性而來，
Till Nature, as she wrought thee, fell a-doting,	但造物者疲德打盹，給你
And by addition me of thee defeated	加了一點，讓我痛失所懷。
By adding one thing to my purpose nothing.	你多了一節，我少了一切，
But since she pricked thee out for women's pleasure,	你既雄峙，可令女人銷魂，
Mine be thy love, and thy love's use their treasure.	把愛給我，把肉體給她們。

　　據推測，莎士比亞認識「美少年」後要求「美少年」代他追求「黑夫人」，順利成了「黑夫人」入幕之賓，卻發現「黑夫人」已先一步引誘「美少年」上床，但莎士比亞

迷戀「黑夫人」肉體，無法自拔，而「黑夫人」個性專斷無情，令莎士比亞痛苦，茲選譯給「黑夫人」的商籟兩首爲例。

第143首：

Lo, as a careful housewife runs to catch One of her feathered creatures broke away, Sets down her babe, and makes all swift dispatch In pursuit of the thing she would have stay Whilst her neglected child holds her in chase, Cries to catch her whose busy care is bent To follow that which files before her face, Not prizing her poor infant's discontent So runn'st thou after that which flies from thee Whilst I thy babe chase thee afar behind. But if thou catch thy hope, turn back to me, And play the mother's part, kiss me, be kind. So will I pray that thou mayst have thy Will, If thou turn back and my loud crying still.	看啊！就像婦人奔跑捉捕 從籠裡逃脫的扁毛牲畜， 她拋下懷中幼兒，用快步 追趕她要抓起來的獵物， 她的幼兒哭喊死命扯絞 她的衣裙，但她全神貫注 追尋那難於企及的目標， 完全忽視她幼兒在嚎哭。 你也是一樣在奔尋追趕， 我像那幼兒從後方求索。 假使你如願，請停身回轉， 像母親一般，吻我，擁抱我。 你如願以償我將會求祈， 如果你回身平撫我涕泣。

第129首：

The expense of spirit in a waste of shame Is lust in action; and till action, lust Is perjur'd, murderous, bloody, full of blame, Savage, extreme, rude, cruel, not to trust; Enjoy'd no sooner, but despised straight; Past reason hunted; and no sooner had, Past reason hated, as a swallow'd bait,	羞愧地消耗浪費精與力 爲滿足肉慾；爲達到目的 肉慾不惜欺騙、血腥淋漓、 極端殘害、粗魯背信、不義； 而一旦滿足，卻即刻自鄙： 瘋狂地需索；而一旦飽饜 又瘋狂排拒，如魚餌牢繫，

On purpose laid to make the taker mad:
Mad in pursuit, and in possession so,
Had, having, and in quest to have, extreme;
A bliss in proof,--and prov'd, a very woe;
Before, a joy propos'd; behind, a dream:
All this the world well knows; yet none knows well
To shun the heaven that leads men to this hell.

故意放置，讓上鉤者痴癲：
索求時瘋邪，到手也一般，
過去、現在、未來，同樣亂狂；
探花入仙境，採畢苦無邊；
事前似幻美，事後夢一場：
此情眾人皆知，但是照樣
追尋引人入陰炙的天堂。

　　莎士比亞劇作大致分四期：第一期為30歲前所作，摹仿古羅馬劇作家、英國中世紀傳統劇作；第二期自30至36歲，先是歷史劇，後喜劇臻於成熟；第三期自36至44歲，寫出經典悲劇；第四期為44歲之後，多浪漫悲喜劇，以救贖為主題。戲班友人集其劇本於1623年刊行，稱為第一對折本（first folio）。茲譯介下列劇本段落：歷史劇《理查三世》（Richard III）、《亨利五世》（Henry V）；喜劇《仲夏夜之夢》（A Midsummer Night's Dream）、《威尼斯商人》（The Merchant of Venice）、《如你所願》（As You Like It）、《第十二夜》（The Twelfth Night）、《暴風雨》（The Tempest）；悲劇：《哈姆雷特》（Hamlet）、《奧賽羅》（Othello）、《李爾王》（King Lear）、《馬克白》（Macbeth）（此四齣合稱四大悲劇）、《羅蜜歐與茱麗葉》（Romeo and Juliet）、《凱撒大帝》（Julius Caesar）。

　　《理查三世》敘述英國玫瑰戰爭，選譯首段：

Now is the winter of our discontent
Made glorious summer by this sun of York;
And all the clouds that lour'd upon our house

如今我的鬱卒有如冬季，
但約克之子光耀如太陽。
曾經壓抑我家族的烏雲

In the deep bosom of the ocean buried.
Now are our brows bound with victorious wreaths;
Our bruised arms hung up for monuments;
Our stern alarums changed to merry meetings,
Our dreadful marches to delightful measures.
Grim-visaged war hath smooth'd his wrinkled front;
And now, instead of mounting barded steeds
To fright the souls of fearful adversaries,
He capers nimbly in a lady's chamber
To the lascivious pleasing of a lute.
But I, that am not shaped for sportive tricks,
Nor made to court an amorous looking-glass;
I, that am rudely stamp'd, and want love's majesty To
strut before a wanton ambling nymph;
I, that am curtail'd of this fair proportion,
Cheated of feature by dissembling nature,
Deformed, unfinish'd, sent before my time
Into this breathing world, scarce half made up,
And that so lamely and unfashionable
That dogs bark at me as I halt by them;
Why, I, in this weak piping time of peace,
Have no delight to pass away the time,
Unless to spy my shadow in the sun
And descant on mine own deformity:
And therefore, since I cannot prove a lover,
To entertain these fair well-spoken days,
I am determined to prove a villain
And hate the idle pleasures of these days.
Plots have I laid, inductions dangerous,
By drunken prophecies, libels and dreams,
To set my brother Clarence and the king
In deadly hate the one against the other:
And if King Edward be as true and just
As I am subtle, false and treacherous,

被驅趕埋藏到海洋深處。
我們額頭冠上勝利桂冠，
百戰刀劍被高掛作獎章，
告急的警訊變成了歌唱，
艱辛的跋涉換作了舞步。
恐怖的戰神修飾了面容，
不騎著披盔戴甲的戰騎
跟凶殘的敵人做殊死戰，
卻伴隨著淫靡的琵琶曲
在婦人睡房裡輕巧舞蹈。
只有我，身形既不便轉騰，
面容又不得攬鏡以自賞；
體態怪異，無法在那妖嬈
的美人眼前展示出身材，
我軀幹短小扭曲，大自然
少給了一副完整的形體。
時辰未到即出生，我殘缺、
不完整，只能算是半個人，
如此醜陋不受歡迎的我，
瘸腿行過狗見了都狂吠。
在今日歌舞昇平的時代，
我除了顧看自己的影子
嘲弄自己殘缺的形體外，
沒有別的娛樂消遣光陰。
在這般美好的日子裡，我
既然缺乏條件追逐聲色，
那就只能選擇做個惡人，
憎惡他人的歡愉享受。
我設計了陰謀，準備害人，
用酒後的謠傳、誹謗、讒言，
讓我的兄弟克拉倫斯和
國王彼此懷疑相互憎恨。
我雖然欺詐不實，但只要
國王執法如山、公正不偏，

> This day should Clarence closely be mew'd up,
> About a prophecy, which says that 'G'
> Of Edward's heirs the murderer shall be.

> 克拉倫斯將會被捕下獄，
> 因為有謠傳，名叫「克」的人
> 將會謀殺國王的眾子孫。

《亨利五世》描述英法戰爭，茲選譯亨利在阿晉固（Agincourt）戰役前激勵英軍以少勝多一段：

> If we are mark'd to die, we are enow
> To do our country loss; and if to live,
> The fewer men, the greater share of honour.
> God's will! I pray thee, wish not one man more.
> By Jove, I am not covetous for gold,
> Nor care I who doth feed upon my cost;
> It yearns me not if men my garments wear;
> Such outward things dwell not in my desires:
> But if it be a sin to covet honour,
> I am the most offending soul alive.
> No, faith, my coz, wish not a man from England:
> God's peace! I would not lose so great an honour
> As one man more, methinks, would share from me
> For the best hope I have. O, do not wish one more!
> Rather proclaim it, Westmoreland, through my host,
> That he which hath no stomach to this fight,
> Let him depart; his passport shall be madeAnd crowns
> for convoy put into his purse:
> We would not die in that man's company
> That fears his fellowship to die with us.
> This day is called the feast of Crispian:

> 如果我們註定要死，國家
> 不能損失更多，如果註定
> 活，越少人分享榮耀越好。
> 老天！多一個人我也不要。
> 我發誓，我絕不希求黃金，
> 也不在意誰佔我的便宜。
> 我不擔心誰穿走我衣服，
> 這些外在物質我不考慮，
> 但如果追求榮耀是罪惡，
> 那我罪大惡極，無與倫比。
> 不！兄弟，多一個人也不要！
> 上帝！即使再多一個人來
> 分享也不行，因為我預期
> 極大的榮耀。一個也不行！
> 相反的，衛摩蘭，你去宣佈
> 不想打仗的人可以自由
> 離去，通行證我們照樣發，
> 路上的盤纏也會照樣給。
> 不願跟我們同生共死的
> 人，我們也不願和他共處。
> 今天是聖克里斯便節日。

He that outlives this day, and comes safe home,
Will stand a tip-toe when the day is named,
And rouse him at the name of Crispian.
He that shall live this day, and see old age,
Will yearly on the vigil feast his neighbours,
And say 'To-morrow is Saint Crispian:'
Then will he strip his sleeve and show his scars.
And say 'These wounds I had on Crispin's day.'
Old men forget: yet all shall be forgot,
But he'll remember with advantages
What feats he did that day: then shall our names.
Familiar in his mouth as household words
Harry the king, Bedford and Exeter,
Warwick and Talbot, Salisbury and Gloucester,
Be in their flowing cups freshly remember'd.
This story shall the good man teach his son;
And Crispin Crispian shall ne'er go by,
From this day to the ending of the world,
But we in it shall be remember'd;
We few, we happy few, we band of brothers;
For he to-day that sheds his blood with me
Shall be my brother; be he ne'er so vile,
This day shall gentle his condition:
And gentlemen in England now a-bed
Shall think themselves accursed they were not here, And
hold their manhoods cheap whiles any speaks
That fought with us upon Saint Crispin's day.

今天能夠活著回家的人
一聽人們提到克里斯便
這天就會企立暨耳傾聽。
今天能夠存活到老的人
每到前夕就會宴享鄰人
說：明天是聖克里斯便節。
他會脫下衣衫，展露傷痕
說：我在克里斯平節受傷。
老人健忘，但是即使其他
忘光了，他也會每年加油
添醋述說這天的事蹟。那
我們名字，由他順口說出，
國王亨利、貝德福、艾克斯特，
沃里克、塔伯特、薩士伯里、
格勞斯特，他向我們敬酒。
這個故事他會代代相傳，
每到聖克里斯便節，打從
今日起一直到世界末日
我們的名字都將被提起──
我們幾個，幾個幸運兒，一群
弟兄。今天跟我共瀝熱血
就是我的弟兄，貧賤出身
也將因今天而高升貴族。
此刻在英國安睡的貴族
將因未能參戰倍感不幸，
今日共襄盛舉的弟兄將
讓他們在人前無法抬頭。

　　《仲夏夜之夢》可能是為1595年德比伯爵（Earl of Derby）史丹利（William Stanley）婚禮而寫，以仲夏日為背景，當晚仙巫歡慶，任何夢境都可能發生成真。三組人物（貴族、仙子、工匠）交叉帶動劇情，主題都是「愛情不受理智操控」。情節如下：萊山德（Lysander）和荷密雅（Hermia）彼此相愛。海倫娜（Helena）愛德米丘（Demetrius），德米丘原先愛海倫娜，如今愛荷密雅。荷密雅的父親伊吉斯（Egeus）

中意德米丘，要求雅典公爵席修斯（Theseus）強迫荷密雅在四天內決定要嫁德米丘、做修女、還是處死。荷密雅和萊山德逃入森林。仙王歐伯朗（Oberon）和仙后泰它妮雅（Titania）在爭吵。歐伯朗打算將迷藥點進泰它妮雅眼睛，使她愛上看到的第一個人。海倫娜和德米丘也進入森林。歐伯朗聽到德米丘罵海倫娜，命令小妖精波克（Puck）將迷藥施用於德米丘，讓他愛上海倫娜。波克錯將藥用在萊山德身上，使萊山德愛上海倫娜。一群工匠準備爲公爵的婚禮上演《皮拉莫與瑟絲比》（Pyramus and Thisbe）。波克惡作劇將匠人巴騰（Bottom）換上驢頭。泰它妮雅醒來就看到並愛上巴騰。歐伯朗施用迷藥於德米丘，讓他看到海倫娜，海倫娜卻以爲萊山德和德米丘都在作弄她。歐伯朗作法讓萊山德再次愛上荷密雅，並和泰它妮雅和解。眾人醒轉返回雅典，以爲做了一場怪夢。巴騰和工匠獻演戲劇。仙子祝福眾人。茲選譯劇尾小妖精波克向觀眾致詞：

If we shadows have offended,	設使吾等冒犯慢怠，
Think but this – and all is mended –	如此設想可堪釋懷：
That you have but slumber'd here	尊駕在此不過小憩，
While these visions did appear.	夢中所見皆幻影戲。
And this weak and idle theme,	此劇不倫而又荒唐，
No more yielding but a dream.,	醒來不過做夢一場。
Gentles, do not reprehend.	貴人請您萬勿責備，
If you pardon, we will mend.	吾等盡力補贖前罪。
And, as I am na honest Puck,	波克我來對天發誓，
If we have unearned luck	如果我們僥倖一時，
Now to scape the serpent's tongue,	得以逃過噓聲憤怒，
We will make amends ere long,	我們將會儘快彌補，
Else the Puck a liar call.	否則儘管罵我詐騙。
So, good night unto you all.	現在跟您說聲晚安，
Give me your hands, if we be friends,	若您喜歡，拍手鼓勵，
And Robin shall restore amends.	我會設法讓您滿意。

莎士比亞

《威尼斯商人》情節為：威尼斯人巴薩紐（Bassanio）向友人安東紐（Antonio）借三千元來追求富家女波霞（Portia），安東紐的錢套牢在航運投資，但向猶太高利貸商夏洛克（Shylock）借錢給巴薩紐。夏洛克仇視安東紐，要求安東紐三個月內要還錢，否則要以身上的一磅肉來償還。波霞父親的遺囑規定追她的人必須在三個盒子裡選一個，如果其中有她的相片就可以娶她，否則追求者必須獨身一世。巴薩紐選對了盒子，預定當晚成婚。巴薩紐的朋友羅倫索（Lorenzo）帶著夏洛克的女兒潔西卡（Jessica）和夏洛克大部分的財產私奔。安東紐有兩艘船遇難，巴薩紐聞訊趕回，波霞也化妝成律師尾隨。夏洛克要求安東紐交出一磅肉。波霞替安東紐辯護，指出一磅肉不得見血，夏洛克因此被判財產一半充公，一半給安東紐。安東紐將他的一半給潔西卡，並要求夏洛克歸依基督教。安東紐其它的商船順利歸來。茲選譯波霞訴諸慈悲向夏洛克求情的一段：

The quality of mercy is not strain'd,	慈悲是自然的，不可勉強，
It droppeth as the gentle rain from heaven	就好像溫柔的雨點，從上
Upon the place beneath: it is twice blest;	降臨到下，受到雙重祝福，
It blesseth him that gives and him that takes:	施者有福，受者亦然有福。
'Tis mightiest in the mightiest: it becomes	在上者慈悲，力量最大，
The throned monarch better than his crown;	它比王冠更彰顯王者之尊。
His sceptre shows the force of temporal power,	權杖代表世俗界的權力，
The attribute to awe and majesty,	王者據以號令天下人眾，
Wherein doth sit the dread and fear of kings;	能使見者心生恐懼敬畏。
But mercy is above this sceptred sway;	但慈悲比權杖位階更高，
It is enthroned in the hearts of kings,	它安坐在王者的胸襟裡，
It is an attribute to God himself;	代表著上帝天父的精神。
And earthly power doth then show likest God's	王者若兼俱慈悲和正義，
When mercy seasons justice. Therefore, Jew,	威望將近似上帝。猶太人，
Though justice be thy plea, consider this,	想想！你要的是正義，就算
That, in the course of justice, none of us	你如願以償，也沒有人會
Should see salvation: we do pray for mercy;	受到福報。我們祈求慈悲，
And that same prayer doth teach us all to render	相對的也應該對人賜予

The deeds of mercy. I have spoke thus much To mitigate the justice of thy plea; Which if thou follow, this strict court of Venice Must needs give sentence 'gainst the merchant there.	慈悲。我說了這許多，就是 要求你慈悲和正義並施。 你如果同意，就算嚴酷的 威尼斯法庭也必將遵循。

《如你所願》敘述貴族少女羅莎琳（Rosalind）之戀情，茲選譯一段獨白：

All the world's a stage, And all the men and women merely players: They have their exits and their entrances; And one man in his time plays many parts, His acts being seven ages. At first the infant, Mewling and puking in the nurse's arms. And then the whining school-boy, with his satchel And shining morning face, creeping like snail Unwillingly to school. And then the lover, Sighing like furnace, with a woeful ballad Made to his mistress' eyebrow. Then a soldier, Full of strange oaths and bearded like the pard, Jealous in honour, sudden and quick in quarrel, Seeking the bubble reputation Even in the cannon's mouth. And then the justice, In fair round belly with good capon lined, With eyes severe and beard of formal cut, Full of wise saws and modern instances; And so he plays his part. The sixth age shifts Into the lean and slipper'd pantaloon, With spectacles on nose and pouch on side,	全世界都是戲臺， 所有男男女女都是演員。 一會兒上臺，一會兒下臺 每個人一輩子角色繁多 隨著年歲演出七幕。首先 是嬰兒，在奶媽懷中哭叫 吐奶。其次是亮眼的學童， 背著書包抗議，以蝸步往 學校趑趄。再來是戀人， 嘆息不斷，賦詩歌詠情人的 眉毛。接著是兵勇，滿口的 難聽粗話，面帶豹鬚虎目， 維護錙銖名譽，動則打架， 為了追求虛名面對炮口 也毫不退讓。第五是官紳， 大腹便便，收受肥雞賄賂， 目光凌厲，鬍鬚修剪齊整， 滿口仁義道德，說的似模 似樣。第六是那乾扁瘦小 耷拉著拖鞋的老頭，鼻上 架著眼鏡，褲袋撐開一旁，

His youthful hose, well saved, a world too wide
For his shrunk shank; and his big manly voice,
Turning again toward childish treble, pipes
And whistles in his sound. Last scene of all,
That ends this strange eventful history,
Is second childishness and mere oblivion,
Sans teeth, sans eyes, sans taste, sans everything.

昔日褲管，保存良好，鬆垮
包住細瘦腳幹，昔日洪亮
嗓音回轉成兒時的尖聲
細氣。最後一幕總結這趟
奇異的旅程，是返老還童，
一切歸零，沒牙齒，沒視力，
沒味覺，任什麼全都沒了。

　　《第十二夜》敘述一對攣生兄妹各自的戀情，茲選譯其中歌詞《我的愛》（Mistress Mine）：

O, mistress mine, where are you roaming?
O stay and hear; your true love's coming,
That can sing both high and low:
Trip no further, pretty sweeting;
Journeys end in lovers' meeting,
Every wise man's son doth know.
What is love? 'tis not hereafter;
Present mirth hath present laughter;
What's to come is still unsure:
In delay there lies no plenty;
Then come kiss me, sweet and twenty,
Youth's a stuff will not endure.

噢，我的愛，你要去何方？
別走，聽我說，你的真愛將來訪，
他會對你婉轉高歌。
別再找了，可愛的女郎，
找到情人，旅途也將收場，
聰明的人都曉得。
愛在哪裡？不在未來，
就在眼前好開懷，
未來事情誰敢說。
等待耽誤沒收穫，
可愛的女郎，來吻我，
青春歲月莫蹉跎。

　　《暴風雨》情節為：米蘭公爵伯斯普洛（Prospero）具有魔法，和女兒密蘭達（Miranda）住在仙島。12年前，伯斯普洛的弟弟安東紐（Antonio）和那不勒斯國王

阿朗所（Alonso）將伯斯普洛和密蘭達放逐海上。伯斯普洛有精靈阿利兒（Ariel）和野人卡力般（Caliban）服侍。伯斯普洛獲知仇人在附近海上，作法以暴風沉船，若干生還者來到島上，其中有阿朗所之子費迪南（Ferdinand），密蘭達一見而鍾情。安東紐和史巴斯欽（Sebastian）計劃殺害阿朗所，被阿利兒所阻。卡力般拉攏史提法諾（Stephano）和秦庫洛（Trinculo）殺害伯斯普洛篡位，被阿利兒報知伯斯普洛。伯斯普洛派阿利兒愚弄安東紐、阿朗所和陰謀篡位的人。費迪南和密蘭達成婚。伯斯普洛要求安東紐歸還他的爵位，決定放棄魔法，解放卡力般和阿利兒，但要阿利兒讓他們順風回返那不勒斯。茲選譯阿利兒所唱《五尋深》（Five Fathoms Deep）歌詞：

Full fathom five thy father lies;	你父親在五尋深處，
Of his bones are coral made;	他的尸骨化作珊瑚，
Those are pearls that were his eyes:	他的眼睛化作珍珠，
Nothing of him that doth fade,	他的一切都被保留，
But doth suffer a sea-change	但是受到大海洗淘，
Into something rich and strange.	轉成一組奇珍異寶。
Sea-nymphs hourly ring his knell:	水仙時刻爲他敲喪鐘，
Ding-dong.	叮—咚，
Hark! now I hear them-Ding-dong, bell.	聽！我聽到鐘聲叮—咚。

　　《哈姆雷特》情節爲：丹麥王子哈姆雷特父親去世，母親格楚德（Gertrude）依例嫁給小叔新王克勞迪斯（Claudius）。哈姆雷特父親亡魂顯靈，宣稱他是被克勞迪斯所殺，要哈姆雷特復仇。哈姆雷特裝瘋，推拒情人歐菲麗雅（Ophelia）。哈姆雷特僱用戲班演出弟弟殺王兄的情節以確定克勞迪斯是兇手。哈姆雷特指責母親嫁給弒夫者，歐菲麗雅的父親波洛紐斯（Polonius）躲在幕後偷聽，哈姆雷特以爲是克勞迪斯，將他刺死。克勞迪斯派哈姆雷特帶信給英國國王，信中要求對方處死哈姆雷特。歐菲麗雅發瘋投河自盡，她哥哥雷提斯（Laertes）返國爲家人復仇。哈姆雷特返國告訴好友荷瑞修（Horatio）他修改信函，反而讓監送他的人被殺。在歐菲麗雅的葬禮上，雷提斯挑

戰哈姆雷特。克勞迪斯安排雷提斯劍尖塗毒，還準備毒酒給哈姆雷特喝。決鬥時，格楚德誤服毒酒，雷提斯刺傷哈姆雷特，自己也被毒劍刺傷。雷提斯供出克勞迪斯的陰謀。哈姆雷特以毒劍刺傷克勞迪斯，再迫他喝下毒酒，之後自己也死去。挪威王子佛亭巴斯（Fortinbras）率軍攻入，下令安葬眾人。哈姆雷特思考人生意義的獨白，有史以來排名第一：

To be, or not to be,—that is the question:—	玉碎，還是瓦全，難題在此。
Whether 'tis nobler in the mind to suffer	哪樣比較偉大？忍耐接受
The slings and arrows of outrageous fortune	命運無情的摧殘和折磨，
Or to take arms against a sea of troubles,	還是奮身對抗如潮打擊，
And by opposing end them?—To die,—to sleep,—	將那打擊終結？結束——安息——
No more; and by a sleep to say we end	消失；以安息終止折磨
The heartache, and the thousand natural shocks	痛楚和人生難免的百般
That flesh is heir to,—'tis a consummation	肉體苦難，——如此結局
Devoutly to be wish'd. To die,—to sleep;—	人人懇切祈求，結束——安息；
To sleep! perchance to dream:—ay, there's the rub;	安息！或可入夢——哎，問題來了：
For in that sleep of death what dreams may come,	當我們擺脫了累贅軀殼
When we have shuffled off this mortal coil,	永恆安息帶來何種夢境？
Must give us pause: there's the respect	這要好好考慮；就是這個
That makes calamity of so long life;	讓人寧願忍耐長壽之災；
For who would bear the whips and scorns of time,	誰會願意承受那時間
The oppressor's wrong, the proud man's contumely,	的鞭笞、強者的暴虐、驕者
The pangs of despis'd love, the law's delay,	的侮慢、失戀的苦痛、律法
The insolence of office, and the spurns	的延宕、官曹的欺凌、還有
That patient merit of the unworthy takes,	被鄉鄙之人辜負的一片善心，
When he himself might his quietus make	假如一支匕首就能自我
With a bare bodkin? who would these fardels bear,	了結，求得安息？誰會揹負
To grunt and sweat under a weary life,	如此重擔，汗流浹背、氣不得喘，
But that the dread of something after death,—	若非我們畏懼死後的未知——
The undiscover'd country, from whose bourn	那不為人知的國度，有去
No traveller returns,—puzzles the will,	無回，——意志為之困頓，讓人

莎士比亞

And makes us rather bear those ills we have	寧可承受已知的辛酸
Than fly to others that we know not of?	也不願面對未知的問題。
Thus conscience does make cowards of us all;	所以：想的越多，膽子越小；
And thus the native hue of resolution	意志和膽識無畏的本色
Is sicklied o'er with the pale cast of thought;	披上了理智灰暗的外衣：
And enterprises of great pith and moment,	原本那活力充盛的偉業
With this regard, their currents turn awry,	一念及此，力道即刻鬆弛，
And lose the name of action.	不復有行動能力。

　　《奧賽羅》情節為：摩爾人奧賽羅是威尼斯將軍，他提升卡西歐（Cassio）為副手，伊亞格（Iago）因妒嫉而決心報復。奧賽羅和威尼斯元老，白人巴班修（Brabantio）的女兒德娣摩娜（Desdemona）秘密結婚。奧賽羅被威尼斯公爵派往塞浦路斯，伊亞格和妻子愛密里雅（Emelia）護送德娣摩娜前往。伊亞格灌醉卡西歐，再鼓動追求德娣摩娜未果的羅德里格（Roderigo）和卡西歐打架，卡西歐因此被罷黜。伊亞格再慫恿卡西歐要求德娣摩娜為他求情。伊亞格讓奧賽羅懷疑卡西歐和德娣摩娜通姦。伊亞格拿到奧賽羅送給德娣摩娜的手巾，放到卡西歐房裡，卡西歐又送給情人，伊亞格讓奧賽羅深化誤解。奧賽羅叫伊亞格殺死卡西歐，伊亞格叫羅德里格下手，羅德里格失手後被伊亞格滅口。奧賽羅勒死德娣摩娜，愛密里雅為德娣摩娜辯護，卻被伊亞格殺死。羅德里格身上的信證實伊亞格的陰謀，奧賽羅自殺在德娣摩娜身旁。奧賽羅殺死德娣摩娜前，看著她在床上安睡，有一段獨白：

It is the cause, it is the cause, my soul,--	是因為這樣，是因為這樣。
Let me not name it to you, you chaste stars!--	對純潔眾星我無法啓口！
It is the cause. Yet I'll not shed her blood;	是因為這樣。別讓她流血，
Nor scar that whiter skin of hers than snow,	也別污毀她潔白勝初雪，

And smooth as monumental alabaster.	潤滑如石膏的美麗肌膚。
Yet she must die, else she'll betray more men.	她必須死，才不會再背叛。
Put out the light, and then put out the light:	撑滅燭光，然後撑滅靈光。
If I quench thee, thou flaming minister,	如果我撑滅蠟燭的火光，
I can again thy former light restore,	萬一後悔，還可以再點燃。
Should I repent me: but once put out thy light,	可是一旦撑滅了大自然
Thou cunning'st pattern of excelling nature,	神奇的靈光，要到那裡去
I know not where is that Promethean heat	尋找普羅米修斯的火種
That can thy light relume. When I have pluck'd the rose,	將你再點燃呢？玫瑰一旦
I cannot give it vital growth again.	摘下，就失去了寶貴生命，
It must needs wither: I'll smell it on the tree.	必然凋謝。摘前先嗅一下。
Ah balmy breath, that dost almost persuade	噢，香啊！幾乎足以說服我
Justice to break her sword! One more, one more.	放棄正義之劍！再來一次。
Be thus when thou art dead, and I will kill thee,	願你死後也如此，讓我先殺你，
Kissing her	吻她
And love thee after. One more, and this the last:	再愛你。最後再一次。
So sweet was ne'er so fatal. I must weep,	甜蜜，卻又惡毒。讓我流下
But they are cruel tears: this sorrow's heavenly;	忍心淚水，既甘美，又創痛，
It strikes where it doth love.	苦樂交攻。

　　《李爾王》情節爲：年邁的英國國王李爾決定將王國平分給三個女兒甘娜瑞（Goneril）、莉根（Regan）、科娣里雅（Cordelia）。甘娜瑞和莉根誇示她們對李爾的愛，科娣里雅只平實的說她愛李爾如女兒愛父親。李爾怒奪科娣里雅的遺產，但法國國王願意娶她，支持科娣里雅的肯特（Kent）伯爵也被放逐。格勞斯特（Gloucester）有兩個兒子，艾格（Edgar）和艾德蒙（Edmund）。艾德蒙欺騙格勞斯特說艾格打算弒父，艾格裝瘋避禍。甘娜瑞和莉根虐待李爾，李爾只有肯特和弄臣陪伴。李爾被逼瘋，在原野中對暴風雨咆哮。格勞斯特幫他們會見由法國帶兵相助的科娣里雅夫婦，卻因此被刺瞎。甘娜瑞先生阿伯尼（Albany）公爵對她不滿，莉根先生去世，兩人都愛上艾德蒙。法軍戰敗，李爾和科娣里雅被俘。艾格決鬥殺死艾德蒙。甘娜瑞爲搶奪艾德蒙毒死莉根，又在艾德蒙死後自殺。科娣里雅被處死，李爾傷心而死，格勞斯特也去世，肯特

和艾格離去，讓阿伯尼統治英國。茲選譯李爾被俘後對科娣里雅所說的一段：

We two alone will sing like birds i' the cage: When thou dost ask me blessing, I'll kneel down, And ask of thee forgiveness: so we'll live, And pray, and sing, and tell old tales, and laugh At gilded butterflies, and hear poor rogues Talk of court news; and we'll talk with them too, Who loses and who wins; who's in, who's out; And take upon's the mystery of things, As if we were God's spies: and we'll wear out, In a wall'd prison, packs and sets of great ones That ebb and flow by the moon.	我們倆像籠中之鳥歌唱， 你求我賜福，我向你下跪 祈求你原諒。我們就如此 過活、唱歌、說故事，嘲笑那 鍍金的蝴蝶，聆聽可憐蟲 傳述宮廷新聞，我們也談 誰輸、誰贏、誰得寵、誰失寵； 探究人間奧秘，彷彿我們 是上帝的密使；我們將在 監獄四壁內，用盡一群群 隨時變換消長風雲人物。

　　《馬克白》情節爲：馬克白是蘇格蘭國王鄧肯（Duncan）手下大將。考多（Cawdor）爵士叛變，馬克白和班扣（Banquo）鎮壓歸來，遇見三個巫婆預言馬克白會受封爲新的考多爵士，進而成爲國王，班扣的兒子也會成爲國王。鄧肯果然提昇馬克白爲考多爵士。馬克白夫人慫恿他做國王。馬克白將來訪的鄧肯被刺殺，把刀放在侍衛手中，再將侍衛殺死。馬克白登基，鄧肯的兒子馬肯（Malcolm）和唐諾貝（Donalbain）逃走，眾人以爲是他們殺了鄧肯，只有班扣懷疑馬克白。馬克白僱人刺殺班扣和他兒子佛利昂（Fleance），佛利昂逃走。馬克白將另一逃到英國的貴族馬克德（Macduff）家人殺死。馬克德和馬肯興兵攻打馬克白。巫婆說要伯南（Birnam）森林來到敦希南（Dunsinane）城堡馬克白才會失勢，而且沒有任何女人生的男子能殺死他。馬克白夫人發瘋夢遊死亡。馬肯的軍隊以伯南森林做掩護逼近。馬克德告訴馬克白他是剖腹產，然後殺死馬克白。馬肯登基。茲選譯馬克白劇尾獨白：

Out, out, brief candle! Life's but a walking shadow, a poor player That struts and frets his hour upon the stage, And then is heard no more; it is a tale Told by an idiot, full of sound and fury, Signifying nothing.	熄滅吧！短暫的蠟燭！ 生命不過是浮略的幻影， 一時在臺上誇叱的劣角， 旋即闃然；是痴人述說的 故事，充滿了喧囂和憤怒， 毫無意義。

　　《羅蜜歐與茱麗葉》情節為：孟它古（Montague）和卡普列（Capulet）家族在維羅那城（Verona）互鬥。城主下令械鬥者處死。孟它古家的羅密歐（Romeo）溜進卡普列家的舞會，看到卡普列的女兒朱麗葉（Juliet），偷進花園向朱麗葉示愛。兩人在和尚勞倫斯（Laurence）協助下準備結婚。朱麗葉的表哥提伯特（Tybalt）發現羅密歐來參加舞會，因此要教訓他。羅密歐避免械鬥，但是他的好友梅庫修（Mercutio）和提伯特鬥劍身亡。羅密歐又將提伯特殺死。城主下令驅逐羅密歐，他向朱麗葉道別，但是預期不久可以重聚。朱麗葉的父親要她嫁給城主的親戚巴里斯（Paris）。朱麗葉服藥令她假死四十二小時，同時勞倫斯派人通知羅密歐來救她。勞倫斯被延誤，羅密歐以為朱麗葉真的去世，在她的墓前見到巴里斯，將他殺死，然後在她身旁服毒自殺。朱麗葉醒來見到羅密歐已死，用他的劍自殺。城主帶著孟它古和卡普列來到。勞倫斯解釋了一切，孟它古和卡普列發誓兩家不再為敵。茲選譯舞會後朱麗葉在窗臺邊獨白：

O Romeo, Romeo! wherefore art thou Romeo? Deny thy father and refuse thy name; Or, if thou wilt not, be but sworn my love, And I'll no longer be a Capulet. ...	羅密歐，為何你是羅密歐？ 拒認你父親，放棄你姓名。 要不，只要你發誓說愛我， 我就放棄卡普列的姓氏。 ……

'Tis but thy name that is my enemy; Thou art thyself, though not a Montague. What's Montague? it is nor hand, nor foot, Nor arm, nor face, nor any other part Belonging to a man. O, be some other name! What's in a name? that which we call a rose By any other name would smell as sweet; So Romeo would, were he not Romeo call'd, Retain that dear perfection which he owes Without that title. Romeo, doff thy name, And for that name which is no part of thee Take all myself.	你的姓名才是我的敵人。 你就是你，你不是孟它古。 孟它古是什麼？非手、非腳、 非臂、非臉，也不是人身上 任何部位。你取別的姓吧！ 姓名算什麼呢？我們稱爲 玫瑰的，換稱呼也一樣香。 同樣的，羅密歐如果換了 名字也一樣會那麼完美。 羅密歐！換掉你的名字吧！ 放棄無關痛癢的名字， 我就把身心全交給你。

《凱撒大帝》敘述凱撒被刺事蹟，茲選譯其中安東尼（Mark Antony）悼念凱撒的演說：

Friends, Romans, countrymen, lend me your ears; I come to bury Caesar, not to praise him. The evil that men do lives after them, The good is oft interred with their bones; So let it be with Caesar. The noble Brutus Hath told you Caesar was ambitious; If it were so, it was a grievous fault, And grievously hath Caesar answer'd it. Here, under leave of Brutus and the rest,— For Brutus is an honourable man; So are they all, all honourable men,— Come I to speak in Caesar's funeral.	朋友、市民、同胞，請聽我說； 我來安葬，而非讚美，凱撒。 人們所做壞事流傳身後， 好事卻常伴隨骸骨入土； 凱撒亦然。君子布魯特斯 告訴你們凱撒富有野心； 若真如此，這是重大缺陷， 凱撒也付出了重大代價。 我，得到布魯特斯等允許， 是的，正人君子布魯特斯； 他們個個，個個都是君子， 來參加凱撒的葬禮致詞。

莎士比亞

He was my friend, faithful and just to me:	凱撒吾友，待我忠誠正直；
But Brutus says he was ambitious;	但布魯特斯說他有野心；
And Brutus is an honourable man.	是的，正人君子布魯特斯。
He hath brought many captives home to Rome,	凱撒為羅馬停獲許多人，
Whose ransoms did the general coffers fill:	他們的贖金全進了國庫；
Did this in Caesar seem ambitious?	他這樣做，像是有野心嗎？
When that the poor have cried, Caesar hath wept;	見到窮人哭喊，凱撒悲泣；
Ambition should be made of sterner stuff:	野心家不會這麼軟弱吧？
Yet Brutus says he was ambitious;	但布魯特斯說他有野心；
And Brutus is an honourable man.	是的，正人君子布魯特斯。
You all did see that on the Lupercal	你們都看到我曾在狼窟
I thrice presented him a kingly crown,	三度向凱撒呈獻上王冠，
Which he did thrice refuse: was this ambition?	被他拒絕；這像有野心嗎？
Yet Brutus says he was ambitious;	但布魯特斯說他有野心；
And, sure, he is an honourable man.	而布魯特斯，當然，是君子。
I speak not to disprove what Brutus spoke,	我不是說布魯斯特說錯，
But here I am to speak what I do know.	我只是說出我所知道的。
You all did love him once, not without cause:	你們大家曾經深愛凱撒；
What cause withholds you then to mourn for him?	為何如今連悲悼也不肯？
O judgment! thou art fled to brutish beasts,	天理啊！你被野獸給吞了，
And men have lost their reason. Bear with me;	人們失去了良知。寬恕我；
My heart is in the coffin there with Caesar,	我心已隨凱撒進入棺木，
And I must pause till it come back to me.	我說不下去，要等它歸來。

　　莎士比亞長詩有《維納斯和阿當那斯》（Venus and Adonis）、《魯克麗絲失貞記》（The Rape of Lucrece），後者描述羅馬古王塔昆（Tarquin）之子賽斯特斯（Sextus）強姦貴族科拉提諾（Collatinus）之妻魯克麗絲之事。

　　莎士比亞於文學技巧無開創但集大成，早期摹仿羅馬作家手法，後期吸收希臘作家意境，編劇襲用現成故事加以改編，身處英國歷史新舊轉折，既出身於中世紀舊傳統，又參與開創近代人本思想；他多方觀察人物世事，藉文藝復興、海路拓展豐富其語彙，成為千古文豪。

圖片來源：IDJ圖庫

1-6
鄧約翰
John Donne

鄧約翰
John Donne

　　鄧約翰（John Donne）1572年生於倫敦天主教家庭，父親爲鐵商公會理事，於他4歲時去世，母親再嫁。鄧約翰1583年入讀牛津大學哈特福學院（Hertford College），1586年轉劍橋大學，1589年肄業，因天主教身份未獲學位。1591年入讀泰維法學院（Thavies Inn），次年轉林肯法學院（Lincoln's Inn），其弟亨利1593年因藏匿天主教士下獄病死，鄧約翰因此質疑自身信仰，改信英國國教。

　　鄧約翰年少揮霍遺產享聲色之娛，遊歷南歐，習意大利、西班牙語，1596-97年參加英西海戰。1597年出任掌璽大臣湯瑪斯·艾格頓爵士（Thomas Egerton）秘書。

　　其早年詩作多描繪男女情色，如《跳蚤》（The Flea）：[1]

Mark but this flea, and mark in this,	你瞧這跳蚤，瞧瞧
How little that which thou deniest me is;	你拒絕我的多微不足道；
It suck'd me first, and now sucks thee,	牠吸我的血，再吸你，
And in this flea our two bloods mingled be.	我倆的血在牠體內合一。
Thou know'st that this cannot be said	你也知道這不構成
A sin, nor shame, nor loss of maidenhead;	罪孽、羞恥、不構成失貞；
Yet this enjoys before it woo,	然而牠未追求即享宴，
And pamper'd swells with one blood made of two;	飽食我倆血液，膨脹自滿；
And this, alas! is more than we would do.	而這，哀哉！比我倆還超前。
O stay, three lives in one flea spare,	住手，一番勿奪三命，
Where we almost, yea, more than married are.	我倆在牠體內幾已成婚。
This flea is you and I, and this	這跳蚤包含我倆，
Our marriage bed, and marriage temple is.	是我倆洞房，是我倆教堂。
Though parents grudge, and you, we're met,	父母和你雖不滿，我們

---

[1] 時人相信男女交合時血液會混而爲一。

And cloister'd in these living walls of jet.	仍在此黑亮教堂裡成婚。
Though use make you apt to kill me,	雖然你順手想將我毀，
Let not to that self-murder added be,	但切勿連帶殺了你自己，
And sacrilege, three sins in killing three.	這是褻瀆，三殺成三罪。
Cruel and sudden, hast thou since	殘忍突擊，你是否
Purpled thy nail in blood of innocence?	以無辜鮮血沾染指手？
Wherein could this flea guilty be,	這跳蚤犯下何罪孽，
Except in that drop which it suck'd from thee?	除了吸了你的一滴血？
Yet thou triumph'st, and say'st that thou	而你炫耀自得說
Find'st not thyself nor me the weaker now.	你我皆未因此而衰弱。
'Tis true; then learn how false fears be;	沒錯；所以你不該恐懼；
Just so much honour, when thou yield'st to me,	你若依我，貞操失去，
Will waste, as this flea's death took life from thee.	受損正如跳蚤之死所取。

再如1654年死後出版的《輓歌 第十九：致情人上床》（Elegy XIX: To His Mistress Going to Bed）：

Come, Madam, come, all rest my powers defy,	來，夫人，來，我精神緊繃不舒，
Until I labour, I in labour lie.	若不能痛幹，我只能痛苦。
The foe oft-times, having the foe in sight,	對敵時經常，當已看到對方，
Is tired with standing, though they never fight.	兀立就疲憊，雖尚未打仗。
Off with that girdle, like heaven's zone glistering	脫掉那腰帶，閃耀如銀河
But a far fairer world encompassing.	但所圍繞的世界更婀娜。
Unpin that spangled breast-plate, which you wear	解開那亮麗護胸，你穿上
That th'eyes of busy fools may be stopped there:	是為阻擋好色者的目光：
Unlace yourself, for that harmonious chime	解開絲帶，那悅耳的聲響
Tells me from you that now 'tis your bed time.	告訴我你現在正該上床。
Off with that happy busk, whom I envy	脫掉幸運的束胸蓋，我羨嫉

◆
鄧
約
翰
◆

That still can be, and still can stand so nigh.

Your gown's going off such beauteous state reveals

As when from flowery meads th'hills shadow steals.

Off with your wiry coronet and show

The hairy diadem which on you doth grow.

Off with those shoes: and then safely tread

In this love's hallowed temple, this soft bed.

In such white robes heaven's angels used to be

Received by men; thou Angel bring'st with thee

A heaven like Mahomet's Paradise; and though

Ill spirits walk in white, we easily know

By this these Angels from an evil sprite:

They set out hairs, but these the flesh upright.

License my roving hands, and let them go

Behind before, above, between, below.

Oh my America, my new found land,

My kingdom, safeliest when with one man manned,

My mine of precious stones, my Empery,

How blessed am I in this discovering thee.

To enter in these bonds is to be free,

Then where my hand is set my seal shall be.

Full nakedness, all joys are due to thee.

As souls unbodied, bodies unclothed must be

To taste whole joys. Gems which you women use

Are as Atlanta's balls, cast in men's views,

That when a fool's eye lighteth on a gem

His earthly soul may covet theirs not them.

Like pictures, or like books' gay coverings made

For laymen, are all women thus arrayed;

Themselves are mystic books, which only we

Whom their imputed grace will dignify

Must see revealed. Then since I may know,

As liberally as to a midwife show

Thyself; cast all, yea this white linen hence.

Here is no penance, much less innocence.

To teach thee, I am naked first: why then

What need'st thou have more covering than a man.

它如此鎮定，如此貼近你。

你衣袍脫落透露如此美景

有似遍野鮮花由山陰現形。

脫下你的金屬頭飾，秀顯

長在你身上的毛髮冠冕。

脫掉鞋子：然後安穩地踏上

愛情神聖的殿堂，這張軟床。

天國使節曾穿著此白袍

受人接待：你這位天使要

帶給人回教般的天堂；雖則

惡靈也著白袍，我們可

輕易將天使與惡靈分出：

後者立人毛髮，前者肌膚。

縱容我的手遊走，走遍

後面、前面、上面、中間、下面。

噢我的亞美利加，我的新土，

我的國度，我獨擁最能守護，

我的玉石寶礦，我的屬地，

我太幸運了得以發現你。

訂下合約許我為所欲為，

我手所及我的印記即在彼。

脫光光，一切快活來自你。

如靈魂離體，肉身也須離衣

才能痛嚐歡樂。女人的珠寶

有如雅特蘭妲的金果，擲拋

引誘男人，看到的人若愚蠢

會想要金果而忘了女人。

像圖畫，也像亮麗的書裝裱

給無知者，女人都打扮精巧；

她們是神秘的書籍，只有應

受其典雅恩賜的我們

才能開卷閱覽。既然如此，

要像面對產婆，儘管展示

你自己；脫光，脫光這白衣裳。

這裡沒有罪罰，更沒有純潔。

為教導你，我先裸體：那麼

你何需穿著較男人更多。

1601年鄧約翰秘密婚娶艾格頓第二任妻子的17歲姪女安‧摩爾（Anne More），因此遭解雇短暫下獄，之後其妻每年一產，靠妻子親戚接濟、並執律師業維生，因生活困苦，1608年甚至撰文為自殺辯護。《成聖》（The Canonization）一詩應是此時寫成：

FOR God's sake hold your tongue, and let me love;	看老天的份上住嘴，讓我愛；
Or chide my palsy, or my gout;	數說我中風，痛風
My five gray hairs, or ruin'd fortune flout;	嘲笑我五莖白髮，我的衰運；
With wealth your state, your mind with arts improve;	你既有錢，學文藝提升心懷；
Take you a course, get you a place,	修個課程，去趟旅程，
Observe his Honour, or his Grace;	觀察大人，巴結貴人；
Or the king's real, or his stamp'd face	國王本人，或其鑄銀
Contemplate; what you will, approve,	端詳；啥給嗨，就去嗨，
So you will let me love.	但別阻撓我愛。
Alas! alas! who's injured by my love?	嗚呼！哀哉！誰被我的愛傷害？
What merchant's ships have my sighs drown'd?	我的悲嘆沉了誰的船？
Who says my tears have overflow'd his ground?	誰抱怨我的淚淹了他田圃？
When did my colds a forward spring remove?	我的傷風可曾阻擋了春天？
When did the heats which my veins fill	充斥我體內的熱血
Add one more to the plaguy bill?	可曾害一人滅絕？
Soldiers find wars, and lawyers find out still Litigious men,	士兵找仗打，律師則尋獵
which quarrels move,	好訟者，他們愛把槓抬，
Though she and I do love.	但她和我只想愛。
Call's what you will, we are made such by love;	隨你怎說，我們如此是因愛；
Call her one, me another fly,	叫她，還有我，做蒼蠅，
We're tapers too, and at our own cost die,	我們也是蠟燭，自斃自焚，
And we in us find th' eagle and the dove.	老鷹、鴿子都在我倆胸懷。
The phoenix riddle hath more wit	鳳凰之謎因我倆當
By us; we two being one, are it;	更有理；我倆二合一，即鳳凰；
So, to one neutral thing both sexes fit.	如此，男女皆屬中性之象。
We die and rise the same, and prove	我倆同死共復生，愛情
Mysterious by this love.	賦予我們奇行。
We can die by it, if not live by love,	我倆可因愛死，若非因愛生，
And if unfit for tomb or hearse	若不得載於墓穴靈車
Our legend be, it will be fit for verse;	我倆的傳奇，可載於詩歌；

And if no piece of chronicle we prove,	若我倆事跡不載於史書，
We'll build in sonnets pretty rooms;	我們可在商籟裡居住；
As well a well-wrought urn becomes	好的骨灰罈裝殮
The greatest ashes, as half-acre tombs,	偉人骨灰，等同廣大墓圍，
And by these hymns, all shall approve	借此詩句，眾皆將贊同
Us canonized for love;	我倆因愛而成聖；
And thus invoke us, "You, whom reverend love	他們將祈求：「你倆，因神聖愛情
Made one another's hermitage;	成爲彼此的隱居所；
You, to whom love was peace, that now is rage;	你倆，因愛得寧靜，此刻雖顚簸；
Who did the whole world's soul contract, and drove	你倆凝縮了世界，將其靈魂
Into the glasses of your eyes;	攝入你倆眼睛；
So made such mirrors, and such spies,	成就如許奇鏡，奇景，
That they did all to you epitomize—	對你倆而言這就是紅塵 —
Countries, towns, courts beg from above	國度、城鎮、宮廷對天乞盼
A pattern of your love."	你倆愛的典範。」

　　1609年鄧約翰與岳父和解，獲得嫁妝，此後詩作漸轉思考生死。1610年賦詩《商籟第十：死神別驕傲》（Sonnet X: Death Be Not Proud）：

Death be not proud, though some have called thee	死神別驕傲，雖然有人稱
Mighty and dreadful, for, thou art not so,	說你偉大、可怕，其實失真，
For, those, whom thou think'st, thou dost overthrow,	因爲你以爲被你扳倒之人，
Die not, poore death, nor yet canst thou kill me.	實未死，哀哉，殺我你也不能。
From rest and sleepe, which but thy pictures bee,	既然休息與睡眠，你的縮影，
Much pleasure, then from thee, much more must flow,	給人安樂，那你必能給人更豐，
And soonest our best men with thee doe goe,	人中英豪最早隨你而行，
Rest of their bones, and souls deliverie.	屍骨得安息，靈魂得平靜。

Thou art slave to Fate, Chance, kings, and desperate men, And dost with poyson, warre, and sicknesse dwell, And poppie, or charmes can make us sleepe as well, And better then thy stroake; why swell'st thou then; One short sleepe past, wee wake eternally, And death shall be no more; Death, thou shalt die.	你是命運、無常、王者、亡命徒之隸， 你和毒物、戰爭、疾病糾纏， 罌粟、符咒也能讓人入眠， 且手腕比你好，你有何神氣； 經過短眠，我們覺醒於永生， 不再有死亡；死神，你將喪命。

1611-12年鄧約翰赴歐前賦詩《道別：不可悲傷》（A Valediction: Forbidding Mourning）給妻子：

As virtuous men pass mildly away, And whisper to their souls to go, Whilst some of their sad friends do say, "Now his breath goes," and some say, "No." So let us melt, and make no noise, No tear-floods, nor sigh-tempests move; 'Twere profanation of our joys To tell the laity our love. Moving of th' earth brings harms and fears; Men reckon what it did, and meant; But trepidation of the spheres, Though greater far, is innocent. Dull sublunary lovers' love —Whose soul is sense—cannot admit Of absence, 'cause it doth remove The thing which elemented it. But we by a love so much refined,	當有德之士平靜逝去， 輕語靈魂該要分離， 某些友人悲傷私語： 「嚥氣了，」別人說：「還沒。」 讓我們消失，輕悄無聲， 不嚎啕，不大聲嘆哀； 那會褻瀆我們的歡情 若告知凡人我等之愛。 地球動搖會傷人嚇人； 人們會猜想其徵兆； 而天上星球的蕩震， 雖更劇烈，但於人無擾。 地上凡人粗俗愛戀 ——其心靈全在感官——不容 分離，因為分離離間 感官，以致心靈也不成。 而我們的愛情極高雅，

鄧約翰

That ourselves know not what it is,	連我們都難以描述，
Inter-assurèd of the mind,	我們彼此互信有加，
Care less, eyes, lips and hands to miss.	不慮眼、唇、手是否接觸。
Our two souls therefore, which are one,	我倆靈魂實爲一體，
Though I must go, endure not yet	不因我遠去而造成
A breach, but an expansion,	分離，反而得以擴溢，
Like gold to aery thinness beat.	有如黃金無限延伸。
If they be two, they are two so	即使其爲二，也如
As stiff twin compasses are two;	圓規堅定之雙腳；
Thy soul, the fix'd foot, makes no show	你的靈魂固定彷彿
To move, but doth, if th' other do.	不動，但隨另足而繞。
And though it in the centre sit,	你的靈魂安坐中心，
Yet, when the other far doth roam,	但當另足出門遠行，
It leans, and hearkens after it,	你傾身追隨聆聽，
And grows erect, as that comes home.	當另足返回，你復歸正。
Such wilt thou be to me, who must,	你我亦如是，我像
Like th' other foot, obliquely run;	圓規另足，離家奔走；
Thy firmness makes my circle just	你的堅定使我圓滿
And makes me end where I begun.	使我得以終歸源頭。

1617年鄧約翰妻子生下第十二胎後去世。

　　當日文人流行爲貴族作詩服務，鄧約翰以此獲寵詹姆士一世，雖不願做國教教士維生，但1615年仍接受詹姆士一世任命爲教士，同年獲得劍橋大學榮譽神學博士學位，出任皇家牧師。1618-20年隨當卡斯特子爵（Viscount Doncaster）出使德國。1621年受任倫敦聖保羅大教堂教長。1623年重病痊癒期間沉思生老病死，寫了一系列文章，隔年以《無常沉思禱書》（Devotions upon Emergent Occasions）爲名出版，其中第17篇有名句「沒有人是孤島，不求自足；人人皆是大陸之一隅，整體之一屬（No man is an island, entire of itself; every man is a piece of the continent, a part of the main）」與「毋須遣人詢問喪鐘爲誰響；它爲你響（send not to know for whom the bell tolls; it tolls for thee）」。

1631年鄧約翰去世，葬於聖保羅大教堂。年輕時詩作多在死後1633年出版。

　　德萊頓（John Dryden）1693年論及鄧約翰：「他不只在諷刺文中，也在情詩裡搬弄玄學，而情詩應以人性為主……」強生博士（Samuel Johnson）1781年因此鑄新詞「玄學派詩人」（metaphysical poets）形容之，此派巧思妙想，善用奇特比喻（conceit），鄧約翰為佼佼者，他還將羅馬諷刺文體（satire）引介入英國。

◆
∙
鄧
約
翰
∙
◆

圖片來源：IDJ圖庫

1-7

安德魯・馬佛

Andrew Marvell

安德魯·馬佛（Andrew Marvell）1621年生於英格蘭東北，父親是國教牧師，馬佛13歲入讀劍橋大學三一學院（Trinity College），獲學士學位，在校期間以希臘、拉丁文作詩。1642年赴歐旅遊，因英國內戰滯留至1647年，習得法、意大利、西班牙語。

　　內戰期間馬佛由保皇逐漸轉爲支持議會，1650-52年任議會派將領湯瑪斯·費法克斯（Thomas Fairfax）女兒家庭教師，此時寫就《致羞澀的情人》（To His Coy Mistress），爲「及時行樂」（carpe diem）詩類代表作：

Had we but world enough, and time,	假使我們時、空夠多，
This coyness, Lady, were no crime	羞澀，女士，不算罪過
We would sit down and think which way	我們可以閒坐慢思
To walk and pass our long love's day.	往何方散步度長日。
Thou by the Indian Ganges' side	你可在印度恆河邊
Shouldst rubies find: I by the tide	尋找紅寶石：我可沿
Of Humber would complain. I would	暗波河岸怨嘆。我會
Love you ten years before the Flood,	從大洪水前十年愛你，
And you should, if you please, refuse	你要的話，可以抵拒
Till the conversion of the Jews.	直到猶太人願皈依。
My vegetable love should grow	我的愛會如植物生長
Vaster than empires, and more slow;	且更慢，比帝國更廣；
A hundred years should go to praise	我會以一百年歌謳
Thine eyes and on thy forehead gaze;	你雙眼，凝視你額頭；
Two hundred to adore each breast,	雙乳各以兩百年讚美，
But thirty thousand to the rest;	三萬年獻給其他部位：
An age at least to every part,	每部份至少用一時代，
And the last age should show your heart.	最後一時代給心懷。
For, Lady, you deserve this state,	因爲，女士，你值得，
Nor would I love at lower rate.	我也不會愛得降格。
But at my back I always hear	但我總在背後聽聞
Time's wingèd chariot hurrying near;	時間的飛車逼近；

And yonder all before us lie	我們前面又是一片
Deserts of vast eternity.	永恆無盡的荒原。
Thy beauty shall no more be found,	於彼你的美貌消亡，
Nor, in thy marble vault, shall sound	你雲石墓室裡，我迴盪
My echoing song; then worms shall try	的歌聲也將不存，蛆蟲
That long preserved virginity,	將享用你多年的守貞，
And your quaint honour turn to dust,	你古樸操守將化為土，
And into ashes all my lust:	我的情慾也將成虛無：
The grave's a fine and private place,	墳墓很好也很私隱，
But none, I think, do there embrace.	但應該沒人在彼相擁。
Now therefore, while the youthful hue	所以，我們要趁朝顏
Sits on thy skin like morning dew,	仍在有如清晨露點，
And while thy willing soul transpires	要趁你心靈欣然
At every pore with instant fires,	遍體透散熱情火焰，
Now let us sport us while we may,	讓我們及時行樂，
And now, like amorous birds of prey,	像歡愛的猛禽，此刻
Rather at once our time devour	將時間一剎痛飲
Than languish in his slow-chapped power.	而非隨之慢嚼凋零。
Let us roll all our strength and all	讓我們將所有氣力
Our sweetness up into one ball,	與親昵捲成球體，
And tear our pleasures with rough strife	將歡愛撕裂衝突
Through the iron gates of life:	闖破生命似鐵戶：
Thus, though we cannot make our sun	如此，我們雖不能阻停
Stand still, yet we will make him run.	太陽，我們可使其狂奔。

1657年馬佛協助目盲的密爾頓（John Milton）擔任共和政府外語大臣。1659年獲選國會議員。查爾斯二世1660年復辟，馬佛避過保皇派懲處，還協助密爾頓免於死刑。1661年續任議員，此後匿名賦詩，批評宮廷腐敗導致1665-67年二次英荷戰爭失利。1678年去世。

馬佛以及時行樂詩《致羞澀的情人》留名後世。

圖片來源：IDJ圖庫

1-8

密爾頓

John Milton

密爾頓
John Milton

　　密爾頓（John Milton）祖父虔信天主教，父親是作曲家，因歸依新教被逐出家門，於1583年遷居倫敦，後從事代書業，密爾頓1608年生於倫敦，幼年受教於信奉長老會的家庭教師，因而傾向極端新教，稍長就讀聖保羅公校（St Paul's School），極用功，1625年入讀劍橋大學基督學院（Christ's College），結識後赴北美創立羅德島州（Rhode Island）首府主賜市（Providence）的羅傑・威廉斯（Roger Williams）。密爾頓鄙視玩樂度日的同學，他們則譏諷他纖弱長髮，稱他為「基督學院的貴婦」。1629年密爾頓畢業，志在成為英國國教牧師，續攻碩士。1630-58年寫就24首商籟。1631年寫就兩首田園詩，描述野外的一天：《快樂的人》（L'Allegro）寫愉悅嬉戲，《沉思的人》（IL Penseroso）寫安靜冥想。1632年獲碩士學位，遷去父親在英格蘭中部達比郡（Derbyshire）的新居，同年寫了紀念莎士比亞的商籟《追悼可敬的劇作家莎士比亞》（Epitaph on the admirable Dramatick Poet, W. Shakespeare）：

What needs my Shakespeare for his honour'd Bones,	我的莎士比亞，其尊貴遺骨，
The labour of an age in piled Stones,	何需勞師動眾壘石砌墓？
Or that his hallow'd reliques should be hid	其神聖遺骸又何需藏匿
Under a Star-ypointing Pyramid?	上指星辰的金字塔之底？
Dear son of memory, great heir of Fame,	你長存記憶，更承載殊榮，
What need'st thou such weak witnes of thy name?	何需卑俗之物見證令名？
Thou in our wonder and astonishment	你，讓我們拍案驚奇嘆喟，
Hast built thy self a live-long Monument.	以一生打造一座紀念碑。
For whilst to th' shame of slow-endeavouring art,	愧煞他人創作緩慢艱辛，
Thy easie numbers flow, and that each heart	你詩文泉湧，讀者各隨心
Hath from the leaves of thy unvalu'd Book,	從你那無價的書頁之中
Those Delphick lines with deep impression took,	展閱你的神諭，受用無窮；
Then thou our fancy of it self bereaving,	你以超凡思擬，使人欸似
Dost make us Marble with too much conceaving;	碑石，人心因此也哀悼不止；
And so Sepulcher'd in such pomp dost lie,	你葬身如此輝煌墓室裡；
That Kings for such a Tomb would wish to die.	王公以身許此猶不可及。

1632-38年密爾頓廣為涉獵，自修文、史、哲科學，學習拉丁、希臘、希伯來、法、西、意、荷、古英語等語言，以備獻身詩作。1634年寫作化妝神話劇《寇魔司》（Comus，酒神之子，歡樂縱慾之神），慶賀布吉瓦特伯爵（Earl of Bridgewater）榮任威爾斯法治委員會（Council of Wales）主席，詩中勸人節制守貞。1637年寫了田園悼詩《萊希達斯》（Lycidas，希臘詩人修克里圖Theocritus田園詩中牧羊人名），又名《悼近遇海難的愛德華・金》（Justa Edouardo King Naufrago），紀念當年死於威爾斯海域船難的大學同窗Edward King，人譽為最佳英語田園詩。1638年密爾頓30歲，宣稱要為英國撰寫史詩，最終於60歲出版巨著《失樂園》（Paradise Lost）。

1638-39年密爾頓遊法、意，在翡冷翠與教廷監禁的伽利略相晤；也參考了威尼斯和日內瓦的精英共和政體。返國時英格蘭、蘇格蘭正交戰，1641年密爾頓參與政治宗教辯論，撰文《論英格蘭宗教改革》（Of Reformation of Church-Discipline in England），批評天主教與蘇格蘭長老會制（Presbyterianism），為英格蘭議會派與清教徒會眾制（Congregationalism）辯護。同年為子姪開辦私校，1644年撰《論教育》（On Education），主張教育應引導啟發、才德並重，培養人才服務政府。1642年英國內戰爆發，這年他33歲，婚娶16歲的瑪麗・包沃（Mary Powell），瑪麗僅留居數月即返娘家，4年後才回來，密爾頓因此撰文宣揚離婚符合道德，主張離婚合法化，引起政府不快，他又因此於1644年撰寫《論言論自由》（Areopagitica，取名自雅典衛城旁Areopagus「戰神山」，為古代法庭辯論之處）主張新教各派應享出版言論自由，但反對無神論者、天主教徒、回教徒、猶太教徒同享此權利。1649年議會派擊潰保皇派，查理一世被處死，密爾頓因支持議會派政教立場，且嫻熟拉丁文，受任外語大臣，負責撰寫外交書信、宣揚政策、控制言論，直到1658年護國主克倫威爾（Cromwell）逝世才去職。1649-54年密爾頓撰寫多篇論文為弒君、為議會派辯護，其拉丁文斐然成章，在歐陸聲譽鵲起。

1652年密爾頓因青光眼失明，此後口述寫作，同年妻子難產去世，留有4子女，親子關係疏隔。1655年由英國國教改信更極端的清教，同年賦寫商籟《論其目盲》（On His Blindness）：

密爾頓

When I consider how my light is spent
Ere half my days in this dark world and wide,
And that one talent which is death to hide
Lodg'd with me useless, though my soul more bent
To serve therewith my Maker, and present
My true account, lest he returning chide,
"Doth God exact day-labour, light denied?"
I fondly ask. But Patience, to prevent
That murmur, soon replies: "God doth not need
Either man's work or his own gifts: who best
Bear his mild yoke, they serve him best. His state
Is kingly; thousands at his bidding speed
And post o'er land and ocean without rest:
They also serve who only stand and wait."

想到人生未半光明已逝
在這廣大的黑暗的世間，
唯一才能（若潛藏定滅湮）
竟不得用，雖然我心亟思
以之侍奉我主，向祂忠實
呈述我的一切，以免責難，
「上帝不賜光明，只允日班？」
我蠢笨提問。耐心，為堵此
牢騷，很快回應：「上帝不需
人以工作或祂所賜回饋：
肩負祂輕軛即是最好。其
國祚皇皇；萬人應命馳驅
跨廣土越四海一刻不息：
但靜候待命也是功績。」

1656年密爾頓賦寫商籟《致凱瑟琳》（Sonnet for Katherine）紀念亡妻：

Methought I saw my late espoused Saint
Brought to me like Alcestis from the grave,
Whom Joves great son to her glad Husband gave,
Rescu'd from death by force though pale and faint.
Mine as whom washt from spot of child-bed taint,
Purification in the old Law did save,
And such, as yet once more I trust to have
Full sight of her in Heaven without restraint,
Came vested all in white, pure as her mind:
Her face was vail'd, yet to my fancied sight,
Love, sweetness, goodness, in her person shin'd

我彷彿見到已成聖亡妻
像愛瑟思娣被帶出墳墓，
由宙斯虎子領還她丈夫，
從死亡搶回但蒼白無力。
我妻好似產後剛得潔洗，
靠舊約律法得拯救去污，
如此，我再度堅信在天府
將來能不受拘束見到伊，
一身白，如她心零般潔淨：
臉罩薄紗，但在我想像裡，
渾身煥發慈愛、甘美、良善

So clear, as in no face with more delight.	如此清晰，面露極度歡喜。
But O as to embrace me she enclin'd,	但，噢，正當她為擁抱俯探，
I wak'd, she fled, and day brought back my night.	我覺醒，她消逝，暗夜重蒞。

　　1656年密爾頓續弦，但續弦妻兩年後也去世。1658-64年密爾頓著手撰寫史詩《失樂園》，自言志在「向人類解釋上帝的作為」（justify the ways of God to men），採無韻五步抑揚格，故事分雙線進行：一敘撒旦被上帝打敗，淪落地獄，為復仇而誘惑上帝新創造的人類；一敘亞當、夏娃情愛糾葛，兩人受誘墮落，被逐出樂園，但上帝預示亞當人類可藉由耶穌獲贖。詩中撒旦一角擇惡固執，為後世負面英雄之濫觴。茲選譯其中三段，第一段是開頭：

OF Mans First Disobedience, and the Fruit	就人類首次抗命，就那禁樹
Of that Forbidden Tree, whose mortal tast	的果實，其貶謫凡俗之味
Brought Death into the World, and all our woe,	致死亡入世間，招來憂患，
With loss of Eden, till one greater Man	失去樂園，直到那一偉人
Restore us, and regain the blissful Seat,	救贖人類，使之重獲所失，
Sing Heav'nly Muse, that on the secret top	唱吧！天上謬思，你在俄立、
Of Oreb, or of Sinai, didst inspire	西奈山巔禁區，曾經靈啟
That Shepherd, who first taught the chosen Seed,	那牧羊人，他又教導選民
In the Beginning how the Heav'ns and Earth	在宇宙之初天地如何從
Rose out of Chaos: Or if Sion Hill	混沌展現；也許錫安山更
Delight thee more, and Siloa's Brook that flow'd	能取悅你，還有西羅亞溪
Fast by the Oracle of God; I thence	流經上帝聖諭；我因此而
Invoke thy aid to my adventrous Song,	祈求你幫助我壯舉歌唱，
That with no middle flight intends to soar	我要飛躍凌駕庸俗之上
Above th' Aonian Mount, while it pursues	要超越艾歐尼亞山，追求
Things unattempted yet in Prose or Rhime.	前人所未達的詩文境界。

And chiefly Thou O Spirit, that dost prefer
Before all Temples th' upright heart and pure,
Instruct me, for Thou know'st; Thou from the first
Wast present, and with mighty wings outspread
Dove-like satst brooding on the vast Abyss
And mad'st it pregnant: What in me is dark
Illumin, what is low raise and support;
That to the highth of this great Argument
I may assert Eternal Providence,
And justifie the wayes of God to men.

神靈啊！你歡喜眷顧純淨
正直心靈超過殿堂廟宇，
指導我，因爲你有知；你從
初始即在，伸展巨大雙翼
鴿子般佇立深淵上沉思
孕育生命其中：我暗昧處
請照亮，我卑微處請提升；
在此鴻文巨構至高之端
助我藉由上帝永恆恩賜，
向人類解釋上帝的作爲。

第二段描述耶穌奉上帝之命與撒旦作戰：

So spake the Son, and into terrour chang'd
His count'nance too severe to be beheld
And full of wrauth bent on his Enemies.
At once the Four spred out thir Starrie wings
With dreadful shade contiguous, and the Orbes
Of his fierce Chariot rowld, as with the sound
Of torrent Floods, or of a numerous Host.
Hee on his impious Foes right onward drove,
Gloomie as Night; under his burning Wheeles
The stedfast Empyrean shook throughout,
All but the Throne it self of God. Full soon
Among them he arriv'd; in his right hand
Grasping ten thousand Thunders, which he sent
Before him, such as in thir Soules infix'd
Plagues; they astonisht all resistance lost,

聖子如此說完，容顏轉爲
震懾使人驚恐不敢直視
面對敵人渾身充滿憤怒。
四智天使即刻展開星翼
下罩可怖陰翳，兇猛戰車
車輪轉動，隆隆作響有如
滔天洪水，或如千軍萬馬。
祂當頭衝向那邪惡敵人
有如暗夜籠罩；戰車火輪
下連磐固的天堂也震動，
惟有上帝寶座安然。頃刻
祂即抵達敵人陣營；右手
抓持萬道雷霆，倏然擲出
有如貫穿其敵人靈魂以
疫癘；敵人震驚潰散逃亡，

All courage; down thir idle weapons drop'd; O're Shields and Helmes, and helmed heads he rode Of Thrones and mighty Seraphim prostrate, That wisht the Mountains now might be again Thrown on them as a shelter from his ire.	失魂落魄;丟其盔棄其甲; 祂駕車踐踏盾牌和盔甲, 敵軍寶座、熾天使皆匍匐, 寧願巨山再次掩蓋其身 阻擋他們不受怒火摧殘。

第三段是夏娃告知吃了禁果後,亞當的反應:

O fairest of Creation, last and best Of all Gods works, Creature in whom excell'd Whatever can to sight or thought be formd, Holy, divine, good, amiable, or sweet! How art thou lost, how on a sudden lost, Defac't, deflourd, and now to Death devote? Rather how hast thou yeelded to transgress The strict forbiddance, how to violate The sacred Fruit forbidd'n! som cursed fraud Of Enemie hath beguil'd thee, yet unknown, And mee with thee hath ruind, for with thee Certain my resolution is to Die; How can I live without thee, how forgoe Thy sweet Converse and Love so dearly joyn'd, To live again in these wilde Woods forlorn? Should God create another Eve, and I Another Rib afford, yet loss of thee Would never from my heart; no no, I feel The Link of Nature draw me: Flesh of Flesh, Bone of my Bone thou art, and from thy State Mine never shall be parted, bliss or woe.	噢!萬物之至美者,上帝所 創造之最後、最好者,臻至 所思所見之極致精華者, 聖然、神如、善良、可親、甜美! 你迷失了,你乍然迷失了, 失神、凋萎了,注定死亡了! 你怎麼會如此屈從犯罪 觸犯禁條,如此大膽食用 神聖禁果!必是某個潛藏 敵人可詛謊言誤導了你, 將你連我一起害了,因為 我決心要和你一同赴死; 我怎能獨自生存,放棄我倆 甜蜜話語,放棄情愛結合, 再次孤單生活在此荒林? 即使上帝再造一夏娃,我 再捐一肋,失去你將使我 心永遠悲痛;不,不,我深感 天性結合之力:你是我的 至親骨肉,你的命運是福 是禍,我都永遠共同面對。

1659年密爾頓撰有《論世俗權力》（A Treatise of Civil Power），反對政府管控教會。克倫威爾1658年去世，共和政府瀕臨解體，密爾頓獨排眾議，堅決支持共和政體，痛罵英國人懦弱反悔，文中甚至主張建立獨裁政權以阻止復辟。1660年查理二世登基，密爾頓短暫入獄，追繳巨額罰款。1662年密爾頓54歲娶了時年24的第三任妻子。1670年撰寫《英國史》（History of Britain），只敘述到1066年諾曼人（Norman）入侵。1671年撰寫史詩《復樂園》（Paradise Regained）與書齋劇《鬥士參生》（Samson Agonistes）。《復樂園》敘述耶穌荒野中抗拒撒旦引誘，終得拯救，宣揚堅忍之美德，暗含密爾頓本人堅信其政治信念終必獲勝。《鬥士參生》描述聖經所敘以色列人參生因神力來源之頭髮被剪，爲非利士人（Philistines）所擒，雙目被盲，但獲天助復仇；顯然密爾頓以參生自喻。1672年撰寫《正信論》（Of True Religion）呼籲寬待拒絕皈依國教的清教徒，而嚴處同樣拒絕皈依的天主教徒，政壇辯論信奉天主教的王儲（詹姆士二世）可否登基時引用此文，有助日後1688年輝格黨（自由黨）推動光榮革命。去世前密爾頓尚有未完成手稿《論基督教義》（De doctrina christiana），陳述其大異主流的看法，包括贊成一夫多妻。

密爾頓自認是英格蘭民族詩人，其《失樂園》之於英國有如維吉爾（Virgil）《埃涅阿斯紀》（Aeneis，英譯Aeneid）之於羅馬；其詩作咸認可同莎士比亞一較高下。

圖片來源：IDJ圖庫

1-9

丹尼爾・德福

Daniel Defoe

丹尼爾‧德福
Daniel Defoe

　　丹尼爾‧德福（Daniel Defoe）1660年生於倫敦，父親是蠟燭商，父母皆爲長老會信徒，不從英國國教。德福在長老會學校受教，成年後從商，雖富有但入不敷出，1684年結婚，次年參與蒙莫斯叛亂（Monmouth Rebellion）推翻詹姆士二世不成但獲赦。1688年光榮革命後，德福成爲威廉三世近臣，爲其潛伺。1692年因欠債被捕，出獄後赴歐陸、蘇格蘭。1695年返英，任酒瓶稅官，次年開辦磚廠，1697年開始著述一系列政治社會評論，1703年因批評安妮女王鎮壓不從國教者而被枷，因同意爲女王的保守黨政府潛伺而獲釋，同年辦雜誌爲政府張目，促成1707年英格蘭、蘇格蘭一統。1714年安妮女王去世後，轉爲自由黨政府揚聲，1724-27年寫就《環遊大不列顚島》（A tour thro' the whole island of Great Britain）全面描述工業革命前夕英國商業狀況。

　　1719年德福出版《魯賓遜漂流記》（Robinson Crusoe），敘述1651年魯賓遜由英格蘭東部出海，於西北非被海盜擄獲，兩年後逃脫隨葡萄牙船赴巴西購置農莊，1659年乘船赴非購買奴隸，於南美東北角遇船難漂流島上，挖山洞自建小屋、打獵、種田、蓄羊、燒瓦，閱讀聖經，自覺惟缺同伴。後發覺偶有食人族帶人來島上烹食，有一人逃脫爲魯賓遜所救，命名「週五」（Friday），教其英語、改信基督教，兩人又救下週五之父與一西班牙人，後兩者潛返大陸求援，期間有英船來到，水手叛變，魯賓遜與船長聯手鎮壓，將叛變者留島上，1686年離島，次年抵英，再赴巴西變賣農莊，返英途中與週五於碧蕊內山（Pyrenees）擊退狼群。初版以魯賓遜爲作者，假託是魯賓遜自傳。書出大賣，開創西方寫實小說文類，流浪荒島之小說蔚爲一時風潮，週五衍生成「傭人」之代名詞。茲選譯三段：

Then to see how like a King I din'd too all alone, attended by my Servants, *Poll*, as if he had been my Favourite, was the only Person permitted to talk to me. My Dog who was now grown very old and crazy, and had found no Species to multiply his Kind upon, sat always at my Right Hand, and two Cats, one on one Side the Table, and one on the other, expecting now and then a Bit from my Hand, as a Mark of Special Favour

看我也像國王一樣單獨用膳，有傭人伺候，只有波爾（鸚鵡），好似倖臣，獲允進言。我的狗年老痴癲，又無匹配子嗣，總是坐在我右首，兩隻貓分坐餐桌兩頭，期待我偶施小惠，以示寵倖。

It happen'd one Day about Noon going towards my Boat, I was exceedingly surpriz'd with the Print of a Man's naked Foot on the Shore, which was very plain to be seen in the Sand: I stood like one Thunder-struck, or as if I had seen an Apparition; I listen'd, I look'd round me, I could hear nothing, nor see any Thing, I went up to a rising Ground to look farther, I went up the Shore and down the Shore, but it was all one, I could see no other Impression but that one, I went to it again to see if there were any more, and to obseve if it might not be my Fancy; but there was no Room for that, for there was exactly the very Print of a Foot, Toes, Hell, and every Part of a Foot; how it came thither, I knew not, nor could in the least imagine. But after innumberable fluttering Thoughts, like a Man perfectly confus'd and out of my self, I came Home to my Fortifcation, not feeling, as we say, the Ground I went on, but terrify'd to the last Degree, looking behind me at every two or three Steps, mistaking every Bush and Tree, and fancying every Stump at a Distance to be a Man;

有天大約中午我去停船處途中，看到海邊沙灘上明顯有人類赤腳足印，大為驚異！我呆立好似雷擊，又好似見了鬼。我傾聽、環視四圍，既無所聞，也無所見。我登上小丘遠望，沿著海灘來回，但都一樣，只有那一個腳印，我再次檢視有無別的，看是否只是幻覺，但確然為真，是個腳印，有腳趾，老天！還有腳的各個部份。這腳印怎麼來的我不知道，也完全無法想像。我思慮紛雜，困惑出神，套句俗話，回堡壘途中渾不覺腳踩實地，而是極度恐懼，每兩三步就回頭張望，恍覺每個樹叢、遠處每個樹幹都是人。

◆ 丹尼爾・德福 ◆

丹尼爾·德福

I learned to look more upon the bright side of my condition, and less upon the dark side, and to consider what I enjoyed, rather than what I wanted : and this gave me sometimes such secret comforts, that I cannot express them ; and which I take notice of here, to put those discontented people in mind of it, who cannot enjoy comfortably what God has given them, because they see and covet something that he has not given them. All our discontents about what we want appeared to me to spring from the want of thankfulness for what we have.

我學會多看事情的光明面，少看黑暗面，多想我擁有的，少想欠缺的，這帶給我心靈的撫慰，大到無法言喻，我在此特地提及此事，就是要提醒那些不滿於上帝所賜、希求他們欠缺之物、不快樂的人。我認為，一切的慾望、不滿都來自對我們已有之物欠缺感恩。

1719年德福出版《魯賓遜歷險續集》（The Farther Adventures of Robinson Crusoe），敘述魯賓遜回到荒島，又去到亞洲。1722年寫就《茉兒·法蘭德斯》（Moll Flanders），敘述主角貧困出生，做過妓女、小偷，還曾亂倫，日後致富歸正善終。

1731年德福去世。

德福參與開創英語小說，《魯賓遜漂流記》廣為世人喜愛。

圖片來源：IDJ圖庫

1-10

翟頓

John Dryden

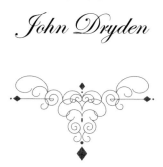

翟頓
John Dryden

翟頓（John Dryden）1631年生於英格蘭中部，曾祖父是次男爵（Baronet），為清教徒。1644年翟頓入讀信奉國教的西敏寺學校，開始寫詩。1650年入讀劍橋三一學院，1654年以第一名畢業，同年父親去世，入克倫威爾政府服務。1660年查爾斯二世復辟，翟頓賦詩《復歸辰御》（Astraea Redux）慶賀。1667年賦詩《神奇的一年》（Annus Mirabilis）記述1666年英國爭奪殖民航海霸權，大敗荷蘭海軍，以及倫敦大火災，成為文壇祭酒，茲選譯首段：

In thriving arts long time had Holland grown,	荷蘭長久以來勃興生計，
Crouching at home and cruel when abroad:	在家蟠據在國外施酷行：
Scarce leaving us the means to claim our own;	對我們不留一絲餘地；
Our King they courted, and our merchants awed.	結納我君王，威嚇我商人。
Trade, which, like blood, should circularly flow,	貿易，如血液，應暢通循環，
Stopp'd in their channels, found its freedom lost:	卻被堵塞，失去了自由：
Thither the wealth of all the world did go,	全世界的財富流向荷蘭，
And seem'd but shipwreck'd on so base a coast.	堆積於其彼岸有如沉舟。
For them alone the heavens had kindly heat;	老天以熱陽獨眷顧荷蘭；
In eastern quarries ripening precious dew:	在東方滋長其珍貴甘露：
For them the Idumæan balm did sweat,	以東畝之膏脂為其流泛，
And in hot Ceylon spicy forests grew.	香料叢林在錫蘭滿佈。
The sun but seem'd the labourer of the year;	太陽成了長年的僱工；
Each waxing moon supplied her watery store,	財物隨滿月流向其國庫，
To swell those tides, which from the line did bear	水漲船高，只見大海負承
Their brimful vessels to the Belgian shore.	滿載商船航向荷蘭本土。

1668年翟頓受封桂冠詩人（Poet Laureate）。共和時期清教主義嚴禁戲劇，復辟後戲禁大開，同年翟頓簽約為國王戲班寫戲，以此維生，所寫喜劇悲劇皆引領風潮。這年還出版《論戲劇創作》（Of Dramatick Poesie）討論古典、英、法戲劇優劣，認為英國伊麗莎白時期戲劇好過古典希臘戲劇，主張莎士比亞是古今最偉大詩人，不學而能。

翟頓最爲人稱道的是虐仿詩（mock heroic），將小事誇大以顯其荒謬，1678年所作《弗列諾之子》（Mac Flecknoe）攻擊同代劇作家夏德維（Thomas Shadwell），宣稱另一文人弗列諾（Richard Flecknoe）是「呆板詩文」（Poetic dullness）之王，王子則是夏德維，茲選譯首段：

All humane things are subject to decay,	人間一切事物注定毀殞，
And, when Fate summons, Monarchs must obey:	當命運召喚，國王也須遵循：
This Fleckno found, who, like Augustus, young	弗列諾終悟此點，如奧古斯都，
Was call'd to Empire, and had govern'd long:	他年少登基，皇祚長久：
In Prose and Verse, was own'd, without dispute	無論韻散詩文，眾人都同意
Through all the Realms of Non-sense, absolute.	在無厘頭國度，他數第一。
This aged Prince now flourishing in Peace,	如今年已老邁，國運昌碩，
And blest with issue of a large increase,	蒙天之幸子女人數眾多，
Worn out with business, did at length debate	他倦煩國事，終於決心
To settle the succession of the State:	安排國家王位繼承人：
And pond'ring which of all his Sons was fit	他思考哪個兒子能繼位，
To Reign, and wage immortal War with Wit;	能承接大統，抗拒智慧；
Cry'd, 'tis resolv'd; for Nature pleads that He	他喊道：就這樣；順天承祚
Should onely rule, who most resembles me:	只有他能統治，他最像我：
Sh— alone my perfect image bears,	只有夏——跟我如出一轍，
Mature in dullness from his tender years.	從小就呆板地很透澈。
Sh— alone, of all my Sons, is he	眾兒子裡，只有夏——是
Who stands confirm'd in full stupidity.	百分之一百的純白痴。
The rest to some faint meaning make pretence,	其他人偶爾會說句人話，
But Sh— never deviates into sense.	只有夏——言語從無章法。
Some beams of wit on other souls may fall,	其他人偶爾還靈光乍現，
Strike through and make a lucid interval;	穿過雲霧讓神志昭顯；
But Shadwell's genuine night admits no ray,	只有夏——腦袋闇黑透透，
His rising fogs prevail upon the day:	光明被霧靄阻隔點滴不漏：
Besides his goodly fabric fills the eye,	此外只見他的華麗衣服，
And seems design'd for thoughtless majesty:	完全搭配這位放空君主：
Thoughtless as monarch oaks, that shade the plain,	放空有如遮蔭的大王橡，

And, spread in solemn state, supinely reign.	伸展枝葉，國王躺著當。
Heywood and Shirley were but types of thee,	跟你比，黑伍、薛利只算小咖，
Thou last great prophet of tautology:	論廢話，先知數你最偉大：
Even I, a dunce of more renown than they,	就連我，雖然也以愚蠢稱著，
Was sent before but to prepare thy way;	也只配給你開道鋪路；
And coarsely clad in Norwich drugget came	我身披諾維區粗服來此
To teach the nations in thy greater name.	奉你之名為世人開示。
My warbling lute, the lute I whilom strung	我曾彈奏那妙琴魯特
When to King John of Portugal I sung,	當我為葡萄牙約翰王獻歌，
Was but the prelude to that glorious day,	但相較於那天則不值一提，
When thou on silver Thames did'st cut thy way,	那天你行舟泰晤士河裡，
With well tim'd oars before the royal barge,	引導王舟船槳律動一同，
Swell'd with the pride of thy celestial charge;	身負重責，滿滿以此為榮；
And big with hymn, commander of an host,	宣唱讚歌，兼且統御軍隊，
The like was ne'er in Epsom blankets toss'd.	此等人從未在艾森被拋起。
Methinks I see the new Arion sail,	我彷彿再見阿里昂航海，
The lute still trembling underneath thy nail.	你指下顫動魯特琴聲籟。
At thy well sharpen'd thumb from shore to shore	你熟練的琴聲傳渡大洋
The treble squeaks for fear, the basses roar:	高音恐怖尖叫，低音狂嚷：
Echoes from Pissing-Alley, Shadwell call,	小便巷內迴音呼喊夏德維，
And Shadwell they resound from Aston Hall.	「夏德維」從艾斯屯居又傳回。

　　1683年翟頓翻譯希臘作家普魯塔克（Plutarch）名著《人物對比》（Parallel Lives），其中首次出現英語「傳記」（biography）一字。1687年翟頓改信天主教，次年光榮革命後拒絕效忠新王，桂冠詩人之位被迫讓給夏德維，此後靠翻譯古羅馬詩文維生，1694-97年翻譯《維吉爾文集》（The Works of Virgil），1700年出版《古今寓言》（Fables Ancient and Modern），翻譯荷馬（Homer）、奧維德（Ovid）、薄伽丘、喬叟作品，序言稱喬叟為英國文學之父（father of English poetry）。同年去世，移葬西敏寺。

　　翟頓主導英國17世紀復辟時期（Restoration）文壇，廣泛使用每兩句押韻的英雄對句（heroic couplet），使之成為英國18世紀最重要格律；翟頓還譯介古典、歐陸文學，在譯作序文裡評論詩文，人稱英國文學批評之父。

翟頓

圖片來源：IDJ圖庫

1-11

喬納森·綏夫特
Jonathan Swift

喬納森・綏夫特（Jonathan Swift）1667年生於愛爾蘭都柏林（Dublin），父親因英國內戰由英格蘭移民愛爾蘭，在綏夫特出生前去世，母親返回英格蘭，將綏夫特留交其夫兄長照顧。1682年綏夫特入讀都柏林大學三一學院，1686年畢業，續攻碩士，但1688年受光榮革命影響被迫返英，母親安排他出任外交官威廉・田普（William Temple）爵士秘書，深受信任。此期間綏夫特結識照顧8歲女孩愛瑟・強生（Esther Johnson），愛瑟母親在田普家工作，綏夫特在詩文中以絲黛拉（Stella）稱呼愛瑟，兩人終身維持親密關係。1690年綏夫特暈眩病初發，纏擾終生。1692年於牛津大學哈特福學院獲碩士，赴愛爾蘭擔任教士，1694年派駐愛爾蘭東北，向同學的妹妹韋玲（Jane Waring）求婚未果，1696年因此返英復任職於田普家。

　　田普爵士1690年出版論文《論古今學問》（Essay upon Ancient and Modern Learning）為古人辯護，遭人批評，綏夫特著《典籍之戰》（Battle of the Books）回應，書中敘述圖書館裡古代、現代書籍打仗，代表現代的蜘蛛織網捕蟲，標榜不靠他人，代表古代的蜜蜂闖入蛛網將之破壞，伊索為古代發言道：「我們贊同蜜蜂，我們一切所有，出自自身的只有雙翅與鳴聲，其他都來自辛勤尋遍大自然每一角落……我們選擇在蜂巢儲藏蜂蜜與蜂蠟，帶給人間兩件至善之物——甘美與光明（sweetness and light），而非蜘蛛儲藏的汙穢與毒液。」「甘美與光明」一語自此常為人引用。

　　田普爵士1699年去世，綏夫特英格蘭謀職不成，再赴愛爾蘭任柏克萊伯爵（Earl of Berkeley）秘書兼牧師，到任後始發覺秘書一職已有人，於是轉赴愛爾蘭東部任教區教士，但大多時間住在都柏林，也常往返英格蘭。1702年獲都柏林大學三一學院神學博士，同年赴英接愛瑟同返。

　　綏夫特1694-97年寫就《木桶的故事》（A Tale of A Tub），1704年匿名出版，以《典籍之戰》為序；《木桶的故事》以寓言諷刺基督教各派，述說三兄弟彼得（聖彼得，代表天主教）、馬丁（路德，代表新教保守的路德會與英國國教）、傑克（約翰・卡爾文，代表新教激進的卡爾文派）各自從父親（上帝）繼承一件漂亮的大衣（基督教教義、儀式），以及父親的遺囑（聖經）；他們結交損友（世俗政治），改動大衣，彼

得以長子身份解讀遺囑，說傭人曾聽父親說大衣上可增添裝飾；傑克照字面解讀遺囑，將大衣拆開重組以回歸原始樣貌，結果走火入魔，閉眼依直覺而行；彼得和傑克殊途而同歸，只有馬丁的大衣較似父親原樣。書名中的木桶指牧師講道的圓形講壇，綏夫特自稱也指行船遇怪獸可拋落海轉移怪獸注意之木桶，以行船喻國家，以怪獸喻危害國家之言論。書中夾雜各種無關主題、無厘頭的討論，為綏夫特典型文風；出版後深受歡迎，綏夫特因此結識博普（Alexander Pope）等文人，1713年共組麥挺弄‧希哩不嚕俱樂部（Martinus Scriblerus Club），專寫諷刺文學。

　　1710年綏夫特因教士福利問題，由自由派改而支持保守派，同年出任保守派刊物《考察家》（The Examiner）編輯。1710-13年綏夫特涉入保守派政府甚深，期間給絲黛拉65封論及政事之信件於死後輯為《致絲黛拉日誌》（A Journal to Stella），1766年出版。同期綏夫特結識另一失怙女孩愛瑟‧范茉里（Esther Vanhomrigh），過從甚密，詩文中稱之為凡妮莎（Vanessa），范茉里1714年追隨綏夫特返愛爾蘭，時年26歲，1723年去世。

　　1713年綏夫特受任都柏林聖派萃克大教堂（St Patrick's）教長，翌年偏好保守派的女王安（Queen Anne）去世，自由派隨新王喬治一世獲寵，綏夫特失意，返回愛爾蘭，開始撰文辯護愛爾蘭利益，包括：1720年出版《普遍使用愛爾蘭製品芻議》（Proposal for Universal Use of Irish Manufacture），建議杯葛英格蘭製品；1724-25年化名出版《布商書簡》（Drapier's Letters），反對英商專利鑄造愛爾蘭銅幣，鼓吹愛爾蘭政治經濟獨立，英國政府為此雇請時任皇家鑄幣廠廠長的大科學家牛頓（Isaac Newton）檢驗此幣成份；1729年綏夫特出版反諷文《一個小小的建議，可免愛爾蘭窮人子女成為父母、政府負擔，並可造福大眾》（A Modest Proposal for Preventing the Children of Poor People in Ireland Being a Burden on Their Parents or Country, and for Making Them Beneficial to the Publick），簡稱《一個小小的建議》（A Modest Proposal），提出荒謬建議改善愛爾蘭經濟：愛爾蘭窮人輸出其1歲嬰兒至英格蘭供人食用，並例舉撒瑪納札（Psalmanazar，18世紀法國人，自稱來自台灣，以此結交權貴）為食人族，以此反襯其真正建議：對居住境外的地主徵稅、使用本土產品、力行簡約、團結境內各派、善待佃農。

1720-25年綏夫特寫就《外科醫生、船長勒謬·格列佛出遊遠國記，共分四冊》（Travels into Several Remote Nations of the World, in Four Parts, by Lemuel Gulliver, first a surgeon, and then a captain of several ships），簡稱《格列佛遊記》（Gulliver's Travels），第一冊《厘厘普遊記1699年5月4日—1702年4月13日》（A Voyage to Lilliput May 4, 1699-April 13, 1702）：格列佛遭船難，漂流到小人國厘厘普（暗喻英國），助其擊敗宿敵布列弗斯庫（Blefuscu，暗喻法國），被控叛國，出逃布列弗斯庫，造船出海，獲救返英。第二冊《伯洛鼎納遊記1702年6月20日—1706年6月3日》（A Voyage to Brobdingnag June 20, 1702 — June 3, 1706）：格列佛出航島上入大人國伯洛鼎納，被農夫擒獲賣給女王，爲國王描述英國國情，被老鷹帶出海，獲救返英。第三冊《拉撲他、巴泥寶鄙、咕嚕嘟椎、捋奶、日本遊記1706年8月5日—1710年4月16日》（A Voyage to Laputa, Balnibarbi, Glubbdubdrib, Luggnagg and Japan August 5, 1706 — April 16, 1710）：格列佛出海遭海盜流放，遇救上到飛天島嶼拉撲他，島上人皆埋頭研究數學、天文、音樂，但不切實際，拉撲他以武力控制其下之島巴泥寶鄙（暗喻英格蘭控制愛爾蘭），巴泥寶鄙人摹仿拉撲他以改變自身制度，但改變不成，百廢待舉。格列佛去到臨近島嶼咕嚕嘟椎，透過島上魔法師與死者交談，覺得古代好過現代、近世名人多虛有其表。格列佛接著去捋奶島，島上有死都不如人（struldbrug）長生不死，但極度衰老。格列佛最後去到日本返英。第四冊《慧駰國遊記1710年9月7日—1715年12月5日》（A Voyage to the Country of the Houyhnhnms September 7, 1710-December 5, 1715）：格列佛出航加勒比海，遭水手叛變棄置荒島，見到貌似人但醜陋粗鄙的野胡（Yahoo），是貌似馬但聰慧理智的慧駰豢養的動物，格列佛與慧駰比較人類、慧駰社會。慧駰議會認定格列佛不得與慧駰雜處，格列佛被迫離開，受葡萄牙船救援返英，格列佛無法再忍受與人類共同生活，買了兩匹馬，終日與其爲伍。本書1726年化名出版，大受歡迎。

愛瑟1728年去世，綏夫特哀傷逾恆。1731年自撰訃聞詩，其中提及要以遺產在愛爾蘭興建精神病院：

He gave the little wealth he had	他以微薄財產興建
build a house for fools and mad;	愚人瘋子的療養院;
And show'd by one satiric touch,	借此捐贈諷刺表達,
No nation wanted it so much.	愛爾蘭對此需求最大。
That kingdom he hath left his debtor,	該國因此欠他的債,
I wish it soon may have a better.	願日後有更好債主來。

1742年綏夫特中風失智,1745年去世,人遵囑修建聖派萃克精神病院(St Patrick's Hospital for Imbeciles),並葬於聖派萃克大教堂愛瑟墓旁,墓誌銘生前以拉丁文自擬:

Hic depositum est Corpus	*Here* is laid the Body of
IONATHAN SWIFT S.T.D.	JONATHAN SWIFT, Dr. of Sacred Theology,
Hujus Ecclesiæ Cathedralis	Dean of this Cathedral
Decani,	Church,
Ubi sæva Indignatio	where fierce Indignation
Ulterius	no longer
Cor lacerare nequit,	the Heart can injure.
Abi Viator	Go forth, Voyager,
Et imitare, si poteris,	and copy, if you can,
Strenuum pro virili	this vigorous (to the best of his ability)
Libertatis Vindicatorem.	Champion of Liberty.

> *此處安置的軀體屬於*
> *喬納森‧綏夫特 神學博士*
> *此大教堂*
> *教長，*
> *在此狂野的憤怒*
> *再也*
> *無法撕裂他的心，*
> *去吧，旅人*
> *去效法，若你有此能耐，*
> *這個盡其力為*
> *尊嚴自由奮鬥的人。*

　　綏夫特以絕妙文筆剖析人性，批評英國政治、宗教，於理性主義當道時，敢於針砭其缺點，為反諷文學大師。

圖片來源：IDJ圖庫

1-12

博普

Alexander Pope

博普（Alexander Pope）1688年生於倫敦天主教家庭，父親經營布匹買賣，1700年法定天主教徒不得居住倫敦周圍，被迫遷居鄉下。博普幼年因骨架結核病而駝背身矮，身高不足1米4，終身未婚。因天主教徒禁上大學，博普在家自修希臘、拉丁、英、法、意大利語言文學，結識倫敦文人。1709年出版詩作《田園詩集》（Pastorals），一舉成名。1711年以英雄對句寫就《論文學批評》（An Essay on Criticism）同受好評，文中主張創作應依據傳統規矩：

True ease in writing comes from art, not chance, As those move easiest who have learned to dance.	作文天成來自鍛煉，非偶發， 正如習舞者舉止最優雅。

　　並多有名句：

To err is human, to forgive, divine.	犯錯乃人性，原諒乃神性。

For fools rush in where angels fear to tread.	天使都懼不踏進之地，蠢人卻衝入。

◆
：
博
普
：
◆

A little learning is a dangerous thing; Drink deep, or taste not the Pierian spring.	淺嘗知識實屬危險之舉； 臨知識之泉，或痛飲，或峻拒。

True wit is nature to advantage dress'd; What oft was thought, but ne'er so well express'd.	真文采乃天賦再加雕琢； 曾有人動念，但無人妙言說過。

　　博普1711年結識保皇派文人綏夫特、亞畢諾（John Arbuthnot）等，共創希哩不嚕俱樂部，撰文嘲諷學究、譏諷淺薄。同時也與自由派文人阿迪生（Joseph Addison）、史迪爾（Richard Steele）相善。1712年出版虐仿史詩（mock epic）《秀髮劫》（The Rape of the Lock），套用史詩文體風格，小題大作，嘲諷一貴族男子剪去貴族女子髮絡之爭執，格律用英雄對句。茲選譯一段：

The Peer now spreads the glittering Forfex wide, T' inclose the Lock; now joins it, to divide. Ev'n then, before the fatal Engine clos'd, A wretched Sylph too fondly interpos'd; Fate urged the Sheers, and cut the Sylph in twain, (But Airy Substance soon unites again) The meeting Points the sacred Hair dissever From the fair Head, for ever and for ever!	男爵此刻將刀剪大開， 圈住髮絡；閉合，將之分裁。 那時，致命利器夾攏之前， 有一可憐精靈誤闖其間； 命運催動刀剪，精靈成兩半， （但屬氣之精靈即刻復原） 剪刀將神聖髮絡絞離 美麗頭頸，永世不復合一！

博普1713年開始翻譯史詩《伊利亞德》（Iliad），1720年完成，賺得巨額稿費，成爲英國第一位得以完全倚文爲生的文人。茲選譯第一段：

Achilles' wrath, to Greece the direful spring	阿基里斯之怒，給希臘造成
Of woes unnumber'd, heavenly goddess, sing!	無盡痛苦，天上女神，歌詠！
That wrath which hurl'd to Pluto's gloomy reign	此怒擲落冥王陰鬱國境
The souls of mighty chiefs untimely slain;	早逝君王豪酋之幽靈；
Whose limbs unburied on the naked shore,	其曝露於海岸的屍骸，
Devouring dogs and hungry vultures tore.	任由飢餓的野狗兀鷹扯拽。
Since great Achilles and Atrides strove,	自從阿基里斯、阿崔烏斯之子
Such was the sovereign doom, and such the will of Jove!	眾英雄出發，宙斯即註定此事！
Declare, O Muse! in what ill-fated hour	宣告啊，謬思！在何不吉時刻
Sprung the fierce strife, from what offended power	萌發此鬥爭，哪個神明不樂，
Latona's son a dire contagion spread,	拉透娜之子女因而生事，
And heap'd the camp with mountains of the dead;	導致堆積如山的死屍；
The king of men his reverent priest defied,	國王對祭司勸告拒而不聽，
And for the king's offence the people died.	爲此罪孽其國人隕命。

1717年博普翻譯中世紀著名情侶愛蘿伊絲（Eloise）與阿貝拉（Abelard）書信集，茲選譯愛蘿伊絲信中部份：

How happy is the blameless vestal's lot!	純淨聖女命運令人羨嫉！
The world forgetting, by the world forgot.	遺世獨立，也爲世人所遺。
Eternal sunshine of the spotless mind!	無垢心靈享有永恆陽光！
Each pray'r accepted, and each wish resign'd.	所祈皆得應，所禱皆得償。
...	……

No, fly me, fly me, far as pole from pole; Rise Alps between us! and whole oceans roll! Ah, come not, write not, think not once of me, Nor share one pang of all I felt for thee.	不，將我飛離、飛離，相距兩極； 以阿爾卑斯阻隔！以大洋分歧！ 啊，勿探訪，勿來信，全勿思及， 也勿有我苦念你之萬一。

　　1719年博普遷新居，並依據神話建造繁複花園地窟。1726年編撰莎士比亞劇本出版，多有增刪，序言認為莎翁劇本廣遭演員篡改，因此需修定。同年與人合作翻譯《奧德賽》（Odyssey）。1727年牛頓去世，博普寫下名句追念：

Nature and nature's laws lay hid in night; God said "Let Newton be" and all was light.	大自然及其法則於黑夜隱藏； 主曰：『讓牛頓出世』，光明乍放。

　　1728年博普寫就諷刺文《論低俗，或稱文學如何沉淪》（Peri Bathous, or the Art of Sinking in Poetry），教人如何寫壞詩文，為英語引介bathos（昇華不成，反而低俗）一詞。

　　1728年博普模仿翟頓《弗列諾之子》，出版長詩《愚人記》（The Dunciad），書名源自13世紀學者蘇格徒（John Duns Scotus），其人好作繁瑣思辯；1729年修改為《愚人眾生相》（Dunciad Variorum），1742年追加《新愚人記》（New Dunciad）；以反諷口吻述說愚人國國王謝投（Elkanah Settle，博普文壇敵手）駕崩，愚蠢女神（Goddess Dullness）遴選逖波（Tibbald，博普另一敵手，本名Lewis Theobald）繼承大位，對逖波讚辭曰：

All nonsense thus, of old or modern date, Shall in thee centre, from thee circulate.	從古至今一切胡言亂語， 歸於爾身，繼而廣播四域。

　　眾人慶祝愚蠢女神及其隨從將駘思愚行與乏味作品帶入大不列顛，舉辦尿盆障礙賽、尿尿射遠、拍馬屁、囈語叫囂、溝渠游泳等比賽。其中嘲諷駘愚文人曰：

While pensive Poets painful vigils keep, Sleepless themselves to give their readers sleep.	詩人通宵達旦苦思不寐， 自己不睡卻讓讀者沉睡。

　　因文中謾罵諸多時人，博普日後出門都攜槍帶犬自衛。

　　1731-35年博普出版《道德論》（Moral Essays），討論財富、人性、女性，其中說道：

Nothing so true as what you once let fall, "Most Women have no Characters at all." Matter too soft a lasting mark to bear, And best distinguish'd by black, brown, or fair.	你曾說過的話可謂經典， 「女性大多毫無個性可言。」 本質軟弱不足以留痕跡， 可分辨者唯膚色黑、棕、或白皙。

1732-34年博普以英雄對句寫就《人論》（Essay on Man），由4封致勃林波克爵士（Lord Bolingbroke）的書信組成，反對人本主義，以「向人類證明上帝的作爲正確」（vindicate the ways of God to Man）爲目的，主張幸福之道在接受上帝安排，始終向善，中有名句：

| Whatever is, is right. | 既存在，即正確。 |

| Hope springs eternal in the human breast. | 人類永遠胸懷希望。 |

另選譯首段：

| Know then thyself, presume not God to scan
The proper study of Mankind is Man.
Placed on this isthmus of a middle state,
A Being darkly wise, and rudely great:
With too much knowledge for the Sceptic side,
With too much weakness for the Stoic's pride,
He hangs between; in doubt to act, or rest;
In doubt to deem himself a God, or Beast;
In doubt his mind and body to prefer; | 認識自己，勿妄想評察上帝
人類才是人該研究的議題。
人類被置於中間的地峽，
聰明又陰暗，粗糙又偉大：
想要懷疑但知道太多，
想要禁慾但弱點難過，
不上不下，猶疑不進不留；
不知該自認是神，或獸；
不知該嚮往靈還是肉； |

博普

Born but to die, and reas'ning but to err;	生而必死,能理解但必錯漏;
Alike in ignorance, his reason such,	有理性,但所知仍極稀,
Whether he thinks too little, or too much;	無論思量太過或不及;
Chaos of Thought and Passion, all confus'd;	理性感性混雜,亂成一團;
Still by himself, abus'd or disabus'd;	獨樹一格,被錯待,或不然;
Created half to rise and half to fall;	本性一半昇華,一半墮壞;
Great Lord of all things, yet a prey to all,	主宰萬物,也受萬物主宰,
Sole judge of truth, in endless error hurl'd;	真理惟一評審,卻不斷出軌;
The glory, jest and riddle of the world.	人世之榮耀、笑柄、不解之謎。

1733-38年博普寫就《仿賀瑞斯》(Imitations of Horace)諷刺詩集,茲選譯序言《書致亞畢諾醫生》(An Epistle to Doctor Arbuthnot)一段:

Let Sporus tremble –"What? that thing of silk,	讓蚖孢孺顫抖——「哼?那絲樣軟腳,
Sporus, that mere white curd of ass's milk?	蚖孢孺,那白白的驢奶酪?
Satire or sense, alas! can Sporus feel?	或諷刺,或講理,蚖孢孺能明瞭?
Who breaks a butterfly upon a wheel?"	誰殺蝴蝶還要用牛刀?」
Yet let me flap this bug with gilded wings,	但這隻塗彩蟲豸我要撥弄,
This painted child of dirt that stinks and stings;	這隻螫人的腥臭抹粉小蟲;
Whose buzz the witty and the fair annoys,	他嗡嗡騷擾言妙容美之人,
Yet wit ne'er tastes, and beauty ne'r enjoys,	自身卻既口拙又貌寢,
So well-bred Spaniels civilly delight	正如文弱長耳犬可笑
In mumbling of the Game they dare not bite.	對獵物嚅嚅卻不敢咬。

此文另有名句「似褒實貶」(Damn with faint praise)。

1742年博普書寫《新愚人記》，以司勃（Colley Cibber）取代遜波作愚人國王，述說司勃：

| Next, o'er his Books his eyes began to roll, In pleasing memory of all he stole. | 接著，他目光投注他的文集， 想起抄襲的文章洋洋得意。 |

司勃對其文集說：

| Unstain'd, untouch'd, and yet in maiden sheets; While all your smutty sisters walk the streets. | 沒人碰過、看過，仍是處女； 他人著作滿街走像妓女。 |

博普1744年去世，爲18世紀英國最著名詩人，妙言辛辣，譯介荷馬史詩、羅馬諷刺詩，精於英雄對句。

圖片來源：IDJ圖庫

1-13

強生博士

Samuel Johnson

強生博士
Samuel Johnson

　　薩慕爾・強生（Samuel Johnson），通稱強生博士（Dr. Johnson），1709年生於英格蘭中部，父親是窮書商，3歲因頸腺腫大開刀，面部留下疤痕。幼習拉丁文，記性奇佳。5歲面部開始抽搐，患妥瑞症候群（Tourette syndrome）。16歲開始寫詩、翻譯。19歲時母親獲遺產一筆，強生因此得入牛津大學彭布羅克學院（Pembroke College），學習法文、希臘文，一年後金盡退學。父親1731年去世，同年強生於小學短暫教書。1734年照顧生病好友，好友去世後不久，追求其妻伊麗莎白（Elizabeth Jervis Porter，暱稱「黛娣」Tetty），後者時年45，攜有三子女。次年黛娣不顧家人反對，嫁給25歲的強生。強生以嫁妝開辦學校，但旋即關門。1737年強生遷居倫敦，替《紳士雜誌》（The Gentleman's Magazine）寫雜文為生，次年於雜文中以「哥倫比亞」（Columbia）代稱美洲，成為慣例。1737-39年強生結識薩維吉（Richard Savage），因恥於依妻生活，離家與薩維吉流浪，1738年薩維吉有意遷居威爾斯（Wales），強生模仿羅馬詩人尤維納里（Iuvenalis，英譯Juvenal），賦長詩《倫敦》（London）相送，茲選譯首段[1]：

Tho' Grief and Fondness in my Breast rebel,	離愁哀思雖在心中翻滾，
When injur'd Thales bids the Town farewell,	泰利斯因傷心而將離城，
Yet still my calmer Thoughts his Choice commend,	平靜後我仍贊成其選擇，
I praise the Hermit, but regret the Friend,	我慕其避世，但哀其分隔，
Resolved at length, from Vice and London far,	他終於決定遠離倫敦惡習，
To breathe in distant Fields a purer Air,	去鄉間呼吸新鮮空氣，
And, fix'd on Cambria's solitary shore,	佇足坎布里亞幽靜海陲，
Give to St. David one true Briton more.	又一不列顛國士歸聖大衛。

---

[1] 末行「聖大衛」為威爾斯守護聖人。

　　薩維吉1743年貧困而死，隔年強生寫就《李查‧薩維吉傳》（Life of Mr Richard Savage）紀念之。

　　1746年強生與出版商簽約編寫英語字典，應承3年交稿，稿費1500基尼金幣（guinea）。法蘭西語文學院曾以40位學者窮40年之功完成法語字典，強生因此誇稱3個英國人足以匹敵1600個法國人。9年後於1755年完成《英語字典》（A Dictionary of the English Language），俗稱《強生字典》（Johnson's Dictionary），共收錄2,773字，例句約114,000條，首創以文學例句說明字詞用法，爲當時字典權威，直到1928年才爲牛津英語字典（Oxford English Dictionary）取代。

　　強生1750年開始於半週刊《漫談》（The Rambler）寫匿名雜文，廣受歡迎。黛娣1752年去世，強生哀痛逾恆。1756年強生出版《以預訂方式出版莎士比亞劇本芻議》（Proposals for Printing, by Subscription, the Dramatick Works of William Shakespeare），其書《莎士比亞劇本》（The Plays of William Shakespeare）1765年出版，注解繁難段落，並評點前人版本；強生於前言強調應細選版本，爲莎士比亞辯護，批評古典三一律（單一地點、單一情節、過程不踰24小時），主張戲劇反映人生，但也批評莎翁言語粗俗、情節矛盾、不顧道德教化。

　　1758-60年強生每週寫撰專欄《閒人》（The Idler）。1759年出版小說《阿比西尼亞王子拉塞拉斯傳》（The History of Rasselas, Prince of Abissinia），敘述拉塞拉斯和妹妹妮卡雅（Nekayah）住在阿比西尼亞的快樂谷，無憂無慮、心想事成，但仍不滿足，遂依哲學家伊沐拉克（Imlac）教導，出外體會人間痛苦，最終返回阿比西尼亞，但不再要求心想事成。

　　1762年強生因《英語字典》獲賜政府年金，得以專心編撰莎士比亞劇本。1763年結識時年22的蘇格蘭青年包斯威爾（James Boswell）。1763年組成《團會》（The Club），成員包括畫家雷諾茲（Joshua Reynolds）、政治哲學家柏克（Edmund Burke）、其早年學生／名演員蓋瑞克（David Garrick）、作家高斯密（Oliver Goldsmith）、經濟學家亞當‧斯密（Adam Smith）、史學家吉本（Edward Gibbon），

強生博士

每週一晚在《土耳其人頭》（Turk's Head）酒館聚會。

1765年強生結識啤酒富商希雷爾（Henry Thrale），應邀入住其家直到1781年希雷爾去世。1773年強生與包斯威爾共遊蘇格蘭，1775年出版《蘇格蘭西方群島遊記》（A Journey to the Western Islands of Scotland）述其事，包斯威爾1786年出版《赫布里底群島遊記》（The Journal of a Tour to the Hebrides）記述同一經歷。

1770年代強生多有政論文章，1775年講述名言：「『愛國』是小人的終極避難所（Patriotism is the last refuge of a scoundrel）」。

1781年強生出版《英國傑出詩人傳記》（Lives of the Most Eminent English Poets），介紹52名當代詩人生平與作品，主張詩的語言要易懂、意象要新鮮。對傳記，強生一反之前歌功頌德之傳統，主張好壞都寫，並主張大小人物都要傳記。

1784年強生去世，葬於西敏寺。1791年包斯威爾出版《法學博士薩慕爾·強生傳記》（The Life of Samuel Johnson, LL.D.），人譽為英語傳記最佳典範，書中稱強生「強生博士」，後世依例稱之。

強生以例句編撰英語字典，改革傳記規範，博學多聞，18世紀後半人稱「強生時代」（Age of Johnson）。

圖片來源：IDJ圖庫

1-14

布雷克

William Blake

布雷克
William Blak

布雷克（William Blake）1757年生於倫敦，父親是襪商，幼年短暫就學，主要在家受教於母親，屬「拒絕歸依英國國教」（non-conformist）家庭，布雷克一生篤信聖經，自幼自稱有靈視，能見上帝、天使、亡靈，從小學習版畫雕刻、繪畫，寫詩，宣稱其創作皆受天使啓發。

1772年布雷克15歲以學徒身份學習版畫，21歲出師，期間於西敏寺臨摹雕像時曾靈視耶穌與聖徒行經。1779年22歲入讀皇家藝術學院（Royal Academy of Arts），主張藝術應表達獨特性而非共通性，顯露其不從眾之個性。

布雷克1782年25歲婚娶20歲的凱瑟琳（Catherine Boucher），婚後教她識字、版畫，兩人終身相倚。1783年布雷克出版《素描詩集》（Poetical Sketches）。次年開辦印刷鋪，與政治異議份子、女權主義者往還，支持美國獨立與法國大革命。1788年發明「凸版蝕刻印刷」（relief etching，以抗酸漆書寫、繪畫，以酸蝕去其餘，然後印刷，成品可以水彩上色），此後作品多採此法。

布雷克根據自創之神話系統表達其宗教、哲學、社會概念，主張靈肉不分、接受慾望、反抗權威、眾生平等，並據以寫作一系列長詩，格律用14音節之長句，其中第一部為《帝列爾》（Tiriel），成於1789年，第二部為《慾望之書》（The Book of Thel），成於1790年。

布雷克詩作爲人熟知者乃早期短詩，有1789年寫就的《純眞之歌》（Songs of Innocence）與1794年寫就的《經驗之歌》（Songs of Experience）。《純眞之歌》共19首，以童稚口吻敘述，茲選譯兩首：

《羔羊》（The Lamb）：

Little lamb, who made thee?	小羔羊，誰造你？
Does thou know who made thee,	你知否誰造你，
Gave thee life, and bid thee feed	賜生命，讓你食飲
By the stream and o'er the mead;	在那草原在河賓；
Gave thee clothing of delight,	賜你愉人的衣裳，
Softest clothing, woolly, bright;	柔軟衣裳，茸茸亮；
Gave thee such a tender voice,	賜你如此嬌柔嗓，
Making all the vales rejoice?	使得山谷齊歡響？
Little lamb, who made thee?	小羔羊，誰造你？
Does thou know who made thee?	你知否誰造你，
Little lamb, I'll tell thee;	小羔羊，告訴你；
Little lamb, I'll tell thee:	小羔羊，告訴你：
He is callèd by thy name,	祂名字和你一樣，
For He calls Himself a Lamb.	因為祂自稱羔羊。
He is meek, and He is mild,	祂很溫柔，祂仁慈，
He became a little child.	祂投身為人稚子。
I a child, and thou a lamb,	你我，羔羊和稚子，
We are callèd by His name.	我們和祂同名字。
Little lamb, God bless thee!	小羔羊，神祝福你！
Little lamb, God bless thee!	小羔羊，神祝福你！

《掃煙囪的孩童》（The Chimney Sweeper）：

When my mother died I was very young,	媽媽去世時我年紀很小，
And my father sold me while yet my tongue	爸爸把我賣了，我連哭叫
Could scarcely cry 'weep! 'weep! 'weep! 'weep!	「嗚！嗚！嗚！嗚！」都還不會。
So your chimneys I sweep, and in soot I sleep.	現在我掃煙囪，睡在煤灰裡。
There's little Tom Dacre, who cried when his head,	小湯姆·達克，頭頸彎彎像羊背，
That curled like a lamb's back, was shaved: so I said,	他剃頭時哭了，我對他安慰：

"Hush, Tom! never mind it, for when your head's bare,
You know that the soot cannot spoil your white hair."
And so he was quiet; and that very night,
As Tom was a-sleeping, he had such a sight, -
That thousands of sweepers, Dick, Joe, Ned, and Jack,
Were all of them locked up in coffins of black.
And by came an angel who had a bright key,
And he opened the coffins and set them all free;
Then down a green plain leaping, laughing, they run,
And wash in a river, and shine in the sun.
Then naked and white, all their bags left behind,
They rise upon clouds and sport in the wind;
And the angel told Tom, if he'd be a good boy,
He'd have God for his father, and never want joy.
And so Tom awoke; and we rose in the dark,
And got with our bags and our brushes to work.
Though the morning was cold, Tom was happy and warm;
So if all do their duty they need not fear harm.

「噓，湯姆，別難過，頭髮剃光
煤灰就不會把白淨頭髮弄髒。」
湯姆聽了平靜下來，當晚
他睡覺時做夢夢到奇觀：
成千個掃煙囱孩童，喬、轟、傑、狄，
全被閉鎖在黑色棺材裡。
來了個天使手握鑰匙帶光，
打開棺材將他們全都釋放；
他們在綠原上跳、笑、奔跑，
在河中沐浴，在陽光下閃耀。
赤身潔白，他們拋下衣物，
在雲端飛升，乘風戲遊；
天使告訴湯姆，只要他乖，
他會有上帝做爸爸，永遠歡快。
湯姆醒來；我們摸黑起身，
拿起掃把包裹去上工。
黎明冷冽，但湯姆快樂暖洋洋；
只要盡責，沒有人需害怕受傷。

《經驗之歌》共26首，茲選譯兩首。

《老虎》（The Tyger）：

Tyger Tyger, burning bright,
In the forests of the night;
What immortal hand or eye.
Could frame thy fearful symmetry?
In what distant deeps or skies,

老虎老虎，灼灼光，
身在暗夜黑林莽；
是何永恆手和眼，
打造你可怕身段？
在何遙遠極高、低處，

Burnt the fire of thine eyes?	燃燒你炯炯雙目？
On what wings dare he aspire?	祂乘何翅發乎至上？
What the hand, dare sieze the fire?	以何手將赤焰握掌？
And what shoulder, & what art,	以何臂膀，何巧技，
Could twist the sinews of thy heart?	揉造你心臟筋肌？
And when thy heart began to beat,	當你心臟開始跳，
What dread hand? & what dread feet?	可怖雙手，可怖腳！
What the hammer? what the chain,	是何鐵錘？何鍊條？
In what furnace was thy brain?	是何火爐鑄你腦？
What the anvil? what dread grasp,	是何砧？何可怖手筆
Dare its deadly terrors clasp!	敢握控你致命煞氣！
When the stars threw down their spears	當眾星擲下長矛
And water'd heaven with their tears:	以淚水澆灌天昊：
Did he smile his work to see?	祂可曾笑視所造？
Did he who made the Lamb make thee?	羔羊是否亦祂造？
Tyger Tyger burning bright.	老虎老虎，灼灼光，
In the forests of the night:	身在暗夜黑林莽：
What immortal hand or eye.	是何永恆手和眼，
Dare frame thy fearful symmetry?	敢造你可怕身段？

《倫敦》（London）：

I wander thro' each charter'd street,	我穿遊過受控街巷，
Near where the charter'd Thames does flow,	在受控泰晤士河旁，
And mark in every face I meet,	見到街上每張面龐，
Marks of weakness, marks of woe.	都顯衰弱，都帶愁相。
In every cry of every Man,	聽到每個人的呼叫，
In every Infant's cry of fear,	每個嬰兒恐懼哭嚎，
In every voice, in every ban,	每個聲音，每個商招，

The mind-forg'd manacles I hear.	都聽到桎梏心靈的銬鐐。
How the Chimney-sweeper's cry	掃煙囪孩童的哭泣
Every black'ning Church appalls;	震驚所有烏黑教堂;
And the hapless Soldier's sigh	還有不幸兵士嘆息,
Runs in blood down Palace walls.	和血流下宮廷牆。
But most, thro' midnight streets I hear	但午夜街巷最常聽悉
How the youthful Harlot's curse	是年輕妓女的詛咒
Blasts the new born Infant's tear,	震懾新生嬰兒眼淚,
And blights with plagues the Marriage hearse.	降下疫病給婚姻靈柩。

　　1793年布雷克寫就長詩《美洲預言》（America a Prophecy），屬其神話系統下大陸預言系列，後有次年的《歐洲預言》（Europe a Prophecy）及1795年有關亞、非的《洛思之歌》（The Song of Los）。其神話系統尚有1794年之《尤里曾之書》（The Book of Urizen）、1795年之《雅哈妮亞之書》（The Book of Ahania）、1790-93年之《天堂與地獄的婚姻》（The Marriage of Heaven and Hell）、1793年之《傲白昂女兒之所見》（Visions of the Daughters of Albion）、1797-1807年的未盡之作《法拉，或曰四左亞》（Vala, or The Four Zoas）、1804-20年之《耶路撒冷：巨人傲白昂之顯像》（Jerusalem: The Emanation of the Giant Albion）。1800年布雷克遷居英格蘭南部斐凡市（Felpham），1804-08年繼續寫作神話系統之《密爾頓》，敘述詩人回返人間修正其生前過錯。1804年遷回倫敦，同年至1820年寫作神話系統之《耶路撒冷》（Jerusalem）。

　　1808年布雷克為喬叟《坎特伯里故事集》人物作版畫《坎特伯里朝聖者》（The Canterbury Pilgrims），並於次年寫就《目錄本事》（Descriptive Catalogue）評論喬叟此詩。

　　1818年年布雷克61歲，結識一群自稱「朔仁[1]古人」（Shoreham Ancients）的年輕藝術家，他們尊奉追隨布雷克，崇古抑今。

　　1823-26年布雷克爲舊約聖經約伯書（Book of Job）作版畫，廣受讚譽。1826年受託爲但丁《神曲》作水彩版畫，次年逝世，僅完成少部份畫作。

　　布雷克生前被視爲異端，今日認爲其以獨創神話、版畫，開英國浪漫時期文學、藝術。

---

[1]　英格蘭南方地名。

圖片來源：IDJ圖庫

1-15

彭斯

Robert Burns

彭斯（Robert Burns）1759生於蘇格蘭西南，父親是自學有成的佃農，彭斯少年在家務農，家貧經常遷徙，主要由父親教育，偶爾出外就學。15歲開始寫情詩，父親1784年去世，同年彭斯結識石匠之女琴（Jean Armour），次年家中女傭為他生下私生女，1782年改寫民謠《穿過麥田》（Comin' Thro' the Rye），帶蘇格蘭方言：

O, Jenny's a' weet, poor body,	噢，珍妮是透濕的可憐女人，
Jenny's seldom dry:	濕濕的整天：
She draigl't a' her petticoatie,	她搭拉著她的襯裙，
Comin thro' the rye!	穿過那麥田！
Comin thro' the rye, poor body,	穿過那麥田，可憐女人，
Comin thro' the rye,	穿過那麥田，
She draigl't a' her petticoatie,	她搭拉著她的襯裙，
Comin thro' the rye!	穿過那麥田！
Gin a body meet a body	如果某人遇到某人
Comin thro' the rye,	穿過那麥田，
Gin a body kiss a body,	如果某人親吻某人，
Need a body cry?	哪需要叫喧？
Gin a body meet a body	如果某人遇到某人
Comin thro' the glen	穿過那山坳
Gin a body kiss a body,	如果某人親吻某人，
Need the warl' ken?	哪需眾人曉？
Gin a body meet a body	如果某人遇到某人
Comin thro' the grain;	穿過那麥子；
Gin a body kiss a body,	如果某人親吻某人，
The thing's a body's ain.	這是他倆的事。
Ilka lassie has her laddie,	每個姑娘都有男人，
Nane, they say, ha'e I	他們說我落單
Yet all the lads they smile on me,	但小伙子全衝我傳情，
When comin' thro' the rye.	當我穿過麥田。

彭斯

1786年琴懷孕生子，同年彭斯為養家打算赴牙買加於農莊任會計，此時又結識瑪麗（Mary Campbell）相戀，不久瑪麗病逝。彭斯為籌措赴牙買加旅費出版詩集《蘇格蘭方言詩集》（Poems, Chiefly in the Scottish dialect），其中《致老鼠》（To A Mouse）一詩描述他犁田時誤毀鼠窩，中有一句：

The best laid schemes of mice and men Go often askew, And leave us nothing but grief and pain, For promised joy!	鼠和人所精心策畫 慣常皆出錯， 只帶給我們傷心痛苦， 而非滿足！

書出一舉成名，彭斯不去牙買加，改赴愛丁堡。1788年結識密友南希（Agnes "Nancy" McLehose），3年後分手，獻詩《溫存的吻》（Ae Fond Kiss）。1787-1802年醉心收集蘇格蘭民謠，編輯出版於《蘇格蘭音樂謬思集》（The Scots Musical Museum），1788年彭斯與琴結婚，同年改寫民謠《舊日時光》（Auld Lang Syne）：

Should auld acquaintance be forgot, and never brought to mind? Should auld acquaintance be forgot, and auld lang syne? For auld lang syne, my jo, for auld lang syne, we'll tak' a cup o' kindness yet, for auld lang syne. And surely ye'll be your pint-stoup! and surely I'll be mine!	我們該忘了舊日同伴， 從不想起來嗎？ 我們該忘了舊日同伴， 和舊日時光嗎？ 為了舊日時光，親愛的， 為了舊日時光， 讓我們舉杯共飲， 為了舊日時光， 你肯定願意買一杯！ 我肯定也幫場！

And we'll tak' a cup o' kindness yet,	讓我們舉杯共飲，
for auld lang syne.	為了舊日時光。
We twa hae run about the braes,	我倆曾跑遍眾山坡，
and pou'd the gowans fine;	採摘菊花眾芳；
But we've wander'd mony a weary fit,	但我們也曾倦遊各地，
sin' auld lang syne.	打從舊日時光。
We twa hae paidl'd in the burn,	我倆曾划船於溪流，
frae morning sun till dine;	從朝早到夜晚；
But seas between us braid hae roar'd	但汪洋湧隔我倆間
sin' auld lang syne.	打從舊日時光。
And there's a hand, my trusty fiere!	我伸出手，忠誠老友！
and gie's a hand o' thine!	也給我你手掌！
And we'll tak' a right gude-willie waught,	讓我們乾杯互祝安康，
for auld lang syne.	為了舊日時光。

1789年彭斯出任稅官，不再務農，1794年改寫民謠《嫣紅玫瑰》（A Red, Red Rose）：

O my Luve's like a red, red rose	噢 我的愛像嫣紅玫瑰
That's newly sprung in June;	於六月新綻放：
O my Luve's like the melodie	噢 我的愛像美妙旋律
That's sweetly play'd in tune.	可以甜美演唱。
As fair art thou, my bonnie lass,	你有多美，漂亮姑娘，
So deep in luve am I:	我就愛你多深切：
And I will luve thee still, my dear,	我會一直愛你，親愛的，
Till a' the seas gang dry:	直到大海枯竭：
Till a' the seas gang dry, my dear,	直到大海枯竭，親愛的，
And the rocks melt wi' the sun:	直到太陽溶化山石：

彭斯

I will luve thee still, my dear,	我會一直愛你，親愛的，
While the sands o' life shall run.	只要生命持續一日。
And fare thee weel, my only Luve	祝你安好，我唯一的愛
And fare thee weel, a while!	祝你安好，適然！
And I will come again, my Luve,	我會再度歸來，我愛，
Tho' it were ten thousand mile.	即使從萬里之遠。

1795年改寫民謠《大丈夫還是大丈夫呵》（A Man's a Man for A' That）：

Is there for honest Poverty	會有人貧窮而誠實，
That hings his head, an' a' that;	卻羞於見人？怎麼的；
The coward slave-we pass him by,	這種膽小賤奴我們不恥，
We dare be poor for a' that!	我們窮就窮！管他的！
For a' that, an' a' that.	管他的，管他的。
Our toils obscure an' a' that,	我們工作卑微又怎的，
The rank is but the guinea's stamp,	高位只是金玉其外，
The Man's the gowd for a' that.	人格才是真金的。
What though on hamely fare we dine,	我們雖然吃的家常，
Wear hodden grey, an' a that;	穿粗毛灰衣，這的那的；
Gie fools their silks, and knaves their wine;	讓蠢人穿綢，無賴飲酒；
A Man's a Man for a' that:	大丈夫還是大丈夫呵：
For a' that, and a' that,	大丈夫呵，大丈夫呵，
Their tinsel show, an' a' that;	他們虛華愛現，又怎的；
The honest man, tho' e'er sae poor,	誠實的人，儘管貧窮，
Is king o' men for a' that.	卻是人上人，說真的。
Ye see yon birkie, ca'd a lord,	你看那闊佬，號稱大爺，
Wha struts, an' stares, an' a' that;	邁步睨視，好不了得；
Tho' hundreds worship at his word,	開口就有百人俯貼，

He's but a coof for a' that:	他只是蠢蛋來著：
For a' that, an' a' that,	蠢蛋來著，蠢蛋來著，
His ribband, star, an' a' that:	他的綬帶、勳章，那些的：
The man o' independent mind	能獨立思考的人
He looks an' laughs at a' that.	看著只覺可笑呢。
A prince can mak a belted knight,	王侯可以賜封騎士啊，
A marquis, duke, an' a' that;	侯爵、公爵啊、什麼的；
But an honest man's abon his might,	但誠實的人更偉大，
Gude faith, he maunna fa' that!	這絕不能忘，眞格的！
For a' that, an' a' that,	眞格的，眞格的，
Their dignities an' a' that;	人格才是眞格的；
The pith o' sense, an' pride o' worth,	明白道理，以己爲傲，
Are higher rank than a' that.	都比地位更要得。
Then let us pray that come it may,	讓我們祈禱祝願，
(As come it will for a' that,)	（此事必然成眞的，）
That Sense and Worth, o'er a' the earth,	願道理、人格，無處不到，
Shall bear the gree, an' a' that.	最終勝出，全部贏得。
For a' that, an' a' that,	全贏得，全贏得，
It's coming yet for a' that,	此事將成眞格的，
That Man to Man, the world o'er,	人與人間，舉世皆然，
Shall brothers be for a' that.	都成兄弟，眞格的。

彭斯支持法國大革命，此詩表達其平等、自由信念。1796年彭斯逝世。

彭斯是蘇格蘭民族詩人，爲英美浪漫文學先驅，集編改寫蘇格蘭民謠。

圖片來源：IDJ圖庫

1-16
史考特
Walter Scott

史考特（Walter Scott）1771年生於蘇格蘭愛丁堡（Edinburgh），父親執律師業，史考特患小兒痲痺1773-75年送至蘇格蘭南方鄉下老家休養，姑母教其識字，聽聞並記錄鄉間傳奇，1779年入讀小學，1783-86年入愛丁堡大學主修古典文學，1786年進父親律師事務所爲學徒，1789-92年再入愛丁堡大學主修法律，準備執業。1802-03年史考特出版《蘇格蘭邊疆民謠》（The Minstrelsy of the Scottish Border），1797年結婚，1799年出任郡法官。

　　1805年史考特出版詩集《吟遊絕響》（The Lay of the Last Minstrel），書出成名。1808年出版長詩《馬靡恩》（Marmion）敘述15世紀貴族馬靡恩企圖強娶一女子不成，最終斃命於英格蘭、蘇格蘭一場戰役。中有名句：

Oh! what a tangled web we weave When first we practise to deceive!	噢！是何等糾纏紊亂 當我們開始去欺騙！

　　1809年史考特協助創辦立場保守的《每季評論》（Quarterly Review）期刊。1810年出版長詩《湖上之女》（The Lady of the Lake）敘述蘇格蘭高地（Highland）、低地（Lowland）間之戰爭、愛情，此書促成19世紀蘇格蘭高地文化復興，美國總統讚歌《領袖頌》（Hail to the Chief）歌詞源於此，舒伯特曾爲德譯本作曲《聖母頌》（Ave Maria）。

　　1814年史考特匿名出版首本歷史傳奇小說《韋佛禮》（Waverley），敘述英國人韋佛禮介入1745年前後之詹姆士起義（Jacobite risings），協助蘇格蘭裔的司圖雅特（Stuart）王朝復辟，最終失敗。此後出版一系列同類作品，本本暢銷，包括1817年之《羅布·羅伊》（Rob Roy）敘述此人參與詹姆士起義之事；1818年之《中洛旬郡

史考特

之心》（The Heart of Midlothian）前半敘述1736年愛丁堡暴民虐殺市政廳衛隊長，後半敘述民女琴妮（Jeanie Deans）徒步至倫敦，為姊求情之事；1819年之《艾凡赫》（Ivanhoe，又譯《撒克遜英雄傳》、《劫後英雄傳》），根據羅賓漢傳奇，敘述12世紀沒落撒克遜貴族艾凡赫，伴隨諾曼人國王理查一世（Richard I）十字軍東征歸來，隨同理查、撒克遜人羅思理（Robin of Locksley，即羅賓漢）鬥爭諾曼貴族，並協助猶太商人父女艾薩克、蕾蓓嘉（Isaac、Rebecca），最終婚娶撒克遜貴族女蘿薇娜（Rowena），此書促成時人對中古時期之興趣，茲選譯兩段：

Chivalry!---why, maiden, she is the nurse of pure and high affection---the stay of the oppressed, the redresser of grievances, the curb of the power of the tyrant ---Nobility were but an empty name without her, and liberty finds the best protection in her lance and her sword.	騎士精神！──要知道，小姐，騎士精神塑造純潔高貴心靈─它保護被壓迫者、平反被冤屈者、拒限暴君權力─貴族少了它就只剩虛名，自由依靠它的劍、矛而得守護。

Norman saw on English oak. On English neck a Norman yoke; Norman spoon to English dish, And England ruled as Normans wish; Blithe world in England never will be more, Till England's rid of all the four.	諾曼鋸齒凌駕英國橡木。 英人頸項扼有諾曼枷梏； 諾曼勺子舀進英國碗碟， 英國任由諾曼控虐； 英國不再有歡樂時光， 除非英國擺脫這四樣。

　　1818年史考特受王儲之託，於愛丁堡塔（Edinburgh Castle）尋獲自17世紀中葉即失蹤的蘇格蘭王冠、權杖、寶劍，因此受封次男爵（Baronet）。1822年受命籌劃盛典，歡迎已登基的王儲喬治四世駕臨蘇格蘭，借此彌補英、蘇百年來的不和。1825年英國金融危機導致史考特欠下巨款，努力寫作還債。1820-32年出任愛丁堡皇家學會會長（President of the Royal Society of Edinburgh），1832年去世。

　　史考特參與開創歷史小說文類，促成蘇格蘭高地文化復興，作品廣受歡迎、影響深遠。

圖片來源：IDJ圖庫

1-17

華茲華士

William Wordsworth

華茲華士（William Wordsworth）1770年生於英格蘭中部湖區（Lake District），父親是律師，爲朗斯岱伯爵（Earl of Lonsdale）服務，長兄也是律師，大弟是東印度公司船長，小弟位至劍橋大學三一學院院長。幼年由父親親授文學，6-7歲和妹妹桃若蘇（Dorothy）就讀小學，與日後的妻子瑪麗（Mary Huthchinson）同窗。8歲喪母，送去寄宿學校，桃若蘇送去北方親戚家寄住，兩人9年後才重聚。華茲華士受寄宿學校校長鼓勵而寫作，閒暇時遊山玩水。13歲父親過世。17歲入讀劍橋大學聖約翰學院（St John's College），21歲畢業。甫入大學即在雜誌刊登商籟，一展文才。大三赴法國、瑞士、意大利北部阿爾卑斯山徒步旅行，大四去威爾斯旅行。

1791年華茲華士大學畢業後再度赴法，時當1789年法國大革命後，他認同了大革命的民主改革思潮，和法國少女安磊特（Annette Vallon）相戀，育有一女卡洛琳（Caroline），此戀情直至1816年才廣爲人知。1793年華茲華士金盡返英，英法隨即因交戰而交通阻絕，直到9年後才得返法。

1792年華茲華士在法遇見同胞司徒爾特（John Stewart），其人曾從印度東部馬德拉斯（Madras）徒步旅行返歐，歷時30年，並融合瑜伽天人一體思想與17世紀荷蘭哲學家史賓諾沙（Spinosa）之泛神論，自成一說，對華茲華士影響甚深。1793年華茲華士23歲首度出版詩集《傍晚漫步》（An Evening Walk）與《素描隨筆》（Descriptive Sketches），之後瀕臨精神崩潰，休養後康復。1795-97年寫了一齣歷史悲情詩劇《邊境之人》（The Borderers），試圖在倫敦柯芬園劇場（Covent Garden）上演未果。

1795年華茲華士照顧肺結核的劍橋同學卡佛特（Raisley Calvert），後者遺贈他900英鎊以供寫作。同年華茲華士和桃若蘇遷居英國西南多石郡（Dorsetshire），結識了事業伙伴柯律治（Samuel Coleridge）。兩年後搬去稍北的暑秣塞郡（Somersetshire）以便親近柯律治。1798年兩人合著出版《抒情歌謠》（Lyrical Ballads），爲英國文學浪漫主義之濫觴，書中20多首作品4首爲柯律治所作，華茲華士寫的第一首《勸告與回應》（Expostulation and Reply），第二首《主客易位》（The Tables Turned）都勸人放下書本，向大自然學習；最後一首《作於帝碇寺上方數哩》（Lines Written a Few Miles above Tintern Abbey），帝碇寺是天主教熙篤會（Cistercian）修院，1536年亨利八世宗教改革時被廢，華茲華士1793年初訪該寺，1798年再訪後寫下此詩，抒發人生的轉化與大自然予人的安慰，全詩以五步無韻體寫就。茲選譯起頭一段：

Five years have past; five summers, with the length	已過了五年；五個夏天，
Of five long winters! and again I hear	還有五個長長的冬天！我又
These waters, rolling from their mountain-springs	再次聽聞此流水，出自那
With a soft inland murmur.--Once again	山泉，帶有內陸幽咽——再次
Do I behold these steep and lofty cliffs,	我目睹這些高峻的山崖，
That on a wild secluded scene impress	賦予了這片僻靜的荒野
Thoughts of more deep seclusion; and connect	更深沉僻靜的幽思，並將
The landscape with the quiet of the sky.	大地連接到天空的寧靜。
The day is come when I again repose	時至今日我再次在這裡
Here, under this dark sycamore, and view	休憩，在這深鬱楓樹下，看
These plots of cottage-ground, these orchard-tufts,	這些茅屋片片，果園樹叢，
Which at this season, with their unripe fruits,	在此季節，果實尚未成熟，
Are clad in one green hue, and lose themselves	呈現一色青綠，掩藏在那
'Mid groves and copses. Once again I see	叢叢樹木中。我再次見到
These hedge-rows, hardly hedge-rows, little lines	排樹分隔，尚非排樹，只是
Of sportive wood run wild: these pastoral farms,	一小行樹木漫溢：這田園
Green to the very door; and wreaths of smoke	農家，綠滿門前；還有圍煙
Sent up, in silence, from among the trees!	由那樹叢裡安靜地飄升。
With some uncertain notice, as might seem	圍煙飄升遲疑，好似在那
Of vagrant dwellers in the houseless woods,	無人的森林中遊民所起，
Or of some Hermit's cave, where by his fire	又似來自隱者洞窟，其中
The Hermit sits alone.	隱者伴火獨坐。

相較之前新古典主義文學，《抒情歌謠》強調以日常語言描述俗民生活，體現法國哲學家盧梭（Rouseau）「崇尚自然純真」之概念。華茲華士深受桃若蘇日記對山水描繪之影響，桃若蘇因此成為詩中對話對象。此書1800年再版，增加多首新詩，另加序文明言其改革宗旨，並定義詩為「自然漫溢的強烈感情，事後於寧靜中回憶」（the spontaneous overflow of powerful emotions recollected in tranquility），再版時作者只列華茲華士一人。1802年三版又增加新詩，再加跋文進一步說明其詩語主張。

1798年華茲華士偕桃若蕬、柯律治赴德旅遊，因思鄉而心情低落，寫了5首以少女露西（Lucy）之死爲主題的詩，茲選譯兩首：

《我曾受襲莫名心緒》（Strange fits of passion have I known）：

Strange fits of passion have I known:	我曾受襲莫名心緒：
And I will dare to tell,	而且我也只敢
But in the Lover's ear alone,	在情人的耳邊傾訴，
What once to me befell.	此一親身經驗。
When she I loved looked every day	當年我的愛日日像
Fresh as a rose in June,	六月新綻玫瑰。
I to her cottage bent my way,	我朝她的小屋往訪，
Beneath an evening-moon.	頭懸夜晚月輝。
Upon the moon I fixed my eye,	我目注那輪月亮，
All over the wide lea;	普照廣闊原野，
With quickening pace my horse drew nigh	加快步伐坐騎趨向
Those paths so dear to me.	小徑眞覺親切。
And now we reached the orchard-plot;	我們前進到達果圍；
And, as we climbed the hill,The sinking moon to Lucy's cot	當上了那山坡，
	月亮落向露西家院
Came near, and nearer still.	越落，越近越迫。
In one of those sweet dreams I slept,	我沉睡於美夢之中，
Kind Nature's gentlest boon!	大自然的恩賞！
And all the while my eyes I kept	同時目光仍然跟蹤
On the descending moon.	往下落的月亮。
My horse moved on; hoof after hoof	坐騎前行；一步一步
He raised, and never stopped:	舉蹄，不曾稍停：
When down behind the cottage roof,	此時小屋後的高處，
At once, the bright moon dropped.	刹時，明月遽隕。

華茲華士

What fond and wayward thoughts will slide Into a lover's head! "O mercy!" to myself I cried, "If Lucy should be dead!"	各樣稀奇古怪念想 潛入情人心思！ 「老天！」我對自己驚嘆， 「萬一露西已死！」

《她佇居之處人跡罕至》（She dwelt among the untrodden ways）：

She dwelt among the untrodden ways Beside the springs of Dove, A Maid whom there were none to praise And very few to love: A violet by a mossy stone Half hidden from the eye! – Fair as a star, when only one Is shining in the sky. She lived unknown, and few could know When Lucy ceased to be; But she is in her grave, and, oh, The difference to me.	她佇居之處人跡罕至 在鴿泉的旁邊， 一方處子無人賞識 更乏人來愛憐 苔石左近一株紫菫 半遮蔽不得見！ ——她燦若星辰，全天屏 只見一星耀閃。 生無人識，更乏人曉 她於何時凋謝； 而她已魂歸墓穴，噢， 於我天壤有別。

　　此期間柯律治鼓勵他：「我希望你寫一首詩，給那些因法國大革命失敗而對人類改進喪失信心、退而沉溺於自我享樂的人」，華茲華士因此寫下自述其心靈成長的長詩《序曲》（Prelude），終其一生不斷修改增益，並稱其爲「給柯律治的詩」；此詩死後才發表，遺孀瑪麗命名爲《序曲》，因爲華茲華士想以之爲巨著《隱者》（The Recluse）的前言，《隱者》最終只完成了此篇與第二冊《出遊》（Excursion），主旨

仍是透過其個人（一位退隱詩人）的感知經歷探討人、社會、大自然之關係，其原定目標在超越密爾頓的《失樂園》。

1799年華茲華士返回湖區，直住到1807年，與詩人瑟西（Robert Southey）往還，時人稱華茲華士、柯律治、瑟西三人為「湖區詩人」（Lake Poets），此時其詩多探討死亡、痛苦、分離等主題。1802年華茲華士收到朗斯岱伯爵積欠父親的4000英鎊，經濟稍有餘裕，準備與青梅竹馬瑪麗結婚，遂偕桃若蘇赴法見舊情人安磊特，並首次見到9歲的女兒卡洛琳（Caroline），賦詩《此夕傍晚日氣佳，平靜，舒闊》（It is a beauteous evening, calm and free），記述和女兒在海邊散步。同年華茲華士結婚，婚禮當天桃若蘇在房中哭泣。

婚後1802-04年華茲華士寫了《頌：憶童年而悟不朽》（Ode: Intimations of Immortality from Recollections of Early Childhood），1815年定稿，詩中認為兒童最具靈性，大自然也同具此特點。序言用了1802年寫的另一首詩《我心雀躍》（My heart leaps up）末三句。《我心雀躍》全詩為：

My heart leaps up when I behold A rainbow in the sky: So was it when my life began; So is it now I am a man; So be it when I shall grow old, Or let me die! The Child is father of the Man; And I could wish my days to be Bound each to each by natural piety.	我心雀躍當我看見 天際彩虹高峙： 我感受之於人之初； 如今成人亦復等如； 願我年老時也不變， 否則寧死！ 孩童乃是成人之父； 願我日復一日終生 敬對自然持之以恆。

1804年華茲華士寫了廣為人知的《我孤獨漫遊像朵雲》（I Wandered Lonely as a Cloud）：

I wander'd lonely as a cloud	我孤獨漫遊像朵雲
That floats on high o'er vales and hills,	飄浮在山與谷峰巔，
When all at once I saw a crowd,	陡然間我見到一群
A host, of golden daffodils;	一簇，金黃色的水仙；
Beside the lake, beneath the trees,	倚傍著湖，上有樹木，
Fluttering and dancing in the breeze.	在微風中瑟瑟起舞。
Continuous as the stars that shine	連綿迢遭有如星辰
And twinkle on the Milky Way,	閃爍在那銀河天漢，
They stretch'd in never-ending line	延伸一線無窮無盡
Along the margin of a bay:	在湖邊的水灣沿岸：
Ten thousand saw I at a glance,	隨意一瞥就以萬計，
Tossing their heads in sprightly dance.	盡情搖擺歡舞身軀。
The waves beside them danced; but they	湖邊波浪也起舞，但
Out-did the sparkling waves in glee:	水仙悅動更勝銀波
A poet could not but be gay,	詩人心情怎能不歡
In such a jocund company:	當他有此快樂同伙：
I gazed--and gazed--but little thought	我注目良久，但不曾
What wealth the show to me had brought:	料到此景豐厚賜贈：
For oft, when on my couch I lie	日後，當我長椅臥偃，
In vacant or in pensive mood,	心中放空或是沉潛，
They flash upon that inward eye	此景常現心靈之眼
Which is the bliss of solitude;	那獨處時幸福之泉；
And then my heart with pleasure fills,	每當此我滿心喜福，
And dances with the daffodils.	隨那水仙歡快起舞。

1805年華茲華士寫就另一名作《獨自刈麥的少女》（The Solitary Reaper）：

Behold her, single in the field,	看啊，她，一人在田中，
Yon solitary Highland Lass!	那孤身的高地少女！
Reaping and singing by herself;	自己一人刈麥歌詠；
Stop here, or gently pass!	停步，或悄然避趨！
Alone she cuts and binds the grain,	她獨自割麥捆麥稈，
And sings a melancholy strain;	同時清唱悲涼哀怨；
O listen! for the Vale profound	聽啊！在此幽深山坳
Is overflowing with the sound.	她的歌聲滿盈繚繞。
No Nightingale did ever chaunt	就連夜鶯婉轉抒啼
More welcome notes to weary bands	都不及其清音撫慰
Of travellers in some shady haunt,	稍憩涼陰的疲憊旅隊
Among Arabian sands:	當身處阿拉伯沙陲：
A voice so thrilling ne'er was heard	憾心妙音人間未悉
In spring-time from the Cuckoo-bird,	春日杜鵑百囀難比，
Breaking the silence of the seas	穿透四海遼闊沉寂
Among the farthest Hebrides.	直達天際赫布里底。
Will no one tell me what she sings?–	誰能告我歌中所思？
Perhaps the plaintive numbers flow	也許是在怨嘆訴泣
For old, unhappy, far-off things,	古老、哀傷、遙遠之事，
And battles long ago:	久遠前的戰役：
Or is it some more humble lay,	或者只是平凡歌詩，
Familiar matter of to-day?	談論日常熟悉瑣事？
Some natural sorrow, loss, or pain,	日常煩憂、得失、苦痛，
That has been, and may be again?	昔日有，來日或再逢？
Whate'er the theme, the Maiden sang	無論為何，少女長歌
As if her song could have no ending;	歌聲曲韻雋永迢邐：
I saw her singing at her work,	我目注她邊做邊唱，
And o'er the sickle bending;--	俯身以鐮刀割刈；
I listened, motionless and still;	我凝神不動側耳聽；
And, as I mounted up the hill	之後，當我爬山前進
The music in my heart I bore,	此曲仍然縈繞我心，
Long after it was heard no more.	縱使歌聲早已不聞。

華茲華士

　　與歐洲年輕人一樣，華茲華士原本崇拜法國大革命，崇拜拿破崙，視其爲理性主義革新之代表，但拿破崙1804年稱帝復辟，導致年輕人理想幻滅，華茲華士政治上轉趨保守。1810年他因柯律治吸食鴉片而與之割席。同年爲稿費寫了《湖區導遊》（Guide Thorough the District of the Lakes）。1813年任稅務官，年薪400鎊，收入終於穩定。1814年出版《隱者》第二冊《出遊》，但中年後詩才漸減。

　　1816年女兒卡洛琳結婚，華茲華士贈予年金30鎊，又於1835年改爲一次性贈予400鎊。1820年華茲華士時年50，循少時途徑再度遊歐，一家在巴黎與安蕾特、卡洛琳相聚。同年，其作品終獲文壇認可，聲譽日增。1823年其好友畫家格林（William Green）逝世，華茲華士因而與柯律治和好，1828年兩人共遊萊茵河。次年桃若蕬生病，從此臥床。1842年華茲華士獲政府頒贈年金300鎊。次年桂冠詩人瑟西過世，政府提名他繼任，起初以年事已高拒絕，政府應承只需掛名才接任。1850年華茲華士去世，葬於湖區，同年遺孀瑪麗出版其鉅作《序曲》，茲選譯第一章一段：

Ye Presences of Nature in the sky	爾等大自然在天上在地下
And on the earth! Ye Visions of the hills!	之展化！爾等山陵之呈現！
And Souls of lonely places! can I think	幽寂處所之靈魂！爾等有
A vulgar hope was yours when ye employed	如此作爲顯然心願絕不
Such ministry, when ye, through many a year	粗鄙，爾等經年累月在我
Haunting me thus among my boyish sports,	童稚於洞窟、樹上，森林中、
On caves and trees, upon the woods and hills,	山丘間玩耍時環繞我身，
Impressed, upon all forms, the characters	賦予雜然萬物或可怖、
Of danger or desire; and thus did make	或可喜之特性；因此而使得
The surface of the universal earth,	全球大地景觀或雄偉、
With triumph and delight, with hope and fear,	或悅目，或誘人、或嚇人，類同
Work like a sea? Not uselessly employed,	那汪洋。我爲了特定目的，
Might I pursue this theme through every change	可否就此主題逐一審視
Of exercise and play, to which the year	細察我的各種冶遊嬉戲，
Did summon us in his delightful round.	伴隨一年季節歡愉輪轉。

華茲華士乘歐洲浪漫主義風潮，偕同柯律治改變英詩主題、風格，以日常語言抒寫俗民之事，融合性靈於大自然，開創一代文風，在英國文壇與密爾頓並列，地位僅次於莎士比亞。

◆
·
華
茲
華
士
·
◆

圖片來源：IDJ圖庫

1-18
柯律治
Samuel Taylor Coleridge

　　柯律治（Samuel Taylor Coleridge）1772年生於英格蘭西南端，父親是國教牧師、小學校長。柯律治自幼喜愛文學，個性孤僻，8歲父親去世，被送入公立慈善學校基督公學（Christ's Hospital）寄讀，結識同窗、另一日後文人藍姆（Charles Lamb）。1791-94年柯律治入讀劍橋大學耶穌學院（Jesus College），其間因失戀或欠債從軍數月。柯律治精神不穩定，可能患有燥鬱症。此時開始服用鴉片止痛。

　　大學時柯律治結識詩人瑟西，共謀於美國創建烏托邦社區未果。1795年兩人先後婚娶一對姐妹，柯律治婚姻不諧，日後與妻分居。同年柯律治結識詩人華茲華士及其妹桃若蕬，其後兩三年定居暑秝塞郡（Somersetshire），詩作豐碩，包括《古舟子詠》（Rime of The Ancient Mariner）、《忽必烈罕，夢中所見片斷》（Kubla Khan, or, A Vision in a Dream, A Fragment）、《翠絲特蓓》（Christabel）首段、還有以對話語氣寫成的「對話詩」（conversation poems）三首：《此檸檬樹亭即我牢房》（This Lime-Tree Bower My Prison）、《午夜凝霜》（Frost at Midnight）、《夜鶯》（The Nightingale），「對話詩」之語氣語法深深影響到華茲華士詩作。

　　《古舟子詠》敘述一艘船被暴風吹至南極，幸賴信天翁引導脫險，但信天翁被一水手射下，眾神怒將船困於無風水域：

Water, water, everywhere, And all the boards did shrink; Water, water, everywhere, Nor any drop to drink.	水啊，水啊，處處水， 船板全都變形； 水啊，水啊，處處水， 但一滴不得飲。

柯律治

眾水手強迫射殺信天翁之同伴將鳥屍掛於頸項，後遇一鬼船，眾水手皆殞命，唯獨射殺信天翁之人注定殘存但生不如死，他見到海中生物，心生祝福：

O happy living things! no tongue Their beauty might declare: A spring of love gushed from my heart, And I blessed them unaware: Sure my kind saint took pity on me, And I blessed them unaware.	噢幸福的生物！言語 無法形容此美景： 一股愛意由我心湧出， 我不覺祝福牠們： 必是守護神憐憫我， 我不覺祝福牠們。

信天翁屍體因此脫落，他得救返鄉，但注定一世流浪講述其經歷，並給人忠告：

He prayeth best, who loveth best All things both great and small; For the dear God who loveth us, He made and loveth all.	善祈禱者乃善愛者， 善愛大小全部： 因為愛我們的上帝， 創造且愛萬物。

此詩包含名句「更憂患也更睿智之人」（a sadder and a wiser man），並衍生出以信天翁為罪孽之象徵。

《忽必烈罕》乃柯律治自承飲用鴉片後昏沉中寫下，描述忽必烈在上都（Xanadu）的宮殿奇景，茲選譯首段：

In Xanadu did Kubla Khan A stately pleasure-dome decree : Where Alph, the sacred river, ran Through caverns measureless to man Down to a sunless sea. So twice five miles of fertile ground With walls and towers were girdled round : And there were gardens bright with sinuous rills, Where blossomed many an incense-bearing tree ; And here were forests ancient as the hills, Enfolding sunny spots of greenery.	忽必烈大罕在上都 敕建宏偉宮殿遊倘： 於阿爾發聖河流經處 穿越神秘未知洞窟 注入陰鬱海洋。 將十英里肥茂土地 以高牆樓塔圍繞起： 中有明艷花園蜿蜒小溪， 樹上繁花似錦散逸馨香； 處處蒼林古木壽與山齊， 片片嬌陽午現青蔥草場。

《翠絲特蓓》描述少女翠絲特蓓在林中遇見自稱被綁架的神秘女子婕偌黛（Geraldine），將婕偌黛帶回家，翠絲特蓓與父親李傲萊（Leoline）爵士皆受婕偌黛吸引。此詩未寫完，茲選譯翠絲特蓓看婕偌黛脫衣準備共眠一段：

Like one that shuddered, she unbound The cincture from beneath her breast: Her silken robe, and inner vest, Dropt to her feet, and in full view, Behold! her bosom and half her side——	彷彿顫慄抖動，她解開 胸部下方的扣帶： 絲質袍子，還有內衣， 墜落腳下，一覽無遺， 看啊！她的雙峰和半側——

1798年柯律治與華茲華士出版《抒情歌謠》，爲英國文學浪漫主義之濫觴，其中《古舟子詠》最受矚目。相對於華茲華士，柯律治詩作多以「異常」爲主題，如《古舟子詠》、《忽必烈罕》、《翠絲特蓓》皆是。

1798年柯律治接受英國陶瓷鉅子「瑋緻活」（Wedgwood）家族提供之150英鎊年金，得以專心寫作。同年偕華茲華士兄妹赴德旅遊，於哥廷根大學（Univ. of Gottingen）接觸並醉心康德（Kant）之唯心主義哲學，以及德國文人萊辛（Gotthold Lessing）之文學批評。1800年柯律治遷居湖區，與相鄰的華茲華士往還，愛上華茲華士日後妻子瑪麗之姊妹莎拉（Sara），未久受困於病痛與婚姻問題，寫下對話詩《詠沮喪》（Dejection: An Ode）。1804-08年柯律治赴意大利與馬爾他，藉南歐天氣治病，擬戒除鴉片煙癮未果。1807年寫就對話詩《致華茲華士》（To William Wordsworth），回應後者詩作《序曲》。

1808年柯律治與妻分居。1809年出版週刊《友人》（The Friend），文章全出自其一人之手，縱論文史哲法各領域，因經營不善只出版25期，但影響文壇頗深。1810年與華茲華士生隙斷交。

1810-20年柯律治在倫敦與英格蘭西南的布里斯托（Bristol）就莎士比亞與密爾頓作系列演講，奠定其文學批評地位，其中1812年討論《哈姆雷特》一場尤為著名，分析哈姆雷特心裡，認為相對於具體，哈姆雷特代表抽象，之前被忽視的《哈姆雷特》因此演講廣受注意。

1814年柯律治託付醫師全面管照，1816年因鴉片煙癮與憂鬱症遷入其醫師於倫敦北郊海格特區（Highgate）住宅，受後輩文人景仰，人稱「海格特智者」（Sage of Highgate）。1815-17年寫就自傳《文學傳記》（Biographia Literaria），記述其文學觀之養成，批評華茲華士主張詩與日常語言無異之論點，書中還提出「擱置不信」（suspension of disbelief）的觀念。此時期其宗教論文影響了稍後國教內主張回歸傳統的牛津運動（Oxford Movement）。1828年柯律治與華茲華士復交，共遊德國萊茵區。1834年去世。

柯律治與華茲華士共同開創英國浪漫主義文學，寫下膾炙人口的《古舟子詠》與《忽必烈罕》；他將德國唯心主義引入英美文化，形成美國超驗主義（Transcendentalism）；對華茲華士與莎士比亞的評論有重大影響。

圖片來源：IDJ圖庫

1-19

珍・奧斯汀

Jane Austen

珍・奧斯汀
Jane Austen

　　珍・奧斯汀（Jane Austen）1775年生於英格蘭南方漢普郡（Hampshire），父親是當地國教牧師，兼營農耕與家教以補充收入，屬小鄉紳階級。奧斯汀有五兄一姊一弟，與姊姊卡珊卓（Cassadra）極親密。三哥為親戚收養；四哥亨利（Henry）初為銀行家，銀行倒閉後任牧師，在倫敦交遊廣闊，是奧斯汀的文學經紀人；五哥和弟弟加入海軍，升至將官。奧斯汀8歲與姊姊一同寄宿牛津市一位老師家受教，兩人感染傷寒，奧斯汀幾乎死去，一年後返家，10歲再與姊姊赴另一寄宿學校，隔年因金盡輟學，在家自修，父兄鼓勵姊妹兩自由發展，此後姊妹兩終身在家。奧斯汀小時候，家人依當時知識分子習俗在家演戲自娛，培養了奧斯汀的文學天份，她也撰寫小說詩文自娛，內容多仿諷時下流行作品。

　　奧斯汀約1795年開始寫小說《愛莉娜與瑪莉安》（Elinor and Marianne），1811年改名《理性與感性》（Sense and Sensibility）出版，敘述達希伍家（Dashwood）姊姊愛莉娜與妹妹瑪莉安於父親死後家道中落，理性的愛莉娜與斐勞斯（Edward Ferrars）互有好感，但費勞斯已秘密訂婚；感性的瑪莉安與率性的韋勒比（John Willoughby）熱戀，結果韋勒比選擇婚娶富家女。矜持節制的愛莉娜最終得與斐勞斯結成正果，瑪莉安也改變自己，接受了大她十多歲，但疼惜她的布蘭登上校（Colonel Brandon）。茲選譯第二章兩姊妹同父異母兄嫂約翰、芬妮（Fanny）繼承其父財產房產後，討論照顧後母一家一段，為縮減篇幅，中有省略：

"It was my father's last request to me...that I should assist his widow and daughters." "He did not know what he was talking of, I dare say; ten to one but he was light-headed at the time. Had he been in his right senses, he could not have thought of such a thing as begging you to give away half your fortune from your own child."	「這是我父親臨終的要求……要我協助他的遺孀和女兒。」 「他自己都不知道自己在說什麼，我敢以10對1打賭他當時已神志不清。他如果神志清醒，不可能要求你將你自己兒子一半的財產交給別人。」

"He did not stipulate for any particular sum...he only requested me, in general terms, to assist them."

...

"Well, then, LET something be done for them; but THAT something need not be three thousand pounds. Consider...that when the money is once parted with, it never can return. Your sisters will marry, and it will be gone for ever. If, indeed, it could be restored to our poor little boy—"

"...The time may come when Harry will regret that so large a sum was parted with. If he should have a numerous family, for instance, it would be a very convenient addition...Perhaps, then, it would be better for all parties, if the sum were diminished one half.—Five hundred pounds would be a prodigious increase to their fortunes!"

"Oh! beyond anything great! What brother on earth would do half so much for his sisters, even if REALLY his sisters! And as it is—only half blood!...There is no knowing what THEY may expect...but we are not to think of their expectations: the question is, what you can afford to do."

...

"As it is, without any addition of mine, they will each have about three thousand pounds on their mother's death—a very comfortable fortune for any young woman."

"To be sure it is; and, indeed, it strikes me that they can want no addition at all. They will have ten thousand pounds divided amongst them. If they marry, they will be sure of doing well, and if they do not, they may all live very comfortably together on the interest of ten thousand pounds."

「他並未明定一個數額⋯⋯他只是籠統地要求我協助她們。」

⋯⋯

「那好，我們就幫她們點什麼吧；但是幫也用不著幫到3000鎊。想想⋯⋯這錢給了就再也回不來了。你的妹妹們將來要嫁人，到時這錢就永別了。反之，要是有辦法讓錢回歸給我們可憐的兒子——」

「⋯⋯有天哈利可能會遺憾我們給出這麼多錢。假定說他將來有個大家庭，有了這筆錢會很趁手⋯⋯這麼說的話，也許我們把數額減半對大家都好。——給她們500鎊已經不得了了！」

「噢！已經好的不得了了！世上有哪個哥哥如此照顧妹妹，即使是親妹妹！而其實——你們是異母！⋯⋯她們期望什麼我們哪知道？我們也不該考慮這個：該考慮的是，你給的起多少？」

⋯⋯

「現況是，就算我不給，她們母親死後姊妹將各得約3000鎊—這對任何少女來說都很夠。」

「說得沒錯；而且，我認為她們根本不需要更多錢。她們總共可以繼承一萬鎊。如果結婚，她們生活一定過得很舒適，就算不結婚，她們可以一起生活，靠一萬鎊的利息也可以過得很舒適。」

"That is very true, and, therefore, I do not know whether, upon the whole, it would not be more advisable to do something for their mother while she lives, rather than for them—something of the annuity kind I mean.... A hundred a year would make them all perfectly comfortable."

His wife hesitated a little, however, in giving her consent to this plan.

"To be sure...it is better than parting with fifteen hundred pounds at once. But, then, if Mrs. Dashwood should live fifteen years we shall be completely taken in."

"Fifteen years!...her life cannot be worth half that purchase."

"Certainly not; but if you observe, people always live for ever when there is an annuity to be paid them; and she is very stout and healthy, and hardly forty. ...I am sure I would not pin myself down to the payment of one for all the world."...." and after all you have no thanks for it. They think themselves secure, you do no more than what is expected, and it raises no gratitude at all. If I were you, whatever I did should be done at my own discretion entirely. I would not bind myself to allow them any thing yearly. It may be very inconvenient some years to spare a hundred, or even fifty pounds from our own expenses."

"I believe you are right, my love;...whatever I may give them occasionally will be of far greater assistance than a yearly allowance, because they would only enlarge their style of living if they felt sure of a larger income, ... A present of fifty pounds, now and then, will prevent their ever being distressed for money, and will, I think, be amply discharging my promise to my father."

「説得很對，所以，也許全盤考量下，更好的做法是趁她們母親還在世的時候協助她們母親，而不是協助她們兩—我意思是說贈予一筆年金……一年100鎊可以讓她們過得很好。」

他的妻子顯得遲疑，沒有馬上贊同這個想法。

「確實……這比一次就給1500鎊要好。但是，假定達希伍女士還能再活15年，那我們就虧大了。」

「15年！……她的命連這一半的錢都不值。」

「當然不值；你只要留意，就知道有年金可拿的人都不會死；她身體很健康，又還不到40歲……要是我可絕不承諾給她年金……況且她們也不會感激你。她們會自覺有保障，認為你只是做了該做的，她們會毫無感激之情。如果是我，我任何付出都要完全由我自己決定。我絕不自我設限每年都要給。有時候我們可能自己手頭不便，一年要給100，甚至給50鎊都難。」

「親愛的，你說的沒錯；……我偶爾給些會比給年金有用地多，因為年金會讓她們覺得收入有保證，會讓她們生活更加奢侈……偶爾給個50鎊不但能讓她們救急，而且也算實踐了我對父親的諾言。」

"...I am convinced within myself that your father had no idea of your giving them any money at all. The assistance he thought of, I dare say, was only such as might be reasonably expected of you; for instance, such as looking out for a comfortable small house for them, helping them to move their things, and sending them presents of fish and game, and so forth, whenever they are in season...Do but consider...how excessively comfortable your mother-in-law and her daughters may live on the interest of seven thousand pounds, besides the thousand pounds belonging to each of the girls, which brings them in fifty pounds a year a-piece, and, of course, they will pay their mother for their board out of it. Altogether, they will have five hundred a-year amongst them...They will live so cheap! Their house-keeping will be nothing at all. They will have no carriage, no horses, and hardly any servants; they will keep no company, and can have no expenses of any kind! Only conceive how comfortable they will be! Five hundred a year! I am sure I cannot imagine how they will spend half of it; ... They will be much more able to give YOU something."

..."I believe you are perfectly right. My father certainly could mean nothing more by his request to me than what you say...When my mother removes into another house my services shall be readily given to accommodate her as far as I can. Some little present of furniture too may be acceptable then."

"...But, however, ONE thing must be considered. When your father and mother moved to Norland, though the furniture of Stanhill was sold, all the china, plate, and linen was saved, and is now left to your mother. Her house will therefore be almost completely fitted up as soon as she takes it."

「……我敢說你父親根本沒想要你給她們錢。我敢說他想要你提供的協助只限於你能合理付出的；譬如說，幫她們尋找一間舒適的小房子，幫她們搬家，偶爾給她們送些時節當令的魚啊、獵物啊什麼的……你要考慮到……你後母和她的女兒有7000鎊滋生的利息，還有她們兩姊妹各自的1000鎊，一年也各有50鎊利息，這樣她們可以活得多麼滋潤，還有，她們姊妹倆可以用這利息支付母親她倆的食宿費。全部算起來，她們一年會有500鎊收入……而且她們簡直沒有支出！她們家裡完全不需要花錢。她們沒有馬車、沒有馬、幾乎沒有傭人；她們不用招待客人，簡直不用花錢！想想她們可以過得多舒服！一年500鎊欸！連一半我都想不出她們要怎麼花；……應該她們給你錢才對。」

……「我認為你說的對極了。我父親臨終的囑託本意一定是如你所說……等母親搬去新家時我一定盡量出力協助。到時也許還可以送她一些傢具之類的小禮物。」

「……再者，還有一件事要考慮。當年你父母搬去諾蘭時，原來司坦希舊家的傢具雖然賣了，但是瓷器、盤碟、被單都沒賣，現在還在你母親手上。所以她的新家完全不需要購置這些。」

"That is a material consideration undoubtedly. A valuable legacy indeed! And yet some of the plate would have been a very pleasant addition to our own stock here."

"Yes; and the set of breakfast china is twice as handsome as what belongs to this house. A great deal too handsome, in my opinion, for any place THEY can ever afford to live in. But, however, so it is. Your father thought only of THEM. And I must say this: that you owe no particular gratitude to him, nor attention to his wishes; for we very well know that if he could, he would have left almost everything in the world to THEM."

This argument was irresistible. It gave to his intentions whatever of decision was wanting before; and he finally resolved, that it would be absolutely unnecessary, if not highly indecorous, to do more for the widow and children of his father, than such kind of neighbourly acts as his own wife pointed out.

「這個確實要考慮。這些家產可值錢了！其中一些盤碟很適合加入我們自己的套件。」

「沒錯；那套早餐瓷器就比我們家的好看兩倍。要我說的話，好看到她們能住得起的房子都配不上。但也沒辦法。你父親就只想到她們。我還要說：你毋須特別感激你父親，也毋須特別在意他的囑託；我們心知肚明，若照他的意思，他會把一切全給她們。」

這個論點令人無法抗拒，消除了他之前任何的猶疑；他終於認定，對他父親的遺孀和女兒，只需給予他妻子所說、一般鄰人的協助，多了完全無必要，反而極不合禮數。

　　1795年奧斯汀20歲，鄰人侄兒勒佛依（Tom Lefroy）大學畢業來訪，交往兩個月，因兩人皆無家產，遭勒佛依家人阻斷。

　　1796-97年奧斯汀寫作《第一印象》（First Impressions），甚受家人喜愛，父親去信出版社詢問出版可能，遭到峻拒。1811年改名《傲慢與偏見》（Pride and Prejudice）出版，敍述女主角伊麗莎白（Elizabeth Bennet）姊妹五人待字閨中，大姐珍（Jane）與新來的鄰居賓里（Bingley）相好，賓里好友達希（Darcy）對伊麗莎白態度傲慢，且阻撓賓里與珍的戀情，伊麗莎白則受到威肯（Wickham）影響，對達希持偏見；達希逐漸愛上伊麗莎白，但求婚被拒；伊麗莎白妹妹莉迪雅（Lydia）隨威肯私奔，達希暗中相助處理，同時鼓勵賓里追求珍；伊麗莎白發現自己的偏見，最終同意達希求婚。茲選譯三段。

小說首句：

It is a truth universally acknowledged, that a single man in possession of a good fortune, must be in want of a wife.	全世界都認同一條真理：一個有錢的單身男人必定需要一個妻子。

珍·奧斯汀

達希在舞會初見伊麗莎白，言語態度傲慢：

"Which do you mean?" and turning round, he looked for a moment at Elizabeth, till catching her eye, he withdrew his own and coldly said, "She is tolerable; but not handsome enough to tempt me; and I am in no humour at present to give consequence to young ladies who are slighted by other men. You had better return to your partner and enjoy her smiles, for you are wasting your time with me."	「你是說哪個？」他回身看了伊麗莎白一會兒，直到兩人目光對接，他才轉頭並冷冷說道：「她還可以，但沒漂亮到足以吸引我，我此刻也沒心情照顧其他男人不理睬的小姑娘。你還是回到你舞伴身邊享受她的微笑吧，你在我這兒只是浪費時間。」

達希首次求婚，伊麗莎白因偏見峻拒：

From the very beginning, from the first moment I may almost say of my acquaintance with you, your manners impressing me with the fullest belief of your arrogance, your conceit, and your selfish disdain of the feelings of others, were such as to form the ground-work of disapprobation, on which succeeding events have built so immoveable a dislike; and I had not known you a month before I felt that you were the last man in the world whom I could ever be prevailed on to marry.	打從一開始，我幾乎可以說，從我第一次見到你，你的言行舉止就讓我深深相信你為人自大、驕傲、自私、枉顧他人感情，我因此對你無法認同，其後的事件進而讓我對你極度厭惡；我認識你不到一個月就認定，你是全世界我最不想婚嫁的男人。

　　1798-99年奧斯汀寫作《蘇珊》（Susan），當時歐洲流行哥德（Gothic）小說，以陰鬱古堡為背景，瘋狂的愛情與謀殺迫害為主題，此作品仿諷之。1803年哥哥亨利以10英鎊將版權售予出版商廓斯比（Benjamin Crosby），但遲未出版，奧斯汀1816年憤而以原價購回，1817年奧斯汀死後改名《諾安格寺》（Northanger Abbey）出版。故事敘述17歲的女主角凱瑟琳（Catherine Morland），應鄰人邀請赴巴池（Bath）過冬，遇見亨利（Henry Tilney），互有好感，又結識輕佻的美少女伊莎貝拉（Isabella）及其粗鄙兄長約翰（John）。約翰正巧與凱瑟琳哥哥詹姆士（James）在大學同窗。凱瑟琳又見到亨利的妹妹愛莉娜（Eleanor）與父親提爾尼將軍。伊莎貝拉與詹姆士訂婚後發覺詹姆士並不富有，趁詹姆士離城購買訂婚戒時與亨利兄長提爾尼上尉公然調情。約翰則視凱瑟琳為禁臠，並破壞她與亨利之關係。提爾尼將軍邀請凱瑟琳至其古老莊園諾安格寺暫住，凱瑟琳嗜讀哥德小說，想像將軍謀害了自己妻子，暗中探查將軍亡妻的臥房，為亨利發現。詹姆士來信告知因伊莎貝拉移情而解除婚約。將軍赴倫敦後突然返家將凱瑟琳逐走。兩天後亨利來訪，說明其父原以為凱瑟琳富有，因發覺並非如此而態度翻轉，亨利堅持婚娶凱瑟琳，與父親決裂，將軍發覺凱瑟琳家也算小有資產，且愛莉娜嫁入富家，可算補償，因此同意亨利婚事。

1800年奧斯汀父親退休，舉家遷至巴池。1802年奧斯汀姊妹赴鄰城訪友，奧斯汀與友人弟弟哈里斯（Harris Bigg-Wither）自幼相識，哈里斯長相平凡、不善交際，但頗有家產，剛從牛津大學畢業，向奧斯汀求婚，奧斯汀初始接受，第二日反悔。1814年奧斯汀去信侄女忠告感情之事：「相較缺乏感情的婚姻，他事皆可忍受。（Anything is to be preferred or endured rather than marrying without Affection）」咸信此為其反悔原因。

1804年奧斯汀開始寫作小說《華生一家》（The Watsons），敘述貧窮牧師與四個未婚女兒一家，次年父親去世後停筆，咸信是因小說情節過於類似奧斯汀自己家庭。因經濟困難，奧斯汀母女們1806年搬去南安普頓（Southampton）與五哥同住。1809年母女遷入英格蘭南方喬屯（Chawton）三哥家附屬的屋子。1811年四哥牽線下《理性與感性》出版，頗受歡迎。1813年《傲慢與偏見》出版，大為暢銷。

1814年《曼斯斐爾莊園》（Mansfield Park）出版，同樣暢銷，故事敘述女主角梵妮（Fanny Price）家食指浩繁，有1兄威廉與弟妹7人，梵妮10歲後寄住嫁給博純次男爵（Baronet Thomas Bertram）的大姨媽家，其莊園名曼斯斐爾。大表哥湯姆（Tom）行為輕率，大表姐瑪麗亞（Maria）、二表姐茱莉雅（Julia）任性傲慢，只有二表哥艾德蒙（Edmund）照顧她，她對艾德蒙暗中日久生情。二姨媽諾里斯夫人（Mrs. Norris）安排瑪麗亞嫁給富家子勒胥沃（Mr. Rushworth）。一對紈褲兄妹亨利與瑪麗‧克勞福（Henry and Mary Crawford）搬到附近，瑪麗開始與艾德蒙交往，亨利初始引誘瑪麗亞，繼則想玩弄梵妮，但作假成真，喜歡上梵妮，梵妮拒絕亨利求婚，造成次男爵不快，梵妮態度軟化，但亨利引誘瑪麗亞私奔，茱莉雅也與湯姆友人私奔，在危機中次男爵一家都依仗忠貞的梵妮支撐。瑪麗企圖為亨利脫罪，艾德蒙發覺自己為瑪麗美貌蒙蔽，最終選了梵妮。

1815年《愛瑪》（Emma）出版，銷路亦佳。愛瑪是奧斯汀小說裡惟一有錢的女主角，20歲，漂亮、聰明、但過於自信，只有姐夫的弟弟，也是鄰居的奈里（George Knightley）敢規勸她。愛瑪幫家庭老師泰勒小姐（Miss Taylor）與鰥夫衛斯敦先生（Mr. Weston）做媒成功，又想替私生女出身的哈莉葉（Harriet Smith）與牧師艾屯（Mr. Elton）做媒，因此要哈莉葉拒絕殷實農人馬丁（Robert Martin）的求婚。艾屯向

愛瑪求婚，愛瑪才驚覺艾屯的目標是自己；艾屯被拒，迅即與富家驕女成婚，哈莉葉傷心失戀。衛斯敦與亡妻的兒子法蘭克（Frank Churchill）過繼給富有的大舅子邱吉爾，如今來訪，似有意追求愛瑪。貧窮村人貝慈小姐（Miss Bates）的侄女，貌美多才的珍（Jane Fairfax）也來訪，珍幼失雙親，為父親友人收養。愛瑪發覺自己不愛法蘭克，又想撮合他和哈莉葉。珍決定出任家庭教師以維生。法蘭克的養母去世，他宣佈早已與珍結婚，因為養母可能反對，祕而不宣，珍之前與他吵架才要做家庭教師。哈莉葉告訴愛瑪她喜歡的是奈里，愛瑪這才發現自己視奈里為禁臠。奈里以為愛瑪遭法蘭克遺棄而安慰她，兩人終於明白彼此情感而成婚。馬丁再次向哈莉葉求婚，這次成功。

奧斯汀四哥的銀行1816年倒閉。同年奧斯汀寫就《勸導》（Persuasion），女主角安（Anne Elliot）是華特次男爵（Baronet Walter）的二女兒，溫柔聰敏似亡母，大姐伊麗莎白（Elizabeth）傲慢似父親，小妹瑪麗（Mary）易小題大作，嫁給鄰居查爾斯（Charles Musgrove）。9年前安曾與英俊有抱負的斐德列（Frederick Wentworth）訂婚，但聽信父親、大姐，因斐德列家貧而退婚，但隨即後悔輕信人言。次男爵因揮霍缺錢被迫租出祖居，攜帶大姐赴巴池租賃昂貴寓所，卻讓安去小妹家借住。不料祖居租客是斐德列的姐姐與姐夫—海軍上將克勞夫（Croft）。斐德列藉英法海戰升官發財，如今貴為艦長，來到姐姐家，對安態度冷淡。瑪麗一家不知安的往事，猜測斐德列要追求查爾斯的妹妹姮列姐（Henrietta）或露意莎（Louisa）。眾人隨斐德列赴海濱城市拜訪其同袍哈維（Harville），在新環境中安恢復生氣美貌，吸引了父親爵位與財產的繼承人艾略特（William Elliot）。露意莎不慎摔倒昏迷，忙亂中安鎮定救傷，另斐德列刮目相看。安赴巴池與父姊團聚，艾略特與斐德列相繼到來。安巧遇老同學史密斯（Smith）太太，承告艾略特是只謀私利的小人，證實了安對艾略特的疑慮。斐德列在酒館裡聽到安對哈維區分男女對待愛情的不同，深受感動，與安再續前緣。

奧斯汀1817年病逝，葬於溫徹斯特大教堂（Winchester Cathedral），《勸導》與《諾安格寺》同年稍後出版。

奧斯汀小說議論小鄉紳家中女性婚嫁事宜，描摹人性刻劃入微。她生前沒沒無聞，1880年代後聲名大噪，粉絲眾多，歷久不衰。

圖片來源：IDJ圖庫

1-20
拜倫
George Gordon Byron

拜倫（George Gordon Byron）1788年生於倫敦，父親是海軍軍官，母親先嫁卡瑪森（Caermarthen）侯爵，後嫁爲財產而娶她的拜倫父親，拜倫出生時右腳略跛，令他一生敏感，2歲隨母返蘇格蘭亞伯丁（Aberdeen）老家，3歲父親去世，幼年即入學，10歲繼承伯父之拜倫男爵爵位，領地位於英格蘭西北蘭卡郡（Lancashire）。13歲入讀哈洛（Harrow）公學。

拜倫早熟，自幼愛恨強烈，15歲愛上同窗瑪麗·查沃斯（Mary Chaworth），爲她作詩《給瑪麗》（To Mary）：

RACK'D by the flames of jealous rage,	妒火中燒備受酷刑，
By all her torments deeply curst,	被她折磨深受詛咒，
Of hell-born passions far the worst,	心受地獄至慘蹂躪，
What hope my pangs can now assuage?	誰能減輕我的苦痛？
I tore me from thy circling arms,	我由你擁抱掙脫出，
To madness fir'd by doubts and fears,	因懷疑恐懼而狂怒，
Heedless of thy suspicious tears,	不顧你可疑的啼哭，
Nor feeling for thy feign'd alarms.	無視你虛僞的驚慌。
Resigning every thought of bliss,	自絕於幸福的念頭，
Forever, from your love I go,	永遠，從你的愛自逃，
Reckless of all the tears that flow,	狠心不顧淚水湧出，
Disdaining thy polluted kiss.	鄙視你不潔的唇口。
No more that bosom heaves for me,	你胸膛不再爲我激抽，
On it another seeks repose,	如今他人伏臥其上，
Another riot's on its snows,	他人於酥胸上狂放，
Our bonds are broken, both are free.	我倆斷交，兩皆自由。
No more with mutual love we burn,	我倆不再彼此熱戀，
No more the genial couch we bless,	不再享用溫馨床褥，
Dissolving in the fond caress;	沉溺彼此柔情愛撫：
Our love o'erthrown will ne'er return.	愛情叛離永不回返。

拜倫

Though love than ours could ne'er be truer,	我倆愛情至真至極，
Yet flames too fierce themselves destroy,	但熱情太過終自毀，
Embraces oft repeated cloy,	擁抱太多令人乏味，
Ours came too frequent, to endure.	物極必反，承受不起。
You quickly sought a second lover,	你未久即琵琶別抱，
And I too proud to share a heart,	而我捍拒與人分享，
Where once I held the whole, not part,	我要獨佔，絕不共嚐，
Another mistress must discover.	於是只能另尋愛業。
Though not the first one, who hast blest me,	你雖非我的初體驗，
Yet I will own, you was the dearest,	但你確實與我最親，
The one, unto my bosom nearest;	你離我的心扉最近：
So I conceiv'd, when I possest thee.	我的確曾如此相看。
Even now I cannot well forget thee,	對你我至今未忘記，
And though no more in folds of pleasure,	雖然我倆不再歡愛，
Kiss follows kiss in countless measure,	擁吻不斷，繾綣滿懷，
I hope you sometimes will regret me.	但願你偶爾有悔意。
And smile to think how oft were done,	我微笑想起我倆常
What prudes declare a sin to act is,	犯老古板所謂罪過，
And never but in darkness practice,	我們總在暗中幹活，
Fearing to trust the tell-tale sun.	怕太陽下曝露行藏。
And wisely therefore night prefer,	聰明人因此好夜晚，
Whose dusky mantle veils their fears,	遮掩恐懼全靠黑幕，
Of this, and that, of eyes and ears,	掩這，掩那，掩耳掩目，
Affording shades to those that err.	為犯錯者提供遮簾。
Now, by my foul, 'til most delight	由我劣行，直臻極樂
To view each other panting, dying,	彼此觀看喘息，仙死，
In love's *extatic posture* lying,	在愛的高潮臥休止，
Grateful to *feeling*, as to *sight*.	所感所見兩皆喜得。
And had the glaring God of Day,	幸好那太陽神不曾，
(As formerly of Mars and Venus)	（像對戰神愛神那般）
Divulg'd the joys which pass'd between us.	洩漏我們倆的偷歡。
Regardless of his *peeping* ray.	儘管太陽讓一切現形。
Of love admiring such a *sample*,	祂們羨慕我倆愛情，
The Gods and Goddesses descending,	男神女神紛紛下凡，
Had never fancied us offending,	不但不覺我倆冒犯，
But *wisely* followed *our example*.	反而效法我倆所行。

此詩雖是少年之作，但頗能代表拜倫風格：言語流暢、格律嚴謹、內容嘲諷激情。

拜倫16歲愛上小他4歲的學弟，17歲入讀劍橋大學三一學院。

1807年拜倫集結早年詩作，出版《散漫時光》（Hours of Idleness），遭《愛丁堡評論》（Edinburgh Review）酷評，1809年拜倫寫就《英格蘭作詩者與蘇格蘭評論者》（English Bards and Scotch Reviewers）反擊，用語刻薄。

1809-11年拜倫出遊南歐，一路不斷有男、女戀情。1812年出版《貴公子哈洛德遊記》（Childe Harold's Pilgrimage）頭兩卷，一舉成名，主角樹立了文學上的「拜倫英雄」（Byronic hero）：才華激情過人、鄙視權位、離經叛道、感情不順、有不光彩的過去、個性矛盾、永不滿足、傾向自我毀滅。這也是拜倫本人的風格。茲選譯此詩兩段：

For he through Sin's long labyrinth had run,	他曾經穿過罪惡的迷宮，
Nor made atonement when he did amiss,	就算犯錯也從未求救贖，
Had sighed to many, though he loved but one,	真愛唯一，但曾多處留情，
And that loved one, alas, could ne'er be his.	與此真愛，奈何，不成眷屬。

But hush! hark! a deep sound strikes like a rising knell!	噤聲！聽！有深沉聲音似鐘響起！
Did ye not hear it?—No! 't was but the wind,	你沒聽到嗎？——沒！那只是風，
Or the car rattling o'er the stony street.	或是車子軋響過石板巷。
On with the dance! let joy be unconfined;	讓舞照跳！大家盡情盡興；
No sleep till morn, when Youth and Pleasure meet	通宵達旦，讓青春歡樂雙雙
To chase the glowing hours with flying feet.	以輕快步伐追趕曙光。

1811年拜倫入上議院，力主社會改革。

1812年與有夫之婦卡絡琳‧蘭姆（Caroline Lamb）相戀，卡絡琳遭棄後仍糾纏不休，曾在拜倫家訪客簿留言：「勿忘我！」（Remember me！）拜倫以詩回應：

Remember thee! remember thee!	勿忘記你！勿忘記你！
Till Lethe quench life's burning stream	直到生命熱流被忘川湮熄
Remorse and shame shall cling to thee,	悔恨羞恥將纏住你，
And haunt thee like a feverish dream!	像瘟疫惡夢恐嚇你！
Remember thee! Aye, doubt it not.	勿忘記你！這說得好。
Thy husband too shall think of thee:	你先生也會記住你：
By neither shalt thou be forgot,	我還有他都忘不掉，
Thou false to him, thou fiend to me!	他——你背叛，我——你追崇！

卡絡琳曾形容拜倫「瘋狂、邪惡、結交了就有害」（mad, bad, and dangerous to know）。

1813年拜倫結識同父異母姐姐歐古絲妲‧蕾（Augusta Leigh），傳聞不倫戀。

1814年拜倫作詩《伊人芳蹤》（She Walks in Beauty）：

SHE walks in beauty, like the night	她行蹤幻美，如暗夜
Of cloudless climes and starry skies;	穹宇清朗星辰滿天；
And all that 's best of dark and bright	光明黑暗極致並列

Meet in her aspect and her eyes:	會聚於其身形、雙眼：
Thus mellow'd to that tender light	熟適溶入輕柔明夜
Which heaven to gaudy day denies.	此景白晝絕不得見。
One shade the more, one ray the less,	增一墨，或減一光線，
Had half impair'd the nameless grace	於莫名優雅皆不宜
Which waves in every raven tress,	烏黑髮絲縷縷彰顯，
Or softly lightens o'er her face;	其人面龐輕泛光輝；
Where thoughts serenely sweet express	祥寧逸思甘美靜恬
How pure, how dear their dwelling-place.	其人純然，可親可貴。
And on that cheek, and o'er that brow,	在其雙頰，在其眉梢，
So soft, so calm, yet eloquent,	柔和、安靜、高雅有致，
The smiles that win, the tints that glow,	含笑引人，顏容明皓，
But tell of days in goodness spent,	顯示其人善良行止，
A mind at peace with all below,	心思全然與世安好，
A heart whose love is innocent!	胸中有愛無垢真摯！

　　1815年拜倫婚娶富家女安娜貝拉（Annabella Millbanke），但仍緋聞不斷，安娜貝拉次年離家分居，拜倫離英，此後未返。拜倫與其私人醫生波里多利（John William Polidori）暫居日內瓦湖畔，再遇其前情人——柯萊爾（Claire）、並結識柯萊爾異母姊瑪麗·高文（Mary Godwin），以及瑪麗日後的先生雪萊（Shelley）。因連日陰寒多雨，眾人困坐屋內讀鬼故事，拜倫提議眾人各寫一篇鬼故事，瑪麗與雪萊合寫了《法藍肯斯坦，又稱現代普羅米修斯》（Frankenstein: or, The Modern Prometheus，又譯《科學怪人》），波里多利受拜倫一篇故事啟發，寫了《吸血鬼》（The Vampyre）。冬季拜倫赴威尼斯，與兩名有夫之婦糾葛，其中一人為他投河。

　　拜倫此時對亞美尼亞（Armenia）文化產生興趣，支持亞美尼亞對抗鄂圖曼土耳其統治，並寫書介紹其歷史語言，為西方研究亞美尼亞之濫觴。

拜倫

1818-20年拜倫撰寫長詩《唐璜》（Don Juan），共17章，未寫完，描述唐璜周遊各國的愛情、冒險經歷，茲選譯三段：

Tis strange,-but true; for truth is always strange;
Stranger than fiction: if it could be told,
How much would novels gain by the exchange!
How differently the world would men behold!

很奇特，但屬實；眞象永遠奇特；
比小說更奇特：若眞象披露，
小說將從中大有所得！
人們也將大改認知的角度！

Wedded she some years, and to a man
Of fifty, and such husbands are in plenty;
And yet, I think, instead of such a ONE
'Twere better to have TWO of five and twenty...

她已結婚若干年，先生年登
五十，如此老公也多得很；
但，我說，與其如此老公一名
不如二十五歲的老公兩人。

When people say, 'I've told you fifty times',
They mean to scold, and very often do;
When poets say, 'I've written fifty rhymes',
They make you dread that they'll recite them too.

人若說：「我已講過五十次，」
他意在罵人，譴責往往跟進；
人若說：「我寫了五十首詩，」
怕的是他接著背給你聽。

　　拜倫邊寫《唐璜》，邊與小12歲的貴秋麗（Guiccioli）伯爵夫人相戀，1819-21年他暫居意大利東部拉文納（Ravenna），據雪萊來訪描述：拜倫下午2點起床，用餐後兩人聊天至下午6點，然後到野外騎馬至8點，晚餐後再聊天至清晨6點；而且拜倫養有10匹馬、8隻巨犬、3隻猴子、5隻貓、5隻孔雀、2隻珠雞、老鷹、獵鷹、烏鴉、埃及鶴各一，動物在家中自由出入。

　　1823年拜倫應邀前往希臘支持對抗土耳其以獨立，次年病歿，享年36。

　　拜倫是英國浪漫文學要角，詩作嘲諷激情，生活放蕩，因支持獨立運動在希臘受尊崇。

圖片來源：IDJ圖庫

1-21
雪萊
Percy Bysshe Shelley

◆
：
雪
萊
：
◆

　　雪萊（Percy Bysshe Shelley）1792年生於英格蘭南方，父親是貴族、自由派國會議員。1804年雪萊入讀伊頓公學（Eton），被視為不合群而遭霸凌。1810年入讀牛津大學大學學院（University College）。同年出版哥德式小說《查斯托奇》（Zastrozzi）宣揚無神論。次年出版論文《無神論實屬必然》（The Necessity of Atheism），因此被退學，又拒絕否認其觀點以復學，因此與父親決裂。1811年19歲的雪萊為仗義保護妹妹16歲同學夏莉葉（Harriet Westbrook）而與之私奔至蘇格蘭成婚，雪萊父親認為女方門第較低，斷絕雪萊金援。雪萊同時與28歲未婚教師伊麗莎白（Elizabeth Hitchener）親密通信，以之為謬思寫就長詩《夢寶仙后》（Queen Mab），構想其心中烏托邦，1813年出版，為英國政治激進主義之濫觴。

　　1812年雪萊透過詩人瑟西（Robert Southey）結識功利主義、無政府主義激進思想家威廉·高文（William Godwin），貧困的高文得知雪萊出身富家，力勸雪萊與父親和解。同年雪萊出遊愛爾蘭，撰文鼓吹愛爾蘭脫離英格蘭、復尊天主教。

　　雪萊與夏莉葉逐漸失合，1814年攜高文16歲女兒瑪麗私奔至日內瓦，一路朗讀莎士比亞、盧梭等人作品。瑪麗母親瑪麗·沃斯東卡（Mary Wollstonecraft）為高文已逝之前妻，著有名作《女權辯護》（A Vindication of the Rights of Woman）。夏莉葉被棄只得返回娘家。雪萊六週後金盡返倫敦，高文憤而拒見，但要求雪萊給錢。1815年雪萊寫就長詩《厄來斯特，又稱孤獨之心靈》（Alastor, or The Spirit of Solitude），敘述詩人神遊。

　　1816年雪萊、瑪麗、瑪麗異母妹柯萊爾（Claire）再赴日內瓦湖畔渡夏，並與柯萊爾的情人、也住附近的拜倫論文賦詩，拜倫由此撰寫長詩《唐璜》。因連日陰寒多雨，眾人困坐屋內讀鬼故事，拜倫提議眾人各自寫一篇鬼故事，瑪麗與雪萊合寫了《法藍肯斯坦，又稱現代普羅米修斯》，拜倫的醫生友人波里多利寫了《吸血鬼》。

　　1816年受孕於新情人的夏莉葉自覺被拋棄而投河，雪萊與瑪麗隨即成婚以便照養雪萊與夏莉葉的子女，高文也因此與瑪麗恢復關係，但法院將夏莉葉子女判給收養家庭。

　　意大利探險家貝佐尼（Giovanni Battista Belzoni）1816年在埃及挖出拉姆西斯二世（Ramesses II）雕像準備運返英國，西元前一世紀希臘史學家刁多羅斯（Diodorus Siculus）曾記載拉姆西斯某雕像下有銘文：「我乃萬王之王，奧西曼達斯。若有人想知道我多偉大，想知道我的地位，讓他超越我任一成就（King of Kings am I, Osymandias. If anyone would know how great I am and where I lie, let him surpass one of my works）」，雪萊1817年因此賦詩《奧西曼達斯》（Ozymandias）：

I met a traveller from an antique land	我見到遠古他方來的旅者
Who said: Two vast and trunkless legs of stone	他說：有兩隻巨大石雕腳腿
Stand in the desert. Near them on the sand,	在沙漠裡。近旁沙堆一側，
Half sunk, a shatter'd visage lies, whose frown	半掩埋，有一破損頭像，其
And wrinkled lip and sneer of cold command	眉蹙、唇抿、睥睨冷笑自得
Tell that its sculptor well those passions read	訴說雕者準確捕捉其心思，
Which yet survive, stamp'd on these lifeless things,	存留至今，表現於石像上，
The hand that mock'd them and the heart that fed.	而雕弄巧手、雕像之心已逝。
And on the pedestal these words appear:	雕像底座有銘文一行：
"My name is Ozymandias, king of kings:	「我名奧西曼達斯，萬王之王：
Look on my works, ye Mighty, and despair!"	瞻我偉業，爾等大人，以致絕望！」
Nothing beside remains: round the decay	此外無物留存：在破殘
Of that colossal wreck, boundless and bare,	巨大雕像四圍，是無垠大荒，
The lone and level sands stretch far away.	極目只見孤寂沙漠互延。

　　1818年雪萊夫妻攜柯萊爾之女愛蕾歌拉（Allegra）赴威尼斯尋其父拜倫，同年雪萊創作詩劇《解放普羅米修斯》（Prometheus Unbound），敘述天神宙斯（Zeus）被推翻，原被宙斯囚困的普羅米修斯得解放。1818-19年雪萊年幼子女去世，夫妻倆陸續旅居斐冷翠、比薩、羅馬等地。

　　1819年英國曼徹斯特（Manchester）聖彼得廣場（St Peter's Field）群眾聚集要求改革國會選舉制度，遭騎兵鎮壓，15人死，數百人傷，史稱彼得盧（比擬1815年滑鐵盧戰

役）屠殺。雪萊大感激憤，賦詩《致英國人》（To the Men of England）、《西風頌》（Ode to the West Wind）、《亂政蒙面劇》（The Masque of Anarchy）等，茲選譯前二者。

《致英國人》：

Men of England, wherefore plough	英國人，你為何幫
For the lords who lay ye low?	欺壓你的貴族耕忙？
Wherefore weave with toil and care	你為何辛勤績紡
The rich robes your tyrants wear?	給暴君穿著華裳？
Wherefore feed and clothe and save,	為何供養、織衣，儉省
From the cradle to the grave,	度日至死從出生，
Those ungrateful drones who would	而那幫公蜂不感謝，
Drain your sweat -nay, drink your blood?	吸你汗—甚至飲你血？
Wherefore, Bees of England, forge	為何，爾等工蜂，鑄鍊
Many a weapon, chain, and scourge,	武器、鎖鏈、皮鞭，
That these stingless drones may spoil	讓無刺公蜂濫用
The forced produce of your toil?	你們被迫的勞動？
Have ye leisure, comfort, calm,	你們有嗎—閒適、安寧、
Shelter, food, love's gentle balm?	住所、食物、慰人愛情？
Or what is it ye buy so dear	你們究竟得到什麼
With your pain and with your fear?	付出如許恐懼苦厄？
The seed ye sow another reaps;	你們播種他人收；
The wealth ye find another keeps;	你的財貨他人留；
The robes ye weave another wears;	你織衣裳他人著；
The arms ye forge another bears.	你造兵器他人握；
Sow seed, -but let no tyrant reap;	播種—但別讓暴君收；
Find wealth, -let no imposter heap;	生財—但別讓怠者留；
Weave robes, -let not the idle wear;	織衣—但別讓懶人著；
Forge arms, in your defence to bear.	造器，要為自衛而握。
Shrink to your cellars, holes, and cells;	回到你的蝸居地窟；
In halls ye deck another dwells.	你建大廈供他人住。
Why shake the chains ye wrought? Ye see	何必自縛手腳又抗議？

The steel ye tempered glance on ye.
With plough and spade and hoe and loom,
Trace your grave, and build your tomb,
And weave your winding-sheet, till fair
England be your sepulchre!

你所鑄刀劍對著你。
用犁耙、鐵鏟、鋤頭、織機，
自掘墳穴，自造墓地，
自織你的裹屍布，
變美麗英國爲你墳墓！

《西風頌》部份：

O, WILD West Wind, thou breath of Autumn's being,
Thou, from whose unseen presence the leaves dead
Are driven, like ghosts from an enchanter fleeing,
Yellow, and black, and pale, and hectic red,
Pestilence-stricken multitudes: O, thou,
Who chariotest to their dark wintry bed
The winged seeds, where they lie cold and low,
Each like a corpse within its grave, until
Thine azure sister of the spring shall blow
Her clarion o'er the dreaming earth, and fill
(Driving sweet buds like flocks to feed in air)
With living hues and odours plain and hill:
Wild Spirit, which art moving every where;
Destroyer and preserver; hear, O, hear!
Thou on whose stream, 'mid the steep sky's commotion,
Loose clouds like earth's decaying leaves are shed,
Shook from the tangled boughs of Heaven and Ocean,
Angels of rain and lightning: there are spread
On the blue surface of thine airy surge,
Like the bright hair uplifted from the head

噢，狂野西風，秋天的氣息，
你隱身藏形，將凋萎枯葉
掃除，像幽靈遭大法師驅離，
黃色、黑色、蒼白、熾紅枯葉，
身染瘟疫的眾生：噢，你，
將其送往暗冬之床眠歇
那帶翅種子，在彼冷臥沉睡，
有如死屍在墓穴，直到
你春天蔚藍的姊妹響吹
號角傳遍酣夢大地，滿罩
（漫天放養甜美種子似羊茁長）
山陵原野以芳香色調：
不羈的精靈，你四處遊盪；
既破壞又保存；聽啊，聽我禱唱！
你一旦湧起，於昊天動盪中，
雲絡似地上枯葉凋逝，
由海天糾結枝椏鬆動，
雷雨的天使：祂們展示
在你湧起的靛藍鋒面上，
像是矗起的亮麗髮絲

Of some fierce Mænad, even from the dim verge

Of the horizon to the zenith's height

The locks of the approaching storm. Thou dirge

Of the dying year, to which this closing night

Will be the dome of a vast sepulchre,

Vaulted with all thy congregated might

Of vapours, from whose solid atmosphere

Black rain, and fire, and hail will burst: O, hear!

Thou who didst waken from his summer dreams

The blue Mediterranean, where he lay,

Lulled by the coil of his crystalline streams,

Beside a pumice isle in Baiæ's bay,

And saw in sleep old palaces and towers

Quivering within the wave's intenser day,

All overgrown with azure moss and flowers

So sweet, the sense faints picturing them! Thou

For whose path the Atlantic's level powers

Cleave themselves into chasms, while far below

The sea-blooms and the oozy woods which wear

The sapless foliage of the ocean, know

Thy voice, and suddenly grow grey with fear, And tremble and

despoil themselves: O, hear!

If I were a dead leaf thou mightest bear;

If I were a swift cloud to fly with thee;

A wave to pant beneath thy power, and share

The impulse of thy strength, only less free

Than thou, O, uncontroulable! If even

I were as in my boyhood, and could be

The comrade of thy wanderings over heaven,

As then, when to outstrip thy skiey speed

Scarce seemed a vision; I would ne'er have striven

As thus with thee in prayer in my sore need.

Oh! lift me as a wave, a leaf, a cloud!

I fall upon the thorns of life! I bleed!

A heavy weight of hours has chained and bowed

One too like thee: tameless, and swift, and proud.

於醉狂酒神女侍頭上，

從陰暗天際到至高九天

暴風的鬈髮將臨。將亡

之年的哀歌，今夜將變

爲你墓穴的高大穹頂，

以你聚合的雲氣張演

撐起，你的氤氳結凝

迸發黑雨、火舌、冰電：噢，聽！

你驚醒他於夏日夢酣

藍色的地中海，他睡躺，

受晶亮洋流循繞催眠，

在巴亞灣裡一座浮石島旁，

夢中見到古老宮殿樓台

在海流晃動裡隨波擺盪，

長滿了青綠水草海苔

如此迷人，想到就暈！爲你修

路開道大西洋以其大能耐

自闢邃谷，在海洋深處

奇花綻放，水下森林身縈

海中無膠汁的莖葉，認出

你的呼嘯，面色悚然轉灰青，

顫抖著凋落枝葉：噢，聽！

願我是枯葉隨你駕乘；

願我是雲絡隨你疾飛；

是海波喘息你威勢下，

共享你衝動的精力，但沒

你自由，噢，不羈的你！但願

我仍是少年郎，還能陪

你並駕齊驅遨遊九天，

那時，我的速度甚至超過你

這不是幻想：若然，我斷

不需急難時來祈求你。

噢！讓我騎乘如波、如葉、如雲！

我跌落生命的荊棘！我血滴！

沉重的時間擊潰綁捆

像你的我：迅疾、驕傲、不馴。

Make me thy lyre, even as the forest is:	森林是你七弦琴,同樣待我:
What if my leaves are falling like its own!	我的綠葉掉落沒關係!
The tumult of thy mighty harmonies	你巨大亂人的共鳴震波
Will take from both a deep, autumnal tone,	形成秋季深沉的主題,
Sweet though in sadness. Be thou, spirit fierce,	甜美而哀傷。狂猛精靈,與我
My spirit! Be thou me, impetuous one!	同心!與我一體,狂烈的你!
Drive my dead thoughts over the universe	將我枯死的思緒傳遍宇宙
Like withered leaves to quicken a new birth!	像枯葉般促成新生命!
And, by the incantation of this verse,	再者,借由這首詩的魔咒,
Scatter, as from an unextinguished hearth	散播,好似從未滅的爐中
Ashes and sparks, my words among mankind!	星火,我的言論於人類吧!
Be through my lips to unawakened earth	對酣睡的世界用我的舌唇
The trumpet of a prophecy! O, wind,	做號角來預言!噢,風啊,
If Winter comes, can Spring be far behind?	若冬天已臨,春天還遠嗎?
...	……
And if then the tyrants dare	如果暴君此時敢
Let them ride among you there,	讓他們騎兵衝陷,
Slash, and stab, and maim, and hew, -	劍刺、斧砍、槍傷、刀劃,——
What they like, that let them do.	他想怎樣,就讓他。
With folded arms and steady eyes,	雙手束胸靜觀察。

《亂政蒙面劇》選譯一段:

And little fear, and less surprise,	不恐懼,也不驚訝,
Look upon them as they slay	看著他們狂殺戮
Till their rage has died away.	直到發洩了憤怒。
Then they will return with shame	他們會面帶羞愧
To the place from which they came,	向其來處而返回,
And the blood thus shed will speak	他們殺戮的血漬

> In hot blushes on their cheek.
> ...
> Rise like Lions after slumber
> In unvanquishable number,
> Shake your chains to earth like dew
> Which in sleep had fallen on you-
> Ye are many — they are few.

> 會使之面紅耳赤。
> ……
> 要奮起如醒獅
> 萬千不屈的戰士，
> 鎖鏈似朝露抖脫
> 它趁你沉睡時附著——
> 他們人少—你們多。

詩中非暴力抵抗的概念後爲美國文人梭羅（Thoreau）及印度聖雄甘地襲用。

1821年雪萊賦詩《阿多尼斯》（Adonais）悼念濟慈（Keats）。同年寫就論文《爲詩文抗辯》（A Defence of Poetry），因皮考克（Thomas Love Peacock）1820年撰文《詩的四個階段》（The Four Ages of Poetry）主張科學興起後文學無用，雪萊回應道：文學想像體現所有學科的精神原型，中有名句：「詩人爲世界立法，但有實無名。（Poets are the unacknowledged legislators of the world）」

1822年雪萊與友人乘船於意大利西北外海遇難，得年30。一說雪萊是因反動著作遇刺。骨灰葬於羅馬新教公墓（Protestant Cemetery）。

雪萊以詩文鼓吹用愛的力量抗強扶弱，是英國浪漫主義文學代表人物之一，其政治理念死後一度遭忽視，如今重新發覺。

圖片來源：維基Richard Rothwell

1-22
瑪麗・雪萊
Mary Shelley

　　瑪麗・雪萊（Mary Shelley）1797年生於倫敦，父親威廉・高文（William Godwin）是激進的政治哲學家，母親瑪麗・沃絲彤卡（Mary Wollstonecraft）是女權運動者，於她出生後數週即去世。瑪麗4歲父親再婚，與後母不洽。瑪麗幼年在家自學，繼承了父親的激進思想，1814年瑪麗時年17，與父親的朋友，已婚的雪萊相戀，私奔法、意、德，數月後返英。

　　1816年雪萊妻子夏莉葉投河，瑪麗隨即與雪萊成婚。同年瑪麗、雪萊、瑪麗異母妹柯萊爾（Claire）再赴日內瓦湖畔渡夏，並與柯萊爾的情人、也住附近的拜倫論文賦詩，因連日陰寒多雨，眾人困坐屋內讀鬼故事，拜倫提議眾人各自寫一篇鬼故事，瑪麗與雪萊合寫了哥德式科幻小說《法藍肯斯坦，又稱現代普羅米修斯》（Frankenstein: or, The Modern Prometheus，又譯《科學怪人》），以書信體敘述探險家沃頓上尉（Captain Robert Walton）在北極見到巨型怪人，並拯救了年輕科學家維多・法藍肯斯坦（Victor Frankenstein），維多告以之前事故：維多是瑞士人，以科學創造了怪人，但驚於其醜陋而棄之，怪人傷心離去。數月後，維多休養康復，獲悉幼弟威廉被殺，疑是怪人所為，而威廉保姆菊絲婷（Justine）遭警方指控被處死。維多退隱山林，怪人尋來解釋：怪人躲入山中，自學說話、看書，試圖結交鄰人不成，憤而焚毀鄰人屋舍、殺死威廉。怪人要求維多給他造一女伴，可隨他隱遁。維多勉強同意，赴蘇格蘭造女怪人，又恐怪人繁衍，將女怪人毀滅。維多原定婚娶父母收養的少女伊麗莎白，怪人威脅要破壞婚禮，又殺害維多好友柯萊法（Clerval），維多卻被疑為兇手遭監禁，卒獲釋返日內瓦。婚禮前怪人殺害伊麗莎白，維多父親傷心而死，維多追逐怪人至北極。敘述完維多不久死於沃頓船上，怪人現身哀悼懺悔，決定自殺，隨即離去不復見。1818年書出成名。20世紀初以來，世人漸以法藍肯斯坦稱呼怪人。茲選譯兩段：

I beheld the wretch — the miserable monster whom I had created. He held up the curtain of the bed; and his eyes, if eyes they may be called, were fixed on me. His jaws opened, and he muttered some inarticulate sounds, while a grin wrinkled his cheeks. He might have spoken, but I did not hear; one hand was stretched out, seemingly to detain me, but I escaped and rushed downstairs. I took refuge in the courtyard belonging to the house which I inhabited, where I remained during the rest of the night, walking up and down in the greatest agitation, listening attentively, catching and fearing each sound as if it were to announce the approach of the demoniacal corpse to which I had so miserably given life.

我看著厭物—這個我造的可憎怪物。他掀起床帷，眼睛，如果那可稱爲眼睛，直視著我。他張開嘴，嘟噥了些聲音，面頰浮現一咧笑容。他也許說了什麼，但我沒聽到，他一手伸出，好像要捉住我，但我逃脱衝下樓，躲到我住房的院子裡，整晚都待在那兒，極度焦躁地徘徊踱步，傾聽任何細微的聲響，怕是那具惡魔般的屍體，那具我該死地賦予生命的屍體，向我接近。

Accursed creator! Why did you form a monster so hideous that even *you* turned from me in disgust? God, in pity, made man beautiful and alluring, after his own image; but my form is a filthy type of yours, more horrid even from the very resemblance. Satan had his companions, fellow devils, to admire and encourage him, but I am solitary and abhorred.

該死的造物者！你爲何造了如此醜陋的怪物，連你都覺噁心，背棄了我？上帝悲憫，以自己的形象造了美麗迷人的人類；而我是你的惡形，因像你而更可怕。連撒旦都有同伙，其他惡魔，來讚美鼓勵他，而我卻孤獨受人憎。

1818年雪萊夫婦赴意大利，1822年雪萊海難去世，次年瑪麗返英，著力宣揚雪萊作品，並寫有多本小說、遊記，1851年去世。

瑪麗‧雪萊以《法藍肯斯坦，又稱現代普羅米修斯》聞名，對後世大眾文化影響重大。

圖片來源：維基共享資源

1-23
濟慈
John Keats

濟慈（John Keats）1795年生於倫敦，父親在一家旅館馬廄工作。8歲入讀寄宿學校，對文史產生興趣。隔年父親意外去世，母親再嫁，濟慈和弟妹依附外婆家。母親1810年去世，濟慈時年14，成為家庭友人醫師／藥劑師學徒，為期3年。1814年濟慈開始寫詩，同年原應收到外公和母親的兩筆遺產，數額頗豐，結果律師未告知，濟慈因此終生手頭拮据。1815年入讀醫學院，不久升任醫師助理。因缺錢，掙扎於行醫、寫作之間，罹憂鬱症。1816年獲醫師／藥劑師執照，同時決定棄醫從文。同年其商籟《噢 孤獨》（O Solitude）刊登於《考察者》（The Examiner）雜誌，並賦詩《首次閱讀查普曼所譯荷馬》（On First Looking into Chapman's Homer）：

Much have I travell'd in the realms of gold,	我在黃金國度閱歷已多，
And many goodly states and kingdoms seen;	已見過許多輝煌的疆域；
Round many western islands have I been	我去過許多西方的島嶼
Which bards in fealty to Apollo hold.	其地詩人皆尊崇阿波羅。
Oft of one wide expanse had I been told	有一大邦我常聽人提說
That deep-browed Homer ruled as his demesne;	為那深眉的荷馬所統御；
Yet did I never breathe its pure serene	我未曾晶聞其莊寧氣宇
Till I heard Chapman speak out loud and bold:	直到聽見查普曼的吟哦：
Then felt I like some watcher of the skies	我感受似觀察星象之士
When a new planet swims into his ken;	驟然發現一顆全新行星；
Or like stout Cortez when with eagle eyes	又似堅毅的鷹眼柯特斯
He star'd at the Pacific — and all his men	目注太平洋—他手下部眾
Look'd at each other with a wild surmise —	以驚疑的目光彼此投視——
Silent, upon a peak in Darien.	默然，看著達里恩的山峰。

濟慈1817年出版第一冊詩集，銷售不佳。1818年與友人徒步旅遊英格蘭湖區、蘇格蘭、愛爾蘭。同年被弟弟傳染肺結核。1818-19年寫就大量成熟詩作，包括《詠賽姬》（Ode to Psyche）、《詠希臘甕》（Ode on a Grecian Urn）、《詠怠惰》

（Ode on Indolence）、《詠憂鬱》（Ode on Melancholy）、《詠寄夜鶯》（Ode to a Nightingale）、《聖愛娜絲節前夕》（The Eve of St. Agnes）、《無情的美女》（La Belle Dame sans Merci）、《亥伯里昂》（Hyperion）、《嫘靡婭》（Lamia）、《致秋天》（To Autumn）。茲選譯其中三首：

濟慈

《詠希臘甕》：

Thou still unravish'd bride of quietness!	你這未經摧殘安寧之新婦！
Thou foster-child of Silence and slow Time,	你這為靜默緩時所收養者，
Sylvan historian, who canst thus express	田園史家，你能如此表述
A flowery tale more sweetly than our rhyme:	華美敘說更勝吾人詩歌：
What leaf-fringed legend haunts about thy shape	何等縈繞傳說環繞你身
Of deities or mortals, or of both,	所飾或仙或凡，或兩者皆屬，
In Tempe or the dales of Arcady?	於潭碧或雅可逖之谷境？
What men or gods are these? what maidens loath?	這是何神何人？何少女驚惡？
What mad pursuit? What struggle to escape?	為何急索？為何掙扎逃奔？
What pipes and timbrels? What wild ecstasy?	是何直笛鈴鼓？是何狂興？
Heard melodies are sweet, but those unheard	樂聲耳聞誠美，但闃然者
Are sweeter; therefore, ye soft pipes, play on;	更美；故此，爾輕巧笛音，勿斷；
Not to the sensual ear, but, more endear'd,	非為人耳，而是，更可貴者
Pipe to the spirit ditties of no tone:	為心靈吹奏那無聲樂章：
Fair youth, beneath the trees, thou canst not leave	俊郎，在樹下，你和曲音
Thy song, nor ever can those trees be bare;	永不分離，那樹也永不凋零；
Bold Lover, never, never canst thou kiss,	大膽情郎，你永不得親吻，
Though winning near the goal—yet, do not grieve;	雖然垂手可得—但，無需傷心；
She cannot fade, though thou hast not thy bliss,	她走不脫，儘管你不得逞，
Forever wilt thou love, and she be fair!	你的愛將永駐，她美貌永存！
Ah, happy, happy boughs! that cannot shed	啊，幸福、幸福的樹枝！永不
Your leaves, nor ever bid the Spring adieu;	落葉，也永不與春道別；
And, happy melodist, unwearied,	還有，幸福的樂手，永不煩苦，
Forever piping songs forever new;	永恆地吹奏永恆新鮮之歌闋；
More happy love! more happy, happy love!	更幸福的愛！幸福、幸福的愛！

Forever warm and still to be enjoy'd,	永恆熱情,仍可享受歡然,
Forever panting and forever young;	永恆在渴求,永恆年少;
All breathing human passion far above,	遠高於所有真實人生情愛,
That leaves a heart high sorrowful and cloy'd,	後者讓人極度傷心厭厭,
A burning forehead and a parching tongue.	讓人額頭燒燙、嘴舌乾燥。
Who are these coming to the sacrifice?	是些什麼人來參加祭典?
To what green altar, O mysterious priest,	赴何青綠祭壇,噢,神秘司祭?
Lead'st thou that heifer lowing at the skies,	你牽引那牛犢哞叫向天,
And all her silken flanks with garlands drest?	牠身披花環覆蓋如絲軀體。
What little town by river or sea-shore,	是哪座傍河或濱海小城,
Or mountain-built with peaceful citadel,	或哪座山城帶安祥城垛,
Is emptied of its folk, this pious morn?	今朝居民盡出參與祭禮?
And, little town, thy streets for evermore	小城啊,你的街巷將永恆
Will silent be; and not a soul to tell	沉默;沒有人會回來訴說
Why thou art desolate, can e'er return.	解釋為何眾人全都出離。
O Attic shape! Fair attitude! with brede	噢,雅典之範型!靚姿!纏繞
Of marble men and maidens overwrought,	以豐繁之大理石男女,
With forest branches and the trodden weed;	還有林木枝幹、腳下雜草;
Thou, silent form! dost tease us out of thought	你,沉默之型!讓我們無語
As doth eternity: Cold Pastoral!	如對永恆:冷默的田園詩!
When old age shall this generation waste,	當我們這代因衰老沒落,
Thou shalt remain, in midst of other woe	你仍將留佇,宥於你自己
Than ours, a friend to man, to whom thou say'st,	的困擾,與人為友,對人說:
"Beauty is truth, truth beauty,"—that is all	「美即是真,真即是美,」——
Ye know on earth, and all ye need to know.	人世間你只知此,也只需知此。

《無情的美女》：

O what can ail thee, knight-at-arms,
Alone and palely loitering?
The sedge has withered from the lake,
And no birds sing.
O what can ail thee, knight-at-arms,
So haggard and so woe-begone?
The squirrel's granary is full,
And the harvest's done.
I see a lily on thy brow,
With anguish moist and fever-dew,
And on thy cheeks a fading rose
Fast withereth too.
I met a lady in the meads,
Full beautiful—a faery's child,
Her hair was long, her foot was light,
And her eyes were wild.
I made a garland for her head,
And bracelets too, and fragrant zone;
She looked at me as she did love,
And made sweet moan.
I set her on my pacing steed,
And nothing else saw all day long,
For sidelong would she bend, and sing
A faery's song.
She found me roots of relish sweet,
And honey wild, and manna-dew,
And sure in language strange she said—
'I love thee true'.
She took me to her Elfin grot,
And there she wept and sighed full sore,
And there I shut her wild wild eyes
With kisses four.
And there she lullèd me asleep,

噢，你為何痛苦，騎士，
面容蒼白獨自漫行？
湖邊蘆草已經枯萎，
也無鳥鳴。
噢，你為何痛苦，騎士，
如此憔悴如此憂抑？
松鼠的糧倉已裝滿，
穀物已收刈。
我見你眉邊有百合，
既含焦鬱又帶濕露，
面頰還有凋謝玫瑰，
正迅疾萎枯。
我在草原遇見女士，
美麗異常—仙女之子，
長髮披肩，腳步輕盈，
眼神狂又熾。
我為她編織了花冠，
還有手環，還有圍巾；
她看著我眼帶愛意，
甜蜜呻吟。
我將她抱上我坐騎，
縱日中不復見他人，
因她側身依偎而唱
仙子歌詠。
她為我尋覓甜美草根，
野生蜂蜜，還有甘露，
她以奇異語言說道—
「我真心愛汝」。
她帶我到她的仙窟，
在彼處她哭泣哀嘆，
我封住她狂熾眼簾
以四親吻。
在彼處她撫慰我入眠，

And there I dreamed—Ah! woe betide!—
The latest dream I ever dreamt
On the cold hill side.
I saw pale kings and princes too,
Pale warriors, death-pale were they all;
They cried—'La Belle Dame sans Merci
Hath thee in thrall!'
I saw their starved lips in the gloam,
With horrid warning gapèd wide,
And I awoke and found me here,
On the cold hill's side.
And this is why I sojourn here,
Alone and palely loitering,
Though the sedge is withered from the lake,
And no birds sing.

在彼處我入夢—嗚呼—
做了我最後一場夢
在冷寂的山麓。
我還見蒼白君王、王子,
蒼白武士,都面容白慘;
他們高呼——「無情的美女
俘獲了你!」
在暗月下其飢涸口唇
大張訴說可怕讒語,
我遂醒來發現身處
在冷寂的山麓。
這是為何我漫行於此,
面容蒼白獨自漫行,
雖然湖邊蘆草已枯萎,
也無鳥鳴。

《詠寄夜鶯》:

My heart aches, and a drowsy numbness pains
My sense, as though of hemlock I had drunk,
Or emptied some dull opiate to the drains
One minute past, and Lethe-wards had sunk:
'Tis not through envy of thy happy lot,
But being too happy in thine happiness,—
That thou, light-winged Dryad of the trees,
In some melodious plot
Of beechen green, and shadows numberless,
Singest of summer in full-throated ease.
O, for a draught of vintage! that hath been

我心痛,昏沉的麻木鈍傷
感官,好像拿毒人參來喝,
也像飲盡了一杯鴉片湯
一分鐘後,沉入遺忘之河:
我並非羨慕你的幸福,
而是為你的幸福深感喜慶,——
你,羽翼輕盈的樹中仙女,
在某悠揚園圃
有青蔥櫸木,有無數幽影,
輕鬆引喉高歌夏日時序。
噢,願飲葡萄酒一杯,在彼

Cool'd a long age in the deep-delved earth,
Tasting of Flora and the country green,
Dance, and Provencal song, and sunburnt mirth!
O for a beaker full of the warm South,
Full of the true, the blushful Hippocrene,
With beaded bubbles winking at the brim,
And purple-stained mouth;
That I might drink, and leave the world unseen,
And with thee fade away into the forest dim:
Fade far away, dissolve, and quite forget
What thou among the leaves hast never known,
The weariness, the fever, and the fret
Here, where men sit and hear each other groan;
Where palsy shakes a few, sad, last gray hairs,
Where youth grows pale, and spectre-thin, and dies;
Where but to think is to be full of sorrow
And leaden-eyed despairs,
Where Beauty cannot keep her lustrous eyes,
Or new Love pine at them beyond to-morrow.
Away! away! for I will fly to thee,
Not charioted by Bacchus and his pards,
But on the viewless wings of Poesy,
Though the dull brain perplexes and retards:
Already with thee! tender is the night,
And haply the Queen-Moon is on her throne,
Cluster'd around by all her starry Fays;
But here there is no light,
Save what from heaven is with the breezes blown
Through verdurous glooms and winding mossy ways.
I cannot see what flowers are at my feet,
Nor what soft incense hangs upon the boughs,
But, in embalmed darkness, guess each sweet
Wherewith the seasonable month endows
The grass, the thicket, and the fruit-tree wild;
White hawthorn, and the pastoral eglantine;
Fast fading violets cover'd up in leaves;

深奧山谷中經久陰涼，
味帶眾花草和鄉村綠意，
帶歡舞、南法歌唱、快樂陽光！
噢，願滿飲一壺溫暖的南方，
滿溢真正、酡紅的龍泉液汁，
杯口全是圓潤泡沫閃凝，
讓人紫沾唇上；
願我飲下，得以悄然遺世，
伴隨你消逝於幽暗森林：
消逝遠颺，溶解，徹底遺忘
你在木葉中從不知的事情，
那厭倦、燥鬱，以及那憂煩
在此，人們坐聽彼此呻吟；
數莖可悲白髮因癱顫抖蕩，
青春變蒼老，瘦臞似鬼，而亡；
只要思想就憂患充斥
和那沉重絕望，
華美無法保住亮麗眼光，
所引至新慕戀也不踰一日。
遠颺！遠颺！我將飛向你，
非乘坐酒神及其伙伴之車，
而是借由詩神隱形之翼，
儘管頭腦思維困惑鈍厄：
既與你同在！夜晚多溫柔，
月亮之后安然穩居寶座，
身邊有眾仙星環繞簇擁；
但我所在處黯幽，
只有天上隨微風所傳落
穿越青綠朦朧蜿蜒苔徑。
我看不到腳下是何花朵，
也不知枝上垂掛何等凝香，
但，在香腴闇暗中，猜測
是何名花隨當季月份綴妝
草原、矮叢、以及野生果樹；
有白山楂，還有野玫瑰；
早凋紫菫為木葉所覆；

And mid-May's eldest child,

The coming musk-rose, full of dewy wine,

The murmurous haunt of flies on summer eves.

Darkling I listen; and, for many a time

I have been half in love with easeful Death,

Call'd him soft names in many a mused rhyme,

To take into the air my quiet breath;

Now more than ever seems it rich to die,

To cease upon the midnight with no pain,

While thou art pouring forth thy soul abroad

In such an ecstasy!

Still wouldst thou sing, and I have ears in vain—

To thy high requiem become a sod.

Thou wast not born for death, immortal Bird!

No hungry generations tread thee down;

The voice I hear this passing night was heard

In ancient days by emperor and clown:

Perhaps the self-same song that found a path

Through the sad heart of Ruth, when, sick for home,

She stood in tears amid the alien corn;

The same that oft-times hath

Charm'd magic casements, opening on the foam

Of perilous seas, in faery lands forlorn.

Forlorn! the very word is like a bell

To toll me back from thee to my sole self!

Adieu! the fancy cannot cheat so well

As she is fam'd to do, deceiving elf.

Adieu! adieu! thy plaintive anthem fades

Past the near meadows, over the still stream,

Up the hill-side; and now 'tis buried deep

In the next valley-glades:

Was it a vision, or a waking dream?

Fled is that music: —Do I wake or sleep?

及五月中新出，

將綻的麝香瑰，飽含露水，

夏夜蚊蠅嗡嗡飛舞。

我在暮色中聆聽；有多次

近乎愛上讓人鬆弛的死亡，

用種種名相輕呼他以詩，

要他將我微息帶向空茫；

死亡此刻較前更富誘惑，

在午夜休止不帶苦痛，

趁你以心靈暢歌傾吐

臻於極樂！

你仍高歌，而我雙耳成空—

對你安魂神曲我已成鈍土。

你非爲死而生，不亡之鳥！

沒有代代飢餓眾生踐踏你；

我今夜所聽聞曲音高妙

爲君王弄臣所聞於往昔：

也許就是同一首歌沁入

路得悲傷心脾，當她思鄉

佇立異域田野中哭泣：

這首歌也幾度

以魔力在浪頭上開啓門窗

在凶險海上，在被棄仙地。

被棄！這句話語像鐘聲

將我由你召回我孤獨自身！

永別了！幻想無法成功愚弄

如眾所傳聞，騙人的精靈。

永別！永別！你幽怨歌曲漸已

穿過那近原，越過那靜溪，

爬上山坡；此刻已悄然埋瘞

在隔鄰山谷草地：

是幻象，還是白晝夢迴？

樂曲已消逝：——我是醒是睡？

濟慈

濟
慈

　　濟慈1818-19年展開兩段戀情，與芬妮‧布朗（Fanny Brawne）尤深，但缺錢結婚，詩作也透露此痛苦。1820年肺結核惡化，遵醫囑赴南歐羅馬養病，次年去世，葬於當地，墓碑依其意未留姓名，但刻有：「躺臥此處者，其名書於水（Here lies One whose Name was writ in Water）。」

　　濟慈困頓早夭，詩作靈犀富感性，於華茲華士之後，領導英國第二代的浪漫詩人。

1-24

卡萊爾

Thomas Carlyle

卡萊爾
Thomas Carlyle

卡萊爾（Thomas Carlyle）1795年生於蘇格蘭南方卡爾文教派（Calvinism）家庭，1809-14年入讀愛丁堡大學（University of Edinburgh），畢業後教數學。1819-21年再入愛丁堡大學，開始質疑基督教，言語寫作辛辣。深受德國唯心主義影響，1824年譯介歌德（Goethe）小說《威廉‧邁斯特之學徒生涯》（Wilhelm Meisters Lehrjahre）。1825年為德國18世紀作家席勒寫就傳記《席勒生平》（Life of Schiller）。1826年婚娶珍‧薇希（Jane Welsh），兩人感情好，但時有勃谿，同代作家巴特勒（Samuel Butler）曾說：「上帝真好，讓卡萊爾夫婦結婚，如此只需兩人而非四人受苦（It was very good of God to let Carlyle and Mrs Carlyle marry one another, and so make only two people miserable and not four）。」

1831年卡萊爾遷居倫敦。1832年結識美國作家艾默生（Emerson）。1831-34年寫就《再裁裁縫師》（Sartor Resartus），借編者（Editor）之名，介紹虛構之德國哲學家戴奧吉尼（Diogenes Teufelsdröckh，意為「神生魔鬼屎」），並評論其書《衣裳：起源及影響》（Clothes, Their Origin and Influence）。《再裁裁縫師》揉雜小說、論文、自傳，批評英國實用主義，並以三部曲陳述卡萊爾自身信仰如何從否定（The Everlasting No），經由漠然（The Centre of Indifference），臻至肯定（The Everlasting Yea）。此書深遠影響美國超驗主義（Transcendentalism），並引領後世存在主義（Existentialism），茲選譯兩段：

Fool! The Ideal is in thyself, the impediment too is in thyself: thy Condition is but the stuff thou art to shape that same Ideal out of: what matters whether such stuff be of this sort or that, so the Form thou give it be heroic, be poetic? O thou that pinest in the imprisonment of the Actual, and criest bitterly to the gods for a kingdom wherein to rule and create, know this of a truth: the thing thou seekest is already with thee, 'here or nowhere,' couldst thou only see!

蠢夫！至善在爾自身，阻隔也在爾自身：爾之現狀即爾塑造至善之原材：原材之屬性，以致塑成之型或為偉人、或為詩人，皆無關緊要。噢，爾等囿於現狀、苦求神賜國度供爾駕馭開創之人，知乎此：爾等所求即在爾身，「非此則不存」，幸求察焉！

卡萊爾

Silence is the element in which great things fashion them-selves together; that at length they may emerge, full-formed and majestic, into the daylight of Life, which they are thenceforth to rule. Not William the Silent only, but all the considerable men I have known, and the most un-diplomatic and unstrategic of these, forbore to babble of what they were creating and projecting. Nay, in thy own mean perplexities, do thou thyself but hold thy tongue for one day: on the morrow, how much clearer are thy pur-poses and duties; what wreck and rubbish have those mute workmen within thee swept away, when intrusive noises were shut out! Speech is too often not, as the Frenchman defined it, the art of concealing Thought; but of quite stifling and suspending Thought, so that there is none to conceal. Speech too is great, but not the greatest. As the Swiss Inscription says: Sprecfien ist silbern, Schweigen ist golden (Speech is silvern, Silence is golden); or as I might rather express it: Speech is of Time, Silence is of Eternity.

沉默之為物，偉業於其中成型，期至脫穎而出，完備宏美，現於人世，駕馭人世。不僅沉默者威廉，我所知每個重要人物，其最不圓滑、最不善計算者，都不侈談其創作、其計劃。不，當你仍身處困惑不明，切記暫勿言說：隔日，你的方向、任務將趨明朗；拒斥囂擾喧譁，沉默的清潔工會清除你心內雜務！許多時候，言語並不（如法國人所說）掩飾思想，而是壓抑滯頓思想，以致無物可掩。言語誠然宏大，但非最宏大者。如瑞士銘文所言：言語是銀，沉默是金；換我的說法：言語從屬時間，沉默從屬永恆。

　　1834年卡萊爾再遷倫敦城西南卻希區，人稱「卻希智者」（Sage of Chelsea）。1837年寫就《法國大革命》（The French Revolution），敘述其起因、結果，書出聲名大噪，狄更斯（Charles Dickens）據以寫作小說《雙城記》（A Tale of Two Cities）。

　　1837-40年卡萊爾為賺錢作系列演講，1840年集編為《論歷史上的英雄、英雄崇拜、英雄業績》（On Heroes, Hero-Worship, and The Heroic in History），討論西方神祇與政治、文學、宗教界偉人，認為他們主控引領歷史潮流，此書影響了尼采（Nietzsche）的超人哲學。中有兩句：

「世界歷史不外偉人的傳記（The history of the world is but the biography of great men）。」

「我說，偉人恆常似天降雷霆，凡間餘人則似薪柴，等待偉人引燃熾燒（I said, the Great Man was always as lightning out of Heaven; the rest of men waited for him like fuel, and then they too would flame）。」

1849年卡萊爾刊文《隨論黑人問題》（Occasional Discourse on the Negro Question），表達支持奴隸制人士之意見，文中稱經濟學為「悲戚學科」（the dismal science）。1850年出版論文集《晚年論文》（Latter-Day Pamphlets），兼批民主政治與傳統貴族統治。1852-65年寫就《普魯士斐德列二世（人稱斐德列大帝）傳記》（The History of Friedrich II of Prussia, Called Frederick the Great），以為偉人之一例。

1866年卡萊爾出任愛丁堡大學校長（Rector），同年妻子去世。次年英國議會決議擴大投票權，卡萊爾撰文《隨尼亞加拉奔流直下：然後？》（Shooting Niagara: and After?），再次質疑民主。1881年去世。

卡萊爾引介德國浪漫文學，繼承英國諷刺文學傳統，主張偉人主導歷史，人視為法西斯先驅，哲學思辯引領20世紀存在主義。

圖片來源：IDJ圖庫

1-25
田尼生
Alfred Tennyson

田尼生
Alfred Tennyson

田尼生（Alfred Tennyson）1809年生於英格蘭東部，父親是鄉村牧師。田尼生與兄弟從少年開始寫詩，1827年入讀劍橋大學三一學院，加入每週聚會討論各種議題的秘密會社「劍橋使徒」（Cambridge Apostles），也結識好友哈藍（Arthur Henry Hallam），同年與哥哥出版詩集。1830年出版個人第一冊詩集。次年父親去世，田尼生輟學幫助養家，哈藍來訪並與妹妹愛米莉雅（Emilia）訂婚。1833年出版個人第二冊詩集，中有《霞落之女》（The Lady of Shalott）：

On either side the river lie	在河流兩岸都延綿
Long fields of barley and of rye,	長遠大麥稞麥田圍，
That clothe the wold and meet the sky;	覆蓋曠野連接天邊，
And thro' the field the road runs by	穿過田野道路伸延
To many-tower'd Camelot;	至眾塔聳立卡美洛；
The yellow-leaved waterlily	有葉色蒼黃的睡蓮
The green-sheathed daffodilly	有草色青綠的水仙
Tremble in the water chilly	於冰冷河水裡抖顫
Round about Shalott.	環繞著霞落。
Willows whiten, aspens shiver.	柳樹轉蒼，白楊顫恍。
The sunbeam showers break and quiver	太陽光線碎裂搖蕩
In the stream that runneth ever	於晝夜不停的水上
By the island in the river	在河中央的小島旁
Flowing down to Camelot.	滾滾流逝向卡美洛。
Four gray walls, and four gray towers	四面灰牆，四座灰塔
Overlook a space of flowers,	圍住片地長滿豔花，
And the silent isle imbowers	寂靜小島中藏人家
The Lady of Shalott.	有女於彼霞落。
Underneath the bearded barley,	在大麥的穗鬚之下，
The reaper, reaping late and early,	刈者早出晚歸收稼，
Hears her ever chanting cheerly,	聽見成日歡唱的她，
Like an angel, singing clearly,	好似天使，歌聲清雅，
O'er the stream of Camelot.	縈繞河上在卡美洛。

Piling the sheaves in furrows airy,
Beneath the moon, the reaper weary
Listening whispers, 'Tis the fairy,
Lady of Shalott.'
The little isle is all inrail'd
With a rose-fence, and overtrail'd
With roses: by the marge unhail'd
The shallop flitteth silken sail'd,
Skimming down to Camelot.
A pearl garland winds her head:
She leaneth on a velvet bed,
Full royally apparelled,
The Lady of Shalott.
No time hath she to sport and play:
A charmed web she weaves alway.
A curse is on her, if she stay
Her weaving, either night or day,
To look down to Camelot.
She knows not what the curse may be;
Therefore she weaveth steadily,
Therefore no other care hath she,
The Lady of Shalott.
She lives with little joy or fear.
Over the water, running near,
The sheepbell tinkles in her ear.
Before her hangs a mirror clear,
Reflecting tower'd Camelot.
And as the mazy web she whirls,
She sees the surly village churls,
And the red cloaks of market girls
Pass onward from Shalott.
Sometimes a troop of damsels glad,
An abbot on an ambling pad,
Sometimes a curly shepherd lad,
Or long-hair'd page in crimson clad,
Goes by to tower'd Camelot:

刈者將麥束置於田畦，
在月光下，力憊身疲
聽了輕語：「是那仙女，
在彼霞落。」
這小島四周全繞圈
玫瑰花籬，處處掛牽
玫瑰：在那無人岸邊
小舟絲帆疾過眼前，
飛馳駛向卡美洛。
她頭戴那珍珠花環：
她舒躺鵝絨床上，
全身如公主著裝，
有女於彼霞落。
她無暇去玩樂耍戲：
成天織造神奇羅匹。
她被詛咒，不得休息
停止織造，不得任意
張望朝向那卡美洛。
她不知道詛咒惡果；
只有日夜織造不輟，
因此全心全意工作，
有女於彼霞落。
她既無歡樂也無憂心。
河流之上，就在附近，
耳中聽到叮噹羊鈴，
她眼前掛著一面明鏡，
映出高聳的卡美洛。
她一邊織出似幻羅錦，
同時看見頑劣村童，
和市集女郎紅衣裙
經過那霞落。
間中一群快樂少女，
一位騎坐慢馬僧侶，
一個頑皮放羊小弟，
或長髮童僕著紅衣，
經此往高聳卡美洛：

田尼生

And sometimes thro' the mirror blue
The knights come riding two and two:
She hath no loyal knight and true,
The Lady of Shalott.
But in her web she still delights
To weave the mirror's magic sights,
For often thro' the silent nights
A funeral, with plumes and lights
And music, came from Camelot:
Or when the moon was overhead
Came two young lovers lately wed;
'I am half sick of shadows,' said
The Lady of Shalott.
A bow-shot from her bower-eaves,
He rode between the barley-sheaves,
The sun came dazzling thro' the leaves,
And flam'd upon the brazen greaves
Of bold Sir Lancelot.
A red-cross knight for ever kneel'd
To a lady in his shield,
That sparkled on the yellow field,
Beside remote Shalott.
The gemmy bridle glitter'd free,
Like to some branch of stars we see
Hung in the golden Galaxy.
The bridle bells rang merrily
As he rode down from Camelot:
And from his blazon'd baldric slung
A mighty silver bugle hung,
And as he rode his armour rung,
Beside remote Shalott.
All in the blue unclouded weather
Thick-jewell'd shone the saddle-leather,
The helmet and the helmet-feather
Burn'd like one burning flame together,
As he rode down from Camelot.

有時映現清澈鏡中
騎士兩兩駕騎同行：
沒有騎士對她效忠，
有女於彼霞落。
但她樂於邊織羅錦
邊觀看那鏡中奇景，
經常當那中夜寂靜
有羽飾火炬，葬禮行進
帶奏樂，來自卡美洛：
有時夜晚明月高懸
新婚戀人相依繾綣；
「鏡中之影我已厭煩，」
霞落之女逑說。
離她閨房一箭之遙，
他在大麥田裡騎駕，
陽光透過碎葉瀧下，
閃耀在他銅製腿甲
無懼爵士蘭斯洛。
紅十字騎士永跪向
女士在他盾牌上，
於金黃田野裡閃亮，
依傍遙遠霞落。
鑲寶馬勒閃閃發光，
像是天上星星一樣
高掛金色銀河之上。
馬鈴晃搖輕快叮噹，
隨他來自卡美洛。
懸掛他盾徽肩帶上
有把銀製號角堂皇，
他邊騎盔甲邊振響，
依傍遙遠霞落。
藍天無雲晴空萬里
馬鞍珠寶金光熠熠，
頭盔還有盔上羽翼
紅焰如火耀眼如一，
隨他來自卡美洛。

As often thro' the purple night,	如同常見紫色夜晚,
Below the starry clusters bright,	蒼穹滿佈星光耀閃,
Some bearded meteor, trailing light,	流星拖帶明亮尾瓣,
Moves over green Shalott.	劃過青綠霞落。
His broad clear brow in sunlight glow'd;	額頭寬廣神采奕奕;
On burnish'd hooves his war-horse trode;	戰馬四蹄光鮮輕移;
From underneath his helmet flow'd	頭盔之下飛揚飄逸
His coal-black curls as on he rode,	烏黑捲髮隨風而起,
As he rode down from Camelot.	隨他來自卡美洛。
From the bank and from the river	從那河流從那岸邊,
He flash'd into the crystal mirror,	他的身影映入鏡面,
'Tirra lirra, tirra lirra:'	「提拉里拉,提拉里連:」
Sang Sir Lancelot.	唱道爵士蘭斯洛。
She left the web, she left the loom	從羅錦、織機她轉向
She made three paces thro' the room	跨出三步穿越閨房
She saw the water-flower bloom,	她見到水中花綻放,
She saw the helmet and the plume,	她見到頭盔和羽裝,
She look'd down to Camelot.	她望向卡美洛。
Out flew the web and floated wide;	羅錦飛出窗外飄捲;
The mirror crack'd from side to side;	鏡子裂開橫貫鏡面;
'The curse is come upon me,' cried	「詛咒對我將要應驗,」
The Lady of Shalott.	哭喊彼女於霞落。
In the stormy east-wind straining,	狂暴東風猛烈吹襲,
The pale yellow woods were waning,	蒼黃樹木不敵偃低,
The broad stream in his banks complaining,	河中波浪翻滾抗議,
Heavily the low sky raining	天幕低垂暴雨不息
Over tower'd Camelot;	覆蓋高聳卡美洛;
Outside the isle a shallow boat	小島之旁小艇停靠
Beneath a willow lay afloat,	漂浮水面垂柳籠罩,
Below the carven stern she wrote,	她在木刻船頭寫道,
The Lady of Shalott.	有女於彼霞落。
A cloudwhite crown of pearl she dight,	她頭戴霞白珍珠冠,
All raimented in snowy white	全身穿著雪白衣裳
That loosely flew (her zone in sight	飄逸(可見腰帶掛懸
Clasp'd with one blinding diamond bright)	上扣一顆炫目寶鑽)
Her wide eyes fix'd on Camelot,	她目光注視卡美洛,

·田尼生·

Though the squally east-wind keenly
Blew, with folded arms serenely
By the water stood the queenly
Lady of Shalott.
With a steady stony glance—
Like some bold seer in a trance,
Beholding all his own mischance,
Mute, with a glassy countenance—
She look'd down to Camelot.
It was the closing of the day:
She loos'd the chain, and down she lay;
The broad stream bore her far away,
The Lady of Shalott.
As when to sailors while they roam,
By creeks and outfalls far from home,
Rising and dropping with the foam,
From dying swans wild warblings come,
Blown shoreward; so to Camelot
Still as the boathead wound along
The willowy hills and fields among,
They heard her chanting her deathsong,
The Lady of Shalott.
A longdrawn carol, mournful, holy,
She chanted loudly, chanted lowly,
Till her eyes were darken'd wholly,
And her smooth face sharpen'd slowly,
Turn'd to tower'd Camelot:
For ere she reach'd upon the tide
The first house by the water-side,
Singing in her song she died,
The Lady of Shalott.
Under tower and balcony,
By garden wall and gallery,
A pale, pale corpse she floated by,
Deadcold, between the houses high,
Dead into tower'd Camelot.

雖然東風猛烈吹襲
她手叉胸前安然佇立
站在河邊皇后姿儀
有女於彼霞落。
她以漠然眼神注視—
有如入定通靈先知，
看到自己未來慘事，
不言不語神情如痴—
她望向卡美洛。
此時太陽即將下沉：
她解開船纜躺下身；
大河將她帶走遠遁，
有女於彼霞落。
如同水手四海流浪，
河上海口遠離家鄉，
身隨波濤高低遊蕩，
天鵝瀕死狂歌高唱，
漂向岸邊；往卡美洛
船頭穩定漂流沿著
多柳山丘和田野之側，
人們聽到她臨終悲歌，
有女於彼霞落。
歌聲悠長，哀傷，肅穆，
時而高昂，時而低俯，
直到她眼前降下黑幕，
直到她面頰漸漸消突，
轉向高聳卡美洛：
她未及隨浪潮進馳
到達河邊首座屋子，
她邊歌唱邊已離世，
有女於彼霞落。
在高塔與陽台下面，
在花園與長廊旁邊，
她慘白身軀慢慢蜿蜒，
極冰冷，在樓閣之間，
死寂漂過高聳卡美洛。

Knight and burgher, lord and dame,
To the planked wharfage came:
Below the stern they read her name,
The Lady of Shalott.
They cross'd themselves, their stars they blest,
Knight, minstrel, abbot, squire, and guest.
There lay a parchment on her breast,
That puzzled more than all the rest,
The wellfed wits at Camelot.
'The web was woven curiously,
The charm is broken utterly,
Draw near and fear not, —this is I,
The Lady of Shalott.'

騎士市民，貴婦大人，
到木架河港齊來臨：
在船頭下看到其名，
有女於彼霞落。
他們胸畫十字，上禱星辰，
騎士、詩人、和尚、鄉紳。
有羊皮紙放置胸衽，
上書難以解釋詩文，
難倒學究於卡美洛。
「很是奇特所織網羅，
詛咒禁制違犯肇禍，
進前勿須恐懼，——是我，
有女於彼霞落。」

1833年哈藍在維也納渡假腦溢血遽逝，田尼生深受打擊，賦詩《悼哈藍》（In Memoriam A.H.H.），中有名句「寧可曾愛過再失去，不可一生從未愛過」（Tis better to have loved and lost, Than never to have loved at all——）。1837年田尼生全家搬去英格蘭東南居住。次年作長篇田園詩《王者之歌》（Idylls of the King），以圓桌武士傳奇比喻世事興衰，田尼生寫詩習慣不斷修改，此作直修改到1888年。1840年投資失利，搬去倫敦。1842年出版詩集二冊，包括《洛克斯里居》（Locksley Hall）、《憂里希思》（Ulysses）等，廣受歡迎，前者描述年輕人心中愛恨糾纏，後者描述希臘神話人物憂里希思流浪返家後不安於室，再次出外闖蕩，結尾有名句「奮鬥、追求、發現、絕不屈服」（To strive, to seek, to find, and not to yield）。

1850年田尼生繼華茲華士榮任桂冠詩人，同年結婚。次年賦詩《鷹隼》（The Eagle）：

He clasps the crag with crooked hands;	牠以曲爪緊抓峭壁；
Close to the sun in lonely lands,	近逼日頭孤身無匹，
Ringed with the azure world, he stands.	藍天環繞傲然獨立。
The wrinkled sea beneath him crawls;	腳下千尋海波似紋；
He watches from his mountain walls,	牠從懸崖俯視下臨，
And like a thunderbolt he falls.	剎然一動雷霆萬鈞。

1853年田尼生遷居英格蘭南部懷特島（Isle of Wight）。1855年賦詩《輕騎兵衝鋒》（The Charge of the Light Brigade），紀念1854年克里米亞戰爭英軍英勇進攻俄軍陣地，中有形容軍人名句：

Their's not to make reply,	他們責不在回嘴，
Their's not to reason why,	他們責不在質疑，
Their's but to do and die:	他們只知死而後已：

1869年賦詩《牆隙裡生長的花》（Flower in the Crannied Wall）

Flower in the crannied wall,	牆隙裡生長的花，
I pluck you out of the crannies,	我將你拔出自牆隙，
I hold you here, root and all, in my hand,	我拿著你，根連莖，在手裡，

Little flower -but if I could understand What you are, root and all, and all in all, I should know what God and man is.	小花啊—只要我能夠明晰 你是什麼，根連莖，上到下， 我就能了解人和上帝。

1884年田尼生受封男爵（Baron），是英國首位因詩文晉封貴族者。1889年因病自覺近死，賦詩《穿越沙隄》（Crossing the Bar）：

Sunset and evening star, And one clear call for me! And may there be no moaning of the bar, When I put out to sea, But such a tide as moving seems asleep, Too full for sound and foam, When that which drew from out the boundless deep Turns again home. Twilight and evening bell, And after that the dark! And may there be no sadness of farewell, When I embark; For though from out our bourne of Time and Place The flood may bear me far, I hope to see my Pilot face to face When I have crossed the bar.	日暮傍晚金星， 清楚對我呼喚！ 但願沙隄上不會有悲聲， 當我出海離岸， 但願海潮流動卻似沉睡， 飽滿無聲無渣， 當來自無盡深海的那位 再次回家。 暮光傍晚鐘聲， 之後夜幕下降！ 我希望沒有道別的悲情， 當我啟航； 雖將脫離人世時空局限 海潮帶我遠逸， 我期望當面親見導航員 當我穿越沙隄。

田尼生1892年去世，葬於西敏寺。

田尼生詩作音韻優美，朗朗上口，抒情略帶抑鬱，人譽「大眾詩人」（Poet of the People），為維多利亞時期詩人典範。

1-26

布朗寧

Robert Browning

布朗寧
Robert Browning

布朗寧（Robert Browning）1812年生於倫敦，父親是英倫銀行高級職員，收藏大量圖書。布朗寧12歲即寫詩，主要在家受教，14歲已嫻熟希臘、拉丁、意、法語，因心儀雪萊而成爲無神論與素食者，但持續不久。16歲入倫敦大學學院（University College London）攻讀希臘文一年，因父母篤信新教而未入只收國教徒的牛津、劍橋。1833年自費出版長詩《寶玲》（Pauline）。1834年隨俄國領事本考森（Benkhausen）遊聖彼得堡，以16世紀術士巴拉塞斯（Paracelsus）爲題賦詩，次年出版，以此結識英國文人。1841-46年出版《鐘與石榴》（Bells and Pomegranates），其中一冊《對白詩》（Dramatic Lyrics）獲好評，茲選譯其中《我前任公爵夫人》（My Last Duchess）：

Ferrara	費拉拉
That's my last Duchess painted on the wall,	牆上畫是我前任公爵夫人，
Looking as if she were alive. I call	看起來栩栩如生。我稱
That piece a wonder, now: Frà Pandolf's hands	之爲奇蹟，話說：潘道弗弟兄
Worked busily a day, and there she stands.	忙了一整天，而後她現容。
Will't please you sit and look at her? I said	您要不坐下觀看？我提說
'Frà Pandolf' by design, for never read	「潘道弗」是有意，因爲訪客
Strangers like you that pictured countenance,	如你只要看到畫像面容，
The depth and passion of its earnest glance,	看到她的深情、熱切眼神，
But to myself they turned (since none puts by	都會轉向我（因爲除我外
The curtain I have drawn for you, but I)	無人可以將畫像簾幕揭開）
And seemed as they would ask me, if they durst,	好像想問我，如果他們敢問，
How such a glance came there; so, not the first	爲何她眼神如此；所以您
Are you to turn and ask thus. Sir, 'twas not	不是首位發問者。先生，並非
Her husband's presence only, called that spot	只有她丈夫才讓那欣喜
Of joy into the Duchess' cheek: perhaps	表情顯現夫人臉上：也許
Frà Pandolf chanced to say 'Her mantle laps	潘道弗只隨口說：「夫人外衣
Over my lady's wrist too much,' or, 'Paint	遮住您手腕了」，或是「畫筆
Must never hope to reproduce the faint	永遠無法畫出夫人頸頤
Half-flush that dies along her throat:' such stuff	上那淡淡紅暈：」諸如此類
Was courtesy, she thought, and cause enough	客套話，也令她起思，足以

For calling up that spot of joy. She had	讓她面容顯現喜色。她的
A heart – how shall I say – too soon made glad,	心—怎麼說呢—太易欣喜，
Too easily impressed; she liked whate'er	太易受影響；她看到什麼都
She looked on, and her looks went everywhere.	喜歡，而她目光又四處巡遊。
Sir, 'twas all one! My favour at her breast,	先生，對她都一樣！我的眷顧，
The dropping of the daylight in the West,	傍晚太陽西下時的日暮，
The bough of cherries some officious fool	阿諛奉承者爲她在果園
Broke in the orchard for her, the white mule	摘的櫻桃枝，她繞著前院
She rode with round the terrace - all and each	乘騎的白騾—這一切全
Would draw from her alike the approving speech,	會讓她開口說好、讚嘆，
Or blush, at least. She thanked men - good! but thanked	至少臉紅。她感激人——好！但她
Somehow - I know not how - as if she ranked	態度—很難形容—好像把
My gift of a nine-hundred-years-old name	我賜予她的九百年貴姓
With anybody's gift. Who'd stoop to blame	等同他物。誰能降低身份
This sort of trifling? Even had you skill	指責這等小事？就算你
In speech - (which I have not) - to make your will	口才好—（而我口拙）—能對
Quite clear to such an one, and say, 'Just this	這麼個人說明白，說：「你這處
Or that in you disgusts me; here you miss,	那處令我鄙薄；這點不足，
Or there exceed the mark' - and if she let	那點太超過」——就算她願意
Herself be lessoned so, nor plainly set	接受訓話，而不直接和你
Her wits to yours, forsooth, and made excuse,	吵架，找各種理由辯駁，
- E'en that would be some stooping; and I choose	—即便如此也算降格；而我
Never to stoop. Oh sir, she smiled, no doubt,	絕不降格。先生，當我經過，
Whene'er I passed her; but who passed without	她當然會微笑；但誰經過
Much the same smile? This grew; I gave commands;	她不笑？此事滋長；我下了令；
Then all smiles stopped together. There she stands	所有微笑終結。她在此現容
As if alive. Will't please you rise? We'll meet	栩栩如生。您請起身？我們
The company below, then. I repeat,	下樓見其他人吧。我重申，
The Count your master's known munificence	伯爵、令主人以慷慨聞名
Is ample warrant that no just pretence	這保證我任何合理合情
Of mine for dowry will be disallowed;	的嫁妝要求都不會被阻；
Though his fair daughter's self, as I avowed	雖則他美麗女兒，如我最初
At starting, is my object. Nay, we'll go	所誓稱，才是我所要。好，我們
Together down, sir. Notice Neptune, though,	下樓吧。欸，請看這尊海神
Taming a sea-horse, thought a rarity,	馴服海馬雕像，這是稀物，
Which Claus of Innsbruck cast in bronze for me!	是茵斯堡克勞斯爲我銅鑄！

　　布朗寧依靠父母、不事生產，致力寫詩，1845年33歲結識大他6歲、體弱多病的詩人伊麗莎白‧巴列特（Elizabeth Barrett），次年因伊麗莎白父親反對子女結婚而秘密成婚，爲妻子健康定居意大利，依妻生活。1855年出版詩集《男人女人》（Men and Women）。妻子1861年去世，布朗寧次年遷返倫敦。1868-69年出版巨著《戒指與書》（The Ring and the Book），依據12世紀羅馬一宗命案，以十位當事人口吻，從各人角度自訴立場，寫成戲劇獨白詩（dramatic monologue），終得大名。1881年愛好其詩者創立布朗寧學會（Robert Browning Society）。1889年死於威尼斯，葬於西敏寺詩人角。

　　布朗寧在英國19世紀詩人中，排位於田尼生之後，穩居第二，以戲劇獨白詩獨樹一幟，廣受喜愛。

1-27

勃朗蒂三姊妹
夏洛蒂、愛蜜莉、安

Charlotte. Emily. Anne

勃朗蒂三姊妹夏洛蒂（Charlotte）1816年、愛蜜莉（Emily）1818年、安（Anne）1820年生於英格蘭北部鄉村。父親移民自北愛爾蘭，任國教助理牧師（curate），也寫作。母親來自康瓦爾富商家庭，1821年去世，三姐妹姨母遷入幫忙持家。三姐妹上有長姊、二姊，一兄弟，由父親與姨母在家教育。1824年除小妹安之外，其他姐妹入寄宿小學，隔年長姊、二姊因肺結核返家，旋即去世，得年11、10歲，另兩姊妹也返家。眾姐妹自幼與兄弟布藍維（Branwell）根據父親訂閱之季刊詩文自編故事，深受拜倫等作家影響。

夏洛蒂1831-32年再入另間學校，這次師生相處融洽，3年後應邀返校任助教。愛蜜莉時年17，極度害羞，隨之前往入學，三個月後不適返家，由安替代入學至1837年。夏洛蒂1838年辭職返家，之後夏洛蒂、安擔任家庭教師。1842年三姐妹籌劃在家設立女子學校，為此赴比利時布魯塞爾（Brussels）私塾學習法文、德文、鋼琴，因成績優異留校任教。同年姨母去世留贈遺產，次年夏洛蒂仍應邀返布魯塞爾任教，戀上私塾先生未果，一年後返家，而女子學校終未設立。

夏洛蒂曾將詩稿寄給詩人瑟西（Robert Southey）求教，瑟西反應冷淡。1846年三姐妹化名貝爾（Bell）三兄弟柯爾（Currer）、艾利斯（Ellis）、艾克敦（Acton）合刊《詩集》（Poems），僅售出3本。1847年夏洛蒂出版《簡愛》（Jane Eyre），愛蜜莉出版《咆哮山莊》（Wuthering Heights），安出版《愛妮絲·葛雷》（Agnes Grey），書出成名。

《簡愛》以第一人稱敘述女主角簡愛幼年住母舅家受虐，入讀寄宿學校環境不佳，之後於桑費莊園（Thornfield Hall）任家庭教師，與莊主羅徹斯特（Edward Rochester）相戀並決定結婚，婚禮上有人指證羅徹斯特已婚，羅徹斯特承認莊園裡的怪女人是他發瘋的妻子。羅徹斯特要簡愛同赴法南同居，簡愛拒絕，遠走他鄉當老師，獲知伯父留贈她大筆遺產。表親牧師向她求婚，簡愛拒絕但同意隨他赴印度傳教，之後反悔，回到桑費莊園，得知羅徹斯特妻子將莊園焚毀並跳樓，羅徹斯特為救妻子而斷臂目盲，兩人終於結婚。此書首創將詩的激情引入小說，大為暢銷。茲選譯一段簡愛對羅徹斯特所言：

Do you think I am an automaton? — a machine without feelings? and can bear to have my morsel of bread snatched from my lips, and my drop of living water dashed from my cup? Do you think, because I am poor, obscure, plain, and little, I am soulless and heartless? You think wrong! — I have as much soul as you — and full as much heart! And if God had gifted me with some beauty and much wealth, I should have made it as hard for you to leave me, as it is now for me to leave you. I am not talking to you now through the medium of custom, conventionalities, nor even of mortal flesh: it is my spirit that addresses your spirit; just as if both had passed through the grave, and we stood at God's feet, equal — as we are!

你以爲我是機器人嗎？——一個沒感情的機器？可以忍受口邊的麵包被搶走，杯裡的救命水被打翻？你以爲，就因爲我貧窮、卑微、樣貌平凡、只是個小人物，我就沒有靈魂、沒有一顆心嗎？你錯了！——我跟你一樣有靈魂一樣有心！如果上帝有給我少許美貌、大量錢財，我也會讓你無法離開我，正如我此刻無法離開你。我現在不是以俗禮或習慣，甚至不是透過肉體在跟你講話：我是以靈魂對你的靈魂溝通；就像是我們已進了墳墓，靈魂到了上帝跟前，地位平等—如其本然！

《咆哮山莊》敘述洛克伍（Lockwood）去英格蘭北部畫眉田莊（Thrushcross Grange）租屋，暫住莊主希克里夫（Heathcliff）之咆哮山莊，發覺之前有住客名凱瑟琳（Catherine）。女管家奈莉（Nelly Dean）告知洛克伍：30年前山莊主人恩肖（Earnshaw）有子辛利（Hindley）與女凱瑟琳，又收養街童希克里夫，引起辛利嫉妒，但凱瑟琳與希克里夫日漸親密。恩肖去世，辛利與妻子法蘭西絲（Frances）將希克里夫當下人，凱瑟琳與畫眉田莊租客林頓（Edgar Linton）相戀，她更愛希克里夫，但因地位高下無法結婚，希克里夫聽到她說他地位低下，離家出走。3年後凱瑟琳、林頓成婚，希克里夫致富返來，爲林頓妹妹伊莎貝拉（Isabella）所戀，希克里夫借此報復林頓。辛利酗酒貧困，將山莊賣給希克里夫，希克里夫帶伊莎貝拉私奔，返來後凱瑟琳產女凱西（Cathy），隨即去世。伊莎貝拉赴英南產子林頓（與舅同名），辛利去世。12年後凱西長成，希克里夫在老林頓不知情下促成小林頓與凱西結婚，老林頓去世，希克里夫要求凱西與他同住山莊，小林頓去世，凱西抑鬱寡歡，辛利之子海敦（Hareton）與凱西相戀，希克里夫臞死（瘦弱而死），葬於凱瑟琳墓旁。書出毀譽參半。茲選譯一段希克里夫對凱瑟琳所言：

You teach me now how cruel you've been - cruel and false. Why did you despise me? Why did you betray your own heart, Cathy? I have not one word of comfort. You deserve this. You have killed yourself. Yes, you may kiss me, and cry; and wring out my kisses and tears: they'll blight you - they'll damn you. You loved me - what right had you to leave me? What right - answer me - for the poor fancy you felt for Linton? Because misery, and degradation, and death, and nothing that God or Satan could inflict would have parted us, you, of your own will did it. I have not broken your heart - you have broken it; and in breaking it, you have broken mine. So much the worse for me that I am strong. Do I want to live? What kind of living will it be when you - Oh, God! would you like to lie with your soul in the grave?

你教給我的是你極其殘酷—殘酷又虛偽。你為什麼卑視我？你為什麼背叛你自己的心，凱西？我絕不安慰你。你活該。你害死了你自己。沒錯，你可以親我，可以哭泣，可以迫出我的親吻、我的眼淚：我的吻和淚會作祟你——會詛咒你。你愛的是我—那你有什麼權利離開我？憑什麼離開—回答我—去找你自以為喜歡的林頓？因苦、卑賤、死亡、上帝或撒旦的任何手段都無法將我倆分開，是你，你自己造成的。我不曾碎了你的心—是你自己做的；你碎了自己的心，同時也碎了我的。活該我比你堅強。我還要活下去嗎？那會是何種境況，當你已—噢，上帝！你會想要讓靈肉一起躺在墳裡嗎？

《愛妮絲‧葛雷》敘述女主角愛妮絲當家庭教師之經歷，書出遭冷落。

1848年布藍維因酗酒與鴉片癮去世，安1849年出版《荒野莊園的房客》（The Tenant of Wildfell Hall），敘述一女子因先生酗酒家暴而離家，先生臨死前她又返家照顧他至死。家暴、離家等話題當時驚世駭俗，書出大賣但被評粗俗，今日視為女性主義小說濫觴。

1854年夏洛蒂嫁給家鄉的助理牧師，次年去世，愛蜜莉1848年去世，安1849年去世，三人皆死於肺結核。

勃朗蒂姐妹結合陰鬱的哥德（Gothic）小說與激情浪漫小說，開創新文類，廣受歡迎。

1-28

阿諾德

Matthew Arnold

阿諾德
Matthew Arnold

阿諾德（Matthew Arnold）1822年生於英格蘭東南，父親出身中產階級稅官家庭，家教嚴格，曾任勒格比公學（Rugby School）校長，創立現代英國公學典範。1836年阿諾德赴南部溫徹斯特學院（Winchester College）就讀，翌年轉讀勒格比公學，1838年後與弟湯姆編撰雜誌供家人自娛。在校期間屢獲散文、英詩、拉丁詩創作獎。1841-44年獲獎學金入讀牛津大學貝柳學院（Balliol College）主修古典語文。父親1842年心臟病去世。阿諾德畢業後返勒格比任教，旋即獲選牛津大學歐里爾學院（Oriel College）院士。1847年受聘為樞密院主席（Lord President of the Council）蘭茲當勳爵（Lord Lansdowne）私人秘書。1849年起出版數冊詩集。

1851年阿諾德任職政府督學，負責視察英格蘭所有非國教學校，旋即婚娶法官之女法蘭西絲（Frances Lucy Wightman）。據推測1853年前寫就兩首名詩《多佛灘》（Dover Beach）與《大夏圖寺詩章》（Stanzas from the Grande Chartreuse），茲選譯《多佛灘》：

The sea is calm to-night.	今夜大海寧靜。
The tide is full, the moon lies fair	潮水滿漲，月亮靚俔
Upon the straits; —on the French coast the light	映於海峽；——法國海濱光影
Gleams and is gone; the cliffs of England stand,	爍動明滅；英國海崖雄立，
Glimmering and vast, out in the tranquil bay.	閃亮廣闊，於平和海灣彼端。
Come to the window, sweet is the night-air!	來站在窗邊，夜息多甜美！
Only, from the long line of spray	但是，從那一線海浪
Where the sea meets the moon-blanch'd land,	於彼大海交接月白大地，
Listen! you hear the grating roar	你聽！可聞錯軋低吼
Of pebbles which the waves draw back, and fling,	海浪席捲碎石，拋擲，
At their return, up the high strand,	當其回湧，海灘高脊，
Begin, and cease, and then again begin,	起始，停止，接著再次起始，
With tremulous cadence slow, and bring	伴隨緩慢顫抖韻律，引致
The eternal note of sadness in.	那永恆的悲傷音旨。

Sophocles long ago	索福克勒斯古早
Heard it on the Ægæan, and it brought	在愛琴海邊聽過，讓伊
Into his mind the turbid ebb and flow	想起起伏伏滾動翻攪
Of human misery; we	的人類悲苦；我們
Find also in the sound a thought,	也在其中聞悉此意，
Hearing it by this distant northern sea.	於此遙遠北方海之濱。
The Sea of Faith	信仰之海
Was once, too, at the full, and round earth's shore	也曾一度滿漲，環繞大地四周
Lay like the folds of a bright girdle furl'd.	像是亮麗腰巾圍裹包捲。
But now I only hear	但如今我只聽聞
Its melancholy, long, withdrawing roar,	其哀傷、悠長、逝退之低吼，
Retreating, to the breath	撤退，隨著夜風
Of the night-wind, down the vast edges drear	流息，下沿人世荒涼無垠
And naked shingles of the world.	裸露之屋簷瓦片。
Ah, love, let us be true	啊，我愛，願我倆
To one another! for the world, which seems	忠於彼此！因為世界看似
To lie before us like a land of dreams,	美夢一般在我們面前顯示，
So various, so beautiful, so new,	如此紛繁，如此美麗、新穎，
Hath really neither joy, nor love, nor light,	其實並無歡樂、愛心、明光，
Nor certitude, nor peace, nor help for pain;	也無真確、安寧、救贖於苦難；
And we are here as on a darkling plain	我們在此猶如漸暗野原
Swept with confused alarms of struggle and flight,	逐流於迷亂之掙扎逃亡，
Where ignorant armies clash by night.	盲然的軍隊於黑夜衝撞。

　　《大夏圖寺詩章》有名句《徘徊兩個世界之間，其一已死，另一難產》（Wandering between two worlds, one dead, the other powerless to be born）常為人引用以表達當時新舊社會價值青黃不接。

　　1857年阿諾德獲聘牛津大學詩學教授，以政治與社會解讀文學，強調看清事物本相，區分優劣，奉持中道。1859年赴歐陸考察教育，1861年自費出版《法國國民教育》（The Popular Education of France），主張改革英國教育，由國家承擔威權，以適應民

主體制。1865年出版《批評論文：第一集》（Essays in Criticism, First Series），其中一篇《當前批評之功能》（The Function of Criticism at the Present Time）對批評提出著名定義：「超然地學習、提倡世間最好的知識思想（the disinterested endeavor to learn and propagate the best that is known and thought in the world）。」

1869年阿諾得出版《文化與失序》（Culture and Anarchy），「失序」意指西方19世紀面臨危機：聖經受到演化論挑戰，下層民眾要求參與政權；「文化」意指阿諾德提議以文學藝術取代宗教，啓迪民智，以便民主社會正確運作，安定社會。阿諾德特指此人文內容爲前述「古往今來相關議論思辨中之精華」（the best which has been thought and said in the world）。此書引起英國知識分子熱烈討論，其中用語多進入日常語言，如以「蠻族」（Barbarians）指稱貴族、以「非利士人」（Philistines）指稱中產階級。西方語言中「文化」一詞指涉人文、藝術精緻一面大半源於本書。茲選譯一段：

And now to pass to the matters canvassed in the following essay. The whole scope of the essay is to *recommend culture* as the great help out of our present difficulties; culture being a pursuit of our total perfection by means of getting to know, on all the matters which most concern us, *the best which has been thought and said in the world*; and through this knowledge, turning a stream of fresh and free thought upon our stock notions and habits, which we now follow staunchly but mechanically, vainly imagining that there is a virtue in following them staunchly which makes up for the mischief of following them mechanically. This, and this alone, is the scope of the following essay.

現在接著談下列文章所論之事。其主旨在建議以文化解決當前問題；在此我將文化定義爲以下列方法追求完善：對我們切身事務，學習古往今來相關議論思辨中之精華，借此爲我們的積習舊俗注入鮮活新意；我們平日嚴格、機械地遵從積習舊俗，以爲如此即可彌補機械遵從的問題。這就是下文唯一的主旨。

1888年阿諾德病逝。死後出版《批評論文：第二集》（Essays in Criticism, Second Series）。

阿諾德之論文界定英國文學經典範疇，開創西方當代文學批評。詩作沉鬱傷感，反映19世紀英國基督教信仰之消蝕，與田尼生、布朗寧並列英國維多利亞時期三大詩人。

◆ ： 阿諾德 ： ◆

圖片來源：IDJ圖庫

1-29

路易斯・卡若

Lewis Carroll

路易斯·卡若（Lewis Carroll）爲查爾斯·勒維吉·道基生（Charles Lutwidge Dodgson）筆名，源自中名與前名之拉丁化（Ludovicus Carolus），1832年生於英格蘭西部，父親是英國國教牧師。卡若與兄弟姐妹大都口吃，自幼展露數學天賦，也著文賦詩，1850年入牛津大學基督堂（Christ Church）學院，1854年畢業，隔年起終生留校，任教數學。1856年書院迎來新院長李德（Henry Liddell）夫婦及其一子三女哈利（Harry）、珞琳娜（Lorina）、伊娣絲（Edith）、愛麗絲（Alice）。同年卡若迷上時興的攝影，爲諸多名人照相，也常以女童爲主題，引動後人議論其性向，但也有人指出此爲維多利亞時期風潮。

卡若常帶李德家子女划船出遊，1862年某次出遊，卡若依例隨口編造故事娛人，愛麗絲要求他寫下，兩年後《愛麗絲夢遊仙境》（Alice's Adventures in Wonderland）原型面世，1865年初版，大受歡迎。

卡若文學創作多爲無厘頭地玩弄邏輯，兼帶虐仿知名詩歌：《愛麗絲夢遊仙境》述說小女孩愛麗絲跟隨白兔進入地洞，身軀時大時小，遇見各色人物：露齒而笑但隱身的寨郡貓（Cheshire Cat）、瘋癲的三月兔（March Hare）與帽商（Hatter）、稍拂其意即喝令「拖去砍頭！（Off with his head）」的紙牌紅心女王等，最後醒來彷彿夢境一場。茲選譯其虐仿詩歌三首：

其一：

How doth the little crocodile Improve his shining tail, And pour the waters of the Nile On every golden scale!	小小鱷魚眞了不起 會讓尾巴發光， 將尼羅河水來沖洗 好讓鱗片晶亮！

路易斯‧卡若

How cheerfully he seems to grin,
How neatly spreads his claws,
And welcomes little fishes in
With gently smiling jaws!

彷彿解頤開口似哂，
怡然舒展銳爪，
張嘴歡迎小魚光臨
面帶溫柔微笑！

其二：

"You are old, Father William," the young man said,
"And your hair has become very white;
And yet you incessantly stand on your head—
Do you think, at your age, it is right?"
"In my youth," Father William replied to his son,
"I feared it might injure the brain;
But now that I'm perfectly sure I have none,
Why, I do it again and again."
"You are old," said the youth, "As I mentioned before,
And have grown most uncommonly fat;
Yet you turned a back-somersault in at the door—
Pray, what is the reason of that?"
"In my youth," said the sage, as he shook his grey locks,
"I kept all my limbs very supple
By the use of this ointment—one shilling the box—
Allow me to sell you a couple?"
"You are old," said the youth, "And your jaws are too weak
For anything tougher than suet;
Yet you finished the goose, with the bones and the beak—
Pray, how did you manage to do it?"
"In my youth," said his father, "I took to the law,
And argued each case with my wife;

「你老嘍，威廉老爹，」年輕人提起，
「你頭髮已經變得蒼白；
但你還是一天到晚倒立—
你覺得，對老人，這是否應該？」
「年輕時，」威廉老爹回答兒子，
「我怕倒立會傷大腦；
但現在我確信我根本沒腦子，
所以我倒立越多越好。」
「你老啦，」年輕人說，「我一再提念，
而且你肚腩變得非常大；
但你在門口還來了個後空翻—
請問，你這是在幹啥？」
「年輕時，」睿智老人邊晃腦邊說著，
「我保持所有筋骨鬆弛
靠的是這種藥膏——先令一盒——
你要不要買幾盒試試？」
「你老啦，」年輕人說，「你齒牙鬆頹
應該只能吃肥肉了；
但你吃了整隻鵝，連骨帶喙—
請問，你是怎麼辦到的？」
「年輕時，」他爹說，「我對法律鑽研，
所有案件都跟太太論爭；

And the muscular strength which it gave to my jaw,	由此鍛鍊出強大頸部肌腱,
Has lasted the rest of my life."	讓我終身都受用。」
"You are old," said the youth, "one would hardly suppose	「你老啦,」年輕人說,「大家都知道
That your eye was as steady as ever;	你眼力應該比以前衰退;
Yet you balanced an eel on the end of your nose—	但你竟能將鰻魚在鼻端樹高—
What made you so awfully clever?"	你怎麼會那麼厲害?」
"I have answered three questions, and that is enough,"	「我已經答了三個問題,該夠了吧,」
Said his father; "don't give yourself airs!	他爹說,「可別太過分嘍!
Do you think I can listen all day to such stuff?	你以為我有空整天閒聊嗎?
Be off, or I'll kick you down stairs!"	滾蛋,否則我踢你下樓!」

其三:

Speak roughly to your little boy,	對小孩要粗言相向,
And beat him when he sneezes:	揍他若他打噴嚏:
He only does it to annoy,	打噴嚏是製造麻煩,
Because he knows it teases.	他知道這騷擾你。
Wow! wow! wow!	汪!汪!汪!
I speak severely to my boy,	我對小孩疾言相向,
I beat him when he sneezes;	揍他若他打噴嚏;
For he can thoroughly enjoy	因為他會盡情歡享
The pepper when he pleases!	胡椒粉且隨心所欲!

　　1871年卡若出版《愛麗絲夢遊仙境》續集《愛麗絲鏡中奇遇》(Through the Looking-Glass and What Alice Found There),敘述愛麗絲發現可以穿越鏡子,鏡中世界與此界相反,遇見西洋棋紅白皇后、童謠裡的孿生兄弟吹得噹、吹得嘀

（Tweedledum、Tweedledee）和混弟沌弟（Humpty Dumpty）等。茲選譯卡若自作的無厘頭詩《喳吧娃子》（Jabberwocky），多有創新字：

'Twas brillig, and the slithy toves Did gyre and gimble in the wabe; All mimsy were the borogoves, And the mome raths outgrabe. "Beware the Jabberwock, my son! The jaws that bite, the claws that catch! Beware the Jubjub bird, and shun The frumious Bandersnatch!" He took his vorpal sword in hand: Long time the manxome foe he sought— So rested he by the Tumtum tree, And stood awhile in thought. And as in uffish thought he stood, The Jabberwock, with eyes of flame, Came whiffling through the tulgey wood, And burbled as it came! One, two! One, two! and through and through The vorpal blade went snicker-snack! He left it dead, and with its head He went galumphing back. "And hast thou slain the Jabberwock? Come to my arms, my beamish boy! O frabjous day! Callooh! Callay!" He chortled in his joy.	時當焙晚，滑溜蚚鉈 又轉又鑽在蓉坡裡； 破裸鴿可憐且單薄， 喪家冄鼠嘶鳴嚎啼。 「小心喳吧娃子，兒啊！ 牠下顎咬，牠爪子攫！ 小心揪揪鳥，避開那 憤怒瘋狂的邦頭掠！」 他將佛菩劍拿在手： 經久尋找雄壯仇敵— 他在敦敦樹旁休息， 陷入沉思佇立於彼。 當他情緒惡憤佇立， 喳吧娃子目光如炬， 穿越沌密暗林飛抵， 嘴裡啵噥鳴噓！ 二！一，二！刺了再刺 佛菩劍勢犀利嘩啦！ 他殺了牠，砍下腦袋 凱旋而歸光榮駕馬。 「你殺了喳吧娃子嗎？ 讓我抱抱，迸芒小子！ 噢 福極時辰！凱囉！凱咧！」 他扯呵樂滋滋。

卡若1863年疏遠與李德家之關係，原因可能是與李德家女性或家庭老師過從太密。1874年寫了無厘頭詩《搜獵熾老鴞》（The Hunting of the Snark），述說9個不同行業的人和一隻海狸去搜獵怪物熾老鴞。1889年寫就小說《蒔薇與布魯諾》（Sylvie and Bruno）將仙境與英國鄉間做對比，茲選譯其中詩作《瘋狂園丁之歌》（The Mad Gardener's Song）：

路易斯‧卡若

He thought he saw an Elephant,	他以爲見到隻大象，
That practised on a fife:	在練習吹橫笛：
He looked again, and found it was	再看一眼，發覺那是
A letter from his wife.	太太來信手筆。
'At length I realise,' he said,	「我終於明白了，」他說，
'The bitterness of Life!'	「生命的苦淒！」
He thought he saw a Buffalo	他以爲見到隻水牛，
Upon the chimney-piece:	佇立煙囱之頂：
He looked again, and found it was	再看一眼，發覺那是
His Sister's Husband's Niece.	姐夫的女外甥。
'Unless you leave this house,' he said,	「你如果不出去，」他說，
'I'll send for the Police!'	「我就要叫員警！」
He thought he saw a Rattlesnake	他以爲見到響尾蛇
That questioned him in Greek:	以希臘語質疑：
He looked again, and found it was	再看一眼，發覺那是
The Middle of Next Week.	下週三四之際。
'The one thing I regret,' he said,	「惟一可惜的是，」他說，
'Is that it cannot speak!'	「它不會做人語！」
He thought he saw a Banker's Clerk	他以爲見到出納員，
Descending from the bus:	從公車正走下：
He looked again, and found it was	再看一眼，發覺那是
A Hippopotamus.	一隻胖大河馬。
'If this should stay to dine,' he said,	「如果牠來吃飯，」他說，
'There won't be much for us!'	「我們要餓肚啦！」
He thought he saw a Kangaroo	他以爲見到隻袋鼠，
That worked a coffee-mill:	在咖啡磨坊上班：
He looked again, and found it was	再看一眼，發覺那是
A Vegetable-Pill.	一粒蔬菜藥丸。
'Were I to swallow this,' he said,	「如果吞下這個，」他說，
'I should be very ill!'	「我會大病一場！」
He thought he saw a Coach-and-Four	他以爲見到輛馬車，

That stood beside his bed:	在他床邊駐止：
He looked again, and found it was	再看一眼，發覺那是
A Bear without a Head.	隻無頭黑瞎子。
'Poor thing,' he said, 'poor silly thing!	「可憐，」他說，「可憐傢伙！
It's waiting to be fed!'	在等人餵飯吃！」
He thought he saw an Albatross	他以爲見到信天翁，
That fluttered round the lamp:	圍繞檯燈飛馳：
He looked again, and found it was	再看一眼，發覺那是
A Penny-Postage Stamp.	一分錢的郵紙。
'You'd best be getting home,' he said:	「你該趕快回家，」他說，
'The nights are very damp!'	「夜晚很是潮濕！」
He thought he saw a Garden-Door	他以爲見到花園門，
That opened with a key:	有鑰匙可以開：
He looked again, and found it was	再看一眼，發覺那是
A Double Rule of Three:	雙重三數定理。
'And all its mystery,' he said,	「它的一切祕密，」他說，
'Is clear as day to me!'	「我都完全明晰！」
He thought he saw a Argument	他以爲見到一則推論，
That proved he was the Pope:	證明他是教皇：
He looked again, and found it was	再看一眼，發覺那是
A Bar of Mottled Soap.	一塊肥皂帶斑。
'A fact so dread,' he faintly said,	「太可怕了，」他輕吐說，
'Extinguishes all hope!'	「一切希望滅亡！」

卡若1898年病逝。他以荒謬邏輯寫詩寫小說，爲英語新造許多辭彙，獨創異趣，老少咸宜。

圖片來源：IDJ圖庫

1-30

狄更斯

Charles Dickens

狄更斯
Charles Dickens

狄更斯（Charles Dickens）1812年生於英格蘭南端，父親是海軍小職員，狄更斯自幼廣泛閱讀，12歲時父親因欠債入獄，狄更斯被迫寄宿友人家，輟學於鞋蠟工廠打工，此經歷使他日後投身社會改革。數月後狄更斯曾祖母過世，留下小筆遺產，父親得以出獄，母親卻要狄更斯繼續打工，又迭經數月狄更斯才復學入讀私人學堂，老師嚴苛、教學散漫。

1827年狄更斯15歲，任律師事務所小職員，善模仿，迷戀戲劇，自學速記，次年轉職記者，其後4年在法院旁聽、報導，1832年開始報導國會議事。1833年小說首次在雜誌刊登，1835年應《晨紀事報》（Morning Chronicle）樂評侯高思（Hogarth）之邀定期爲該報撰文，1836年結集以筆名波西出版《波西素描集》（Sketches by Boz），頗受歡迎，繼之應邀爲月刊漫畫搭配文章，描述倫敦士紳匹克威克與友人在鄉間遊歷之趣事，大爲暢銷，1836年結集出版爲《匹克威克外傳》（The Pickwick Papers）。同年狄更斯24歲，婚娶侯高思長女凱瑟琳，共育有十子女。婚後凱瑟琳小妹瑪麗遷入同住，數月後病逝，狄更斯哀痛逾恆，日後數度以之爲典範塑造小說主角。

1838年狄更斯出版《孤雛淚》（Oliver Twist），以孩童爲主角，開維多利亞時期先例，茲選譯主角奧利佛在孤兒院要求添粥一段：

The evening arrived; the boys took their places. The master, in his cook's uniform, stationed himself at the copper; his pauper assistants ranged themselves behind him; the gruel was served out; and a long grace was said over the short commons. The gruel disappeared; the boys whispered each other, and winked at Oliver; while his next neighbours nudged him. Child as he was, he was desperate with hunger, and reckless with misery. He rose from the table; and advancing to the master, basin and	時屆傍晚；眾男童就位。院長著廚師裝，站在大鐵鍋前；助理們排列身後；粥分好，長長的感恩禱迴響於短短的大廳裡。粥頃刻見底；眾男童交接耳語，對奧利佛眨眼；他身旁的人暗推他。小小年紀的他饑餓至極，不顧一切。他站起身，走向院長，手拿碗匙，對自己的膽子也有點驚訝，

spoon in hand, said: somewhat alarmed at his own te-merity: "Please, sir, I want some more." The master was a fat, healthy man; but he turned very pale.

He gazed in stupified astonishment on the small rebel for some seconds, and then clung for support to the copper. The assistants were paralysed with wonder; the boys with fear. "What!" said the master at length, in a faint voice. "Please, sir," replied Oliver, "I want some more."

說道：「求求你，大人，我還想要。」院長胖胖的，身體健壯；但此刻面色轉青白。

他震驚地看著眼前的小逆賊，幾秒鐘都說不出話來，接著抓住鐵鍋以免暈倒。助理們驚呆了；眾男童則嚇呆了。「你說什麼！」院長終於輕聲吐出。「求求你，大人，」奧利佛回答：「我還想要。」

　　1843年狄更斯為關懷弱勢，寫就《聖誕歌聲》（A Christmas Carol），敘述守財奴史古基（Scrooge）受訪於幽靈而成為善人，為有史以來最受歡迎之聖誕故事，書中用語「聖誕快樂」（Merry Christmas）廣被襲用，聖誕也因此由宗教節日漸轉為家庭節日。

　　1846年狄更斯應銀行業富家女庫慈（Angela Burdett Coutts）之請，在倫敦主辦妓女收容教養所，13年間協助約百名妓女婚嫁、移民。1850年狄更斯寫就《塊肉餘生記》（David Copperfield），具自傳性質，他自承最喜此作。1854年寫就《苦日子》（Hard Times）描述下層工人階級生活。約此時狄更斯再度沉迷劇場，自寫自演，1857年狄更斯45歲，愛上18歲女演員愛倫‧特能（Ellen Ternan），1858年與妻分居。同年為支助慈善醫院而朗讀作品，聲調入戲，所獲甚豐。此後10年主要以巡迴朗讀作品維生。

　　1859年狄更斯寫就《雙城記》（A Tale of Two Cities），以法國大革命為背景，首句膾炙人口：

狄更斯

It was the best of times, it was the worst of times, it was the age of wisdom, it was the age of foolishness, it was the epoch of belief, it was the epoch of incredulity, it was the season of Light, it was the season of Darkness, it was the spring of hope, it was the winter of despair, we had everything before us, we had nothing before us, we were all going direct to Heaven, we were all going direct the other way - in short, the period was so far like the present period, that some of its noisiest authorities insisted on its being received, for good or for evil, in the superlative degree of comparison only.

那是最好的時代，也是最壞的時代，是睿智的時代，也是愚蠢的時代，是信仰的時代，也是難以置信的時代，是光明的時代，也是黑暗的時代，是帶來希望的春天，也是令人絕望的冬天，我們前景無窮，我們前途無望，我們將直上天堂，我們將直下地獄─簡言之，當時與今日如此相似，以致對其最善鼓噪發聲者堅持，或好或壞，對此時代只能以極端形容之。

　　1861年狄更斯寫就《遠大前程》（Great Expectations），兩書皆暢銷。1867-68年赴美朗讀。1870年中風去世，葬於西敏寺。

　　狄更斯是英國維多利亞時期最著名小說家，書作等身，生活面廣，接觸的人、事多寫入小說，善於漫畫式描繪人物，創造了耳熟能詳的角色：《聖誕歌聲》裡為富不仁的史古基、可憐的殘障小孩小提姆（Tiny Tim）、《孤雛淚》裡的孤兒奧利佛（Oliver Twist）、小扒手「妙手空空」（The Artful Dodger）、扒手頭兒費根（Fagin）、流氓塞克斯（Bill Sikes）、《遠大前程》裡憤世的哈維善老小姐（Miss Havisham）、《塊肉餘生記》裡好心但天真的麥考伯先生（Mr. Micawber）、邪惡的尤賴爾·希普（Uriah Heep）、《匹克威克外傳》裡不諳世事卻執意遊歷的士紳匹克威克（Samuel Pickwick）等。狄更斯以週刊、月刊連載寫作，用低廉售價開拓下層社會讀者，作品內容揭露下層生活真象，推動英國工業革命後社會改革。

圖片來源：IDJ圖庫

1-31

王爾德
Oscar Wilde

王爾德
Oscar Wilde

　　王爾德（Oscar Wilde）1854年生於愛爾蘭都柏林（Dublin）英裔家庭，父親是醫生，母親是詩人。幼年隨家庭老師習德、法語。1871-74年入都柏林三一學院主修希臘、羅馬文學。成績優異，1874年獲獎學金入牛津大學茉德蓮學院（Magdalen College），受文藝評論家佩特（Walter Pater）與羅斯金（John Ruskin）影響，主張唯美主義（aestheticism），認爲藝術至上、美即是善，並投身相關的頹廢時尚（decadent movement），誇張修飾打扮，1878年獲學士學位。1882-83年王爾德赴美巡迴演講。1884年婚娶法官之女康絲疊（Constance Lloyd），育有兩子。1886年左右受當時17歲、日後的文評家洛思（Robert Ross）引誘轉爲同性戀。1887-89年出任《婦女世界》（The Lady's World）雜誌編輯。1888年出版童話故事《快樂王子及其他》（The Happy Prince and Other Tales）。1890年出版小說《葛雷的畫像》（The Picture of Dorian Gray），敘述葛雷年輕時請人作畫，祈願永保青春，讓畫像代他衰醜，葛雷隨性一生，死前割裂畫像，本人恢復老態而亡。

　　1891年王爾德結識牛津大學學生道格拉斯（Alfred Douglas），兩人熱戀，並經由道格拉斯幽會下層社會男妓。同年在巴黎以法文根據聖經故事寫就劇本《莎樂美》（Salome）。接著寫作一系列喜劇，諷刺維多利亞社會假正經，包括1892年《溫夫人的扇子》（Lady Windermere's Fan）、1893年《無足輕重的女人》（A Woman of No Importance）、1894年《理想丈夫》（An Ideal Husband）與《非正經不可》（The Importance of Being Earnest），後者爲其代表作，大受歡迎，敘述居住倫敦的年輕貴族阿傑農（Algernon）謊稱有友人班伯里（Bunbury）住鄉下，阿傑農每要避離倫敦就藉口班伯里生病要探訪。阿傑農至交恩斯特（Ernest Worthing，恩斯特雙關語義爲「正經」）住鄉間，某次來訪阿傑農，不慎遺留香菸匣，上刻：「給親愛的傑克叔叔，愛你的西希莉（Cecily）」。恩斯特承認在鄉間自稱約翰（亦稱傑克），謊稱在倫敦有常需照顧的兄弟恩斯特，鄉間有18歲少女西希莉受傑克照顧，是他已逝繼父的孫女。傑克進倫敦即以恩斯特名義花天酒地。傑克想娶阿傑農表妹莧德琳（Gwendolen），但莧德琳只喜歡取名恩斯特者，而且莧德琳母親布萊納夫人（Lady Bracknell）反對，因爲傑克是火車站撿獲的棄嬰。阿傑農爲見西希莉而拜訪傑克，宣稱自己是傑克倫敦友人恩斯特。西希莉一向聽說恩斯特是壞男人，因此著迷。傑克原想改邪歸正，打算宣佈恩斯特

病死巴黎,不料阿傑農(恩斯特)來訪。西希莉也喜歡恩斯特這個名字,因此阿傑農與傑克都要查士博牧師(Dr. Chasuble)幫他們改名恩斯特。莨德琳來找傑克,西希莉與莨德琳都堅持是恩斯特的未婚妻,傑克與阿傑農謊言遂被拆穿。布萊納夫人追尋女兒而來,覺得西希莉不配其外甥阿傑農,傑克也反對西希莉嫁給窮小子阿傑農,並以此脅迫布萊納夫人同意他娶莨德琳。布萊納夫人認出西希莉保姆普里沐小姐(Miss Prism)是以前家中保姆,28年前帶著布萊納夫人另一外甥失蹤。普里沐小姐說她當年誤將嬰兒留置火車站,原來傑克是阿傑農哥哥,本名就是恩斯特。傑克/莨德琳、阿傑農/西希莉、查士博/普里沐三對戀人歡聚,布萊納夫人責備傑克言行輕佻,傑克回應:「我此刻才發現非正經(恩斯特)不可。」

1895年道格拉斯父親昆斯伯里侯爵(Marquess of Queensbury)公開辱指王爾德同性戀,王爾德控告侯爵誹謗,反遭定嚴重猥褻罪,判苦役兩年(1895-97年),並因訴訟宣告破產。王爾德在獄中反思人生,寫就致道格拉斯的長信《出自深處》(De Profundis)。出獄後王爾德隨即赴法,1897年寫就《瑞丁監獄歌謠》(The Ballad of Reading Gaol),敘述獄中故事。同年與道格拉斯重聚,但未久為雙方家人分離。康絲曇也不讓王爾德與自己或兒子見面。

王爾德1900年困居巴黎小旅館,但不忘玩世,曾就醜陋的房間說:「壁紙和我正在生死一搏,不是它死,就是我亡。(My wallpaper and I are fighting a duel to the death. One of us has got to go)」不久病逝,葬於巴黎。

王爾德自承「天賦用於生活,僅以才能寫作(I put all my genius into my life; I put only my talent into my works)」,是維多利亞晚期唯美主義作家,劇本諷世,多有警句名言,如:

「自由若是雙手沾血而來,我們也難與之握手。(When liberty comes with hands dabbled in blood it is hard to shake hands with her)」

王爾德

「男人可與任何女人幸福過日，只要他不愛她。（A man can be happy with any woman as long as he does not love her）」

「一個人再多錢也買不回做過的事。（No man is rich enough to buy back his past）」

「上帝創造女人是為讓人疼愛，而非理解。（Women are made to be loved, not understood）」

「男人都想做女人的初戀—女人都想做男人的終戀。（Men always want to be a woman's first love-women like to be a man's last romance）」

圖片來源：IDJ圖庫

1-32

蕭伯納

George Bernard Shaw

　　蕭伯納（George Bernard Shaw）1856年生於愛爾蘭都柏林英裔家庭，父親是清貧的公務員，母親是音樂老師。幼年讀過多間學校，厭惡學校教學，1871年父母分居，母親遷至倫敦，蕭伯納任地產公司職員，1876年遷往倫敦依母，1879-83年在大英圖書館廣泛閱讀，立志寫作，寫就多本小說，未能出版，靠父母接濟生活。蕭伯納此時投身社會主義政壇，1884年參加主張漸進社會改革的費邊社（Fabian Society）。1880年代後期，為報章撰寫音樂評論，推崇華格納，經濟得以自立；為《週六評論》（Saturday Review）撰寫戲劇評論，引介挪威劇作家易卜生（Henrik Ibsen）社會寫實概念，名利雙收。1881年開始食素。

　　蕭伯納劇作多為推廣其社會主義概念，劇本前皆有長篇引言，1892年第一齣劇本《鰥夫的房產》（Widowers' Houses）上演，抨擊貧民窟房東。1893年寫就《華倫夫人的職業》（Mrs. Warren's Profession），聲張女權，敘述薇薇（Vivie Warren）剛由劍橋大學畢業，不知其母華倫夫人經營妓院維生，薇薇男友父親曾與華倫夫人有染，可能是薇薇父親，華倫夫人向女兒解釋她賣淫是為撫養薇薇，薇薇最初讚揚母親，但因母親不願放棄經營而斷絕母女關係，華倫夫人天倫夢碎；此劇至1925年才獲准上演。茲選譯一段：

People are always blaming their circumstances for what they are. I don't believe in circumstances. The people who get on in this world are the people who get up and look for the circumstances they want, and if they can't find them, make them.	人們總是將其現況歸罪於環境。我不相信環境的力量。世上能夠前進的人都能尋找自己需要的環境，要是找不到就自己創造。

　　因之前劇本賣座不多，1894年蕭伯納寫就喜劇《武器與人》（Arms and the Man），嘲諷戰爭。

1895年蕭伯納協助創辦具社會主義理想的倫敦政治經濟學院（London School of Economics and Political Science）。1898年寫就《凱撒與克柳姵婷》（Caesar and Cleopatra）。同年婚娶富家女、女權運動者夏洛蒂（Charlotte Payne-Townshend）。1900年協助創立工黨（Labor Party）。

1903年蕭伯納寫就《人與超人》（Man and Superman），敘述一對男女之戀情，借由尼采的超人理論（主張人類會演化成超人）表達蕭伯納自己的生命力（Life Force）理論，認為女性主導有目的之演化；1905年寫就《芭芭拉少校》（Major Barbara），敘述基督教救世軍（Salvation Army）少校芭芭拉與分居多年的軍火鉅子父親重逢，父親捐款給救世軍，芭芭拉因其來自軍火拒絕，但救世軍上司接受，芭芭拉對救世軍幻滅，參觀父親工廠後，決定與其救濟窮人對之傳教，不如對有錢人傳教更能有效救世。中有一句：「他一無所知，卻自以為無所不知。顯然適合從政。（He knows nothing; and he thinks he knows everything. That points clearly to a political career.）」

1912年蕭伯納寫就《畢馬龍》（Pygmalion），根據希臘神話裡雕刻家畢馬龍愛上自己的雕像的故事，敘述語言學家希金斯（Henry Higgins）與友人打賭，訓練倫敦貧民窟賣花女伊萊莎（Eliza Doolittle），將其下層考克尼（Cockney）口音轉為上流口音，使人誤認其為貴族，伊萊莎成功轉換形象，但希金斯仍視其為無足輕重的女性，兩人生隙；此劇1956年改為百老匯音樂劇《窈窕淑女》（My Fair Lady），1964年拍成同名電影，三者皆廣受歡迎。

1914年蕭伯納撰文反對一次大戰，政治主張由民主漸進改革轉為強人領導，但二次大戰後此想法也幻滅。

1920年蕭伯納寫就《回到瑪土撒拉》（Back To Methuselah，瑪土撒拉為聖經裡的古人，享壽969年）鼓吹人需活300歲才有足夠經驗治理現代社會，中有一句：「你見到某事某物，問：『為何？』我夢想到不曾存在的事物，問：『有何不可？』（You see things; and you say, "Why?" But I dream things that never were; and I say, "Why not?"）」1923年寫就《聖女貞德》（Saint Joan），認為15世紀英法交戰雙方都依據信仰行事，

造成貞德之死是難以避免的悲劇。

1925年蕭伯納獲諾貝爾文學獎，此後仍不斷寫作。1931年訪問蘇聯，盛讚其制度。

1950年去世。

蕭伯納是20世紀初諷刺喜劇作家，以幽默口吻書寫諷刺題材，宣揚社會改革理念。另舉數例蕭伯納趣言：

「英美兩國因同一語言而分隔。（England and America are two countries divided by a common language.）」

「任何人20歲時不信共產主義必是笨蛋。任何人30歲還信共產主義必是超級笨蛋。（Any man who is not a communist at the age of twenty is a fool. Any man who is still a communist at the age of thirty is an even bigger fool.）」

「能者，行之。不能者，以之教人。（He who can, does. He who cannot, teaches.）」

「缺錢乃萬惡之源。（Lack of money is the root of all evil.）」

「她失去了談天之藝術，不幸的是，沒失去說話的能力。（She had lost the art of conversation, but not, unfortunately, the power of speech.）」

1-33

哈地

Thomas Hardy

　　哈地（Thomas Hardy）1840年生於英格蘭西南，父親是石匠，以造房爲生，哈地幼年由知書的母親教育，8歲入學，16歲爲建築師學徒，1862年遷居倫敦，入讀倫敦大學國王學院（King's College London）主修建築，對社會主義產生興趣，1867年遷返老家，決心寫作，1874年結婚，同年寫就《遠離塵囂》（Far from the Madding Crowd），敘述牧羊人蓋布里（Gabriel Oak）向美麗驕傲的芭絮芭（Bathsheba Everdene）求婚不成，芭絮芭經其他感情磨難，最終與蓋布里成眷屬。此書與哈地其他小說多以英格蘭西南的西撒克遜地區（Wessex）爲背景。書出大賣，哈地得以專心寫作。

　　1878年哈地寫就《還鄉》（The Return of the Native），以古典悲劇形式敘述三男兩女感情糾葛：想返鄉教書的柯林（Clym）娶了想到城市居住的優妲霞（Eustacia），愛上優妲霞的戴蒙（Damon）娶了湯瑪莘（Thomasin），導致一連串不幸。

　　1885年寫就《卡德橋市長》（The Mayor of Casterbridge），敘述兩對男女之經歷：農夫亨徹（Michael Henchard）醉酒將妻、女伊麗莎白—珍（Elizabeth-Jane）賣掉，醒後發誓21年不沾酒，18年後亨徹事業成功成爲市長，提拔年輕人法費里（Donald Farfrae），並與少女呂瑟（Lucette）有染。亨徹妻女返來。法費里與伊麗莎白—珍相戀，事業蒸蒸日上。亨徹事業沒落，並發覺伊麗莎白—珍是其妻後來所生同名女，非其親生，再次酗酒。呂瑟來尋，與法費里相戀但病逝。亨徹醜聞揭發、破產病逝，法費里與伊麗莎白—珍結婚。

　　1891年寫就《德博家的苔絲》（Tess of the d'Urbervilles，又譯《黛絲姑娘》），敘述農家女苔絲被富家子亞列克（Alec d'Urberville）強姦，之後與安傑（Angel Clare）結婚，安傑獲知前情後出走巴西，苔絲爲養家成爲亞列克情婦，安傑返來欲重圓，苔絲殺死亞列克，與安傑逃亡至巨石陣（Stonehenge）被捕，苔絲被處死。論者解讀苔絲象徵大自然，與現代社會不相容。

　　1895年寫就《無名者裘德》（Jude the Obscure），敘述石匠出身的裘德（Jude Fawley）想進大學成爲學者，但被膚淺女子雅拉蓓拉（Arabella Donn）誘騙成婚，不

諧分手，雅拉蓓拉移居澳洲，裘德與表親秀（Sue Bridehead）相戀，但秀與裘德老師費利臣（Phillotson）結婚，秀發覺自己厭惡婚姻與性愛，返回裘德身邊，雅拉蓓拉返來，告知裘德與她有一子，個性嚴肅陰鬱似老人家，綽號「歲月小老爺」（Little Father Time）。秀與裘德產下二子女，但未結婚而處處受逐，「歲月小老爺」覺得起因於父母所生子女，遂殺死另兩人並自殺，留有字條說：「因為我們人太多了。（Done because we are too menny）」秀認為上帝因她離開費利臣而懲罰她，遂與費利臣再婚，裘德也在雅拉蓓拉算計下與之再婚，不久病死。此書批評維多利亞時期英國教育、宗教、婚姻，書出被指不道德。此後哈地專注作詩。茲選譯書中一段：

People go on marrying because they can't resist natural forces, although many of them may know perfectly well that they are possibly buying a month's pleasure with a life's discomfort.	人們結婚是因為無法抗拒天生慾望，儘管很多人清楚這是以一生的不快換取一個月的歡樂。

　　1898年哈地出版首冊詩集，1902年作反戰詩《他所殺的人》（The Man He Killed）：

Had he and I but met By some old ancient inn, We should have sat us down to wet Right many a nipperkin! But ranged as infantry, And staring face to face, I shot at him as he at me,	若他與我相遇 於某古老酒館， 我們當會同坐將杯舉 共飲甘醇若干盞！ 但置身於步兵， 又面對面對立， 我們彼此開槍互拼，

And killed him in his place.	我將他當場擊斃。
I shot him dead because —	我殺他的原因—
Because he was my foe,	因為他是敵人，
Just so: my foe of course he was;	就這樣，他當然是敵人；
That's clear enough; although	這很明白；雖然
He thought he'd 'list, perhaps,	他當初參軍，或許是，
Off-hand like — just as I —	隨意之舉—與我相同—
Was out of work — had sold his traps —	因為失業—賣了家什—
No other reason why.	沒別的原因。
Yes; quaint and curious war is!	沒錯；戰爭是很奇特！
You shoot a fellow down	你槍殺的老兄
You'd treat if met where any bar is,	若在酒館相遇你會請客，
Or help to half-a-crown.	或是借他點零用。

　　哈地婚姻後期不諧，妻子1912年去世。1914年哈地74歲，婚娶35歲的秘書，同年出版《呼聲》（The Voice）追憶前妻：

Woman much missed, how you call to me, call to me,	我牽念的女人，如此對我呼喚，呼喚，
Saying that now you are not as you were	說你如今已不同於以前
When you had changed from the one who was all to me,	那時你變了，不再是我的全然，
But as at first, when our day was fair.	如今你回歸我們最初樂園。
Can it be you that I hear? Let me view you, then,	是你在喚我嗎？那現身讓我一窺，
Standing as when I drew near to the town	就像當初我進城的時分
Where you would wait for me: yes, as I knew you then,	你在那兒等我，是，正如當初的你，
Even to the original air-blue gown!	穿的也須是當初的天青裙！
Or is it only the breeze, in its listlessness	或許這只是風聲，懨懨地
Travelling across the wet mead to me here,	吹拂過濕原來到我這裡，

You being ever dissolved to wan wistlessness,	而你仍永恆消逝於蒼白憂鬱，
Heard no more again far or near?	無論遠近皆無消息？
Thus I; faltering forward,	如此我，蹣跚前行，
Leaves around me falling,	環身樹葉殞落，
Wind oozing thin through the thorn from norward,	風由北方稀滯穿過棘荊，
And the woman calling.	那女人在喚我。

　　1928年哈地去世。遵其遺囑將他的心臟與第一任妻子同葬，但骨灰則葬於西敏寺詩人角。

　　哈地以寫實手法批評維多利亞時期英國社會對人性束縛造成悲劇，描寫鄉村沒落，詩作今日評價甚高。

圖片來源：維基共享資源

1-34

康拉德
Joseph Conrad

康拉德（Joseph Conrad）本名約瑟夫・寇曾紐斯基（Józef Teodor Konrad Korzeniowski），1857年生於烏克蘭（Ukraine）北方波蘭裔貴族家庭，當時地屬俄國（波蘭1795年被俄、普魯士、奧地利瓜分），父親是作家、抗俄人士，1861年因反俄被囚，次年全家放逐莫斯科北方，1863年獲赦返回烏克蘭。1865年母親病逝。康拉德幼年在家閱讀受教，習法文。1867年全家遷至奧屬波蘭，父親1869年病逝。康拉德由舅舅照顧，課業、身心兩差，舅舅計劃讓他由水手進而成為商人，康拉德自己也想出海，1874年赴法國馬賽（Marseilles）開始跑船去加勒比海，1878年被發現未獲俄國批准被迫下船，同年欠債自殺未遂，轉赴英國發展，已20出頭才學英文，跑船赴澳洲、東南亞、南亞，逐步升至船長。

　　1886年康拉德入籍英國，1889年赴非洲剛果河（Congo）流域接出生病的白人商人，日後據以寫就《黑暗之心》（Heart of Darkness）。1894年結束跑船生涯，專注寫作，次年出版首部小說《奧邁爾的荒誕》（Almayer's Folly），初次使用筆名「康拉德」，敘述荷蘭商人奧邁爾於婆羅洲之事；英文生硬帶波蘭味。讀者頗好其異國情調。由此至1913年為康拉德創作第一期，其名作多成於此時，包括《「水仙」號上的黑仔》（Nigger of the 'Narcissus'）、《黑暗之心》、《吉姆大人》（Lord Jim）、《諾斯托莫》（Nostromo，意大利文nostro uomo縮寫，意為「我們的人」）、《間諜》（The Secret Agent）、《在西方俯視下》（Under Western Eyes）。

　　1896年康拉德婚娶小他16歲的英國藍領階層女子婕西（Jessie George）。

　　《「水仙」號上的黑仔》1897年出版，敘述來自西印度群島的黑人水手在印度開往英國的船上生病，船上同伴試圖救他之事；探討同情心與責任之矛盾。

　　《黑暗之心》1899年出版，英國船長馬洛（Charles Marlow）敘述他去中非溯河而上，接返生病的公司駐地大員庫茨（Kurtz），庫茨原先教養好，受重用，但在非洲日久性格大變，土人與船員開戰，庫茨病死於回程途中，馬洛回英探訪庫茨未婚妻，謊稱馬洛臨終呼喚她的名字。茲選譯兩段，一為馬洛沿河而上時觀察岸邊土人：

康拉德

| It was unearthly, and the men were—No, they were not inhuman. Well, you know, that was the worst of it—the suspicion of their not being inhuman. It would come slowly to one. They howled and leaped, and spun, and made horrid faces; but what thrilled you was just the thought of their humanity—like yours—the thought of your remote kinship with this wild and passionate uproar. Ugly. Yes, it was ugly enough; but if you were man enough you would admit to yourself that there was in you just the faintest trace of a response to the terrible frankness of that noise, a dim suspicion of there being a meaning in it which you—you so remote from the night of first ages—could comprehend. And why not? | 那景象不屬人世，那些人—不，不能說他們不是人。哦，你知道，最糟的是—你覺得不能說他們不是人。我慢慢才察覺此點。他們嗷叫、騰跳、翻滾、表情可怖；但撼人的正是想到他們是人—和你一樣—想到你和這野蠻激狂遙遙相繫。醜惡。沒錯，是很醜惡；但你如果夠勇敢，你會承認自身對那可怖的本性嗷叫有幾乎無法察覺的呼應，有你—雖然你距離原初暗夜如此遙遠—能夠辨識的意義。反思之，你不是本該有反應嗎？ |

一爲庫茨臨終時：

| He cried in a whisper at some image, at some vision--he cried out twice, a cry that was no more than a breath: "The horror! The horror!" | 他對著某個意想、某個景象低聲喊道—連續兩次，喊聲輕如氣息：「恐怖！恐怖！」 |

　　《吉姆大人》1900年出版，敘述英國船員吉姆於船難時棄職潛逃，因羞愧躲避馬來群島，成爲當地領袖，人稱「大人」。土匪擊斃酋長兒子，吉姆自願犧牲讓酋長息怒，以贖前愆。《諾斯托莫》1904年出版，敘述忠誠的諾斯托莫在南美動蕩的政局中被政治與金錢腐化，探討殖民現象。《間諜》1907年出版，敘述某國間諜在倫敦開書店，爲錢於格林威治村放炸彈，誤炸了智障的小舅子，因而被妻子殺死。

1910年康拉德獲賜英國政府年金100鎊，經濟始稍穩定。

《在西方俯視下》1911年出版，敘述在日內瓦念書的俄國學生拉朱莫夫（Razumov）出賣其革命派俄國同窗哈丁（Haldin），之後因愛上哈丁姊妹而招供，最終傷殘返俄。

康拉德寫作第二期1913至18年，作品開始受大眾青睞。1914年曾返波蘭探訪。第三期由1918至1924年去世，作品與心靈趨於平靜。

康拉德因家世背景，對政治有超越時人的體悟，將此體悟透過海洋、殖民地、反面英雄（anti-hero），以詩意語言寫入小說，描寫人痛苦自覺，生存於漠然的世界，勉強以忠誠對抗。人謂其小說預示了20世紀世局走向。

1-35

葉慈

葉慈（W.B. Yeats）1865年生於愛爾蘭都柏林新教家庭，父親是英裔愛爾蘭人，由律師轉而習畫，母親爲愛爾蘭西北思立勾（Sligo）地區富商家女。葉慈出生不久舉家遷往思立勾，他視之爲家鄉。葉慈自小喜好愛爾蘭民間傳說，對靈異現象深感興趣。1867年家人隨父親工作遷居英格蘭，葉慈於彼接觸印度哲學，1880年返回都柏林，1883年決定獻身寫詩，1884-86年就讀大都會藝術學院（Metropolitan School of Art），詩作最早刊於1885年《都柏林大學評論》（Dublin University Review），早期詩作景緻豐茂，1888年賦詩《湖島茵尼斯》（The Lake Isle of Innisfree）述故鄉之思：

I will arise and go now, and go to Innisfree,	我現將起身出發，去茵尼斯湖島，
And a small cabin build there, of clay and wattles made;	在那裡建造小屋，用泥土和荊叢；
Nine bean rows will I have there, a hive for the honey bee,	我將有九隴豆子，和蜜蜂住的蜂巢，
And live alone in the bee loud glade.	獨居嗡嗡蜂鳴林原中。
And I shall have some peace there, for peace comes dropping slow,	在彼我將安寧，因爲安寧總緩臨，
Dropping from the veils of the morning to where the cricket sings;	從那朝霧緩緩降臨到蟋蟀歌唱之處；
There midnight's all a glimmer, and noon a purple glow,	午夜穹蒼光朦朧，天色泛紫日中，
And evening full of the linnet's wings.	傍晚滿空紅雀飛舞。
I will arise and go now, for always night and day	我現將起身出發，因爲晝夜昏曉
I hear lake water lapping with low sounds by the shore;	我總是聽見水波柔聲緩拍湖岸；
While I stand on the roadway, or on the pavements grey,	無論我立身路中，或在灰色行道，
I hear it in the deep heart's core.	我心至深處總聽見。

　　1889年葉慈出版詩集《歐伊辛漫遊記及餘詩》（The Wanderings of Oisin and Other Poems），典涉愛爾蘭神話。同年葉慈愛上23歲、投身愛爾蘭建國運動的英格蘭演員莫德・耿（Maud Gonne），1891年求婚被拒，1899年、1900年、1901年陸續遭拒。1892年葉慈改寫法國16世紀詩人洪薩（Ronsard）詩作《當你老去》（Quand Vous Serez Bien Vieille/When You Are Old），暗喻莫德：

葉慈

When you are old and grey and full of sleep,	當你老去、髮白、昏昏欲睡，
And nodding by the fire, take down this book,	在爐邊打盹，請取下此書，
And slowly read, and dream of the soft look	緩緩閱讀，遙想你當年有
Your eyes had once, and of their shadows deep;	的溫柔眼神，和目光深遠；
How many loved your moments of glad grace,	多少人醉戀你年輕歡愉，
And loved your beauty with love false or true,	醉戀你美貌，以假或真情，
But one man loved the pilgrim Soul in you,	獨有一人愛你虔敬心靈，
And loved the sorrows of your changing face;	愛你變幻臉容所顯憂鬱；
And bending down beside the glowing bars,	你在火紅的木柴旁俯身，
Murmur, a little sadly, how Love fled	輕嘆囁語愛情如何消逝
And paced upon the mountains overhead	如何徘徊於頭頂山峰間
And hid his face amid a crowd of stars.	遮掩其面目於眾多星辰。

　　1896年葉慈結識辛（J. M. Synge）、歐給希（Seán O'Casey）等愛爾蘭文人，推動愛爾蘭文藝復興運動。1899年葉慈協助創立愛爾蘭文學劇院（Irish Literary Theatre），旨在演出本土劇本，1901年倒閉，1904年演變爲愛爾蘭國家劇院（又名艾比劇院Abbey Theatre，因位於修院街Abbey street，音譯艾比），葉慈終身爲其寫作劇本。

　　1900年左右葉慈詩作進入第二期，以自身經驗爲社會寫實。莫德1903年嫁給愛爾蘭民族主義者麥布萊上尉（John MacBride），改信天主教，葉慈深受打擊，賦詩《無特洛伊第二》（No Second Troy）：

Why should I blame her that she filled my days	我何必怪她就因她讓我
With misery, or that she would of late	日日痛苦？因她近來教
Have taught to ignorant men most violent ways,	無知的人極端暴力運作？
Or hurled the little streets upon the great,	將那小街區擲向大街區，

Had they but courage equal to desire?	只要前者勇氣慾望相若？
What could have made her peaceful with a mind	如何能讓她平和？她心靈
That nobleness made simple as a fire,	因高貴而得以單純如火,
With beauty like a tightened bow, a kind	她美貌似滿張勁弓，於今日
That is not natural in an age like this,	已顯得與潮流不諧和,
Being high and solitary and most stern?	她的美尊貴孤傲且嚴峻。
Why, what could she have done, being what she is?	故曰，其人如此，你能奈她何？
Was there another Troy for her to burn?	豈再有特洛伊供其火焚？

　　莫德婚姻不諧，1905年與夫分居，1908年終與葉慈上床，雙方反應都平淡，葉慈說：「性交是悲劇，因其使得靈魂永遠是處子。（the tragedy of sexual intercourse is the perpetual virginity of the soul）」，20年後賦詩《一個少／老男人》（A Man Young and Old），其中一節追憶此事：

My arms are like the twisted thorn	我雙臂似荊棘扭曲
And yet there beauty lay;	但美躺臥其中；
The first of all the tribe lay there	人類之母躺臥其中
And did such pleasure take;	盡情享受歡愉；
She who had brought great Hector down	擊垮猛士赫克托並
And put all Troy to wreck.	毀滅特洛伊的她。

　　1909年葉慈結識美國詩人龐德（Ezra Pound），經龐德認識日本能劇，影響其劇作。1916年賦詩《復活節，1916》（Easter, 1916）悼念同年為愛爾蘭建國起義被處死者（包括莫德之夫麥布萊），末句「有一可怖的美誕生」（A terrible beauty is born）預

見了日後愛爾蘭獨立戰爭之血腥。時年51，葉慈興念結婚生子，第五度向莫德求婚，被拒後立即轉而追求莫德婚前與情夫、法國報業人士密爾瓦（Lucien Millevoye）生的女兒，21歲的伊瑟德（Iseult）。伊瑟德15歲時曾想嫁給葉慈，但1917年轉而拒絕。同年葉慈向25歲的喬琪（Georgie Hyde-Lees）求婚，婚後幸福，葉慈晚年多情人，但喬琪說：「你身後人們會議論你的婚外情，但我會緘口，因為我會記得你以此自傲。」婚後夫妻倆透過靈媒寫作，1925年出版《靈視》（The Vision），認為人世每兩千年一循環（gyre），1920年葉慈作詩《二度降臨》（The Second Coming），有人解讀為預視到西方文明之沒落：

Turning and turning in the widening gyre	迴旋再迴旋圈子越飛越遠
The falcon cannot hear the falconer	獵鷹已經聽不到放鷹人
Things fall apart; the centre cannot hold;	情勢崩潰；中心已經失控；
Mere anarchy is loosed upon the world,	徹底失序散漫於全世界，
The blood-dimmed tide is loosed, and everywhere	血暗的海潮在漫延，處處
The ceremony of innocence is drowned.	純真的行為、儀式都被淹沒。
The best lack all conviction, while the worst	精英了無信念，而渣滓則
Are full of passionate intensity.	全然充滿那狂熱的激情。
Surely some revelation is at hand;	無疑某種啟示即將到來；
Surely the Second Coming is at hand.	無疑二度降臨即將到來。
The Second Coming! Hardly are those words out	二度降臨！這幾個字剛出口
When a vast image out of Spiritus Mundi	就有巨物來自世界靈魂
Troubles my sight: somewhere in sands of the desert	赫現眼前：在沙漠中某處
A shape with lion body and the head of a man,	其形狀為獅之身人之頭，
A gaze blank and pitiless as the sun,	其目光空白無情如太陽，
Is moving its slow thighs, while all about it	正緩慢移動腿腳，在其四周
Reel shadows of the indignant desert birds.	眈恕的沙漠禽鳥陰影飛旋。
The darkness drops again; but now I know	黑暗再臨；但如今我知曉
That twenty centuries of stony sleep	二十個世紀似石的沉睡
Were vexed to nightmare by a rocking cradle,	被那晃動的搖籃擾以噩夢，
And what rough beast, its hour come round at last,	是何暴獸，其時刻終到臨，
Slouches towards Bethlehem to be born?	蹣跚爬向伯利恆要出世？

1922年愛爾蘭建國,葉慈任上議院議員直到1928年,期間爲其身屬的少數族群新教徒發聲。1923年獲頒諾貝爾文學獎,他借機宣揚愛爾蘭國。1924年負責國幣設計,選定非政治的動物與文藝圖像。1926年賦詩《航向拜占庭》(Sailing to Byzantium)以藝術永恆對比人生老病:

That is no country for old men. The young	那個國度老人不宜。年輕人
In one another's arms, birds in the trees	互相擁抱,鳥兒在樹上
– Those dying generations – at their song,	——一代代正走向死亡——在歌詠,
The salmon falls, the mackerel crowded seas,	鮭魚躍瀑,鯖魚滿佈海洋,
Fish, flesh, or fowl, commend all summer long	魚類、動物、禽鳥,整夏季不停
Whatever is begotten, born, and dies.	爲了生育、分娩、死亡奔忙。
Caught in that sensual music all neglect	專注感官妙樂,他們全遺忘了
Monuments of unageing intellect.	智識永恆的紀念碑。
An aged man is but a paltry thing,	人年老了就瑣碎不足觀,
A tattered coat upon a stick, unless	像細棍上掛著破衣,除非
Soul clap its hands and sing, and louder sing	靈魂鼓掌歌唱,越唱越響
For every tatter in its mortal dress,	對應肉身衣裳每個破隙,
Nor is there singing school but studying	此歌唱無處學,只能鑽研
Monuments of its own magnificence;	其自身那輝煌的紀念碑;
And therefore I have sailed the seas and come	因此我橫渡了大海到臨
To the holy city of Byzantium.	這座神聖的都城拜占庭。
O sages standing in God's holy fire	噢,聖人們置身上帝聖火
As in the gold mosaic of a wall,	如同牆上金色拼圖所繪,
Come from the holy fire, perne in a gyre,	從聖火降臨,似紡錘旋陀,
And be the singing masters of my soul.	來教導啓示我靈魂歌藝。
Consume my heart away; sick with desire	將我心帶走;因慾望病弱
And fastened to a dying animal	我心羈絆於將死之軀體
It knows not what it is; and gather me	無自知之明;請將我攜赴
Into the artifice of eternity.	那人文藝術的永恆國度。
Once out of nature I shall never take	一旦超脫色身我將永不再
My bodily form from any natural thing,	投入任何凡塵之肉體,
But such a form as Grecian goldsmiths make	我只投身希臘金匠所鑄
Of hammered gold and gold enamelling	以金打造、飾以金釉之器

To keep a drowsy Emperor awake;	供瞌睡欲眠的皇帝開目；
Or set upon a golden bough to sing	或擺放金枝上獻唱歌藝
To lords and ladies of Byzantium	助拜佔庭大人貴婦興致
Of what is past, or passing, or to come.	吟詠過去、現在、未來之事。

1928年葉慈據希臘神話賦詩《麗達與天鵝》（Leda and the Swan）：

A sudden blow: the great wings beating still	猛然被襲：巨翅仍在扇撲
Above the staggering girl, her thighs caressed	於踉蹌少女身上，撫摩腿股
By the dark webs, her nape caught in his bill,	的暗蹼，頸項被鳥喙叼住，
He holds her helpless breast upon his breast.	將她無助的胸部抵胸部。
How can those terrified vague fingers push	受驚軟弱十指哪能推拒
The feathered glory from her loosening thighs?	漸鬆的腿股間雄崤的榮耀？
And how can body, laid in that white rush,	置於白色茅草中的體軀
But feel the strange heart beating where it lies?	只能躺臥感受奇異心跳。
A shudder in the loins engenders there	下腹一陣抽動迸產生
The broken wall, the burning roof and tower	殘垣、焚燒的望樓和屋子
And Agamemnon dead. Being so caught up,	和阿伽門農之死。如此被箝，
So mastered by the brute blood of the air,	被天降的血淋蠻物擺弄，
Did she put on his knowledge with his power	她有否隨他力量獲其知識
Before the indifferent beak could let her drop?	在那鳥喙漠然拋下她之前？

一次大戰與1929年經濟大恐慌後，葉慈政治立場轉趨保守，質疑民主制度能否處理經濟與社會衝突，傾向集權體制。1934年時年69，葉慈接受手術恢復性能力，與多名少女交往。1936年賦詩《女傭之歌一》（The Chambermaid's First Song）、《女傭之歌二》（The Chambermaid's Second Song）。

《女傭之歌一》：

HOW came this ranger	何來此浪子
Now sunk in rest,	現已偃伏，
Stranger with stranger,	彼此不相識，
On my cold breast?	臥我冷乳？
What's left to sigh for?	尚有何可嘆？
Strange night has come;	異夜已臨；
God's love has hidden him	主愛掩藏了他
Out of all harm,	免於傷痛，
Pleasure has made him	歡享使得他
Weak as a worm.	弱似蠕蟲。

《女傭之歌二》：

From pleasure of the bed,	床笫歡享之後，
Dull as a worm,	呆似蠕蟲，
His rod and its butting head	他的男根及其凸首
Limp as a worm,	軟似蠕蟲，
His spirit that has fled	他的精氣已溜走
Blind as a worm.	盲似蠕蟲。

　　1936年葉慈主編《牛津版現代詩集1892-1935》（Oxford Book of Modern Verse, 1892-1935）。1939年死於法國，遵其遺囑先就地埋葬，1948年遷葬老家思立勾，墓誌銘出自其晚年詩作《顎山腳下》（Under Ben Bulben）[1]：

Cast a cold Eye On Life, on Death. Horseman, pass by!	投視冷凝 對生，對死。 騎士，續行！

　　葉慈以傳統格律、現代意象作詩，不落俗套，領導愛爾蘭當代文藝復興，為現代文學大詩家。

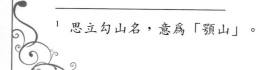

[1] 思立勾山名，意為「顎山」。

圖片來源：IDJ圖庫

1-36
伍爾芙
Virginia Woolf

伍爾芙
Virginia Woolf

　　伍爾芙（Virginia Woolf）1882年生於倫敦，父親是史學家，母親以貌美著稱，父母皆爲再婚，伍爾芙童年曾被同母異父兄性侵。父親第一任妻子是作家薩克雷（William Makepeace Thackeray）之女，伍爾芙從小在家受教，浸淫文藝氣息中，夏天依例到英格蘭西南康瓦爾（Cornwall）海邊渡假。1895年13歲母親去世，1897年同母異父姐絲黛拉（Stella）也去世，導致伍爾芙精神崩潰，此後終身爲憂鬱症纏擾。1897-1901年在倫敦大學國王學院（King's College London）修課。父親1904年去世，伍爾芙再次崩潰，大姐凡妮莎（Vanessa）決定搬家到倫敦城內圍榮蒔里（Bloomsbury），結識文藝人士，包括藝評家克萊夫·貝爾（Clive Bell）、猶太裔作家雷納德·伍爾夫（Leonard Woolf）、經濟學家凱因斯（John Maynard Keynes）等，每週四晚聚會，人稱圍榮蒔里小集（Bloomsbury Group）。大姐1907年婚嫁對前衛藝術同感興趣的貝爾。伍爾芙1912年嫁給雷納德·伍爾夫，從此冠夫姓，感情融洽。1915年出版第一本小說《出航》（The Voyage Out）。1917年創辦荷佳思出版社（Hogarth Press），出版伍爾芙自己以及艾略特（Eliot）、佛洛伊德（Freud）等人作品。圍榮蒔里小集對性愛態度開放，伍爾芙1922年與作家薇妲·薩克威—韋斯特（Vita Sackville-West）同性戀。

　　1925年伍爾芙出版《戴洛薇夫人》（Mrs. Dalloway），敘述一次大戰後倫敦社交名媛戴洛薇夫人一天之事：早上開始準備當晚晚宴，以意識流（stream of consciousness）描寫，反思少年時期，選擇嫁給可靠的先生而非迷人的彼得（Peter Walsh）、還有與莎莉（Sally Seton）一段同性戀情。彼得當天來訪過，對她仍有意。彼得早上還在公園見到退役軍人戚提莫斯（Septimus Warren Smith），後者勞工出身，在一戰中心靈受創，經常憶起戰死的同袍艾文斯（Evans），稍後被送入精神療養院，跳樓尋短。晚宴客人都是戴洛薇夫人舊識，包括彼得和莎莉。有人提起戚提莫斯之事，戴洛薇夫人聽了很欽佩，認爲他這樣保存了自己的幸福。此書有典型伍爾芙風格：故事平淡、以意識流抒情反思人生感受與際遇。茲選譯近尾一段：

> She felt somehow very like him—the young man who had killed himself. She felt glad that he had done it; thrown it away. The clock was striking. The leaden circles dissolved in the air. He made her feel the beauty; made her feel the fun. But she must go back. She must assemble.

> 她不知爲何，但自覺與他很像—那個自殺的年輕人。她慶幸他自殺，把包袱拋開。此時鐘鳴響。似鉛迴音蕩散漸渺。他讓她體會到其中的美；讓她體會到其中的快感。但此刻她不得不回去。她不得不從眾。

　　1927年伍爾芙出版《燈塔行》（To the Lighthouse），敘述藍希（Ramsey）一家及友人1910年、1920年兩度在蘇格蘭史開（Skye）島避暑，其中各一天的經歷。客人畫家莉莉（Lily Briscoe）因爲身爲女性，對天份缺乏信心。一次大戰期間藍希家女兒難產去世，兒子戰死，藍希太太也去世。1920年莉莉再度來做客，藍希先生也帶著剩下的一對兒女再度來臨，藍希先生要兒女陪他乘船去燈塔，莉莉試圖完成十年前開始，爲藍希太太作的畫像，同時回想往事，終於完成畫作。茲選譯第一章結尾描述藍希夫婦一段：

> She could not say it. Then, knowing that he was watching her, instead of saying anything she turned, holding her stocking, and looked at him. And as she looked at him she began to smile, for though she had not said a word, he knew, of course he knew, that she loved him. He could not deny it. And smiling she looked out of the window and said (thinking to herself, Nothing on earth can equal this happiness)-- "Yes, you were right. It's going to be wet tomorrow. You won't be able to go." And she looked at him smiling. For she had triumphed again. She had not said it: yet he knew.

> 她説不出口。她知道他在看她，因此拿著絲襪轉身看他。邊看邊展露笑容，因爲她雖然什麼都沒説，但他知道，他當然知道—她愛他。這他無法否認。她笑看著窗外説（心中想道：世上幸福以此爲最）：「沒錯，你説對了。明天會下雨。你沒法子去了。」她看著他笑，因爲她又贏了。她沒説出來：但他也心知。

1928年伍爾芙創作小說《奧蘭多》（Orlando）獻給薇姐，等同情書，主角奧蘭多即代表薇姐。故事始於1588年，貴族子弟奧蘭多成為伊麗莎白女王的大臣與情人；到了詹姆士一世時代，奧蘭多與俄國公主莎霞（Sasha）談戀愛，相約私奔，但莎霞將他拋棄；查爾斯二世任命奧蘭多出使伊斯坦堡，適逢民眾造反，奧蘭多一覺醒來變成女人，乘船赴英，此時已是18世紀，結識詩人翟頓、博普；到19世紀奧蘭多嫁給船長薛莫丁（Shelmerdine）作結，時為1928年。茲選譯第二章一段：

Nature, who has played so many queer tricks upon us, making us so unequally of clay and diamonds, of rainbow and granite, and stuffed them into a case, often of the most incongruous, for the poet has a butcher's face and the butcher a poet's; nature, who has so much to answer for besides the perhaps unwieldy length of this sentence, has further complicated our task and added to our confusion by providing...a perfect rag-bag of odds and ends within us--a piece of a policeman's trousers lying cheek by jowl with Queen Alexandra's wedding veil--but has contrived that the whole assortment shall be lightly stitched together by a single thread. Memory is the seamstress and a capricious one at that.	大自然對我們開了許多奇怪的玩笑，造某些人以土、另一些以鑽石，某些以彩虹、另一些以硬岩，又常將這些材質塞入極不搭調的外殼，結果詩人長得像屠夫，屠夫長得像詩人；大自然要負責的可多了，包括為何此句如此冗長，而大自然更加重了我們的負擔、加深了我們的困惑，因為大自然賦予我們零亂不協的內涵—以警察制服褲搭襯丹麥皇后亞莉珊卓的婚紗—又單只用一條細線將這一切雜碎勉強串起。負責縫紉串起的女紅就是回憶，而這女紅脾氣又善變。

1929年伍爾芙根據前一年在劍橋大學新創立的葛屯（Girton）與紐南（Newnham）女子學院的系列演講《女性與小說》（Women and Fiction）出版論文《自己的房間》（A Room of One's Own），為女性爭取權利，假想莎士比亞有才華相等的姐妹茱蒂思（Judith），因身為女性不得就學，在家操勞，為逃避強迫婚姻離家出走，在外懷孕自殺。中有一句：「女性要想寫小說就必須有自己的錢、有自己的房間。（A woman must have money and a room of her own if she is to write fiction）」

1931年伍爾芙出版小說《浪潮》（The Waves），由六個角色獨白構成。1937年出版小說《歲月》（The Years），探討帕提哲（Partiger）一家從1880到1930年代的變化。1938年出版論文《三枚金幣》（Three Guineas）探討戰爭與女權。1941年出版劇本《劇幕之間》（Between the Acts）探討英國歷史。

1941年伍爾芙因憂鬱症自沉家附近渼氾河（Ouse）中。

伍爾芙與喬伊斯（Joyce）同為現代小說典範作家，以意識流與實驗性手法探討心理、感知、時間、社會，為女性發聲。

伍
爾
芙

圖片來源：IDJ圖庫

1-37

詹姆士・喬伊斯

James Joyce

詹姆士・喬伊斯（James Joyce）1882年生於愛爾蘭都柏林天主教家庭，弟妹九人，父親是稅官。6歲入耶穌會寄宿學校就讀，9歲即賦詩悼念愛爾蘭政治家帕內爾（Charles Stewart Parnell），同年父親因酗酒破產。隔年輟學，1893年獲獎學金復學，1898-1902年於都柏林大學學院（University College Dublin）主修英、法、意語言文學，活躍於市內戲劇、文學界，1900年刊文於《雙週評論》（Fortnightly Review）讚譽易卜生（Ibsen）新劇《當我們死者復活》（When We Dead Awaken），為與易卜生通信而學挪威文。畢業赴法習醫，旋即放棄，後因母親病危返回，母親要他去教堂辦告解，他因質疑天主教而拒絕，母親死後也拒絕下跪為母祈禱。1904年喬伊斯22歲，試圖出版自傳式小說《藝術家畫像》（A Portrait of the Artist）未果，後改寫為《青年藝術家畫像》（A Portrait of the Artist as a Young Man）於1914-15年出版，以意識流手法描述年輕藝術家史迪芬・達道勒斯（Stephen Daedalus，達道勒斯為希臘神話巧匠，為逃離克里特島Crete而研創翅膀）之心靈成長，叛離其天主教養成，最終離開愛爾蘭赴巴黎追尋藝術。

1904年6月16日喬伊斯與日後的妻子娜拉（Nora）首度約會，娜拉時任女傭。此日期成為其巨著《憂里希思》（Ulysses）[1]描述之日期。喬伊斯某次酗酒與人在都柏林聖史迪芬公園（St Stephen's Green）打架，為其父友人送回家，此人傳聞是妻子出軌的猶太人，諸如此事日後皆寫入《憂里希思》。後不久偕娜拉渡海赴奧匈帝國，落腳崔市地（Trieste）教授英文。1909年暫返都柏林出版《都柏林人》（Dubliners），並代表崔市地投資者在都柏林開辦愛爾蘭首家電影院，未久歇業。1912年又為《都柏林人》返回，兩次都出版未果，此後未再返愛爾蘭。

《都柏林人》共15篇短篇小說，全以都柏林為背景，主角由兒童到成年。第三篇《阿拉比》（Araby）寫於1905年，描述少年主角暗戀年長少女，為她遠赴市集購禮，終而幻滅，茲選譯一段：

---

[1] 此希臘名可能源自「哭泣」之意。

Or if Mangan's sister came out on the doorstep to call her brother in to his tea, we watched her from our shadow peer up and down the street. We waited to see whether she would remain or go in and, if she remained, we left our shadow and walked up to Mangan's steps resignedly. She was waiting for us, her figure defined by the light from the half-opened door. Her brother always teased her before he obeyed, and I stood by the railings looking at her. Her dress swung as she moved her body, and the soft rope of her hair tossed from side to side.

或是曼耿的姊姊在他家門口喚他吃午茶，我們在陰影處看著她搜尋街道。我們等著看她是進屋還是待在那兒，要是待著，我們就乖乖離開陰影走上曼耿家門階。她等著我們，光線由半開的門瀉出，透現她的輪廓。她弟弟總是先逗她一下才進去，我就站在扶手邊看著她。她的裙裳隨身軀擺動，輕柔的髮辮來回蕩漾。

　　末篇《死者》（The Dead）描述主角參加每年一度的晚宴，過程每年相同，主角激勵賓客要真正活出來，但自己連妻子死去的情人都無法戰勝。全書呈現都柏林沉滯癱瘓之感。

　　喬伊斯引介多名弟妹至崔市地工作。學生史密茨（Ettore Schmitz，筆名Italo Svevo）為猶太裔天主教徒，也為其寫入《憂里希思》。1915年喬伊斯因一次大戰移居瑞士蘇黎士（Zurich），結識英國畫家薄君（Frank Budgen），與之切磋創作。美國作家龐德（Ezra Pound）為其介紹英國出版家荷莉葉（Harriet Shaw Weaver），後者助其出版《青年藝術家畫像》，並長期提供生活費，便其專心寫作。戰後喬伊斯返回崔市地，1920年赴巴黎，寫作《憂里希思》，因眼力退化數次開刀，女兒露夏（Lucia）被精神分析大師容格（Carl Jung）診斷為精神分裂，容格讀了《憂里希思》認為喬伊斯患有同病。《憂里希思》1921年出版，同名希臘神話描述主角海上漂流十年的經歷，喬伊斯此書則描述猶太裔愛爾蘭人、廣告業務員李奧波・布隆（Leopold Bloom），以及因母病由巴黎返回都柏林之藝術家史迪芬・達道勒斯，於1904年6月16日從早上8點到半夜2點的經歷，共18章，每章涵蓋一小時，章節主題與神話章節對應。若干章節模仿不同文體，第14章模仿不同時期、不同作家的英語風格。布隆和達道勒斯父親相識，路遇達道勒斯醉酒給予援手。布隆知道妻子歌唱家茉莉（Molly）當天與經紀人布雷茲・

波伊藍（Blazes Boylan）相約偷情。書尾以意識流描寫茉莉憶起當初布隆求婚場景：「他問我我會否說好說好我的山花我先環抱他好讓他俯身感觸我的雙乳佈滿香水好他滿心激狂好我說好我願意好。（he asked me would I yes to say yes my mountain flower and first I put my arms around him yes and drew him down to me so he could feel my breasts all perfume yes and his heart was going like mad and yes I said yes I will Yes）」喬伊斯自述：「我要描述都柏林，詳細到假使都柏林有一天從地球消失也能根據我的書重建。」書中因描寫手淫1922-33年在美國遭禁，在英也禁至1930年代。

喬伊斯1926年於巴黎結識美國文化人周拉斯夫婦（Eugene, Maria Jolas），他們也提供經濟支助，並協助於1939年出版《芬尼根守靈》（Finnegans Wake），此書多用意識流、自由聯想、雙關語、新創語，脫離傳統佈局，因此廣受批評。全書首句為「河流，經過亞當夏娃的，從海濱轉到海灣，把我們從便利循環之區帶回豪司堡附近。（riverrun, past Eve and Adam's, from swerve of shore to bend of bay, brings us by a commodius vicus of recirculation back to Howth Castle and Environs）」末句為「一條一獨一終一愛一長這。（A way a lone a last a loved a long the）」連接到首句循環不斷，反映喬伊斯此時的看法，認為世事反復循環。書名來自愛爾蘭民謠，述說挑磚工芬尼根醉酒跌下高梯致死，眾人為其守靈，混亂中威士忌灑落其身，芬尼根因此復活。第一章描述芬尼根化身為書中主角HCE（可做各種解讀，或為姓名「韓福瑞・欽普登・伊耳鼬蝌 / Humphrey Chimpden Earwicker」，或為「凡人亮相 / Here Comes Everyman」，或為「到處生子 / Haveth Childers Everywhere」等等），其妻ALP（或為姓名「安娜・莉薇雅・普拉蓓兒 / Anna Livia Plurabelle」，或為「可笑的一群 / A Laughable Party」等等），二子其一作家閃（Shem）、另一郵差尚（Shaun），一女伊西（Issy）。HCE夢到在公園犯下原罪，繼而受謠傳毀謗，ALP為其脫釋不成，兒子企圖取代他，書尾是ALP獨白。有人將全書解讀為愛爾蘭史，有人解讀為人類歷史，有人解讀為一場夢。學者認為喬伊斯以雙關語和人物身份變換表達世間萬物相關。其語言變幻莫測，茲舉近起頭一句為例：「噢在此在此如何匍匐匿行遇見暮塵通姦之父但，（噢我閃亮的星星和身體！）如何神聖伸展最高穹宇那天上招示柔軟廣告！（O here here how hoth sprowled met the duskt the father of fornicationists but, (O my shining stars and body!) how hath fanespanned most high heaven the skysign of soft advertisement!）」有人解讀此句旨在界

定時間（傍晚）、地點（有廣告牌的空曠處）、架構（夢中）。

1931年喬伊斯與娜拉在倫敦成婚。1940年因二次大戰避居蘇黎士。次年胃潰瘍手術後病逝，葬於蘇黎士。

喬伊斯以出格語言、意識流、對歷代文體模仿擺弄、嚴謹佈局，爲現代文學樹立典範。

詹姆士‧喬伊斯

圖片來源：維基共享資源

1-38

勞倫斯

D. H. Lawrence

勞倫斯
D. H. Lawrence

　　勞倫斯（D. H. Lawrence）1885年生於英格蘭中部，父親是礦工，母親是小學老師，父母不和，1898年獲獎學金入中學，1901年輟學入工廠工作，1902-06年任小學老師，1908年於諾丁漢大學學院（University College, Nottingham）獲教師執照。同年赴倫敦，邊教書邊寫作，1910年出版第一本小說《白孔雀》（The White Peacock），同年母親病逝。次年辭去教職全心寫作。1912年結識其諾丁漢大學現代語文教授之妻，大他6歲的芙莉妲（Frieda Weekley），後者出身德國貴族，兩人都對佛洛伊德（Freud）的精神分析理論深感興趣，未久私奔赴德、意旅遊。

　　1913年勞倫斯出版帶自傳性質的小說《兒子與情人》（Sons and Lovers），敘述出身中產階級的葛楚（Gertrude Coppard）與粗獷礦工（Walter Morel）相戀結婚，婚姻不諧，葛楚將感情投注於長子威廉，導致威廉無法正常發展而早逝，葛楚繼而關注次子保羅（Paul），保羅在前後兩位情人與母親間掙扎，最終母親去世。茲選譯一段保羅對母親的想法：

He feels that "sometimes he hated her, and pulled at her bondage. His life wanted to free itself of her. It was like a circle where life turned back on itself, and got no farther. She bore him, loved him, kept him, and his love turned back into her, so that he could not be free to go forward with his own life, really love another woman.	他感覺「有時恨她，要逃脫她的束縛。他的生命冀求獨立於她。生命像個圓圈，總是回歸原點，無法遠離。她生下他、愛護他、養育他，以致他的愛總是回歸於她，以致他的生命無法獨立前進，無法真正的愛另一個女人。」

　　1914年勞倫斯返英成婚，1916年暫寓康瓦爾（Cornwall），結識農夫亨利（Henry Hocking）並相戀，1915年出版小說《彩虹》（The Rainbow），敘述英格蘭一工農家庭三代之事。二戰期間勞倫斯被英國政府疑為德國間諜，艱困度日。1920年出版《彩

虹》續集《戀愛中的女人》（Women in Love），探討現代社會下之人際關係，兩書皆因坦白描述性愛而延遲出版。1919年戰後勞倫斯離英，流浪於意、法、德，1922年轉赴錫蘭、澳洲，最終定居美國新墨西哥州（New Mexico）陶斯市（Taos），並數度走訪墨西哥，1923年寫就《經典美國文學研究》（Studies in Classic American Literature），有助於鉤沉梅維爾（Herman Melville）作品，1926年寫就《羽蛇》（The Plumed Serpent），探討20世紀初墨西哥的政治、宗教。1925年因肺結核移居意大利，1928年寫就《查泰萊夫人的情人》（Lady Chatterley's Lover），敘述年輕的查泰萊夫人先生因戰傷下半身不遂，且情感冷漠，查泰萊夫人與園丁梅勒斯（Oliver Mellors）有婚外情，查泰萊夫人因此發覺靈肉缺一不可。此書因言語「淫穢」直到1960年才得以在英出版。茲選譯查泰萊夫人與園丁初次幽會一場：

She lay quite still, in a sort of sleep, in a sort of dream. Then she quivered as she felt his hand groping softly, yet with queer thwarted clumsiness, among her clothing. Yet the hand knew, too, how to unclothe her where it wanted. He drew down the thin silk sheath, slowly, carefully, right down and over her feet. Then with a quiver of exquisite pleasure he touched the warm soft body, and touched her navel for a moment in a kiss. And he had to come in to her at once, to enter the peace on earth of her soft, quiescent body. It was the moment of pure peace for him, the entry into the body of the woman. She lay still, in a kind of sleep, always in a kind of sleep. The activity, the orgasm was his, all his; she could strive for herself no more. Even the tightness of his arms round her, even the intense movement of his body, and the springing of his seed in her, was a kind of sleep, from which she did not begin to rouse till he had finished and lay softly panting against her breast. Then she wondered, just dimly wondered, why? Why was this necessary? Why had it lifted a great cloud from her and given her peace? Was it real?

她靜靜躺著，好似睡著，好似入夢。接著顫抖，感覺他的手，笨拙生硬，輕探她的衣裙。儘管如此，那手仍然知道如何解開她的衣裙。他輕緩、小心地將薄絲裙褪到直下腳踝。接著他顫動著、樂極地撫觸她柔暖的軀體，輕輕觸吻她肚臍。他即刻進入她的身體，她柔軟、安靜的身體，進入人間的安寧。對他而言，這是純淨安寧的時刻，進入她的剎那。她靜靜躺著，好似睡著，恆常好似睡著。主動、高潮都是他的，全是他的；她已無法自主。連他緊緊環抱她的手臂，連他高亢的抽動，連他射入她的種子，對她都好似睡夢，直到他結束，躺在她胸上輕喘，她才醒來。這時她心想，模糊地想，為什麼？為什麼必需這樣？為什麼這揭開了掩蓋她的雲霧，給了她安寧？這是真的嗎？

1930年勞倫斯肺結核去世。

勞
倫
斯

勞倫斯出身勞工階層，醉心佛洛伊德心理分析理論，探討現代工業社會下的人際關係，認爲靈肉應完滿結合，對性愛直白描述，爲英國20世紀初重要小說家。

圖片來源：IDJ圖庫

1-39

艾略特

T.S. Eliot

　　艾略特（T.S. Eliot）1888年生於美國密蘇里州聖路易（St. Louis）市，父親爲製磚公司總裁，祖父由東北遷此以創辦聖路易一神派（Unitarian，否認神性分爲三位一體）教會。艾略特幼好文藝，習拉丁、希臘、法、德諸文，1906-09年入哈佛大學主修比較文學，在校刊發表詩作，1910-11年入英美文學碩士班，於巴黎大學進修哲學。1911年入哈佛哲學博士班研究佛學、梵文、巴利文，同年寫就現代詩傑作《J‧阿弗瑞德‧普魯弗洛克的情歌》（The Love Song of J. Alfred Prufrock），以中年男子口吻述說想對心儀之人表白卻遲疑[1]：

S'io credesse che mia risposta fosse	假如我相信我的回答是給
A persona che mai tornasse al mondo,	一個有可能回到人世的人，
Questa fiamma staria senza piu scosse.	這火焰就會停住不再游移。
Ma perciocche giammai di questo fondo	但是因爲自此深淵從未能
Non torno vivo alcun, s'i'odo il vero,	有一人生還，如果傳聞是眞，
Senza tema d'infamia ti rispondo.	我就無需顧慮惡名而可回應。
Let us go then, you and I,	我們走吧，你和我，
When the evening is spread out against the sky	當日暮開展呈現對著天廓
Like a patient etherized upon a table;	像病人被麻醉躺臥手術台；
Let us go, through certain half-deserted streets,	我們走，穿過些半被棄街巷，
The muttering retreats	喁喁角落收藏
Of restless nights in one-night cheap hotels	一宿廉價旅館的不安夜晚
And sawdust restaurants with oyster-shells:	和滿地木屑蠔殼的餐館：
Streets that follow like a tedious argument	街道綿延好似煩瑣的論述
Of insidious intent	引人暗入歧途
To lead you to an overwhelming question...	將你帶向那不勝負荷的一問……
Oh, do not ask, "What is it?"	噢，別問我：「哪一樁？」
Let us go and make our visit.	讓我們前往去拜訪。

---

[1] 前六行引文出自但丁神曲地獄第八層貴多（Guido da Montefeltro）對但丁所言。

In the room the women come and go
Talking of Michelangelo.
The yellow fog that rubs its back upon the window-panes,
The yellow smoke that rubs its muzzle on the window-panes,
Licked its tongue into the corners of the evening,
Lingered upon the pools that stand in drains,
Let fall upon its back the soot that falls from chimneys,
Slipped by the terrace, made a sudden leap,
And seeing that it was a soft October night,
Curled once about the house, and fell asleep.
And indeed there will be time
For the yellow smoke that slides along the street,
Rubbing its back upon the window-panes;
There will be time, there will be time
To prepare a face to meet the faces that you meet;
There will be time to murder and create,
And time for all the works and days of hands
That lift and drop a question on your plate;
Time for you and time for me,
And time yet for a hundred indecisions,
And for a hundred visions and revisions,
Before the taking of a toast and tea.
In the room the women come and go
Talking of Michelangelo.
And indeed there will be time
To wonder, "Do I dare?" and, "Do I dare?"

Time to turn back and descend the stair,
With a bald spot in the middle of my hair—
[They will say: "How his hair is growing thin!"]

My morning coat, my collar mounting firmly to the chin,
My necktie rich and modest, but asserted by a simple pin—
[They will say: "But how his arms and legs are thin!"]

廳堂裡女人來去穿梭
談論著米開朗基羅
黃色霧靄將其背脊磨蹭於窗玻璃，
黃色煙塵將其口鼻磨蹭於窗玻璃，
以其舌舔拭日暮各個角落，
逗留於排水口水灘滯積，
讓煙囪飄落的灰塵降於其背脊，
閃過陽台，突然縱身一竄，
看到那是溫柔的十月夜晚，
蜷繞屋子一圈，沉沉入眠。
肯定將會有時間
讓黃色煙塵隨著街道延伸，
將其背脊磨蹭於窗玻璃；
會有時間，會有時間
準備面容對應你將對應的面容；
會有時間殺，會有時間生，
有時間讓雙手為其所為
提起一問落放你盤碟中；
有時間給你我，
還有時間斟酌一百個遲疑，
一百種推臆和一百種改臆，
斟酌完之後才進用茶果。
廳堂裡女人來去穿梭
談論著米開朗基羅。
肯定將會有時間
臆想：「我敢嗎？」疑慮：「我敢嗎？」

有時間轉身將樓梯下，
頭頂中間有一塊已經禿髮—
（她們說：「他頭髮越來越少！」）

我的晨禮服，直抵下巴衣領挺傲，
領帶富麗而含蓄，但以簡單帶夾挺翹——
（她們說：「他手臂腿腳真細小！」）

Do I dare	我敢嗎？
Disturb the universe?	讓全宇宙驚動？
In a minute there is time	一分鐘裡有時間
For decisions and revisions which a minute will reverse.	作出決定、改變決定、一分鐘後又否定。
For I have known them all already, known them all—	因我已全都熟識她們，全熟識—
Have known the evenings, mornings, afternoons,	熟識那日暮、早晨、那下午，
I have measured out my life with coffee spoons;	我用咖啡勺將生命點滴付出；
I know the voices dying with a dying fall	我熟識那殞落的語音殞逝
Beneath the music from a farther room.	在音樂聲下自遠房傳來。
So how should I presume?	那我該如何推臆？
And I have known the eyes already, known them all—	而且我已熟識那眼神，全熟識—
The eyes that fix you in a formulated phrase,	那眼神以慣常語句將你定型，
And when I am formulated, sprawling on a pin,	而我一旦被定型，癱於大頭針刺，
When I am pinned and wriggling on the wall,	一旦被釘住在牆上蠕滯，
Then how should I begin	我還怎能開始
To spit out all the butt-ends of my days and ways?	吐訴我生活我習性瑣碎種種？
And how should I presume?	那我該如何推臆？
And I have known the arms already, known them all—	而且我已熟識那手臂，全熟識—
Arms that are braceleted and white and bare	手臂上穿帶著鐲子，赤裸白淨
[But in the lamplight, downed with light brown hair!]	（但檯燈光下，帶棕色細絨！）
Is it perfume from a dress	是衣裝上的香氣
That makes me so digress?	讓我如此走題？
Arms that lie along a table, or wrap about a shawl.	手臂或枕放在桌上，或以圍巾纏飾。
And should I then presume?	然則我該推臆？
And how should I begin?	我該如何開始？
...	......
Shall I say, I have gone at dusk through narrow streets	我該說，我曾於日暮穿過狹巷
And watched the smoke that rises from the pipes	觀看煙灰從那煙囪升起
Of lonely men in shirt-sleeves, leaning out of windows?	孤單人們穿著裡衫，探身出窗戶？
...	......
I should have been a pair of ragged claws	我原應生而為一對粗螫
Scuttling across the floors of silent seas.	碎步穿越那寂靜的海底。
...	......

And the afternoon, the evening, sleeps so peacefully!	還有下午，日暮，能沉睡安詳！
Smoothed by long fingers,	長手指撫順，
Asleep... tired... or it malingers,	睡著……疲憊……或是裝病，
Stretched on the floor, here beside you and me.	趴伸地上，在此你我身旁。
Should I, after tea and cakes and ices,	我，在茶點冰飲之後，應該
Have the strength to force the moment to its crisis?	鼓起勇氣迫使此刻一決成敗？
But though I have wept and fasted, wept and prayed,	雖然我哭泣拒食，哭泣祈禱，
Though I have seen my head [grown slightly bald] brought in upon a platter,	雖然我曾見我頭（已變略禿）盛放盤中送至，
I am no prophet—and here's no great matter;	我不是先知─這也不是大事；
I have seen the moment of my greatness flicker,	我曾見到我的關鍵時刻動搖，
And I have seen the eternal Footman hold my coat, and snicker,	我也曾見那永恆僕從持我大衣，並冷笑，
And in short, I was afraid.	簡單說，我是膽小。
And would it have been worth it, after all,	這一切是否值得呢，終究，
After the cups, the marmalade, the tea,	在碗杯後，在果醬後，茶後，
Among the porcelain, among some talk of you and me,	在磁器之間，在你我的談論之間，
Would it have been worth while,	一切是否得值，
To have bitten off the matter with a smile,	若還面帶微笑硬對此事，
To have squeezed the universe into a ball	若將宇宙擠迫壓縮成球
To roll it toward some overwhelming question,	將它滾向某不勝負荷的一問，
To say: "I am Lazarus, come from the dead,	說道：「我是拉撒路，由死返生，
Come back to tell you all, I shall tell you all"—	返回告知所有，我將告知所有」─
If one, settling a pillow by her head,	若某人，邊調適頭旁靠枕，
Should say: "That is not what I meant at all.	邊說：「這意思我完全沒有。
That is not it, at all."	完全沒有，沒有。」
And would it have been worth it, after all,	這一切是否值得呢，終究，
Would it have been worth while,	一切是否得值，
After the sunsets and the dooryards and the sprinkled streets,	在那日落、那前院、那灑水街道之後，
After the novels, after the teacups, after the skirts that trail along the floor—	在那些小說、那茶杯、那迤邐地面的裙腳之後─
And this, and so much more?—	還有這個，和不盡餘事後？──
It is impossible to say just what I mean!	我絕望於說出我心中所想！

艾略特

But as if a magic lantern threw the nerves in patterns on a screen:
Would it have been worth while
If one, settling a pillow or throwing off a shawl,
And turning toward the window, should say:
"That is not it at all,
That is not what I meant, at all."
...
No! I am not Prince Hamlet, nor was meant to be;

Am an attendant lord, one that will do
To swell a progress, start a scene or two,
Advise the prince; no doubt, an easy tool,
Deferential, glad to be of use,
Politic, cautious, and meticulous;
Full of high sentence, but a bit obtuse;
At times, indeed, almost ridiculous—
Almost, at times, the Fool.
I grow old... I grow old...
I shall wear the bottoms of my trousers rolled.
Shall I part my hair behind? Do I dare to eat a peach?
I shall wear white flannel trousers, and walk upon the beach.
I have heard the mermaids singing, each to each.
I do not think that they will sing to me.
I have seen them riding seaward on the waves
Combing the white hair of the waves blown back
When the wind blows the water white and black.
We have lingered in the chambers of the sea
By sea-girls wreathed with seaweed red and brown
Till human voices wake us, and we drown.

但就算有一盞魔燈將我心思映照
銀幕上：
一切是否得值
若某人，邊調適頭枕或將披肩解收，
邊轉頭向窗，說道：
「完全沒有，沒有，
這意思我完全沒有。」
⋯⋯
不！我不是哈姆雷特，這本非我宿命；

我只是陪臣，至多只堪
隨隊充充數，偶爾開個場，
給點意見；當然，很好使用，
恭敬有加，樂於效命，
世故，謹慎，且辦事周詳；
能說善道，但略微遲鈍；
有時，甚至，幾近可笑荒唐—
幾近，有時，弄臣。
吾老矣⋯⋯吾老矣⋯⋯
我著長褲會把褲腳管捲起。
頭髮後梢該分梳？桃子我是否敢吃？
我要去海灘散步，穿白法蘭絨褲子。
我曾聽見美人魚歌詠，彼對此。
我不認爲她們會對我唱。
我曾見她們乘浪濤出海
梳撫回捲的浪頭白髮
風吹海面水花黑白交雜。
我們在海中廳堂滯留延宕
依傍頭冠紅棕色海草海女
直到被人語驚醒，遂沉溺。

　　艾略特1914年赴牛津大學默頓（Merton）學院研究希臘哲學，在倫敦結識美國詩人龐德。艾略特時年26，信中自承仍是處男，隔年結識任職家教的薇薇安（Vivienne Haigh-Wood），與她註冊結婚，但婚姻不諧。1916年寫成博士論文，因戰亂未返美口試。1917年入羅伊德（Lloyds）銀行任職員，1920年於巴黎結識喬伊斯（Joyce）。1922年出版現代詩經典《荒原》（The Waste Land），當時婚姻不睦，夫妻倆精神皆陷低潮，艾略特自承此詩表述其心境，時人則解讀為表達一次戰後西方文明之幻滅。此詩以意識流手法，不斷變換時、地、敘述觀點，受法國象徵派影響，用典多，包含英、希臘、拉丁、意大利、德、法、梵文等語文，為現代詩典範。詩分五段：一、埋葬死者（The Burial of the Dead），二、棋局（A Game of Chess），三、火誡（The Fire Sermon），四、死於水（Death by Water），五、雷霆之言（What the Thunder Said）。茲選譯首段和末段，首段：

April is the cruellest month, breeding	四月是最殘酷月份，孳生
Lilacs out of the dead land, mixing	紫丁香於死寂荒原，摻混
Memory and desire, stirring	回憶和慾望，撥弄
Dull roots with spring rain.	鈍根以春雨。
Winter kept us warm, covering	冬季溫暖我們，覆掩
Earth in forgetful snow, feeding	大地以白茫茫雪，餵養
A little life with dried tubers.	枯萎根莖以苟延生命。
Summer surprised us, coming over the Starnbergersee	夏日令人意外，在史當貝湖上
With a shower of rain; we stopped in the colonnade,	突然驟雨來襲；我們暫佇於柱廊，
And went on in sunlight, into the Hofgarten,	待陽光才復出，去到皇宮庭園，
And drank coffee, and talked for an hour.	喝咖啡，聊了一小時。
Bin gar keine Russin, stamm' aus Litauen, echt deutsch.	我不是俄國人，來自立陶宛，純德國人。
And when we were children, staying at the archduke's,	我們小時候，在大公爵家，
My cousin's, he took me out on a sled,	我表哥家，他帶我去滑雪，
And I was frightened. He said, Marie,	我很害怕。他說，瑪麗，
Marie, hold on tight. And down we went.	瑪麗，抓緊了。我們滑下。
In the mountains, there you feel free.	在高山中，覺得自由。
I read, much of the night, and go south in the winter.	我看書，大半夜晚，到冬天就去南方。

末段：

Then spoke the thunder	這時雷霆發聲
Da	達
Datta: what have we given?	給達：我們給了什麼？
My friend, blood shaking my heart	朋友，我心血激動
The awful daring of a moment's surrender	驚天一注於關鍵一刻之捨身
Which an age of prudence can never retract	即使一世之謹慎也無法挽回
By this, and this only, we have existed	依此，惟有依此，我們才存在
Which is not to be found in our obituaries	這在我們的訃聞裡不會寫入的
Or in memories draped by the beneficent spider	在蜘蛛善意編織的回憶裡也沒有
Or under seals broken by the lean solicitor	精瘦律師破開的印記下也見不到
In our empty rooms	在我們清空的房裡
Da	達
Dayadhvam: I have heard the key	心達：我聽見鎖匙
Turn in the door once and turn once only	在門裡轉動且只轉一次
We think of the key, each in his prison	我們念著鎖匙，在各自牢中
Thinking of the key, each confirms a prison	念著鎖匙，各人自塑牢房
Only at nightfall, aetherial rumours	惟當夜晚，虛幻的傳言才
Revive for a moment a broken Coriolanus	讓破碎的科留拉努暫時復神
Da	達
Damyata: The boat responded	控達：小船愉悦
Gaily, to the hand expert with sail and oar	回應，嫻熟風帆船槳之手
The sea was calm, your heart would have responded	海面平靜，你的心也會愉悦
Gaily, when invited, beating obedient	回應，當受邀時，律動服從
To controlling hands	控制之手
I sat upon the shore	我坐在岸上
Fishing, with the arid plain behind me	釣魚，身後是乾涸原野
Shall I at least set my lands in order?	我是否至少該整頓家園？
London Bridge is falling down falling down falling down	倫敦橋就要垮了要垮了要垮了
Poi s'ascose nel foco che gli affina	然後他藏身於淨化人的火中
Quando fiam ceu chelidon—O swallow swallow	何時我才會化為燕子—噢燕子燕子
Le Prince d'Aquitaine à la tour abolie	廢棄城塔裡的雅基坦王子
These fragments I have shored against my ruins	這些殘句我堆砌以撐住廢墟
Why then Ile fit you. Hieronymo's mad againe.	那就隨你意吧。海洛尼莫又瘋了。
Datta. Dayadhvam. Damyata.	給達。心達。控達。
Shantih shantih shantih	圓靜 圓靜 圓靜

1925年艾略特轉任費博／枴爾（Faber and Gwyer）出版社編輯，同年賦詩《空心人》（The Hollow Men），絕望心情臻於谷底，末句爲「世界將如此結束／非以驚爆而以嗚咽（This is the way the world ends/Not with a bang but a whimper）」。1927年艾略特39歲由一神論教改信英國國教，並歸化英籍。1930年賦詩《聖灰星期三》（Ash Wednesday）借由宗教信仰恢復希望。1932-33年應邀於哈佛講學一年，借機與薇薇安分居，此後僅短暫見過一面，薇薇安1938年被兄長送入精神療養院，1947年去世。

艾略特愛貓，1939年出版詩集《老負鼠[2]論世故貓經》（Old Possum's Book of Practical Cats）描述貓生百態，1981年作曲家韋伯（Andrew Lloyd Webber）改編爲音樂劇《貓》（Cats）。1936-42年艾略特賦詩《四重奏四首》（Four Quartets）探討時間的意義，包含四部分：《火焚後的諾頓莊園》（Burnt Norton）、《東寇科》（East Coker）、《三荒礁》（The Dry Salvages）、《小吉町》（Little Gidding）。1948年獲諾貝爾文學獎。1957年艾略特68歲，婚娶他的秘書艾絲美（Esmé Valerie Fletcher，時年30）。1965年病逝於倫敦。

艾略特融合傳統與個人典故，訴說西方文明與其個人感情困境，爲英美詩打造新語言，樹立現代英詩典範。

2　龐德對艾略特之稱呼。

1-40

奧威爾

George Orwell

奧威爾（George Orwell）本名亞瑟‧卜列（Eric Arthur Blair），1903年生於印度東北，曾祖輩是貴族，至父輩已沒落，父親在印度政府鴉片部門任公務員，母親成長於緬甸，有法國血統。奧威爾1歲隨母返英格蘭中部定居，自幼志於寫作，5歲入讀天主教小學，1912年父親退休返英，8歲轉讀南部貴族私校，因家貧自覺受歧視。1917-21年以獎學金入讀伊頓公學（Eton），因缺錢未入大學，考入大英帝國警隊。因外祖母在緬甸，1922年選擇赴緬工作，學會緬語，親睹殖民壓迫，1927年因登革熱返英格蘭東部休假，辭去警職專注寫作。同年遷居倫敦，化名體驗東區貧民窟生活以備寫作，1928年遷居巴黎，繼續探索下層生活。1929年返英。

1931年奧威爾短文《絞刑》（A Hanging）刊於雜誌，敘述在印度監視絞刑，透露反對死刑之意。同年為體驗監獄，犯輕罪入獄兩天。次年在倫敦西部中學任教。1933年以喬治‧奧威爾筆名出版《巴黎倫敦落魄記》（Down and Out in Paris and London），頗受歡迎。次年因肺炎返英格蘭東部休養，1934年出版小說《緬甸歲月》（Burmese Days）描述殖民之惡。1936年奧威爾赴北英格蘭調查礦工生活，因此被英國特勤局監視至1948年。奧威爾1936年成婚，寫就短文《射象》（Shooting an Elephant），描述在緬射殺發狂大象之事。同年赴西班牙東北助共和政府與法西斯派作戰，喉部中槍，因共和政府派系傾軋遭迫害而返英，從此抨擊共產黨，但仍堅定支持社會主義。

1945年二戰爆發，其妻任職於政府負責宣傳與監控媒體的資訊部（Ministry of Information）。1940年奧威爾加入防衛本土的國民軍（Home Guard），1941年入英國廣播公司（BBC）對印度宣傳，同年辭去廣播與國民軍工作，出任左派期刊《論壇》（Tribune）編輯，1945年任《觀察家》（Observer）報戰地記者，採訪法、德，妻子同年於手術中意外去世。

1945年一篇論文中奧威爾首創「冷戰」（cold war）一詞。同年《動物農莊：童話故事》（Animal Farm: A Fairy Story）出版，敘述農莊上動物領袖公豬「老少校」（Old Major）要動物對人類革命，去世後兩隻公豬雪球（Snowball）和拿破崙（Napoleon）繼位，趕走人類，改農莊名為「動物農莊」，定下7條教條，至要者為「所有動物地位

平等」（All animals are equal）。豬作為領導層享受較好待遇，人類反攻但被擊退，拿破崙在奪權中趕走雪球，攬功諉罪，以狗迫害其他動物，以謊言惑眾。豬模仿人類享受，與人類結盟，將前述條改為「所有動物地位平等，但有些動物比其他動物更平等」（All animals are equal, but some animals are more equal than others）。此書影射蘇聯、史達林，書出大賣。茲選譯一段：

Man is the only creature that consumes without producing. He does not give milk, he does not lay eggs, he is too weak to pull the plough, he cannot run fast enough to catch rabbits. Yet he is lord of all the animals. He sets them to work, he gives back to them the bare minimum that will prevent them from starving, and the rest he keeps for himself.	只有人這種動物光消費不生產。人不產奶、不下蛋、力不足以拉犁、速度不足以補兔。但人卻掌控所有動物，使牠們工作，只給予極少口糧讓牠們不至於餓死，其他收穫人類全據為己有。

　　1946年奧威爾遷居蘇格蘭西部朱拉島（Jura），書寫《一九八四》（Nineteen Eighty-Four），1947年肺結核發作，1949年《一九八四》殺青，敘述世界分裂為大洋（Oceania）、歐亞（Eurasia）、東亞（Eastasia）三大國，大洋國由老大哥（Big Brother）獨裁，其下有內黨員（Inner Party）、外黨員（Outer Party）、普羅民眾（Proles），政府和平部（Ministry of Peace）負責戰爭、富足部（Ministry of Plenty）負責管控糧食物資、愛民部（Ministry of Love）負責洗腦虐囚、真理部（Ministry of Truth）負責管控媒體、偽造新聞歷史。思想警察（Thought Police）在各處設有監視器監控「思想犯罪」（thought crime），處處有標語「老大哥在看著你」（BIG BROTHER IS WATCHING YOU）。溫斯頓（Winston Smith）是外黨員，任職真理部，因研究歷史而質疑黨的教條，與同具思想犯罪的同事朱莉雅（Julia）相戀。溫斯頓誤認上司歐伯良（O'Brien）身屬反抗組織「兄弟會」（The Brotherhood），其實歐伯良是思想警察，溫斯頓與朱莉雅被捕，兩人受刑屈服，最終彼此背叛。洗腦後溫斯頓出獄，不分真偽，樂於接受現狀。此書嘲諷獨裁政權，廣獲好評，其中新創用語大為流傳。茲

奧威爾

選譯兩段：

War is peace. Freedom is slavery. Ignorance is strength.	戰爭就是和平。 自由就是奴役。 無知就是力量。

"You are a slow learner, Winston." "How can I help it? How can I help but see what is in front of my eyes? Two and two are four." "Sometimes, Winston. Sometimes they are five. Sometimes they are three. Sometimes they are all of them at once. You must try harder. It is not easy to become sane."	「溫斯頓，你太遲鈍了。」 「我沒辦法，我只能看到雙眼所見。2加2就是4。」 「這有時正確，有時候2加2是5。有時候是3。有時候既是4，又是5，又是3。你要更努力。想要成為正常人沒那麼容易。」

1949年奧威爾再婚，1950年肺結核去世。

奧威爾以小說批評獨裁體制，預見20世紀世局發展，創造多例新用語。

～ *American Literature 20 scholars* 美國文學20大家 ～

圖片來源：IDJ圖庫

2-1

霍桑

Nathaniel Hawthorne

霍桑（Nathaniel Hawthorne）1804年生於美國麻州（Massachusetts）綏聯市（Salem），祖上曾在17世紀綏聯女巫案（Salem witch trial）任法官。父親是船長，1808年病逝海外，一家依附住緬因州（Maine）的母舅生活。1820年開始寫詩作文，1821-25年入讀鮑登學院（Bowdoin College），結識詩人朗費羅（Longfellow）。1828年出版第一本小說。陸續寫了一些短篇小說，包括1835年的《年輕良人布朗》（Young Goodman Brown，goodman爲中世紀用語，指殷實人家之主）、1836年的《牧師的黑面罩》（The Minister's Black Veil），1837年結集出版爲《複述的故事》（Twice-Told Tales），頗受好評；《年輕良人布朗》以17世紀綏聯市爲背景，年輕良人布朗離別妻子「信仰」（Faith）於夜間深入森林，途遇老人（撒旦）及其他鎮民，午夜到達林中，衆人舉辦黑色彌撒，全鎮皆已歸依，新信徒只有布朗夫婦，布朗求上帝相助，一切驀然消逝，布朗返家，但失去對妻子、對周遭鎮民信心。《牧師的黑面罩》敘述牧師胡珀先生（Mr. Hooper）突然戴起黑面罩，引起鎮民疑懼，未婚妻也棄他而去，但胡珀如此反而更吸引信衆，臨死前說世人其實全都戴有黑面罩；一般解讀此兩篇小說在探討霍桑祖上清教徒信仰之原罪（original sin）概念。

1839年霍桑任職波士頓海關，1841-42年爲了省錢加入烏托邦的布魯克農莊（Brook Farm）。1842年結婚，遷居麻州康科德市（Concord），結識作家艾默生（Emerson）、梭羅（Thoreau）。

1843年霍桑寫就短篇小說《胎記》（The Birth-Mark），敘述科學家艾莫（Aylmer）婚娶面有掌形胎記的美女喬佳娜（Georgiana），艾莫著迷於去除胎記，讓喬佳娜飲下藥水，胎記漸隱，但喬佳娜也隨之死去。1844年寫就短篇小說《拉帕奇尼的女兒》（Rappaccini's Daughter），敘述中世紀意大利藥學家拉帕奇尼善培養有毒植物，女兒碧雅翠絲（Beatrice）照料這些植物，因而免疫，但自身帶毒，青年喬凡尼（Giovanni）愛上碧雅翠絲，給她飲藥解毒，她卻因此而死。此兩篇作品探討神意與人類知識之衝突。

1846年霍桑出任綏聯港稅收督察，1848年因政黨輪替去職，同年出任綏聯論壇

（Salem lyceum）秘書，該論壇負責舉辦系列公開演講。1850年出版長篇小說《紅字》（The Scarlet Letter），敘述17世紀波士頓女子海絲特‧普林（Hester Prynne）產下私生女，市民罰她穿上紅色A字（代表Adultery通姦），但她拒絕透露情人身份。她原以為死於海難的年長先生出現，他化名崔林沃醫師（Roger Chillingworth）報復海絲特不忠，脅迫她不得透露其身份。海絲特以針黹養大女兒珀兒（Pearl）。牧師丁姆斯代（Arthur Dimmesdale）受市民愛戴但有心臟病，崔林沃醫師入住牧師家照料，懷疑牧師就是情人，並窺見牧師胸膛也印有A字，牧師對崔林沃認罪，海絲特將崔林沃身份告知牧師，力勸牧師與她共赴歐洲開展新生活，牧師講道後當眾認罪，死於海絲特懷中，崔林沃不久也去世，留給珀兒大筆遺產。多年後海絲特回到波士頓，重新穿上紅字，死後葬於牧師左近。書出大賣，茲選譯兩段：

She had wandered, without rule or guidance, into a moral wilderness. Her intellect and heart had their home, as it were, in desert places, where she roamed as freely as the wild Indian in his woods. The scarlet letter was her passport into regions where other women dared not tread. Shame, Despair, Solitude! These had been her teachers-stern and wild ones-and they had made her strong, but taught her much amiss.

她無人帶領，無準則可循，漫遊入道德野地。可以說，她的理智、感情都置身荒漠，游走其中她好似森林裡的印地安人。紅字成了她的護照，讓她得以進入其他女人不敢觸碰的地域。恥辱，絕望，孤單！這些成了她的導師—嚴厲、狂野的導師—使她堅強，但帶她走上歧途。

"Mother," said little Pearl, "the sunshine does not love you. It runs away and hides itself, because it is afraid of something on your bosom. ... It will not flee from me, for I wear nothing on my bosom yet!"

「母親，」小珀兒說，「陽光不愛你。它逃跑躲避你，它怕你胸膛上的什麼東西……陽光不會躲避我，我胸膛上什麼都還沒有！」

"Nor ever will, my child, I hope," said Hester.	「我兒，但願你永遠也不會有，」海絲特說。
"And why not, mother?" asked Pearl, stopping short. …	「為什麼呢，母親？」珀兒問，稍停再續……
"Will it not come of its own accord, when I am a woman grown?"	「它不會自己出現嗎，等我長大成為女人時？」

　　1850年霍桑遷居雷諾克斯市（Lenox）與作家梅維爾（Herman Melville）為鄰。1851年寫就長篇小說《七角屋》（The House of the Seven Gables），以18世紀綏聯市一棟孽緣糾纏的七角屋為背景，敘述屋主荷西芭‧平洵（Hepzibah Pyncheon）在屋角開店迎養因謀殺坐監30年的哥哥克利佛（Clifford）。美麗活潑的表親菲比（Phoebe）來訪暫住，與房客侯格雷（Holgrave）相戀，侯格雷在為平洵家族作史。平洵家族得到七角屋是因前屋主馬修（Matthew Maule）被控行巫術處死，據說馬修死前詛咒平洵家族。平洵家一位法官遠親來訪，驟死屋中。證據顯示克利佛坐了冤獄。侯格雷是馬修後代，但因與菲比相戀而無報復心，眾人遷至鄉間開始新生活。

　　1852年霍桑根據布魯克農莊經驗寫就小說《福谷傳奇》（The Blithedale Romance）。同年遷回康科德與艾默生、梭羅為鄰，並為年輕時的好友、正競選總統的皮爾思（Franklin Pierce）撰寫傳記美化形象，皮爾思1853年當選，酬之以美國駐英國利物浦（Liverpool）領事，1857年隨皮爾思卸任，之後旅遊法、意，1860年返美，同年寫就小說《大理石牧神》（The Marble Faun），以意大利為背景敘述兩男兩女之事。1864年病逝。

　　霍桑為美國19世紀重要小說家，以新英格蘭為背景，以象徵手法探討祖上清教徒文化心理，作品歸類為「黑暗傳奇」（Dark Romanticism），引領美國心理描述之小說。

圖片來源：IDJ圖庫

2-2

華盛頓・厄文
Washington Irving

華盛頓·厄文（Washington Irving）1783年生於美國紐約市，父母皆爲蘇格蘭移民，從商，1798年紐約市爆發黃熱病，厄文時年16，送至紐約市北邊塔里城（Tarrytown）避疫，聽聞鄰近沉睡谷（Sleepy Hollow）的荷蘭移民傳說。厄文還曾沿赫德遜河（Hudson River）進入卡茨奇山區（Catskill），日後以此爲短篇小說《李伯大夢》（Rip Van Winkle）場景。

　　厄文19歲開始撰文投報，1804-06年遊歐，磨練了圓熟社交技能，返美後習法，1806年考取律師執照，次年創辦文藝雜誌《雜燴》（Salmagundi），中有一文稱紐約市爲「羔城」（Gotham，古英語意謂「羊城」），延用至今。1809年厄文以幽默筆調寫就《紐約史—由太初至荷蘭殖民結束，狄椎奇·尼克博克著》（History of New-York from the Beginning of the World to the End of the Dutch Dynasty, by Diedrich Knickerbocker），廣受歡迎，Knickerbocker（荷蘭人穿的燈籠褲）此後成爲紐約市民代稱。

　　1813年厄文任雜誌編輯，曾印發美國詩人法蘭西斯·史考特·基（Francis Scott Key）1812年美英戰爭時所作詩《保衛麥亨利堡》（Defense of Fort McHenry），其詩句後成爲美國國歌。因家族生意受戰爭影響，厄文1815年赴歐挽救不成，滯歐至1832年。

　　1818年厄文在英寫就《李伯大夢》，敘述荷裔美人李伯隨和懶散，某日爲躲避妻子嘮叨上卡茨奇山蹓躂，遇身著荷蘭古裝之人，李伯助其負酒上山，見一群相類之長鬚老人玩保齡球，李伯飲其酒醉臥，醒來發覺獵槍生鏽、鬍鬚尺長，下山返家則妻子已逝、親友無蹤，兒子已長大成人，據測他在山中所見可能是17世紀初走失的英國探險家赫德遜船長（Hendrick Hudson）和手下，他離家20多年，其間美國已獨立，他住到女兒家中，一復常態。此篇收錄於1819-20年出版的《傑弗瑞·奎昂先生的素描本》（The Sketch Book of Geoffrey Crayon, Gent.），茲選譯兩段：

A tart temper never mellows with age, and a sharp tongue is the only edged tool that grows keener with constant use.

辛辣脾氣不隨年齡趨緩，銳器中唯有尖舌愈用愈利。

Rip Van Winkle, however, was one of those happy mortals, of foolish, well-oiled dispositions, who take the world easy, eat white bread or brown, which ever can be got with the least thought or trouble, and would rather starve on a penny than work for a pound...If left to himself, he would have whistled life away, in perfect contentment, but his wife kept continually dinning in his ears about his idleness, his carelessness, and the ruin he was bringing on his family.

但是，李伯是那種笨笨的、個性隨和的樂天凡人，這種人隨遇而安，不在乎吃的是白麵包還是棕麵包，只看哪種得來最不費力，寧願身留一文而挨餓，不願爲了一鎊而工作……要照他的意，他會一輩子無所事事吹吹胡哨，一樣滿足，但是他老婆在他耳邊數落他懶散，數落他漫不經心，數落他沒有好好養家。

　　書中另一篇爲《沉睡谷傳奇》（The Legend of Sleepy Hollow），敘述獨立戰爭中沉睡谷有一德國僱傭兵頭顱被炮彈擊落，其幽靈夜夜騎馬找頭，1790年膽小的外來鄉村教師伊克包・奎恩（Ichabod Crane）與當地浪蕩子「鐵骨布隆」（Abraham "Brom Bones" Van Brunt）手求富家女卡翠娜（Katrina Van Tassel），伊克包某晚參加卡翠娜家派對，求婚不成，騎馬返家途中遇無頭騎士頭置鞍上，伊克包催趕駑馬逃命，被無頭騎士擲頭擊中，次早眾人遍尋伊克包不著，只見路上有一碎裂南瓜。卡翠娜後嫁布隆，每當人們提起此事，布隆總面帶曖昧表情，當地則傳說伊克包遭鬼帶走。《傑弗瑞・奎昂先生的素描本》大賣，厄文成爲早期在英受歡迎的美國作家，中有一句：「良好坦誠的幽默是快樂聚會的調味油酒，小小的玩笑和多多的笑聲最能讓人同樂。（Honest good humor is the oil and wine of a merry meeting, and there is no jovial companionship equal to that where the jokes are rather small and laughter abundant）」《紐約史》與《傑弗瑞・奎昂先生的素描本》裡對聖誕節的描述影響及美國的聖誕文化。

1826年厄文應前美國駐西班牙大使之邀前往馬德里，以西班牙殖民美洲為題寫書，1828年出版《哥倫布傳》（A History of the Life and Voyages of Christopher Columbus），虛實相雜，例如虛構中世紀歐洲人相信地球扁平。1829年厄文遷入西班牙南部格拉納達（Granada）阿罕布拉宮（Alhambra）寫作，隨即受任美國駐倫敦使館秘書，1831年辭秘書職，次年出版《阿罕布拉故事集》（Tales of the Alhambra）。

1832年厄文49歲返美，多人指責其作品歐化，不夠本土，厄文以三本美西背景之作品回應：1835年之《草原遊記》（A Tour on the Prairies）、1836年之《亞斯托里亞》（Astoria，敘述美國富豪約翰·亞斯托（John Jacob Astor）1811-13年出資探索美國西北皮毛生意）、1837年之《邦維上尉探險記》（The Adventures of Captain Bonneville）。

1842-46年厄文受任美國駐西班牙大使，1855-59年出版《華盛頓傳》（The Life of George Washington），亦虛實相雜，但流傳甚廣。厄文1859年去世。

厄文生於美國獨立後不久，改寫民間傳說廣受歡迎，享譽歐洲，人譽美國首位文人、美國短篇小說之父。

◆ 華盛頓·厄文 ◆

圖片來源：IDJ圖庫

2-3

朗費羅

Henry Wadsworth Longfellow

朗費羅（Henry Wadsworth Longfellow）1807年生於美國緬因州波特蘭市（Portland），父親是律師，外祖父是國會議員。朗費羅自幼入學，嫻熟拉丁文，喜好閱讀，13歲首度刊登詩作，15歲入緬因州鮑登學院，祖父是創校元老之一，大四立志創作。1825年畢業，應邀留母校擔任首位歐洲現代語言文學教授，1826-29年赴歐學習德、法、西班牙、意大利、葡萄牙等語文，返美後自編語文教科書，將歐洲文學譯為英語。1831年婚娶瑪麗‧波特（Mary Storer Potter），1834年應邀赴哈佛大學執教，同年至1836年再赴歐學習德、荷蘭、丹麥、瑞典、芬蘭、冰島等語文。

　　妻子1835年小產去世，1838年朗費羅作詩《天使足聲》（Footsteps of Angels）紀念。1839年出版翻譯與創作詩集《夜之聲》（Voices of the Night），1841年出版《民謠等詩作》（Ballads and Other Poems），廣受歡迎。1842年寫就《人生過半》（Mezzo Cammin），標題來自但丁《神曲》首句：「當我來到我們人生的半途」（Nel mezzo del cammin di nostra vita），聖經詩篇（Psalms）90章10節：「我們一生的年日是七十歲（The days of our years are threescore years and ten）」，所以人生的一半是35歲，正是朗費羅此時年齡，茲譯出：

Half of my life is gone, and I have let	我人生過了一半，而我讓
The years slip from me and have not fulfilled	歲月空虛流逝，沒有完成
The aspiration of my youth, to build	年輕時的志向，建立一棟
Some tower of song with lofty parapet.	詩歌之塔，上有高聳胸牆。
Not indolence, nor pleasure, nor the fret	非因懶散、或貪玩、或焦躁
Of restless passions that would not be stilled,	浮動，沒辦法平息的情緒，
But sorrow, and a care that almost killed,	而是因憂鬱，致命的憂鬱，
Kept me from what I may accomplish yet;	阻礙了我仍求企及的目標：
Though, half-way up the hill, I see the Past	上山已半，我回望過往
Lying beneath me with its sounds and sights,--	在腳下，聲囂景致歷歷，
A city in the twilight dim and vast,	暮露裡的城市朦朧漫延，

| With smoking roofs, soft bells, and gleaming lights,--
 And hear above me on the autumnal blast
 The cataract of Death far thundering from the heights. | 囪煙飄，鐘聲迴，燈火瑰麗，
 而上方傳來秋日爆響震天
 是死神的瀑布由高處轟墜。 |

1843年朗費羅婚娶第二任妻子芬妮（Fanny Appleton）。1845年作詩《日暮之星》（The Evening Star）獻給芬妮。同年出版《歐洲詩人詩作》（The Poets and Poetry of Europe）介紹歐洲文學。

1845年朗費羅寫就詩作《箭與歌》（The Arrow and the Song）：

| I shot an arrow into the air,
 It fell to earth, I knew not where;
 For, so swiftly it flew, the sight
 Could not follow it in its flight.
 I breathed a song into the air,
 It fell to earth, I knew not where;
 For who has sight so keen and strong,
 That it can follow the flight of song?
 Long, long afterward, in an oak
 I found the arrow, still unbroke;
 And the song, from beginning to end,
 I found again in the heart of a friend. | 我射了一箭飛入高空，
 它落於地，不知所蹤；
 因為，箭速飛快，目光
 無法追隨它飛翔。
 我吟唱一曲傳入高空，
 它落於地，不知所蹤；
 因為，誰的眼力夠尖夠強，
 足以追隨歌聲遠揚？
 許久許久後，在橡樹幹
 上我找到箭，仍未斷；
 而那首歌，從頭直到尾，
 我在友人的心中尋回。 |

1847年朗費羅出版長詩《伊凡潔琳》（Evangeline），敘述一對戀人被迫分離。因出版收入頗豐，1854年朗費羅47歲由哈佛退休，專心寫作。1855年作長詩《海俄瓦薩之

歌》（Song of Hiawatha），敘述原住民酋長海俄瓦薩之事。1860年作詩《親子時辰》（The Children's Hour）：

朗費羅

Between the dark and the daylight,	在白日與黑夜之間，
When the night is beginning to lower,	當夜幕將要低垂降臨，
Comes a pause in the day's occupations,	一日之繁忙暫得休止，
That is known as the Children's Hour.	此時稱爲親子時辰。
I hear in the chamber above me	我聽到樓上房間傳來
The patter of little feet,	小小腳步劈啪響，
The sound of a door that is opened,	聽到房門打開的聲音，
And voices soft and sweet.	還有稚嫩甜蜜語腔。
From my study I see in the lamplight,	我從書房樓燈光下看到，
Descending the broad hall stair,	沿著大廳梯而至，
Grave Alice, and laughing Allegra,	肅靜愛麗絲，歡笑愛樂嘉，
And Edith with golden hair.	和金髮的伊迪絲。
A whisper, and then a silence:	一陣低語，隨即沉默：
Yet I know by their merry eyes	但我見其目光喜點
They are plotting and planning together	看出他們有所圖謀打算
To take me by surprise.	要讓我意外驚詫。
A sudden rush from the stairway,	從階梯突然湧入，
A sudden raid from the hall!	從大廳衝進重圍！
By three doors left unguarded	穿過三道無人門關
They enter my castle wall!	他們闖入我的堡壘！
They climb up into my turret	他們爬入我的塔樓
O'er the arms and back of my chair;	翻越我的扶手椅背，
If I try to escape, they surround me;	他們包圍阻止我逃跑；
They seem to be everywhere.	他們無所不在。
They almost devour me with kisses,	他們以親吻幾乎將我吞噬，
Their arms about me entwine,	他們纏繞我以手臂，
Till I think of the Bishop of Bingen	令我想起賓根的主教

In his Mouse-Tower on the Rhine!	在他萊茵河邊的鼠塔裡！[1]
Do you think, O blue-eyed banditti,	你們這群藍眼強盜，以爲
Because you have scaled the wall,	你們翻越了塔城，
Such an old mustache as I am	我這個捲鬍老頭
Is not a match for you all!	就對付不了你們！
I have you fast in my fortress,	你們被我困在堡中，
And will not let you depart,	我不放你們離開，
But put you down into the dungeon	把你們禁閉在地牢裡，
In the round-tower of my heart.	關進我的心塔要塞。
And there will I keep you forever,	把你們永遠關在那裡，
Yes, forever and a day,	沒錯，永永遠遠，
Till the walls shall crumble to ruin,	直到塔牆碎成廢墟，
And moulder in dust away!	發黴化爲灰煙！

1860年朗費羅作詩《保羅・李維爾夜奔》（Paul Revere's Ride），敘述美國獨立革命時，波士頓人保羅・李維爾奔走告知英軍來襲之事，雖與史實不甚符合，但此作廣爲傳誦，成爲美國造國神話一環。

1861年芬妮意外燒傷去世，朗費羅拯救妻子時面頰灼傷，此後蓄鬚掩飾。朗費羅哀痛近痴，1879年作詩《雪十字》（The Cross of Snow）紀念芬妮。1864-67年翻譯但丁《神曲》，每週三晚邀請文友來家討論譯稿，稱爲「但丁小集」（Dante Club），1882年去世。1884年英國西敏寺置其半身像，美國詩人唯朗費羅有此殊榮。

朗費羅廣泛譯介歐洲文學，由此仿習多種詩律，文字音韻優美，用語通俗，廣受大眾喜愛，他首譯《神曲》，爲美國19世紀最受歡迎詩人。

---

[1] 10世紀德國麥茵茨（Mainz）哈托二世（Hatto II）大主教暴虐，相傳被鼠群咬死塔中。

圖片來源：IDJ圖庫

2-4

愛倫坡

Edgar Allan Poe

　　愛倫坡（Edgar Allan Poe）1809年生於美國波士頓市，父母皆為演員，父親次年離家，母親1811年去世，愛倫坡為維吉尼亞州（Virginia）首府里奇蒙市（Richmond）富商愛倫夫婦收養，1815年舉家赴英，1825年返美，次年入讀維吉尼亞大學，賭博欠債，養父拒絕寄錢，一年後退學，1827年入伍，出版首冊詩集，1829年養母去世，次年入讀西點軍校，因養父私生子與再婚問題決裂，1831年故意犯錯退學，立志寫作，但盜版盛行，難以維生。1835年任期刊編輯，因酗酒解職，同年婚娶13歲的表妹薇琴妮雅（Virginia Clemm），復任編輯。

　　1838年寫就小說《來自南特奇的亞瑟·戈登·皮姆之故事》（The Narrative of Arthur Gordon Pym of Nantucket），敘述主角偷乘捕鯨船出海，往南極途中各種冒險，法國科幻作家居勒·韋爾納（Jules Verne）曾為之寫續集。

　　1839年愛倫坡寫就短篇小說《厄佘家宅之崩壞》（The Fall of the House of Usher），敘述羅德列（Roderick Usher）與妹妹瑪德琳（Madeline）居住祖宅，羅德列神經衰弱，瑪德琳患癲癇，羅德列覺得祖宅有感知能力，瑪德琳去世，葬於祖宅地下墓穴，後數日夜晚暴風雨，羅德列與來訪友人朗讀小說，書中情節應和祖宅地下異聲，羅德列驚覺他活埋了瑪德琳，渾身帶血的瑪德琳破門而入，撲倒羅德列，雙雙死去，祖宅中裂沉入沼澤。茲選譯瑪德琳即將破門而入的一段：

"Not hear it?—yes, I hear it, and have heard it. Long—long—long—many minutes, many hours, many days, have I heard it—yet I dared not—oh, pity me, miserable wretch that I am!—I dared not—I dared not speak! We have put her living in the tomb! Said I not that my senses were acute? I now tell you that I heard her first feeble movements in the hollow

「沒聽到？——我有聽到，聽到很長一段時間了。很久—很久—很久了—無數分鐘，無數鐘頭，無數日子，我聽到了—但我不敢——可憐我吧—我是個廢物！——我不敢—不敢承認！我們活埋了她！我不是說我感官靈敏嗎？我告訴你她在棺材裡一開始微動

coffin. I heard them—many, many days ago—yet I dared not—1 dared not speak! And now — to-night — Ethelred—ha! ha!—the breaking of the hermit's door, and the death-cry of the dragon, and the clangor of the shield! —say, rather, the rending of her coffin, and the grating of the iron hinges of her prison, and her struggles within the coppered archway of the vault!

Oh, whither shall I fly? Will she not be here anon? Is she not hurrying to upbraid me for my haste? Have I not heard her footstep on the stair? Do I not distin-guish that heavy and horrible beating of her heart? Madman!"— here he sprang furiously to his feet, and shrieked out his syllables, as if in the effort he were giving up his soul—"Madman! I tell you that she now stands without the door!"

我就聽到了。我聽到了—許多，許多天以前—但我不敢—我不敢承認！而今—今晚—艾瑟雷—哈！哈！——破開隱士的門，惡龍垂死的哀嚎，盾牌掉地之聲！——其實，是她破開棺材，推開墓穴鐵柵樞紐，掙扎爬上地穴銅鑄梯道之聲！

噢，我能逃去何方？她不是馬上就到來了嗎？她不正趕來責怪我忙中出錯嗎？我不是聽到她的腳步上樓嗎？我不是聽出她那沉重可怕的心跳嗎？瘋子！」——他狂然躍起，尖聲喊叫，好似要將靈魂吐出——「瘋子！我告訴你她現在就在門外！」

　　1841年愛倫坡寫就小說《金甲蟲》（The Gold-Bug），涉及密碼學，引起一般讀者興趣。同年寫就偵探小說《末閣街凶殺案》（The Murders in the Rue Morgue），敘述一對母女陳屍於密閉的公寓，私家偵探杜班（C. Auguste Dupin）成功解謎，指出凶手是一隻紅毛猩猩。此作公認是舉世第一篇偵探小說，建立此文類典範：天才私家偵探、偵探的友人敘述故事、警察無能、結尾解謎。

　　1842年薇琴妮雅患肺結核。1844年愛倫坡指控詩人朗費羅（Longfellow）剽竊他人詩作，朗費羅不作回應。1845年愛倫坡出版詩作《烏鴉》（The Raven），敘述主角失去愛人蕾娜（Lenore），冬夜在書房聽到敲門，門外無人，但一隻烏鴉由窗飛入，停駐門頂雕像上，口吐：「永失落！（Nevermore!）」主角對烏鴉悲傷自語，但烏鴉只重複：「永失落！」茲選譯首段與中間一段：

Once upon a midnight dreary, while I pondered weak and weary,	我曾於某沉悶午夜，疲憊神衰展卷思閱，
Over many a quaint and curious volume of forgotten lore,	許多珍本古籍、為人遺忘遠年奇異傳說，
While I nodded, nearly napping, suddenly there came a tapping,	我打盹幾乎要睡著，突然聽到一聲叩敲，
As of some one gently rapping, rapping at my chamber door.	好像有人輕輕抓撓，抓撓我的書房門廊。
``'Tis some visitor,' I muttered, `tapping at my chamber door -	「來客人了，」我自語道，「在叩敲書房門廊——
Only this, and nothing more.'	如此而已，沒什麼。」

Then, methought, the air grew denser, perfumed from an unseen censer	然後，好似，空氣滯凝，由無形香爐傳清芬
Swung by Seraphim whose foot-falls tinkled on the tufted floor.	晃動在小天使手中，於地墊上步娑娑。
'Wretch,' I cried, 'thy God hath lent thee - by these angels he has sent thee	「可憐人，」我驚呼，「你主賜你一派下天使賜予你
Respite - respite and nepenthe from thy memories of Lenore!	安息—安息、忘憂，不再困於憶念蕾娜！
Quaff, oh quaff this kind nepenthe, and forget this lost Lenore!'	痛飲，痛飲這忘憂液，忘掉你失去的蕾娜！
Quoth the raven, 'Nevermore.'	烏鴉說道，「永失落。」

詩出一舉成名。

1847年薇琴妮雅病逝。1849年愛倫坡於巴爾地摩市（Baltimore）街頭失智遊蕩，送醫數日後去世。文壇宿敵格瑞斯沃（Rufus Wilmot Griswold）撰文捏造信件，謊稱愛倫坡為邪惡嗑藥瘋子，廣為人信，近年始稍平反。

愛倫坡一生窮困，鬻文維生，善寫哥德式恐怖小說，開創偵探小說，引領科幻小說。法國詩人波德萊爾（Charles Baudelaire）譯述其作，在法國廣受歡迎。為美國19世紀重要小說家、詩人。

圖片來源：IDJ圖庫

2-5

哈麗葉・碧澈・絲朵

Harriet Beecher Stowe

哈麗葉‧碧澈‧絲朵（Harriet Beecher Stowe）1811年生於美國康乃狄克州（Connecticut）西部，父親是卡爾文教派（Calvinism）牧師，絲朵5歲母親去世，1824年入讀姊姊辦的哈特福女子學院（Hartford Female Seminary），學習語文、數學，1832年父親遷至中部俄亥俄州（Ohio）辛辛那提市（Cincinnati）任雷恩神學院（Lane Theological Seminary）院長，絲朵隨父遷居，開始寫作。1829-41年辛辛那提愛爾蘭裔勞工三度與黑人勞工衝突，絲朵也曾訪問逃奴，進一步了解黑奴處境。1836年絲朵與神學院教師結婚，夫婦兩都力主廢奴，協助南方黑奴向北逃亡。1850年國會通過奴隸逃亡法（Fugitive Slave Law），嚴禁協助逃奴。同年其夫出任緬因州鮑登學院（Bowdoin College）教授，全家東遷。

　　1851年絲朵聽道時動念以黑奴為題寫小說，同年一歲半的幼子去世，切身感受黑奴家毀之痛，之前1849年逃奴韓生（Josiah Henson）出版自傳，絲朵也受啟發，1851-52年絲朵寫就《湯姆叔叔的小屋》（Uncle Tom's Cabin）於報紙連載，內容敘述肯德基州（Kentucky）農夫薛比（Arthur Shelby）因欠債出售黑奴湯姆與哈利（Harry），中年人湯姆已有妻女，薛比之子喬治一向視為師友，哈利則是薛比妻子之女傭伊萊莎（Eliza）之子。伊萊莎母子逃亡，湯姆被賣到南方，河船上為聖柯萊（Augustine St. Clare）買下帶往新奧爾良（New Orleans），湯姆與與聖柯萊女兒伊娃（Eva）都虔信基督教，成為好友。伊萊莎母子遇見之前逃跑的先生，將搜捕黑奴的洛克（Tom Loker）擊傷，出於基督教慈悲，又將其送醫，洛克感動信神。兩年後伊娃病逝，死前見到天國，聖柯萊承諾釋放湯姆但驟逝，其妻背信將湯姆賣給路易斯安那州（Louisiana）農莊主勒圭（Simon Legree），湯姆拒絕鞭打其他黑奴，被勒圭酷虐，但湯姆堅信基督愛心，並安慰眾黑奴，包括曾被販家毀，因而殺死自己嬰兒的女奴凱西（Cassy）。湯姆鼓勵凱西逃跑，被勒命工頭殺害，但死前仍寬恕勒圭及工頭，勒圭與工頭感動信神。喬治‧薛比要贖買湯姆但來遲，返家後釋放所有黑奴。凱西遇見伊萊莎，發覺是自己之前的女兒，全家赴加拿大獲自由後，返居非洲賴比瑞亞（Liberia）。1852年書出大賣，成為美國19世紀最暢銷小說，南方作家為反擊，紛紛出書描述奴制優點。此書遭批塑造黑人刻板印象：逆來順受的黑奴、慈祥的黑人保母、天真幼稚的黑人小孩等。1862年絲朵赴華盛頓謁見林肯總統，據稱林肯說：「原來你就是寫書造成這場大戰的小婦人（So you are the little woman who wrote the book that started this great war）。」茲選譯兩段，其一爲湯姆被鞭前對勒圭所言：

Mas'r, if you was sick, or in trouble, or dying, and, if taking every drop of blood in this poor old body would save your precious soul, I'd give 'em freely, as the Lord gave his for me. Oh, Mas'r! don't bring this great sin on your soul! It will hurt you more than't will me! Do the worst you can, my troubles'll be over soon; but, if ye don't repent, yours won't never end!	主倫，鹵果你生病，或有困難，或快死掉，而偶口以救你，偶會給你偶心裡的血；鹵果把這個老舊身體裡的每一滴血都給你口以救你寶貴的靈魂，偶會全送給你，就像主耶穌把祂的給偶。噢，主倫！不要造下這個大罪！這給你的傷害大過給偶的！你口以儘量懲罰偶，偶的痛苦不久會結束，但你鹵果不懺悔，你的痛苦永遠沒完！

其二爲喬治釋放黑奴前所言：

It was on his grave, my friends, that I resolved, before God, that I would never own another slave, while it is possible to free him; that nobody, through me, should ever run the risk of being parted from home and friends, and dying on a lonely plantation, as he died. So, when you rejoice in your freedom, think that you owe it to that good old soul, and pay it back in kindness to his wife and children. Think of your freedom, every time you see Uncle Tom's Cabin; and let it be a memorial to put you all in mind to follow in his steps, and be as honest and faithful and Christian as he was.	是在他的墳前，朋友們，我在上帝面前發誓永遠不再蓄養任何奴隸，發誓只要我能釋放奴隸，就不會有任何人因爲我，而可能被迫離家、被迫與友人分隔、被迫孤獨死於農莊，像湯姆那樣。所以，當你們歡慶獲得自由時，別忘了你們要感謝那個善良的心靈，別忘了要報答他的妻子兒女。每當你們看到湯姆叔叔的小屋，都要想到你們的自由；讓這小屋做個紀念，提醒你們記得效法他，跟他一樣誠實、一樣忠心、一樣做個好基督徒。

內戰後絲朵轉而鼓吹已婚婦人應有獨立財產權，1868-69年出任早期婦女雜誌《家爐》（*Hearth and Home*）主編，1873年遷居康州哈特福市，先生1886年去世，絲朵1896年去世。

哈麗葉‧碧澈‧絲朵以寫作《湯姆叔叔的小屋》聞名，促成美國黑奴解放。

圖片來源:IDJ圖庫

2-6
艾默生
Ralph Waldo Emerson

艾默生（Ralph Waldo Emerson）1803年生於美國波士頓市，父親是基督教一神派牧師，1811年病逝。艾默生由母親與姑姑帶大，1812年入學，1817-21年入讀哈佛大學，畢業後與兄長在家辦學。1825年入哈佛神學院，次年爲健康南下佛羅里達州，開始寫詩。1829年任波士頓第二教堂牧師，同年結婚，1831年妻子病逝，深受打擊，開始質疑牧師工作，次年辭職。1833年赴歐旅遊，參觀巴黎植物園時看到植物科學分類，開始關注科學；在英結識哲學家卡萊爾（Thomas Carlyle），深受其自然神論（Deism，認爲上帝造物後即不再現身，人只能透過大自然了解上帝）影響。返美後開始以演講維生，收入頗豐，次年遷居麻州康科德市。1835年再婚。

1836年艾默生籌組「超驗集社」（Transcendental Club），探討超驗主義（Transcendentalism，主張個人根據直覺可上合天道）。同年發表論文《自然》（Nature），立論一個人單獨時可與自然完全溝通，體會自然之神性，以之滋養人；1833年一次演講表達了此論點精髓：

Nature is a language and every new fact one learns is a new word; but it is not a language taken to pieces and dead in the dictionary, but the language put together into a most significant and universal sense. I wish to learn this language, not that I may know a new grammar, but that I may read the great book that is written in that tongue.	自然是一種語言，我們所學每項新知即一新詞；此語言非字典裡破碎的死語言，而是以宇宙組成的重要語言。我要學這語言，不是爲了多學一種文法，而是爲了閱讀以此語言寫就的巨著。

1837年艾默生演講《美國學者》（The American Scholar），鼓勵同胞創建不同於歐洲、獨屬美國的文風。同代詩人老奧利弗·溫德爾·霍姆斯（Oiver Wendell Holmes, Sr.）稱之爲美國「知識界的獨立宣言」（Intellectual Declaration of Independence）。1838年艾默生應邀於哈佛大學神學院演講，指聖經述說的奇蹟不實，耶穌是人非神，被教會指責爲無神論者。

1840年「超驗集社」發行期刊《日晷》（The Dial）。1841年《論文：初集》（Essays: First Series）出版，其中《自立》（Self-Reliance）一文受印度一元論哲學影響，主張個人必須遵從自己良心，不可從眾，中有一句：「卑微的心靈崇於愚蠢從眾，格局小的政客、哲學家、神學家最好此道。（A foolish consistency is the hobgoblin of little minds, adored by little statesmen and philosophers and divines）」；《大靈魂》（The Over-Soul）一文主張人類靈魂至美常存，彼此相繫，具有神性。《圓》（Circles）一文表述大自然處處體現圓，首句為：「第一個圓是眼睛；第二個圓是眼睛所見視野；此原型不斷重複，充斥整個大自然。（The eye is the first circle; the horizon which it forms is the second; and throughout nature this primary figure is repeated without end）」；書出享譽歐洲。

1842年艾默生長子去世，次年「超驗集社」社友奧科特（Bronson Alcott，其女露意莎Louisa May Alcott寫有小說《小婦人》Little Women）在麻州創立烏托邦農場「果莊」（Fruitlands）失敗，艾默生1945年為奧科特一家在康科德置房居住。

《日晷》1844年停刊，同年《論文：次集》（Essays: Second Series）出版，其中《詩人》（The Poet）一文呼籲美國詩人寫作美國文化，直接啟發了惠特曼（Walt Whitman）；《經驗》（Experience）一文強調感性對經驗之影響，反對將生活過度理性化，因此反對烏托邦社區。

1847-48年艾默生赴英格蘭、蘇格蘭、愛爾蘭、法國旅遊。1872年家裡失火，同年出現失語現象，此後較少演講，再赴歐陸、埃及旅遊。艾默生此時地位崇高，人稱「康科德聖人」（Concord Sage）。1879年後逐漸失智，1882年去世。艾默生終身寫日記，共16冊，1960-82年陸續出版，人比之為美國的蒙田（16世紀法國散文家）。

艾默生受德國唯心主義（Idealism）與印度哲學影響，提倡超驗主義、個人主義，引領19世紀美國本土文化、宗教、文學。

圖片來源：IDJ圖庫

2-7
梭羅

梭羅

梭羅
Henry David Thoreau

　　梭羅（Henry David Thoreau）1817年生於美國麻州康科德市，父親開鉛筆工廠，1833-37年入讀哈佛大學，畢業後返家結識艾默生，因其引導開始寫日記，曾短暫教書，因不願體罰而辭職。1838年與兄長辦學，引入踏青、參訪工商門號等觀念，1840年其文初次刊於艾默生「超驗集社」之期刊《日晷》，1841-44年遷入艾默生家，擔任助理、家教。1842年兄長病逝，次年開始在父親的鉛筆工廠工作。

　　1845年7月4日至1847年9月6日梭羅遷入艾默生莊園上華騰湖（Walden Pond）旁梭羅自建的小屋，自述：

I went to the woods because I wished to live deliberately, to front only the essential facts of life, and see if I could not learn what it had to teach, and not, when I came to die, discover that I had not lived.	我前往森林居住，目的在明確體驗生活，面對生命的基本要素，試圖從中學習，以免臨死前才發覺從未眞正活過。

　　1854年梭羅出版《華騰湖，或稱林中的生活》（Walden, or Life in the Woods，又譯《湖濱散記》），將兩年的經驗濃縮爲一年，中有一句：

If a man does not keep pace with his companions, perhaps it is because he hears a different drummer. Let him step to the music which he hears, however measured or far away.	若有人步伐異於同儕，也許是因爲他聽到另一種鼓聲節奏。讓他照他的節奏行進吧，無論這節奏是何形態、有多飄渺。

1846年梭羅居住華騰湖時反對美國入侵墨西哥以擴張蓄奴地盤，拒絕繳稅，因此入獄，隔日有人代為繳稅而釋出。1849年他以此經驗寫就論文《公民抗命》（Resistance to Civil Government，又稱Civil Disobedience），中有兩句：

There will never be a really free and enlightened State until the State comes to recognize the individual as a higher and independent power, from which all its own power and authority are derived, and treats him accordingly.	不可能有真正自由開明的政府，除非政府承認個人有更高、獨立的權力，承認政府權力來自個人，並以此對待個人。

That government is best which governs not at all.	最好的政府就是完全不管事的政府。

1849年梭羅寫就《康科德與梅里馬克河一週遊》（A Week on the Concord and Merrimack Rivers），紀念1839年和兄長出遊；梭羅聽從艾默生意見，自費請艾默生的出版社印刷1000本，結果只賣出不到300本，因此欠債。

1846年起梭羅在美國東北、中西部、魁北克旅遊，1851年起著迷於植物學，觀察記錄康科德四季生態變化，出版多本遊記、生態書籍，勸人「以旅人心態居住家鄉。（live at home like a traveler）」

1859年激進廢奴主義者約翰·布朗（John Brown）劫持聯邦軍火庫鼓動黑奴造反，因而處死，梭羅獨排眾議，堅決支持布朗，扭轉相當輿論。

1860年梭羅深夜觀察林木遇雨生病，延至1862年去世。

梭羅是西方個人主義典型，《湖濱散記》塑造了美國文化親近自然之風氣，引領生態科學與環保運動；《公民抗命》的非暴力抵抗影響了印度聖雄甘地與美國黑人民權運動領袖馬丁‧路德‧金（Martin Luther King）。

梭
羅

圖片來源：IDJ圖庫

2-8

惠特曼
Walt Whitman

惠特曼
Walt Whitman

　　惠特曼（Walt Whitman）1819年生於美國紐約州長島（Long Island）農家，11歲輟學，任當地週報印刷工學徒，工餘去圖書館自學，參加辯論社，看戲劇演出，在雜誌發表詩作。1835年遷居紐約市，次年失業搬回長島，兼職教書，1838-39年自辦報紙。其後至1848年在紐約市任報紙編輯。生活散漫，作息不定。1848年參加「自由土地黨」（Free Soil Party），宗旨是反對美西新成立的州施行奴隸制。

　　1855年惠特曼自費出版詩集《草葉集》（Leaves of Grass），志在書寫「美國史詩」，採無韻體，語言節奏模仿聖經，第一首是長詩《自我之歌》（Song of Myself），茲選譯首段與中間一段：

I celebrate myself, and sing myself, And what I assume you shall assume, For every atom belonging to me as good belongs to you. I loafe and invite my soul, I lean and loafe at my ease observing a spear of summer grass. My tongue, every atom of my blood, formd from this soil, this air, Born here of parents born here from parents the same, and their parents the same, I, now thirty-seven years old in perfect health begin, Hoping to cease not till death. Creeds and schools in abeyance, Retiring back a while sufficed at what they are, but never forgotten, I harbor for good or bad, I permit to speak at every hazard,	我慶祝我自己，歌頌我自己， 我的心思就是你的心思， 因為屬於我的每個分子也屬於你。 我遊蕩，邀靈魂同行， 我悠晃閒逛觀察一莖夏日之草。 我舌頭、血液每個分子，出自這土、這氣， 我生於這裡，父母同樣生於這裡， 他們的父母也同樣生於這裡， 我，現年三十七歲，健康極佳，此刻開始， 希望到死才停止。 信條、教派退避一旁， 暫時留置不去顧、不去問，但絕未忘記， 我身具或善或惡，我任意開口言論，

Nature without check with original energy. ... Walt Whitman, an American, one of the roughs, a kosmos, disorderly, fleshly, and sensual, no sentimentalist, no stander above men or women or apart from them, no more modest than immodest.	我是自然不設限,有自生能量。 …… 華特‧惠特曼,一個美國人,一個粗人,一個宇宙,散亂的,肉體的,感性的,不濫情,既不高於男人、女人,也不不同於他們,既不謙虛,也不不謙虛。

　　書出遭人評爲淫穢,但作家艾默生主張美國需要本土文學,見書後大爲讚賞。次年再版增加20首詩。惠特曼一生有多位親密男性友人,1860年三版(又稱《菖蒲版》Calamus,菖蒲形似陽具,在希臘神話中代表男同性戀)加入「菖蒲」、「亞當之子」(Enfants dAdam)兩章,「菖蒲」描述男男感情,茲選譯一段:

We two boys together clinging, One the other never leaving, Up and down the roads going, North and South excursions making, Power enjoying, elbows stretching, fingers clutching, Armd and fearless, eating, drinking, sleeping, loving. No law less than ourselves owning, sailing, soldiering, thieving, threatening, Misers, menials, priests alarming, air breathing, water drinking, on the turf or the sea-beach dancing, Cities wrenching, ease scorning, statutes mocking, feebleness chasing, Fulfilling our foray.	我們兩男孩纏抱一起, 彼此之間從不分離, 去到這裡去到那裡, 南方北方一塊出行, 享受活力,肘臂伸遞,指掌握緊, 攜械無懼,饑食,渴飲,倦眠,愛戀。 不遵從低於自身的法令,駕船,當兵, 偷竊,威脅, 小氣,卑賤,不守誡命,有生息, 慣喝水,在草原、海灘上跳舞歡慶, 絞扭都會,鄙視安逸,嘲弄法律, 對軟弱迫迫欺凌, 我們成功出擊。

「亞當之子」一章描述男女感情，選譯一段：

A woman waits for me, she contains all, nothing is lacking,	有個女人在等我，她涵有一切，什麼都不缺，
Yet all were lacking if sex were lacking, or if the moisture of the right man were lacking.	但若沒有性愛則一切都缺，若沒有合適男人的潤澤也一樣。
Sex contains all, bodies, souls,	性愛包涵一切，肉體，靈魂，
Meanings, proofs, purities, delicacies, results, promulgations,	意義，證明，純淨，精緻，結果，繁衍，
Songs, commands, health, pride, the maternal mystery, the seminal milk,	歌唱，命令，健康，自尊，母性的神秘，精液，
All hopes, benefactions, bestowals, all the passions, loves,	一切希望，行善，賜予，一切激情，摯愛，
beauties, delights of the earth,	華美，世間歡享，
All the governments, judges, gods, followd persons of the earth,	一切政府，法官，神明，世上個個領袖，
These are contain in sex as parts of itself and justifications of itself.	這些全包涵於性愛，為性愛一部份，為性愛之理由。

　　1867年內戰結束後《草葉集》出四版，1871年南方重建期出五版，1876年美國建國百年出六版，1881年出七版，1889年出八版，1892年出九版（又稱「臨終版」Deathbed Edition），每版皆有改動。

　　惠特曼弟弟喬治在南北戰爭北方軍隊服役，1862年報載傷亡士兵名單有名字近似喬治，惠特曼往南方前線尋找，發現弟弟只是輕傷，但親見士兵傷亡慘重，決定南下華盛頓照顧傷兵，同時在陸軍部兼職，1865年在內政部找到專職，未久或因《草葉集》情色詩文被新任部長解職，隨即在友人作家歐康納（William Douglas O'Connor）協助下轉職司法總長辦公室（Attorney Generals office）直到1872年。

1865年林肯被刺，惠特曼寫就《噢 船長！我的船長》（O Captain! My Captain!）痛悼，爲其唯一傳統格律詩作：

O Captain! my Captain! our fearful trip is done;	噢船長！我的船長！我們險途已終；
The ship has weatherd every rack, the prize we sought is won;	船經受各種擊盪，我們目的已成；
The port is near, the bells I hear, the people all exulting,	港口已近，鐘聲已聞，眾人都在歡慶，
While follow eyes the steady keel, the vessel grim and daring:	大家目注船體穩進，船身肅穆武勇：
But O heart! heart! heart!	但，噢，心啊！心啊！心啊！
O the bleeding drops of red,	噢滴出的鮮血，
Where on the deck my Captain lies,	甲板上我的船長橫躺，
Fallen cold and dead.	僵臥已殞滅。
O Captain! my Captain! rise up and hear the bells;	噢船長！我的船長！起來聆聽鐘聲；
Rise up—for you the flag is flung—for you the bugle trills;	起來—旗幟爲你飄揚—號角爲你響動；
For you bouquets and ribbond wreaths—for you the shores a-crowding;	爲你有花束、綴絲花環—爲你岸邊人群麋集；
For you they call, the swaying mass, their eager faces turning;	爲你呼喚，熱切群眾，殷切目光期冀；
Here Captain! dear father!	船長在此！至親之父！
This arm beneath your head;	我手將你頭枕接；
It is some dream that on the deck,	我疑似夢，在甲板上，
You've fallen cold and dead.	你僵臥已殞滅。
My Captain does not answer, his lips are pale and still;	我的船長不回應，雙脣蒼白不動；
My father does not feel my arm, he has no pulse nor will;	我父無法感知我手，心脈意識皆空；
The ship is anchord safe and sound, its voyage closed and done;	船已下錨安全無虞，航程已完畢；
From fearful trip, the victor ship, comes in with object won;	經歷艱險，船得勝利，入港已達目的；
Exult, O shores, and ring, O bells!	歡慶，噢港岸，傳響，噢鐘聲！
But I, with mournful tread,	但我，腳步悲切，
Walk the deck my Captain lies,	彳亍船長倒臥的甲板，
Fallen cold and dead.	他僵臥已殞滅。

同年另寫就長詩《當丁香上回在門口綻放》（When lilacs last in the dooryard bloomd）紀念林肯，林肯4月被刺，是丁香花季，茲選譯第一段：

When lilacs last in the dooryard bloomd,	當丁香上回在門口綻放，
And the great star early droopd in the western sky in the night,	當金星暮色初降即懸掛西方天際，
I mournd, and yet shall mourn with ever-returning spring.	我哀悼，未來每當春回都將哀悼。
Ever-returning spring, trinity sure to me you bring,	每當春回，此三者你必然帶到，
Lilac blooming perennial and drooping star in the west,	丁香年年綻放，星垂西方天際，
And thought of him I love.	思念我敬愛的他。

1866年歐康納寫就傳記《善良的白髮詩人》（The Good Gray Poet）將惠特曼形象由浪蕩子重塑為道德愛國長者。1868年《惠特曼詩集》（Poems of Walt Whitman）在英出版，廣受歡迎。1873年惠特曼中風，遷入新澤西州坎登市（Camden）喬治家休養，1892年去世。

惠特曼《草葉集》志在為美國創作本土建國文學，為無韻詩語法、美國本土內涵樹立典範，人稱「民主詩人」（Poet of Democracy）、「無韻詩之父」（Father of Free Verse）；其浪蕩生活方式引領20世紀頹廢（Beat generation）與嬉皮（Hippies）世代。

圖片來源：IDJ圖庫

2-9

梅維爾

Herman Melville

梅維爾
Herman Melville

梅維爾（Herman Melville）1819年生於美國紐約市，父母祖上都參加過獨立戰爭。父親從事法國乾貨生意，揮霍無度，1830年遷居紐約州奧伯尼市（Albany）。梅維爾自幼好學，1831年家貧輟學，父親1832年破產，隨即病逝，伯父安排梅維爾做銀行職員，1834年轉往大哥的皮貨廠任職。1835年以外祖母遺產復學，1837年美國經濟衰退，大哥破產，梅維爾再度輟學，暫任教師。

1839年梅維爾在報章刊文，顯露其獨特文風：多用典故（聖經、莎士比亞、密爾頓）、語氣誇飾、略顯遊戲之姿。同年大哥安排他上英國商船做水手赴利物浦。1841年在麻州上船捕鯨赴南太平洋，1842年在馬克薩斯群島（Marquesas）跳船潛逃，與泰皮族（Typee）土人共處三週，後上澳洲捕鯨船赴大溪地（Tahiti），參與叛變短暫被捕，數月後又乘捕鯨船赴檀香山。1844年在美國軍艦上做水手返美。梅維爾自述此次海上旅程為他開展了新生命，讓他接觸到下層階級和異族文化，啟發日後哲學思考。

1845年梅維爾以泰皮族背景寫就小說《泰皮》，開太平洋冒險小說濫觴，書出大賣。1847年依據大溪地經驗寫就小說《歐木》（Omoo），同年婚娶麻州最高法院法官之女伊麗莎白（Elizabeth Knapp Shaw），定居紐約市。1849年出版小說《瑪地》（Mardi），多哲學討論，滯銷。同年依據1839年赴利物浦船程寫就小說《雷本》（Redburn）。1850年依據美國軍艦背景寫就小說《白夾克》（White-Jacket），同年遷居麻州匹茲斐爾德市（Pittsfield），與作家霍桑為鄰，並著文《霍桑及其青苔》（Hawthorne and His Mosses）評論霍桑短篇小說集《古宅青苔》（Mosses from an Old Manse），中有一句：

It is better to fail in originality, than to succeed in imitation. He who has never failed somewhere, that man can not be great. Failure is the true test of greatness. And if it be said, that continual success is a proof that a man wisely knows his powers, — it is only to be added, that, in that case, he knows them to be small. Let us believe it, then, once for all, that there is no hope for us in these smooth pleasing writers that know their powers.

寧可原創而失敗，也好過模仿而成功。從未失敗的人，不可能偉大。惟有失敗才能驗證偉大。如果說恆常的成功證明其人知其所能，——我們可以再加一句：此人必知其所能者卑小。由此可以確認：我們不能寄望於此等知其所能、安穩討好的作家。

　　1850-51年梅維爾寫就小說《白鯨記》（Moby Dick，又名《莫比敵》），敘述主角以實瑪利（Ishmael）加入捕鯨船「皮夸德」號（Pequod）赴南太平洋捕鯨，但船長阿哈伯（Ahab）之前因白色巨鯨莫比敵失去一腿，一心追逐白鯨復仇，最終全船只有以實瑪利生還。歷來文評家賦予白鯨多種象徵：上帝、命運、撒旦、大自然、各人追逐的終極目標等，書出滯銷，今日則視爲文學巨著，茲選譯第一段：

Call me Ishmael. Some years ago - never mind how long precisely - having little or no money in my purse, and nothing particular to interest me on shore, I thought I would sail about a little and see the watery part of the world. It is a way I have of driving off the spleen and regulating the circulation. Whenever I find myself growing grim about the mouth; whenever it is a damp, drizzly November in my soul; whenever I find myself involuntarily pausing before coffin warehouses, and bringing up the rear of every funeral I meet; and especially whenever my hypos get such an upper hand of me, that it requires a strong moral principle to prevent me from deliberately stepping into the street,

叫我以實瑪利。若干年前—別管到底幾年—我身上分文不名，對陸地上一切覺得無趣，想說出海走走，看看水上世界。我都靠這方法驅趕煩悶，調整身心。每當我自覺表情日沉，每當我心靈呈現十一月的潮濕雨季，每當我不由自主佇立棺材倉庫前，遇到喪葬隊伍即尾隨其後，尤其是每當我情緒失控，要強忍才不至於上街逐一打掉人們的帽子—這時，

and methodically knocking people's hats off - then, I account it high time to get to sea as soon as I can. This is my substitute for pistol and ball. With a philosophical flourish Cato throws himself upon his sword; I quietly take to the ship. There is nothing surprising in this. If they but knew it, almost all men in their degree, some time or other, cherish very nearly the same feelings towards the ocean with me.

我自覺該儘快出海了。我以此代替手槍和子彈。卡托口述長篇大論飲刃自盡，我則悄悄上船。這不奇怪。大多數人若有自覺，或多或少，或早或晚，都會發現他們也有我對海洋的感情。

　　1852年梅維爾寫就小說《皮耶》（Pierre），內容晦澀，書出滯銷，紐約報紙甚至報導他精神錯亂。梅維爾因經濟困難精神憂鬱，1853-56年轉為雜誌寫作短篇小說，包括《錄事巴托比》（Bartleby the Scrivener），敘述紐約華爾街律師事務所錄事（文抄員）巴托比日漸拒絕與世人溝通，對任何要求皆應以「我選擇不要」（I would prefer not to），最終蜷曲餓死監獄裡，此文探討人與人間溝通之困難。

　　1856年梅維爾接受岳父支助赴英國與中東旅遊，1857年出版最後一本長篇小說《詐騙者》（The Confidence-Man），敘述一名騙徒在密西西比河遊輪上試探騙取乘客信任，此作探討世事表裡虛實。

　　1860年後梅維爾棄文從詩，1863年遷居紐約市，1866年透過岳家關係獲任紐約市海關稽察員，據說是該海關唯一清廉關員，因經濟穩定精神也逐漸穩定。其出版生涯雖告終，但仍致力創作長詩《凱拉若》（Clarel），藉由主角凱拉若在中東聖地旅遊探討宗教與信仰，共18,000行，於美國文學裡長度第一。

　　1886年梅維爾退休，晚年復歸小說，寫作《水手比利·巴德》（Billy Budd, Sailor），敘述貌美心善的比利·巴德被英國軍艦強徵入伍做水手，遭人誣陷，意外將誣陷者打死，被判吊死，此作探討善惡賞罰問題，至1891年去世仍未完成，1924年由學者編輯出版。

梅維爾以美國的莎士比亞自期，以語言風格、象徵指涉探討永恆價值、存在意義，引領20世紀荒謬（absurdist）文學，爲美國文學巨匠。

梅維爾

圖片來源：IDJ圖庫

2-10

愛茉莉・荻金蓀

愛茉莉·荻金蓀（Emily Dickinson）1830年生於美國麻州中部安姆赫斯特市（Amherst）望族，祖父創立了當地名校安姆赫斯特學院（Amherst College），父親為該學院財物長，曾任眾議員。荻金蓀自幼受良好教育，就讀安姆赫斯特中學（Amherst Academy），受教於校長亨復禮（Leonard Humphrey）。1844年因密友病逝大受打擊，深切感受死亡。1847年入讀賀柳山女修院（Mount Holyoke Female Seminary），未滿一年即被接回家，原因不明。次年經家庭友人、年輕律師紐騰（Benjamin Franklin Newton）引介，開始閱讀華茲華士與艾默生詩作，深受啓發。1850年時年25的亨復禮病世，善感的荻金蓀再次深受打擊，日後詩作多探討死亡，茲選譯此類作品4首。其一：

I never lost as much but twice,	我曾兩度如此痛失，
And that was in the sod.	所失葬於地下。
Twice have I stood a beggar	兩度我曾為乞丐
Before the door of God!	佇求上帝門闔！
Angels — twice descending	天使—兩度降臨
Reimbursed my store —	裝滿我的倉廩—
Burglar! Banker — Father!	小偷！掌櫃—父親！
I am poor once more!	我此刻又輸盡！

其二：

My life closed twice before its close—	我生命終結前曾兩次掩闔—
It yet remains to see	現在還未知

If Immortality unveil A third event to me So huge, so hopeless to conceive As these that twice befell. Parting is all we know of heaven, And all we need of hell.	上天是否將揭示 如此之事第三次 巨大，完全無法想像 如同此前兩次。 分離——對天堂我們僅此認知， 對地獄則僅需此。

其三：

I heard a Fly buzz — when I died — The Stillness in the Room Was like the Stillness in the Air — Between the Heaves of Storm — The Eyes around — had wrung them dry — And Breaths were gathering firm For that last Onset — when the King Be witnessed — in the Room — I willed my Keepsakes — Signed away What portion of me be Assignable — and then it was There interposed a Fly — With Blue — uncertain stumbling Buzz — Between the light — and me — And then the Windows failed — and then I could not see to see—	我聽到蠅嗡—當我臨終— 房間裡的沉靜 有如空氣裡的沉靜— 在陣陣風暴間— 四周眼目—已被絞乾— 氣息復聚重整 以備最後進襲—當君王 來露面—於房中— 我吩咐遺物—給出 我能夠給出 的部份—就在此刻 一隻蒼蠅擋路— 靛藍—翅翅嗡嗡頓折— 隔斷光明—與我— 接著窗戶轉暗—接著 我失去張看的意圖——

其四：

Because I could not stop for Death—	因我無法停接死亡—
He kindly stopped for me—	他好意停接我—
The Carriage held but just Ourselves—	馬車裡只有我們倆—
And Immortality.	以及永恆不朽。
We slowly drove—He knew no haste,	我們緩馳—他毫不急，
And I had put away	我也放下了
My labor and my leisure too,	我的忙碌、我的休閒，
For His Civility—	因他禮數嫻熟—
We passed the School, where Children strove	車過學校，學童下課
At recess—in the ring—	漫遊—在操場—
We passed the Fields of Gazing Grain—	車過田野，參莖注目—
We passed the Setting Sun—	車過西下夕陽
Or rather—He passed Us—	或該說—夕陽越過我們—
The Dews drew quivering and chill—	寒露使人骰餗打顫—
For only Gossamer, my Gown—	薄如蟬翼，我的外衣—
My Tippet—only Tulle—	我披肩—只有輕紗—
We paused before a House that seemed	我們停在一棟屋前
A Swelling of the Ground—	有如地面墳起—
The Roof was scarcely visible—	屋頂幾乎看不見—
The Cornice—in the Ground—	屋簷—在地底—
Since then—'tis centuries— and yet	迄今—已數百年—但是
Feels shorter than the Day	感覺短過那一天
I first surmised the Horses' Heads	當日我初次估判馬首
Were toward Eternity—	朝向永恆方位——

1853年荻金蓀密友、中學同窗蘇珊（Susan Gilbert）與荻金蓀哥哥奧斯丁（Austin）訂婚，1856年結婚。1855年荻金蓀偕母親和妹妹出遊華府，在費城結識長老會牧師瓦茲沃斯（Charles Wadsworth），成為好友。1850年代中母親健康逐漸惡化，此後為照顧母親荻金蓀幾乎足不出戶。1850年代末結識《春田共和報》（Springfield Republican）總編輯博爾思（Samuel Bowles），兩人書信往還，荻金蓀生前極少發表詩作，但博爾思刊登了幾首，其中1865年一首詠蛇：

愛茉莉‧荻金蓀

A narrow Fellow in the Grass	草叢中一個細長傢伙
Occasionally rides -	偶爾越經—
You may have met Him - did you not	你可能見過—沒有嗎
His notice sudden is-	發現他很突然—
The Grass divides as with a Comb -	草叢兩分有如梳開—
A spotted shaft is seen -	斑點長條顯露—
And then it closes at your feet	隨即在腳下復掩
And opens further on -	繼續前行分剖—
He likes a Boggy Acre	他喜愛溼地田畝
A Floor too cool for Corn,	地面種黍太涼，
Yet when a Boy, and Barefoot -	但是小時，打赤腳—
I more than once at Noon	我多次在午間
Have passed, I thought, a Whip lash	走過，我以為，一條長鞭
Unbraiding in the Sun	在日頭下散垂
When stooping to secure it	我蹲下要撿起
It wrinkled and was gone -	它扭動離去
Several of Nature's People	大自然若干居民
I know, and they know me -	我認識，他們也認識我—
I feel for them a transport	我對他們抱有
Of cordiality -	一種友好情懷—
But never met this Fellow,	但每當遇到這傢伙，
Attended, or alone	或有伴，或一人
Without a tighter breathing	我都胸腔一緊
And Zero at the Bone-	而且骨髓冰冷——

1860年代初荻金蓀創作達高峰。1867年後極少露面，只與人隔牆交談，但仍積極通信，在家料理家事，種花蒔草，通常著白色衣裳，1861年有一首小詩論及此：

愛茉莉・荻金蓀

A solemn thing – it was – I said – A Woman – White – to be – And wear – if God should count me fit – Her blameless mystery –	莊重大事—這是—我說— 一個女人—白色—成為— 穿著—若上帝認為我配— 她無垢的神秘——

　　1872-73年荻金蓀結識麻州最高法院法官羅德（Otis Phillips Lord），魚雁往還，討論文學。哥哥婚姻不諧，1882年愛上安姆赫斯特學院教員之妻梅波（Mabel Loomis Todd），同年母親、瓦茲沃斯去世，1883年荻金蓀最鍾愛的8歲侄子病逝，1884年羅德去世，荻金蓀說：「這些死亡淹沒了我，我心尚未浮出前者，後者又來。（The Dyings have been too deep for me, and before I could raise my Heart from one, another has come）」

　　1886年荻金蓀病逝，生前要求妹妹銷毀書信，但未提及詩作，妹妹發現詩作後將之收集，部份於1890年出版，大受歡迎。全集1955年出版，遵照荻金蓀原稿編排。

　　茲再譯荻金蓀小詩一首：

I'm Nobody! Who are you? Are you — Nobody — Too? Then there's a pair of us! Don't tell! they'd advertise — you know! How dreary — to be — Somebody! How public — like a Frog — To tell one's name — the livelong June — To an admiring Bog!	我是無名小卒！你是誰？ 你也是—無名小卒—歟？ 那我倆是一對！ 別嚷！他們會傳開—知道嗎！ 好累—成為—大人物！ 要公然—像青蛙— 廣告身份—漫長六月— 對著仰慕的沼窪！

　　荻金蓀一生寫了近1,800首詩，以獨創標點、斷句、意象，探討死亡、永生、大自然，生前沒沒無聞，如今視爲現代詩先驅，爲19世紀美國重要詩人。

圖片來源：IDJ圖庫

2-11
馬克・吐溫
Mark Twain

　　馬克‧吐溫（Mark Twain）原名撒姆爾‧克雷蒙斯（Samuel Langhorne Clemens），1835年生於美國密蘇里州佛羅里達市（Florida），同年哈雷彗星（Halley's Comet）來訪。父親為律師，吐溫4歲遷居密西西比（Mississippi）河畔漢尼拔市（Hannibal）。父親1847年去世，吐溫次年輟學至印刷廠做學徒，1851年在兄長歐萊恩（Orion）所辦《漢尼拔日報》（Hannibal Journal）任排版工，並撰寫幽默短文。18歲赴美國東部、中西部做印刷排版，晚間在公立圖書館廣泛閱讀自修。1857年返家學習做密西西比河導航員，日後筆名馬克‧吐溫（Mark Twain）由此而來，意為「標記：二」，2尋（fathom）約3.66公尺，為河輪安全通過深度。吐溫攜帶弟弟亨利上船工作，後者1858年因河輪爆炸燒傷去世，吐溫自責甚深。

　　1861年美國內戰開始，河運銳減，歐萊恩時任內華達地區（Nevada）區務卿（Secretary），吐溫投奔兄長，暫任礦工，隨即轉任記者，1863年首度以筆名馬克‧吐溫於報紙刊文。1864年赴舊金山，仍任記者，曾說：「我平生遭遇最冷的冬天，是在舊金山的某個夏天。（The Coldest Winter I ever spent in my life, was a Summer in San Francisco）」吐溫刊文為弱勢發聲遭解職，貧困幾至自殺，次年根據在採金礦區聽到的故事於紐約一家週報發表短篇小說《卡縣的馳名跳蛙》（The Celebrated Jumping Frog of Calaveras County），敘述兩人姓名相似造成混淆，以諷刺幽默一舉成名，為典型吐溫風格。1866年為《沙加緬度聯合報》（Sacramento Union）赴夏威夷寫遊記，並據此演講賺錢。次年再為報紙赴地中海寫遊記，結集為《鄉巴佬出國記》（The Innocents Abroad），1869年出版，大為暢銷。途中結識查爾斯‧藍登（Charles Langdon），1870年婚娶其姊歐麗薇雅（Olivia）。歐麗薇雅出身富貴前衛家庭，吐溫因此結識一批前衛思想家。婚後定居紐約州水牛城（Buffalo），任職《水牛城快報》（Buffalo Express），1871年遷居康乃狄克州哈特福市（Hartford），1873年出版小說《鍍金時代》（The Gilded Age），描述美國19世紀後期極度繁榮，此辭彙後普遍為人使用。1874年於哈特福自起豪華新屋遷入。

　　1876年吐溫根據小時在漢尼拔市的生活寫就《湯姆歷險記》（The Adventures of Tom Sawyer），茲選譯一段：

> Tom said to himself that it was not such a hollow world, after all. He had discovered a great law of human action, without knowing it – namely, that in order to make a man or a boy covet a thing, it is only necessary to make the thing difficult to attain. If he had been a great and wise philosopher, like the writer of this book, he would now have comprehended that Work consists of whatever a body is obliged to do, and that Play consists of whatever a body is not obliged to do.

> 湯姆自言道原來世界並不那麼無趣。他無意中發現了人世一條重要定律—即是：要讓成人或男孩渴求某事物，只需讓該事物難以到手。如果湯姆是偉大睿智的哲學家，有如本書作者，他當會明白工作即是你必須做的事，而嬉戲即是不必做的事。

1881年吐溫出版《乞丐與王子》（The Prince and the Pauper），描述長相相似的乞丐與王子對調身份，批評階級社會。1884年出版《哈克歷險記》（Adventures of Huckleberry Finn），描寫內戰前美國南方，敘述《湯姆歷險記》主角之一哈克與友人黑奴吉姆（Jim）順著密西西比河而下的各種經歷，批評奴隸制度，首創以方言、地方色彩書寫，例如首句：「你打是沒看過《湯姆歷險記》作本書你就不曉得俺；但不要緊。（You don't know about me without you have read a book by the name of The Adventures of Tom Sawyer; but that ain't no matter）」茲選譯一段，哈克決定寧下地獄，也要遵照良心，不向吉姆主人告發吉姆，為哈克轉變之關鍵段落：

> It was a close place. I took ... up [the letter I'd written to Miss Watson], and held it in my hand. I was a-trembling, because I'd got to decide, forever, betwixt two things, and I knowed it. I studied a minute, sort of holding my breath, and then says to myself: "All right then, I'll go to hell" —and tore it up. It was awful thoughts and awful words, but they was said. And I let them stay said; and never thought no more about reforming.

> 地方狹窄。俺拿起……（寫給華生太太的信），在手中，渾身打顫，因為俺必須做個選擇，沒得反悔，俺心裡明白。俺看著信一陣子，屏住氣，告訴自己：「好吧，俺就下地獄」——然後把信撕掉。這樣想、這樣說，感覺糟透了，但俺還是說了。以後也沒收回來，也沒再想過要「學好」。

此書人譽為第一部偉大的美國小說，海明威（Hemingway）曾說：「所有美國現代文學都出自《哈克歷險記》。（All modern American literature comes from *Huck Finn*）」

1889年吐溫出版歷史科幻小說《美國佬誤闖亞瑟王廷》（A Connecticut Yankee in King Arthur's Court），描述19世紀美國人返至亞瑟王時期的英國，並帶去先進科技，批評封建社會。

吐溫書多賺錢，但投資新科技虧損，1891年因此迫遷歐洲，1893年結識石油業鉅子羅傑斯（Henry Huttleston Rogers），後者勸其1894年宣告破產，並代掌理財務。

1894年吐溫寫就《漿糊腦袋威爾生》（Pudd'nhead Wilson），敘述一黑一白嬰兒出生時被掉包，批評種族歧視。1895年為還債環球旅行演講，1900年還清所有欠款，遷回美國。1896年吐溫最鍾愛的幼女蘇西（Suzy）驟然病逝，吐溫寫作漸轉憤世，妻子1904年也逝世。

吐溫年輕時支持美國殖民夏威夷，晚年幡然改變，痛批美國殖民菲律賓，也批評歐洲對非洲殖民，1901年任反帝國主義聯盟（Anti-Imperialist League）紐約分會副會長。約此時寫就短篇小說《戰爭禱文》（The War Prayer），表達基督教教義與戰爭之矛盾，雜誌社拒絕刊登。1900年義和團事件後美國傳教士在中國徵收賠償，次年吐溫發表文章《給坐在黑暗中的人》（To the Person Sitting in Darkness）抨擊美國帝國主義，標題引自馬太福音4章16節：「那坐在黑暗裡的百姓看見了大光（The people who sat in darkness have seen a great light）」，嘲諷帝國主義給落後民族帶來光明的主張，中有名句：「基督如果今日重現世上，祂絕不會做一基督徒。（If Christ were here now there is one thing he would not be——a Christian）」吐溫晚年反帝國主義文章當時多半不得發表。

1910年哈雷彗星再臨，隔日吐溫去世。

　　吐溫出身美國南方鄉下，將方言、鄉土文化以幽默口吻帶入文學，晚年仗義為世界弱勢族群發聲，其幽默諷刺文風處處可見，茲僅舉一例：「世上可笑之事甚多；其一為白種人以為自己不如其他蠻族野蠻。（There are many humorous things in this world; among them the white man's notion that he is less savage than the other savages）」

馬克・吐溫・

2-12

亨利·詹姆士

亨利・詹姆士（Henry James）1843年生於美國紐約市，祖父是銀行家，父親不憂衣食，專研哲學，1855-60年全家數度遊歐，亨利在家受教，習得法文，1860年全家返美定居羅德島（Rhode Island）新港市（New Port），亨利在此閱讀法國文學，受巴爾扎克（Balzac）影響。1862年短暫入讀哈佛法學院，1864年時年21歲全家遷至波士頓，同年出版第一篇短篇小說，1870年出版第一本長篇小說，1869-70年遊歐，首次去到羅馬，1869年26歲定居倫敦，為雜誌寫連載小說，主要銷售對象為年輕婦女，此後極少返美。

　　詹姆士早期作品平鋪直敘，著重比較歐美文化，1877年寫就長篇小說《美國人》（The American），敘述貧困出身、善良單純的美國商人紐曼（Christopher Newman）致富後遊法尋找結婚對象，追求年輕貴族寡婦可萊爾（Claire de Cintré），與之訂婚，但可萊爾母親、兄長鄙視紐曼出身，強迫她嫁給富有的貴族表親，可萊爾決定出家，紐曼獲知她父親死於妻、兒之手，以此脅迫對方，最終仍放棄可萊爾返美。1878年詹姆士寫就《歐洲人》（The Europeans），敘述一對在歐洲長大的美國兄妹返美與波士頓的表兄妹交往，凸顯歐洲與美國女性差異。1878年寫就短篇小說《黛西・米勒》（Daisy Miller）廣受歡迎，敘述歐化美國男子溫特彬（Winterbourne）想追求旅歐美國女子黛西，但黛西過於直率大膽，遭到滯歐美國人抵制，最終黛西病死。同年詹姆士寫就專書《法國詩人與小說家》（French Poets and Novelists），中有一句：

Life is, in fact, a battle. Evil is insolent and strong; beauty enchanting, but rare; goodness very apt to be weak; folly very apt to be defiant; wickedness to carry the day; imbeciles to be in great places, people of sense in small, and mankind generally unhappy. But the world as it stands is no narrow illusion, no phantasm, no evil dream of the night; we wake up to it, forever and ever; and we can neither forget it nor deny it nor dispense with it.	生命，其實，是一場戰鬥。邪惡：粗暴而強大；華美：迷人但少見；善良：極可能弱小；愚蠢：極可能傲慢；歹毒：極可能勝出；笨蛋：極可能居高位，智者：極可能居低位，大部份人：極可能不幸。但是現實世界不是局部的錯覺，不是幻象，不是夜晚惡夢；我們醒來就面對之，永遠如此；我們對之既無法忘懷，無法否認，也無法免除。

亨
利
‧
詹
姆
士

　　1881年詹姆士寫就《女士肖像》（The Portrait of a Lady），探討個人自由與責任，敘述美國女子伊莎蓓兒（Isabel Archer）前往英國探望姨母，因追求獨立自由拒絕多人求婚，姨夫留給她大筆遺產，她赴歐陸，受梅爾夫人（Madame Merle）操弄而接受美國人吉伯特（Gilbert Osmond）求婚，婚姻不諧，但她甚喜吉伯特女兒潘西（Pansy），後發現潘西是吉伯特與梅爾夫人私生女。伊莎蓓兒赴英照顧垂死的表兄，之後仍返回歐陸，但不知決定未來忍受吉伯特，還是攜潘西離去。書出廣受好評，許為詹姆士創作第一期巔峰作。1884年詹姆士寫就論文《小說的藝術》（The Art of Fiction），主張小說家應自由發揮題材、形式。

　　詹姆士中期作品受當時法國寫實主義與自然主義（Naturalism，將人當動物觀察）影響，有1886年寫就的《波士頓人》（The Bostonians）與《卡撒瑪西瑪公主》（The Princess Casamassima）、1897-98年寫就的哥德式靈異故事《螺絲擰緊》（The Turn of the Screw，又譯《碧廬冤孽》）。《波士頓人》探討女性地位，敘述政治立場保守的美南人士冉森（Basil Ransom）與波士頓女權主義者歐莉芙（Olive Chancellor）爭取波士頓少女薇莉娜（Verena Tarrant）效忠。《卡撒瑪西瑪公主》敘述私生子海咢辛（Hyacinth Robinson）猶疑於激進政治與享受人生之間。《螺絲擰緊》轉述英國一名家庭老師／保姆記載她照顧兩兄妹之事，她見到可能是幽靈的一對男女，懷疑是已逝的前任家庭老師傑瑟小姐（Miss Jessel）及其男友彼得（Peter Quint），傑瑟與彼得之前與兩兄妹關係親密，家庭老師懷疑兩兄妹與幽靈有來往，試圖阻止，最終彼得幽靈現身，男孩死於她懷中。《波士頓人》與《卡撒瑪西瑪公主》銷路不佳，詹姆士因此心情憂鬱，1890年代寫劇本也失敗。

　　詹姆士晚期作品以冗長語句描述角色心理，有1902年的《鴿之翼》（The Wings of the Dove，又譯《慾望之翼》）、1903年的《奉使記》（The Ambassadors）、1904年的《金碗》（The Golden Bowl）。《鴿之翼》敘述一對英國戀人——凱特（Kate Croy）與鄧舍（Merton Densher）——缺錢成家。身患重病、曾暗戀鄧舍的美國富家女密莉（Milly Theale）來訪，不知凱特、鄧舍已訂婚。凱特慫恿鄧舍為遺產婚娶即將病死的密莉，密莉獲知真象疏遠鄧舍，隨後病逝但遺贈鄧舍一筆錢，鄧舍拒收，並要求凱特就錢與結婚擇一。

《奉使記》（The Ambassadors）敘述單純的中年美國男子史崔瑟（Lewis Lambert Strether）同意為富有的未婚妻去巴黎將她迷戀歐洲的兒子查德（Chad Newsome）帶返美國繼承家業，途徑倫敦認識了歐化美國女子瑪麗亞（Maria Gostrey）。在巴黎史崔瑟經由查德結識一對美麗雅致的法國母女—瑪麗（Marie de Vionnet）與嬋（Jeanne），史崔瑟自己也開始迷戀歐洲，其未婚妻另派人來帶返兒子。史崔瑟於鄉間旅館撞見查德與瑪麗，至此才明白兩人私情。他勸查德返美，自己也進一步了解了歐洲。他拒絕瑪麗亞提婚，之後返美。

《金碗》敘述貧窮的意大利貴族亞美利戈（Amerigo）去倫敦婚娶美國富家女瑪姬（Maggie Verver），遇見舊情人、瑪姬好友夏洛蒂（Charlotte Stant），婚後瑪姬擔心父親亞當寂寞，安排夏洛蒂嫁他，亞美利戈與夏洛蒂舊情復燃被瑪姬獲悉，瑪姬私下安排父親與夏洛蒂返美，亞美利戈訝於瑪姬世故的處理，擁她入懷。

1915年詹姆士歸化英籍，隔年去世。

詹姆士以心理寫實引領20世紀現代文學，探討美歐文化差異，對比純真與世故，描摹體驗之危險，他本人也觀察多於體驗，一生未婚，為美國19世紀重要小說家。

2-13
佛洛斯特
Robert Frost

佛洛斯特（Robert Frost）1874年生於美國加州舊金山市，父親是教師、報紙編輯，1885年病逝，家人遷居麻州東北依祖父生活，祖父監管磨坊。佛洛斯特高中開始在校刊刊登詩作，曾短暫就讀達特茅斯學院（Dartmouth College），隨即輟學打工，立志寫詩。1894年首次以詩作賺得稿費，次年結婚，有子女6人，4人先佛洛斯特而逝。1897-99年入讀哈佛大學文科，因病中輟。由於遺傳，母親、他本人、妹妹、女兒都患憂鬱症。母親1900年去世。祖父為他於新漢普夏州（New Hampshire）東南購置農場，佛洛斯特於此每日早起寫詩，白晝耕作。因經營不善，1906年改於當地平克頓中學（Pinkerton Academy）教英文，1911年再轉新漢普夏州中部普利茅斯市（Plymouth）新漢普夏師範學院（New Hampshire Normal School）任教。

1912年佛洛斯特覺得窮困文人宜居英國，舉家遷往倫敦近郊，次年出版詩集《少年的意向》（A Boy's Will），標題出自朗費羅詩作《我失去的青春》（My Lost Youth）其中一句：「少年的意向是風的意向／少年的冥想悠長綿延」（A boy's will is the wind's will / And the thoughts of youth are long, long thoughts），1914年出版詩集《波士頓以北》（North of Boston），頗受歡迎。1915年因一次大戰返回新州購買農莊，邊教書邊寫作，次年起任教麻州安姆赫斯特學院，1916年作詩《火與冰》（Fire and Ice）與《未擇之路》（The Road Not Taken）。

《火與冰》：

Some say the world will end in fire,	有人說世界將毀於火，
Some say in ice.	有人說冰。
From what I've tasted of desire	因我對慾望也嚐過
I hold with those who favor fire.	我贊同火這一說。
But if it had to perish twice,	但若世界要毀兩次，
I think I know enough of hate	我對仇恨也有了解

| To say that for destruction ice
Is also great
And would suffice. | 可說冰的毀滅力度是
同樣劇烈
也能成事。 |

《未擇之路》：

| Two roads diverged in a yellow wood,
And sorry I could not travel both
And be one traveler, long I stood
And looked down one as far as I could
To where it bent in the undergrowth;
Then took the other, as just as fair,
And having perhaps the better claim,
Because it was grassy and wanted wear;
Though as for that the passing there
Had worn them really about the same,
And both that morning equally lay
In leaves no step had trodden black.
Oh, I kept the first for another day!
Yet knowing how way leads on to way,
I doubted if I should ever come back.
I shall be telling this with a sigh
Somewhere ages and ages hence:
Two roads diverged in a wood, and I—
I took the one less traveled by,
And that has made all the difference. | 兩條路分岔於黃色林木，
我遺憾無法兩條都選
而維持單一身份，我久佇
凝目遠望其中一條盡處
於彼，路在樹叢中彎轉；
我走上另一條，同具美景，
且也許更應有人蹤，
因為草多需人踩行；
可是說到這事，路人
踩踏兩者程度略同，
兩者那天早上同樣滿是
樹葉，尚未踐化為泥。
噢，我保留第一條待他日！
但我知路會再岔出別支，
我自疑將來能返回此地。
我將歎氣把此事述說
久遠之後在某地某日：
兩條路分岔於林中，而我—
我選的較少人走過，
日後一切差異皆源於此。 |

1921年起佛洛斯特也在佛蒙特州（Vermont）明德學院（Middlebury College）、密西根大學（University of Michigan）任教。1922年作詩《落雪暮晚停駐森林邊》（Stopping by Woods on a Snowy Evening）：

Whose woods these are I think I know.	這森林屬誰我約略知悉。
His house is in the village though;	他家可是在村子裡；
He will not see me stopping here	他不會見到我停這裡
To watch his woods fill up with snow.	觀看他的森林被雪覆披。
My little horse must think it queer	我的小馬定覺怪異
To stop without a farmhouse near	停駐之地沒有農居
Between the woods and frozen lake	兩旁是森林與冰凍湖水
The darkest evening of the year.	於一年暮色最暗日期。
He gives his harness bells a shake	牠晃動彎上的鈴墜
To ask if there is some mistake.	問我是否有問題。
The woods are lovely, dark and deep.	森林誘人，黑暗深邃。
The only other sound's the sweep	此外餘聲僅有拂吹
Of easy wind and downy flake.	輕風與柔軟的雪絮。
But I have promises to keep,	但我有承諾需信兌，
And miles to go before I sleep,	有遠路要走才能休息，
And miles to go before I sleep.	有遠路要走才能休息。

1923年作詩《金黃事物不留》（Nothing Gold Can Stay）：

Nature's first flower is gold,	自然初蕾色金，
Her hardest green to hold.	是最難留的初青。
Her early leaf's a flower;	早發脈葉是朵花；

But only so an hour.	但只綻放一刹。
Then leaf subsides to leaf.	葉葉漸次垂落。
So Eden sank to grief,	如此伊甸悲墮,
Dawn goes down to day.	朝早墜化白晝。
Nothing gold can stay.	金黃事物不留。

　　佛洛斯特生平出版多冊詩集。1961年應甘迺迪（Kennedy）總統邀請於總統就職典禮朗誦其詩。1963年去世。

　　佛洛斯特遵循傳統格律，以新英格蘭鄉間作背景，以口語對白入詩，探討現代人生疏離落寞，體現英美詩19、20世紀轉折。

2-14

尤金・歐尼爾

Eugene O'Neill

尤金·歐尼爾
Eugene O'Neill

　　尤金·歐尼爾（Eugene O'Neill）1888年生於美國紐約市，父親是愛爾蘭裔演員，酗酒；母親患精神疾病。歐尼爾自幼寄讀天主教學校，寄情閱讀，1906年入讀普林斯頓大學（Princeton University），酗酒蹺課，次年遭退學。一生有三段婚姻，1909年首次結婚，未久任商船水手出海，3年後離婚，患憂鬱症，自殺未遂。1912-23年因肺結核，休養期間決定寫作劇本，1914年於哈佛大學修習相關課程一年，結識紐約市格林威治村（Greenwich Village）文藝人士，1916年參加麻州東岸普文市劇團（Provincetown Players），創作劇本。1920年《越過地平線》（Beyond the Horizon）於百老匯上演，評語甚佳，《鐘斯大帝》（The Emperor Jones）同年上演，敘述非裔美人統治加勒比海島國，不得善終；廣受歡迎。1922年《安娜·柯莉絲蒂》（Anna Christie）上演，敘述妓女從良不成。

　　1923年歐尼爾哥哥傑米（Jamie）酗酒去世。1924年《榆樹下的慾望》（Desire Under the Elms）上演，以希臘神話題材描寫亂倫、殺嬰。1928年《奇異插曲》（Strange Interlude）上演，敘述一女子複雜的感情生活。

　　1929年歐尼爾遷居法國中部，數年後返美，1931年《依烈姐其悼也美》（Mourning Becomes Electra）上演，改寫希臘依烈姐神話，敘述美國內戰後拉薇妮雅（Lavinia Mannon）父親艾札（Ezra）、弟弟歐仁（Orin）解甲歸來，母親克莉絲汀（Christine）與船長亞當（Adam Brant）有染，兩人毒死艾札，拉薇妮雅說服歐仁擊斃亞當，克莉絲汀自殺，歐仁因戀母自殺，拉薇妮雅孤獨存活。

　　1936年歐尼爾獲諾貝爾文學獎，1937年遷居北加州。1941-42年寫就自傳性巨著《漫漫長途漸入夜》（Long Day's Journey Into Night，又譯《日暮途遠》），敘述1912年8月泰榮（Tyrone）一家在康乃狄克州（Connecticut）海邊從早上8點30分到午夜一天之事，父親詹姆士（James）、長子艾德蒙（Edmund）、次子傑米（Jamie）發現母親瑪麗（Mary）嗎啡癮復發，瑪麗喜好回憶少女時光，父子三人酗酒，艾德蒙患肺結核，傑米想當作家，四人彼此扞格，全劇大多是兩兩對話。1956年上演，廣受好評，茲選譯兩段，第一段是瑪麗所說：

| None of us can help the things life has done to us. They're done before you realize it, and once they're done they make you do other things until at last everything comes between you and what you'd like to be, and you've lost your true self forever. | 沒有人能改變生命加諸我們的事物。等你發覺時一切都已定型，這些事又迫使你做另一些事，最後阻隔了你真的想做的事，你因此永遠失去真正的你。 |

第二段是艾德蒙引述法國詩人波德萊爾（Charles Baudelaire）：

| Be always drunken. Nothing else matters: that is the only question. If you would not feel the horrible burden of Time weighing on your shoulders and crushing you to the earth, be drunken continually. Drunken with what? With wine, with poetry, or with virtue, as you will. But be drunken. | 要長醉不醒。其他一切都不重要：人生只有這個問題。如果你不想感受時間可怕的重擔壓在你肩上，將你軋進土裡，那就要長醉不醒。醉於何物？醉於酒、醉於詩、醉於道德，隨你選。但一定要醉。 |

1943年歐尼爾時年18的女兒烏娜（Oona）嫁給54歲的演員卓別林（Charles Chaplin），歐尼爾斷絕父女關係。

1939年歐尼爾寫就《賣冰人來了》（The Iceman Cometh），1946年上演，敘述1912年在侯普（Harry Hope）酒館，酒客白天宿醉酣睡，夜間睜眼酗酒，等待一年光臨一次的希奇（Theodore "Hickey" Hickman）來請他們喝酒，希奇來到一改前態，勸大家為夢想打拚，眾人為其說服，但奮鬥一天後毫無進展，在酒客、前無政府主義者賴里（Larry）催問下，希奇承認殺妻自首，賴里來訪的私生子派瑞特（Parritt）也在承認出賣了自己母親後自殺，眾人回復酗酒，人生黑暗無出路。

1947年劇本《月照不幸人》（A Moon for the Misbegotten）上演，是《漫漫長途漸入夜》續集，敘述1923年詹姆士（James Tyrone，影射歐尼爾哥哥）與房客酒友候根（Phil Hogan）的女兒宙姬（Josie）月下傾談，戲尾詹姆士赴紐約闖蕩劇場，未久酗酒而死。

1950年歐尼爾長子自殺，1953年本人病逝。

歐尼爾將歐洲劇作寫實主義引入美國，善描寫社會邊緣人掙扎幻滅，為美國20世紀重要劇作家。

圖片來源：IDJ圖庫

2-15
費茲傑羅
Francis Scott Key Fitzgerald

費茲傑羅（Francis Scott Key Fitzgerald）1896年生於美國明尼蘇達州（Minnesota）聖保羅市（Saint Paul）愛爾蘭裔天主教家庭，父親任職於日用品大廠寶僑（Procter & Gamble），家人1898年定居紐約州水牛城（Buffalo），1908年遷返明尼蘇達。費茲傑羅自幼展露文才，1913年入讀普林斯頓大學，開始酗酒，終生不改；因寫作荒廢學業，1917年退學從軍，次年在阿拉巴馬州（Alabama）結識18歲的法官之女婕妲（Zelda Sayre）。1918年一戰結束，次年費茲傑羅退役，任職紐約廣告公司，婕妲因其收入不豐廢除婚約。費茲傑羅返回聖保羅，修改1917年寫就的近自傳小說《浪漫的利己主義者》（The Romantic Egoist），更名為《樂園在彼》（This Side of Paradise），1920年出版大賣，得以婚娶婕妲。1920年代夫婦倆多次旅遊法國，結識了海明威（Hemingway）等作家，費茲傑羅為雜誌寫短篇小說賺錢，但出手闊綽，入不敷出。1922年寫就小說《亮麗與沉淪》（The Beautiful and Damned），反映其自身生活。

1923-25年費茲傑羅精心寫就《偉大的蓋茨比》（The Great Gatsby，又譯《大亨小傳》），敘述1922年一戰退伍軍人尼克（Nick Carraway）於紐約長島（Long Island）租屋，結識鄰居年輕富翁蓋茨比（Jay Gatsby），蓋茨比5年前的舊情人黛西（Daisy）是尼克表親，已嫁與粗俗富人湯姆（Tom Buchanan），湯姆有情婦茉桃（Myrtle Wilson），蓋茨比深戀黛西，希望以豪奢派對吸引黛西重投懷抱，蓋茨比透過尼克與黛西再結舊緣，湯姆抨擊蓋茨比財富來路不正，黛西最終選擇湯姆，回家途中蓋茨比的車撞死茉桃，尼克獲悉開車的是黛西而非蓋茨比，但蓋茨比自願認罪，茉桃的先生懷疑開車者即其妻情夫，因此擊斃蓋茨比後自殺，尼克對美東奢華文化幻滅，遷返中西部。茲選譯兩段，第一段描述蓋茨比對黛西的幻戀：

There must have been moments even that afternoon when Daisy tumbled short of his dreams — not through her own fault, but because of the colossal vitality of his illusion. It had gone beyond her, beyond everything. He had thrown himself into it with a creative passion, adding to it all the time, decking it out with every bright feather that drifted his way. No amount of fire or freshness can challenge what a man will store up in his ghostly heart.

就連那天下午，黛西也必然有某些時刻未能臻至他的夢幻標準—非因她本身的問題，而是因為他夢幻的巨大生命力。這夢幻超越了她，超越了一切。他以創造熱情全心投入，隨時增益之，以偶遇的每簇艷羽綴飾之。再大的火焰、再多的清新，都無法除淨男人幽秘的心藏。

第二段是書尾尼克的獨白：

And as I sat there brooding on the old, unknown world, I thought of Gatsby's wonder when he first picked out the green light at the end of Daisy's dock. He had come a long way to this blue lawn and his dream must have seemed so close that he could hardly fail to grasp it. He did not know that it was already behind him, somewhere back in that vast obscurity beyond the city, where the dark fields of the republic rolled on under the night. "Gatsby believed in the green light, the orgastic future that year by year recedes before us. It eluded us then, but that's no matter--tomorrow we will run faster, stretch out our arms farther.... And one fine morning—
"So we beat on, boats against the current, borne back ceaselessly into the past.

我坐著沉思這古老、莫明的世界，想到初初辨出黛西家碼頭那端的綠光時蓋茨比的入神。他歷經長途，來到這片青藍草地，一定覺得離夢想近到觸手可得。卻不知夢想已擦身而過，去到城外無邊的迷離中，於彼，共和國的暗野在黑夜裡翻動。「蓋茨比相信那個綠光、那個將要到來的高潮，高潮卻在我們面前逐年退卻。那時我們捕捉不到，但沒關係—明天我們可以跑得更快、手伸得更遠……。直到某個美好清晨——」因此，我們繼續鼓桿，逆流而上，卻被潮流不停沖回。

書出有好評但未大賣，今日人譽爲象徵美國夢（The American Dream）的「偉大美國小說」（Great American Novel）。

1930年婕妲精神分裂，1932年入住馬里蘭州（Maryland）巴爾的摩市（Baltimore）醫院治療，費茲傑羅在郊區租屋寫作，其作品多取材於自身生活，婕妲也想以此材料寫作，遭其夫阻止。1934年費茲傑羅出版《夜晚多溫柔》（Tender Is the Night），敘述心理分析醫師狄克（Dick Diver）婚娶其病人、曾與父親亂倫的富家女妮蔻（Nicole），住在法南蔚藍海岸與滯法美國人交往，狄克與年輕女演員蘿絲瑪麗（Rosemary Hoyt）有染，因酗酒事業不振，蘿絲瑪麗逐漸疏遠狄克，妮蔻與湯米（Tommy Barban）有染，離婚另嫁湯米，狄克繼續沉淪。茲選譯蘿絲瑪麗與狄克相戀一段：

They were still in the happier stage of love. They were full of brave illusions about each other, tremendous illusions, so that the communion of self with self seemed to be on a plane where no other human relations mattered. They both seemed to have arrived there with an extraordinary innocence as though a series of pure accidents had driven them together, so many accidents that at last they were forced to conclude that they were for each other. They had arrived with clean hands, or so it seemed, after no traffic with the merely curious and clandestine.	他們仍身處戀愛較快樂的階段。他們充滿對彼此勇敢的幻想，幻想大到兩人眼中只有對方，他人彷彿都不存在。他們以超常的純眞臻至此境，好似一連串巧合將他們驅向彼此，巧合多到他們不得不認定這是命中注定。他們純淨地來到此境，至少看似如此，不摻雜任何好奇、任何私暗。

1937年費茲傑羅遷居好萊塢爲電影製片廠寫劇本，同時寫作小說《末代大亨之戀》（The Love of the Last Tycoon），一般認爲反映好萊塢大亨邵伯格（Irving Thalberg）生平事蹟，死後於1941年由好友威爾遜（Edmund Wilson）編輯更名《末代大亨》（The Last Tycoon）出版。

1940年費茲傑羅潦倒病逝 ，婕妲1948年死於北卡羅來納州（North Carolina）療養院一場火災。

費茲傑羅身屬一戰後西方喪失理想而失落的一代（Lost Generation），人譽爲爵士年代（Jazz Age，美國1920年代）代表作家，其形容爵士年代「是奇蹟的年代，是藝術的年代，是肆越的年代，是嘲諷的年代。（It was an age of miracles, it was an age of art, it was an age of excess, and it was an age of satire）」費茲傑羅文筆華麗，善寫年少得意，老大不佳，反映美國1920年代心想事成、紙醉金迷，30年代夢想幻滅、蕭條窘困，爲美國20世紀小說大家。

◆
費
茲
傑
羅
◆

圖片來源：IDJ圖庫

2-16

福克納

William Faulkner

福克納（William Faulkner）1897年生於美國密西西比州拉法葉郡（Lafayette County）新奧伯尼市（New Albany），父親任家族鐵路公司財務長，1902年搬到牛津市（Oxford），福克納終生居此，據以虛構「游納派套分郡」（Yoknapatawpha County），爲日後所有作品背景。

　　福克納自幼由黑人家傭照顧，熟聞美國南方歷史與自身家族史，曾祖父經商有成，是內戰英雄；母親習畫，重閱讀；父親教他漁獵。高中無心學業未畢業，1918年爲參加一戰自稱報名加拿大空軍，戰事旋即結束退伍。1919年入讀密西西比大學（University of Mississippi），喜好作詩，次年退學。1925年開始出版小說，1927年寫小說《旗墮塵土》（Flags in the Dust），次年更名《薩托里斯家族》（Sartoris）出版，敘述一戰後南方貴族薩托里斯家族之衰敗。

　　1929年出版《喧囂與憤怒》（The Sound and the Fury），敘述1898-1928年南方貴族康普生家族（Compson）之衰敗，第一部從智障的班吉（Benjamin "Benjy" Compson）觀點，敘述姊姊凱娣（Caddy）出軌離婚被逐；第二部敘述班吉長兄昆亭（Quentin Compson）拯救凱娣不成而自殺；第三部從班吉二哥傑生（Jason）觀點，敘述他賺錢養活一家子，個性扭曲憤世；第四部敘述黑傭娣希（Dilsey）帶班吉上教堂，凱娣私生女捲款私奔。此書標題出自莎士比亞劇本《馬克白》（Macbeth）：

Life's but a walking shadow, a poor player That struts and frets his hour upon the stage And then is heard no more: it is a tale Told by an idiot, full of sound and fury, Signifying nothing.	生命不過是浮略的幻影， 一時在臺上誇叱的劣角， 旋即闃然：是癡人述說的 故事，充滿了喧囂與憤怒， 毫無意義。

福克納

茲選譯一段昆亭的回憶：

When the shadow of the sash appeared on the curtains it was between seven and eight o' clock and then I was in time again, hearing the watch. It was Grandfather's and when Father gave it to me he said I give you the mausoleum of all hope and desire; it's rather excruciatingly apt that you will use it to gain the reducto absurdum of all human experience which can fit your individual needs no better than it fitted his or his father's. I give it to you not that you may remember time, but that you might forget it now and then for a moment and not spend all your breath trying to conquer it. Because no battle is ever won he said. They are not even fought. The field only reveals to man his own folly and despair, and victory is an illusion of philosophers and fools.

簾帶投影於窗簾，時值7、8點之間，我聽聞鐘錶走動，回身復處時間之中。這原是爺爺的錶，父親傳給我時說，我給你的是希望和慾求的陵墓；既痛苦又真切的是，你將以之獲取終顯荒謬的人生識見，而這識見既不合你父祖，也不合你個人需求。我給你這錶不是要你記住時間，而是要你偶爾忘掉時間，要你不至於費盡氣息想征服時間。因為沒有任何戰役可以打勝，他說。甚至沒有戰役可打。戰場只顯示給人看人的愚蠢、絕望，勝利是哲學家、是蠢人的幻象。

1929年福克納婚娶離婚的大學情人愛絲窕（Estelle Oldham），夜間任職密西西比大學鍋爐間，白日寫作，次年出版小說《我彌留之際》（As I lay Dying），標題出自荷馬史詩《奧迪賽》（The Odyssey）11冊阿嘎曼農（Agamemnon）對奧迪修斯（Odysseus）說其妻柯萊藤妮妃（Clytemnestra）之事：「我彌留之際，去陰曹途中，那個狗眼的女人不幫我闔眼。（As I lay dying, the woman with the dog's eyes would not close my eyes as I descended into Hades）」，小說敘述鄉下貧家老母親愛蒂（Addie Bundren）死後，家人遵囑帶棺歸葬老家，一路多舛，荒謬錯亂。

1930年福克納還寫有短篇小說《玫瑰一朵給愛密莉》（A Rose for Emily），敘述南方沒落貴族女愛密莉（Emily Grierson）拒嫁門第不等之人，老大後心智異常，父親死後任其屍陳屋內，之後與北方工人荷馬（Homer Barron）相好，荷馬自言不婚，失蹤後屋內有臭味傳出，多年後愛密莉去世，鎮民入屋發現荷馬骷髏躺在床上，旁邊枕上有

愛密莉髮絲。

　　同年福克納以短篇小說稿費於牛津市購屋。1932年爲賺錢赴好萊塢爲米高梅製片廠寫劇本，同年出版《八月秋光》（Light in August），探討南方種族、政治、宗教、性別等問題，敘述懷孕少女莉娜（Lena Grove）來尋找其私逃男友盧卡斯（Lucas Burch），北方移民後代喬安娜（Joanna Burden）被殺，盧卡斯供出友人周（Joe Christmas）與喬安娜交往，且帶黑人血統，鎮民拜倫（Byron Bunch）愛上莉娜，尋求被黜牧師海陶（Gail Hightower）協助莉娜生產，周逃入牧師家，但被民警擊斃閹割。

　　1936年福克納出版《押沙龍，押沙龍！》（Absalom, Absalom!），透過多人觀點回憶湯瑪斯（Thomas Sutpen）家族歷史，湯瑪斯在西印度群島結婚生子查爾斯（Charles），發現妻子有黑人血統而棄家，赴美南創建家業，再婚生育一子亨利（Henry）、一女茱蒂絲（Judith），查爾斯與亨利大學同窗，不知情的茱蒂絲與查爾斯相戀，亨利原先贊同，獲知查爾斯帶黑人血統後反對，擊斃查爾斯逃逸，內戰後湯瑪斯爲重建家園與15歲佃農女密莉（Milly）生育，因生女嬰將母女逐出，密莉祖父憤而殺死湯瑪斯與密莉母女，自己也被民警擊斃，最終湯瑪斯一家死絕，只剩查爾斯智障的孫子。標題用聖經大衛王家族亂倫、與子押沙龍相殘之典故。茲選譯茱蒂絲的一段話：

<table>
<tr>
<td>You get born and you try this and you don't know why only you keep on trying it and you are born at the same time with a lot of other people, all mixed up with them, like trying to, having to, move your arms and legs with strings only the same strings are hitched to all the other arms and legs and the others all trying and they don't know why either except that the strings are all in one another's way like five or six people all trying to make a rug on the same loom only each one wants to weave his own pattern into the rug; and it can't matter, you know</td>
<td>你出生，你試圖努力，你不知道爲什麼，你只是盡力做，跟你同時出生還有好多人，跟你混在一起，好像你試著要、必須要用繩子牽動手腳，但是繩子也繫在別人手腳上，別人也試圖努力、也不知道爲什麼，繩子彼此阻絆像5、6個人用同一架織機織毯子，但每個人都要織自己的花紋；一切都沒意義，這點你知道，否則</td>
</tr>
</table>

> that, or the Ones that set up the loom would have arranged things a little better, and yet it must matter because you keep on trying or having to keep on trying and then all of a sudden it's all over.

> 架設織機的人會安排地好些，但是這又必須有意義，因為你不斷努力、或說你不得不努力，接著一剎間一切都結束。

福克納1940年出版《村落》（The Hamlet），1957年出版《城鎮》（The Town），1959年出版《豪廈》（The Mansion），三者敘述斯諾普家族（Snopes）歷史，合稱「斯諾普三部曲」（Snopes Trilogy）。福克納1949年獲諾貝爾文學獎，1962年病逝。

福克納以意識流、多重觀點、時空交錯等前衛手法，透過美南游納派套分郡一地家族歷史，書寫人性社會，引領中南美魔幻寫實文學，作品躋身英美文學經典。

圖片來源：IDJ圖庫

2-17
海明威
Ernest Hemingway

　　海明威（Ernest Hemingway）1899年生於美國伊利諾州芝加哥郊區橡園市（Oak Park），父親行醫，母親是音樂家，自幼隨父於野外漁獵，高中從事各種體育運動，修習新聞寫作，投稿校刊，畢業後在《堪薩斯市星報》（The Kansas City Star）任記者，遵從該報寫作原則：「用短句。第一段要簡潔。語言要有力。用正面敘述，避免否定。（Use short sentences. Use short first paragraphs. Use vigorous English. Be positive, not negative）」半年後於1918年，18歲的海明威赴意大利參加一戰，開救護車，同年受傷送至米蘭休養，與26歲護士愛涅絲（Agnes von Kurowsky）相戀，隔年返美，原定結婚，但愛涅絲毀約別戀。1919年海明威赴加拿大任《多倫多星報》（Toronto Star）記者，次年返芝加哥，結識長他8歲的哈德蕾（Hadley Richardson），1921年結婚，未久赴巴黎任《多倫多星報》駐巴黎記者，結識了一戰後美國滯法、喪失理想，被稱為「失落的一代」（The Lost Generation）的作家、藝術家，此稱謂透過其1926年第一本小說《太陽依舊升起》（The Sun Also Rises）廣為流傳。1923年海明威參加西班牙龐貝洛納城（Pamplona）聖費明奔牛節（Festival of San Fermín），次年帶友人再訪。海明威認為死亡直面生死，賦予生命意義，作品多探討死亡，也因此熱衷鬥牛。

　　1924年海明威出版短篇小說《印地安營地》（Indian Camp），敘述男童尼克（Nick Adams）隨醫生父親赴印地安營地，協助為難產孕婦剖腹生產，產婦先生割喉自殺。語言簡練、敘事低調，廣受好評。次年海明威於巴黎結識費茲傑羅，同時與時尚雜誌作家寶琳（Pauline Pfeiffer）有染。《太陽依舊升起》1926年出版，敘述一群滯法英人美人由巴黎赴西班牙參加聖費明奔牛節，因戰傷失去性能力的記者傑克（Jake Barnes）與兩度離婚、多男友的貴婦布蕾特（Brett Ashley）相戀，布蕾特與傑克友人寇恩（Robert Cohn）有染，又引誘19歲的鬥牛士羅梅洛（Romero），傑克與布蕾特陷於無望的戀情。

　　1927年海明威離婚婚娶寶琳。1928年返美定居佛羅里達州（Florida）南端西礁島（Key West），同年父親自殺。1929年出版小說《永別戰事》（A Farewell to Arms，又譯《戰地春夢》），敘述美國人費佳克（Frederic Henry）於一戰在意大利開救護車受傷，與英國護士凱瑟琳（Catherine Barkley）相戀，費佳克傷癒返前線，兵敗撤退時處

決抗命屬下，遭憲兵執訊，費佳克逃脫尋獲懷孕的凱瑟琳，一起逃往瑞士，凱瑟琳產下死胎，失血身亡。書出大賣，中有一段費佳克的話：

I was always embarrassed by the words sacred, glorious, and sacrifice and the expression in vain. We had heard them ... and had read them... now for a long time, and I had seen nothing sacred, and the things that were glorious had no glory and the sacrifices were like the stockyards at Chicago if nothing was done with the meat except to bury it. There were many words that you could not stand to hear and finally only the names of places had dignity.... Abstract words such as glory, honor, courage or hallow were obscene beside the concrete names of villages, the numbers of roads, the names of rivers, the numbers of regiments and the dates.	神聖、光榮、犧牲等字眼，和無謂付出這個用詞，一向讓我感到難堪。長久以來這些話有人說……有人寫，但我見到的事物毫不神聖，所謂光榮的事情並不光榮，血肉若不另處置，只遭掩埋，那犧牲與芝加哥的屠宰場也無異。許多字眼都令人無法忍受，最終只有地名仍保有尊嚴……相對於具體的村名、道路代號、河名、軍團代號、日期等，抽象字眼如光榮、榮譽、勇氣、神聖等都顯得汙穢。

1930年代海明威多天住西礁島，夏天住懷俄明州（Wyoming），呼朋引伴打獵釣魚，1933年赴東非狩獵，1934年購船「妣拉」號（Pilar）巡遊加勒比海。1936年寫就短篇小說《乞力馬扎羅山的雪》（The Snows of Kilimanjaro，又譯《雪山盟》），敘述作家哈利（Harry）與富妻海倫（Helen）在非洲狩獵，哈利受傷染壞疽，回憶生平，自覺未發展潛力，而是依靠一系列富妻生活，哈利夢中自覺獲救，海倫半夜發現哈利已死。

海明威1936年在美結識記者瑪莎（Martha Gellhorn），次年赴西班牙報導內戰。1939年駕船赴古巴，次年離婚另娶瑪莎，此後夏居愛達荷州（Idaho），冬居古巴。1940年出版小說《喪鐘為誰響》（For Whom the Bell Tolls，又譯《戰地鐘聲》），敘述美國人喬登（Robert Jordan）參加西班牙內戰為共和派效力，奉命帶領游擊隊潛入敵後炸毀橋梁，愛上年輕游擊隊員瑪麗亞（Maria），游擊隊隊長巴布羅（Pablo）畏死將

炸藥引信拋棄，喬登被迫以手榴彈引爆炸藥，於逃離時受傷，決定犧牲拒敵以便瑪麗亞與游擊隊撤退。書出大賣。

海明威

1941年海明威偕瑪莎赴中國採訪中日戰爭，美日開戰後，他駕妣拉號於古巴外海搜尋德國潛艇，1944年赴倫敦報導二戰，結識記者瑪麗（Mary Welsh），並觀察諾曼第登陸，隨軍進入巴黎時參戰，違反記者公約被訴，獲判無罪。1945年第三度離婚，次年另娶瑪麗。因酗酒與多次意外受傷，1940年代開始健康逐漸惡化。1952年出版《老人與海》（The Old Man and the Sea），敘述老漁夫聖地牙哥（Santiago）久無漁獲，在古巴外海釣到巨大馬林魚（marlin），搏鬥三晝夜，終將魚繫於船邊，鯊魚聞腥而來，殺之不盡，馬林魚被吃到只剩骨架，聖地牙哥返家力盡沉睡，醒來答應會再度帶徒弟馬諾林（Manolin）出海。書出廣獲好評，茲選譯首段：

He was an old man who fished alone in a skiff in the Gulf Stream and he had gone eighty-four days now without taking a fish. In the first forty days a boy had been with him. But after forty days without a fish the boy's parents had told him that the old man was now definitely and finally salao, which is the worst form of unlucky, and the boy had gone at their orders in another boat which caught three good fish the first week. It made the boy sad to see the old man come in each day with his skiff empty and he always went down to help him carry either the coiled lines or the gaff and harpoon and the sail that was furled around the mast. The sail was patched with flour sacks and, furled, it looked like the flag of permanent defeat.

他是個老人，自駕小船在灣流捕魚，已經84天隻魚未獲。頭40天有個男孩跟著。但接連40天隻魚未獲後，父母跟男孩說老人肯定、絕對是「salao」，就是最糟的霉星高照，男孩遵父母命換船出海，頭個星期就捕獲三條好魚。見到老人每天空船回港，男孩心裡難過，總是幫忙搬繩捆、長鉤、魚叉、捲繞船桅的風帆等等。風帆以麵粉袋修補，捲起來就像永遠戰敗的降旗。

1954年海明威再赴非洲狩獵，飛機失事受傷，同年獲諾貝爾文學獎，得獎答詞有一段論及寫作：

Writing, at its best, is a lonely life. Organizations for writers palliate the writer's loneliness but I doubt if they improve his writing. He grows in public stature as he sheds his loneliness and often his work deteriorates. For he does his work alone and if he is a good enough writer he must face eternity, or the lack of it, each day.	寫作，在最佳情況下，是孤獨事業。各類作家協會可以舒緩此孤獨，但無助於寫作本身。作家地位越上升孤獨越少，但作品也常越差。這是因為寫作是個人之事，及格的作家每日都須面對永恆，或者面對自己的無能。

1956年海明威尋獲早年寄存巴黎的手稿，次年據此書寫回憶錄《移動的盛宴》（A Moveable Feast），1959年書成。1960年聽聞革命領袖卡斯楚（Fidel Castro）要沒收外國人財產，因而離開古巴。1961年於愛達荷因憂鬱症飲彈自殺。

海明威是美國20世紀重要小說家，透過戰爭、死亡探討生命意義，語言簡潔凝鍊，開創美國現代主流文風，對寫作有著名的「冰山理論」（Iceberg theory）：

If a writer of prose knows enough of what he is writing about he may omit things that he knows and the reader, if the writer is writing truly enough, will have a feeling of those things as strongly as though the writer had stated them. The dignity of movement of an ice-berg is due to only one-eighth of it being above water. A writer who omits things because he does not know them only makes hollow places in his writing.	小說作家若熟知題材，寫作時可以省略其所知，假使寫作真誠，讀者可感知其所省略，強度恍如未省略一般。冰山移動時，其莊嚴來自僅有八分之一露出水面。作家若因不熟悉題材而省略，作品只顯空洞。

圖片來源：IDJ圖庫

2-18

史坦貝克

John Steinbeck

史坦貝克（John Steinbeck）1902年生於美國加州中部近海薩林納斯市（Salinas），父親是當地蒙特利郡（Monterey County）財務長，母親是教師，年少暑期在家鄉農場打工，結識了許多中南美移民工。1919年入讀史丹福大學（Stanford University）主修英美文學，1925年肄業，移居紐約市邊工作邊寫作，1928年返加州太浩湖（Lake Tahoe）任導遊，1930年於洛杉磯結婚，經營塑膠模特兒廠失敗，遷返蒙特利市，靠父親支持寫作，同年結識海洋生態學家李克茨（Ed Ricketts），李克茨在海濱開有海洋生物實驗室，兩人成為密友。經濟大恐慌期間，史坦貝克自購小船捕魚、種菜為食，也領取救濟。1933-36年出版小說《小紅馬》（The Red Pony）敘述男孩周弟（Jody Tiflin）在父親加州農場成長覺醒，包括照顧一匹小紅馬不善以致小馬病死。

1935年史坦貝克出版《煎餅坪》（Tortilla Flat），以圓桌武士為喻，敘述一戰後蒙特利一群流浪漢偷竊飲酒作樂之生態，書出成名。1937年出版《鼠與人》（Of Mice and Men），標題源自蘇格蘭詩人彭斯（Robert Burns）詩作《致老鼠》，敘述大恐慌時期流浪到加州的農工喬治（George Milton）未讀過書但聰明，磊尼（Lennie Small）高壯但智障，喜愛撫摸柔軟的小動物，卻粗手粗腳常將其弄死，之前磊尼在別城曾緊抓女子衣裙而被控性侵。喬治自任保護磊尼，磊尼則常要求喬治複述他們自購農莊的夢想。農場主之子柯戾（Curley）矮小好鬥，其妻貌美嬌縱，讓磊尼撫摸頭髮，因磊尼力大而尖叫，磊尼情急無意中將其頸拗斷，喬治尋獲磊尼，邊複述其夢想，邊開槍將之擊斃，以免被柯戾折磨。

1939年史坦貝克寫就巨著《憤怒的葡萄》（The Grapes of Wrath），標題源自聖經啓示錄14章19-20節：

So the angel swung his sickle to the earth and gathered the clusters from the vine of the earth, and threw them into the great wine press of the wrath of God.	那天使就以鐮刀在地上割刈，收取了大地葡萄藤的果串，將其擲入神之怒的大酒醡。

以及1862年《共和國戰歌》（The Battle Hymn of the Republic）歌詞：

Mine eyes have seen the glory of the coming of the Lord: He is trampling out the vintage where the grapes of wrath are stored; He hath loosed the fateful lightning of His terrible swift sword: His truth is marching on.	我曾雙眼親見上帝駕臨之光耀： 祂正在踩踏其中貯存憤怒的葡萄； 祂已釋出祂可怖快劍的致命閃矯： 祂的真理勇往直前。

　　內容敘述經濟大恐慌時期俄克拉何馬州（Oklahoma）佃農周茲（Joads）一家被迫隨流民遷離老家前往加州，到了卻發現人多工少，被大農業公司剝削，隨行的牧師凱西（Casy）籌組工會，其他家人去打工，違犯工會罷工，勞資雙方暴力衝突，湯姆眼見凱西被害，憤而殺死兇手逃亡。周茲一家躲避澇災，在廢棄穀倉見到瀕於餓死的兩父子，周茲家女兒沙龍玫瑰（Rose of Sharon）剛產下死胎，以母乳哺育拯救之。書出大賣，但遭農場主與保守人士批評，於若干地區圖書館被禁兩年。茲選譯兩段：

This is the beginning—from "I" to "we". If you who own the things people must have could understand this, you might preserve yourself. If you could separate causes from results, if you could know that Paine, Marx, Jefferson, Lenin were results, not causes, you might survive. But that you cannot know. For the quality of owning freezes you forever into "I", and cuts you off forever from the "we".	這是開始—從「我」到「我們」。如果你們擁有必需品之人了解這點，你們或可自保。如果你們能夠區分因與果，如果你們知道裴恩、馬克思、傑佛遜、列寧是果而非因，那你們或可生存。可是正是此點你們無法知道。因為擁有將你們凍結於「我」，將你們永遠割離於「我們」。

Wherever they's a fight so hungry people can eat, I'll be there. Wherever they's a cop beatin' up a guy, I'll be there. If Casy knowed, why, I'll be in the way guys yell when they're mad an'—I'll be in the way kids laugh when they're hungry n' they know supper's ready. An' when our folks eat the stuff they raise an' live in the houses they build—why, I'll be there. See? God, I'm talkin' like Casy. Comes of thinkin' about him so much. Seems like I can see him sometimes.

哪裡在鬥爭好讓肚子餓的人有的吃，我就在那裡。哪裡有警察亂打人，我就在那裡。如果凱西知道，那，那我會在人們憤怒的叫喊裡—我會在餓肚子的小孩知道有東西吃發出的歡笑裡。當人們吃自己種的糧、住自己蓋的屋—我也會在那裡。你看，老天，我現在講話都像凱西。因為我整天都在想他。有時好像都能見到他。

　　1930年代至1941年史坦貝克常隨李克茨出海，1951年出版《科特斯海日誌》（The Log from the Sea of Cortez）。1941年離婚，遷居紐約，1943年任《紐約先鋒論壇報》（New York Herald Tribune）歐洲戰地記者。1945年出版《製罐巷》（Cannery Row），敘述大恐慌時期，蒙特利市沙丁魚製罐廠街區，流浪漢頭子麥克（Mack）一幫人為好友海洋學家「博士」（Doc）籌辦派對之事。1947年史坦貝克赴蘇聯旅遊，次年出版《遊俄日記》（A Russian Journal），同年李克茨車禍去世，史坦貝克哀痛逾恆。

　　1952年史坦貝克出版《伊甸之東》（East of Eden），標題源自創世紀第4章16節：「於是該隱離開上帝，住到伊甸之東挪得之地（And Cain went out from the presence of the Lord and dwelt in the land of Nod on the east of Eden）。」內容敘述漢彌頓（Hamilton）與查斯克（Trask）兩家之事，以聖經該隱殺害弟弟亞伯（Abel）之事探討善惡，認為上帝予人選擇之權，書出大賣。

　　1960年史坦貝克駕車攜狗查理周遊美國，出版《與查理同遊》（Travels with Charley），次年出版《我們鬱卒的冬季》（The Winter of Our Discontent）批評美國道德沒落。1962年獲諾貝爾文學獎，但廣遭批評。1967年赴越南報導越戰。1968年去世。

史坦貝克小說以聖經爲喻，描述美國社會農工階級所受欺壓，客觀刻劃加州各族裔生活形態，爲美國20世紀重要小說家。

◆
．
史
坦
貝
克
．
◆

圖片來源：IDJ圖庫

2-19

田納西・威廉斯

Tennessee Williams

　　田納西‧威廉斯（Tennessee Williams）1911年生於美國密西西比州哥倫布市（Columbus），父親常年在外售鞋，酗酒家暴，母親出身上層階級；威廉斯幼隨長老會牧師祖父居住，身體孱弱，溺於母親關照，8歲全家隨父工作定居密蘇里州聖路易市（St. Louis），17歲短篇小說刊於雜誌，同年隨祖父遊歐，1929年入讀密蘇里大學新聞系，自承同性戀，隔年首度發表劇本。1931年軍訓不及格，父親令他退學任職鞋廠，他厭惡鞋廠工作，夜晚寫作，24歲精神崩潰離職。1930年代中父母分居，1936年威廉斯入讀聖路易華盛頓大學（Washington University in St. Louis），1937年轉讀愛阿華大學（University of Iowa）主修英文，同年姊姊若絲（Rose）精神分裂，隔年威廉斯大學畢業，1939年遷居新奧爾良（New Orleans），為經濟大恐慌時協助就業的「公家計劃行政署」（Works Progress Administration）寫作，以父親老家田納西為筆名。1942年遷居紐約市，打零工維生，次年母親讓若絲接受前額腦葉切除（prefrontal lobotomy），若絲此後終身嚴重智障，威廉斯為此責怪父母。

　　1944年威廉斯劇本《玻璃動物園》（The Glass Menagerie）上演，敘述青年湯姆（Tom）回憶：出身南方沒落大家之母親愛曼達（Amanda Wingfield）與女兒蘿拉（Laura）、兒子湯姆於聖路易租賃陋居，蘿拉膽怯腳瘸，整天在家摩玩收集的玻璃動物造型，湯姆任職鞋廠養家，志在寫作，愛曼達要湯姆幫蘿拉介紹男友，湯姆帶同事吉姆（Jim）返家，碰巧吉姆是蘿拉高中心儀對象，飯後吉姆溫言鼓勵蘿拉，兩人慢舞時吉姆不慎觸落玻璃獨角獸，獨角斷裂，吉姆親吻蘿拉後坦言已訂婚，接受蘿相贈的破碎獨角獸離去，湯姆不知吉姆已訂婚，但被愛曼達責怪，不久後湯姆離家，從此未返。戲出威廉斯一舉成名，茲選譯一段蘿拉與吉姆的對話：

LAURA: Little articles of it, they're ornaments mostly! Most of them are little animals made out of glass, the tiniest little animals in the world. Mother calls them a glass menagerie! Here's an example of one, if you'd like to see it! ... Oh, be careful—if you breathe, it breaks! ... You see how the light shines through him?	蘿拉：玻璃做的小東西，大多是裝飾！大多是玻璃做的小動物，全世界最小的動物。母親說是玻璃動物園！這裡有一隻，要是你想看的話！……噢，小心─連呼吸都會讓它碎裂！……你看到光線如何穿透他嗎？
JIM: It sure does shine!	吉姆：真亮！
LAURA: I shouldn't be partial, but he is my favorite one.	蘿拉：我不該偏心，可是他是我的最愛。
JIM: What kind of a thing is this one supposed to be?	吉姆：這個究竟是什麼樣的東西呢？
LAURA: Haven't you noticed the single horn on his forehead?	蘿拉：你沒看到他額頭上有支獨角嗎？
JIM: A unicorn, huh? —aren't they extinct in the modern world?	吉姆：喔，是獨角獸？──他們在現代世界不是絕種了嗎？
LAURA: I know!	蘿拉：正是！
JIM: Poor little fellow, he must feel sort of lonesome.	吉姆：可憐的小傢伙，他一定有點孤單。

　　1947年其劇本《慾望街車》（A Streetcar Named Desire）上演，敘述南方沒落大家女、30出頭的白蘭詩（Blanche DuBois）在中學教英文，先生因同性戀被發覺自殺，白蘭詩欠債失去祖宅「幻夢」（Belle Reve），又因與學生上床解職，赴新奧爾良依附懷孕的妹妹思蝶拉（Stella），謊稱請假出遊，妹夫史坦力（Stanley Kowalski）是粗俗工人，白蘭詩結識其同事米奇（Mitch），互有好感；史坦力酒醉家暴，姊妹兩上鄰家躲避，史坦力酒醒，喚得妻子情動回家；史坦力獲知白蘭詩真象，告知米奇，米奇拒絕白蘭詩，思蝶拉赴院生產，史坦力強姦白蘭詩，後者精神崩潰，對送她入院的醫師說：「無論您是哪位，我一向倚仗陌生人的慈悲。（Whoever you are, I have always depended upon the kindness of strangers）」劇本廣受歡迎，茲選譯白蘭詩述說失去「幻夢」一段：

There are thousands of papers, stretching back over hundreds of years, affecting Belle Reve as, piece by piece, our improvident grandfathers and father and uncles and brothers exchanged the land for their epic fornications—to put it plainly!   The four-letter word deprived us of our plantation, till finally all that was left—and Stella can verify that!—was the house itself and about twenty acres of ground, including a grave-yard, to which now all but Stella and I have retreated.

有數以千計的文件，綿延數百年，我們不事生產的父祖兄叔以之將「幻夢」片片裂解，交換他們洪濤無匹的濫交──講白了就是這樣！……那個難以出口的字眼奪走了我們的莊園，最後只剩─這點有思蝶拉爲證──大廈本身和20畝地，包括一個墳場，家人全退居其中，只差思蝶拉和我。

1950年代威廉斯不斷遷居旅遊，1955年劇本《燙鐵皮屋上的貓》（Cat on a Hot Tin Roof，又譯《朱門巧婦》）上演，敘述美南棉花大王「老爸」（Big Daddy Pollitt）健檢無恙後慶生，其實子女知道他患癌不治，小兒子、前足球明星布里克（Brick）因好友斯基波（Skipper）發覺自己同性戀而自殺，布里克因此酗酒，與出身貧困的美妻「貓」瑪姬（Maggie the "Cat"）不洽，布里克告知老爸病情眞象，大兒子古伯（Gooper）與大兒媳圖謀搶奪家產，瑪姬爲遺產謊稱懷孕，劇尾瑪姬對布里克承諾將假變眞。

1960、1970年代威廉斯寫作風格轉含蓄，劇本不再賣座，同時酗酒嗑藥，1983年去世。

《慾望街車》是美國20世紀最著名劇本之一，威廉斯多部劇本拍成電影，廣爲人知。

2-20

亞瑟・米勒

Arthur Miller

亞瑟·米勒
Arthur Miller

　　亞瑟·米勒（Arthur Miller）1915年生於美國紐約市，父母皆來自今日波蘭東部，父親經營女裝製衣廠，1929年經濟大恐慌破產。1934年米勒入讀密西根大學（University of Michigan）新聞系，寫了第一齣劇本，轉攻英美文學，1938年獲學士學位，任職政府協助就業的「聯邦劇場計劃」（Federal Theater Project）寫作，次年該計劃中止，米勒入海軍船塢打工，1940年結婚，同年第一齣劇本上演，評論不佳。

　　米勒因之前足球膝傷二戰免役，1947年作品《人皆吾子》（All My Sons）上演，此劇受挪威劇作家易卜生《野鴨子》（Vildanden）影響，敘述商人製造不良飛機零件售予美國政府致飛行員死亡，商人兒子以此質疑其父，商人自殺。演出甚受歡迎。

　　1948年寫就《推銷員之死》（Death of a Salesman），次年上演，敘述旅行推銷員委里·洛曼（Willy Loman）返家途中險出車禍，妻子玲達（Linda）要他跟老闆要求免除旅行。洛曼長子畢夫（Biff）曾撞見父親出軌，指責父親是騙子，因此只想做農夫，但洛曼覺其才能遠不止此。當晚洛曼回憶往事，開始自言自語，原來因收入不敷支出，洛曼曾企圖自殺。畢夫打算跟之前的僱主貸款創業。次日，洛曼不但未能免於旅行，反遭解雇，畢夫也貸款不成，洛曼藉幻想逃避現實，畢夫坦言他們一家都活在幻想中，父子擁抱，但洛曼仍覺畢夫為失敗者。洛曼決定撞車自殺，領取壽險以助畢夫，喪禮上無人來祭弔。畢夫決定誠實面對自己，不隨父從商，但其弟哈皮（Happy，意為「無憂」）決定繼承父親志向。此劇質疑美國夢幻想多過實幹，與尤金·歐尼爾之《漫漫長途漸入夜》、田納西·威廉斯之《慾望街車》並列20世紀美國三大劇作。茲選譯兩段：

And when I saw that, I realized that selling was the greatest career a man could want. 'Cause what could be more satisfying than to be able to go, at the age of eighty-four, into twenty or thirty different cities, and pick up a phone, and be remembered and loved and helped by so many different people?	我看到此事，明白了推銷是一個人能追求的最偉大的事業。你到了84歲，去到二、三十個不同的城市，拿起電話一打，就會受到各式各樣的人憶念、關愛、幫助，有什麼比這更令人心滿意足呢？

I don't say he's a great man. Willie Loman never made a lot of money. His name was never in the paper. He's not the finest character that ever lived. But he's a human being, and a terrible thing is happening to him. So attention must be paid. He's not to be allowed to fall in his grave like an old dog. Attention, attention must finally be paid to such a person.	我不是說他偉大。委里・洛曼從沒賺過大錢。他名字從沒上過報。他不是有史以來最好的人。但他是一個人，現在碰到了很糟的事。所以我們必須關懷他。我們不能讓他像條老狗一樣死去。關懷，我們必須對這樣一個人給予關懷。

1952年米勒好友名導卡贊（Elia Kazan）在眾議院非美活動調查委員會（House Un-American Activities Committee）指控影藝界共黨人士，兩人絕交，至1964年才復交。

1953年米勒劇作《煉獄》（The Crucible）上演，根據1692年麻州綏聯市（Salem）女巫迫害案改編，影射非美活動調查委員會。1955年《橋上一瞥》（A View from the Bridge）上演，次年改編再次上演，劇名之橋指俯瞰紐約市布魯克林區（Brooklyn）之布魯克林大橋，內容探討告密與背叛，敘述港口搬運工艾迪（Eddie）迷戀甥女凱瑟琳（Catherine），為阻止非法移民的親戚羅多夫（Rodolpho）與凱瑟琳相戀，密告移民局逮捕羅多夫及其兄馬克（Marco），於決鬥中被馬克刺死。

1956年米勒拒絕為眾議院非美活動調查委員會指控他人，被判藐視國會（Contempt of Congress），1958年平反。1956年米勒離婚再娶明星瑪麗蓮夢露（Marilyn Monroe），1961年離婚。次年第三度結婚。2005年去世。

米勒以劇作探討人與家庭、社會之關係，為美國20世紀重要劇作家。

國家圖書館出版品預行編目資料

英美文學60大家／姜葳著.
－－初版.－－臺北市：五南, 2016.05
　面；　公分
ISBN 978-957-11-8604-7（平裝）

1.英國文學　2.美國文學　3.文學史

873.9　　　　　　　　　　105006504

1XOR

英美文學60大家

作　　　者 — 姜葳

發 行 人 — 楊榮川

總 編 輯 — 王翠華

主　　編 — 朱曉蘋

封面設計 — 陳翰陞

出 版 者 — 五南圖書出版股份有限公司

地　　　址：106台北市大安區和平東路二段339號4樓

電　　　話：(02)2705-5066　　傳　　真：(02)2706-6100

網　　　址：http://www.wunan.com.tw

電子郵件：wunan@wunan.com.tw

劃撥帳號：01068953

戶　　　名：五南圖書出版股份有限公司

法律顧問　林勝安律師事務所　林勝安律師

出版日期　2016年5月初版一刷

定　　　價　新臺幣420元